THE INLAND SEA

THE INLAND SEA

Sam Clark

Rootstock Publishing

First Printing:

The Inland Sea
Copyright © 2020 by Sam Clark
All Rights Reserved.

Release Date: November 9, 2020
Softcover ISBN: 978-1-57869-032-9
eBook ISBN: 978-1-57869-033-6
LCCN: 2020902121

Published by Rootstock Publishing
an imprint of Multicultural Media, Inc. 27 Main Street, Suite 6
Montpelier, VT 05602 USA www.rootstockpublishing.com
info@rootstockpublishing.com

Interior design by Eddie Vincent (ed.vincent@encirclepub.com)
Cover design by Deirdre Wait/Enc Graphic Services
Printed in the USA

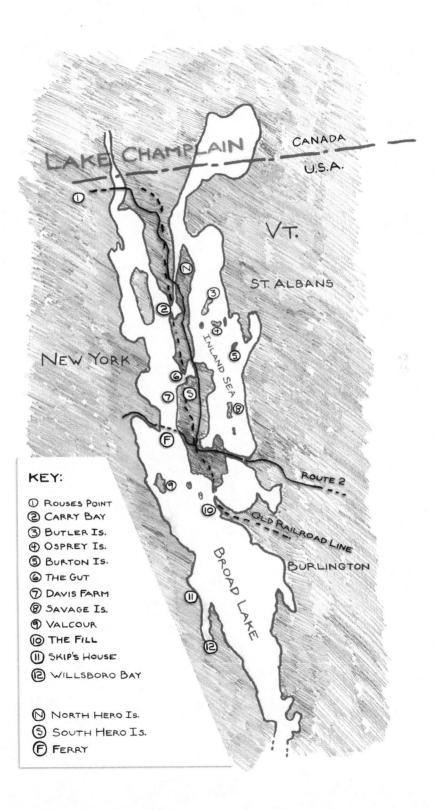

LAKE CHAMPLAIN

CANADA
U.S.A.

VT.

ST. ALBANS

NEW YORK

INLAND SEA

ROUTE 2

OLD RAILROAD LINE

BURLINGTON

BROAD LAKE

KEY:

① ROUSES POINT
② CARRY BAY
③ BUTLER IS.
④ OSPREY IS.
⑤ BURTON IS.
⑥ THE GUT
⑦ DAVIS FARM
⑧ SAVAGE IS.
⑨ VALCOUR
⑩ THE FILL
⑪ SKIP'S HOUSE
⑫ WILLSBORO BAY

Ⓝ NORTH HERO IS.
Ⓢ SOUTH HERO IS.
Ⓕ FERRY

PREFACE

Lake Champlain, one hundred twenty-five miles long, runs south to north between Vermont and New York. At the Canadian border, the lake drains into the Rivière Richelieu, which leads to the St. Lawrence River, and from there—everywhere. At the south, the Champlain Canal links the lake to the Hudson, and from there—everywhere. Looking west toward the sunset, the Adirondack Mountains, large and forbidding, seem to come right down to the lakeshore. Along the eastern shore is the Champlain Valley, where the big farms are, and beyond that, the more gentle Green Mountains. At the northern end of the lake, two large islands, North Hero and South Hero, separate the water into two parts. To the west is the major section known as the Broad Lake. To the east, on the Vermont side, is a miniature version of the lake, a mere forty miles long, known as the Inland Sea. The northern lobe, Missisquoi Bay, bulges eight miles up into Canada.

In the late nineteenth century, a railroad was built to connect mainland Vermont to the islands, and from there to Canada. The railroad causeways created a stone necklace around the Inland Sea. The railroad is gone, but the necklace is still there. Three openings, each about one hundred feet wide, where there were once drawbridges, let boats in and out. At the southern end, the gap lets boats into Malletts Bay, but the delta of the Lamoille River and its sandbar keep the larger boats from proceeding farther north, except at high water.

The best entrance is at the Gut, a pond that separates North and South Hero. Boats enter through another gap in the causeway, cross the Gut, and then wait for the Route 2 drawbridge to lift every half hour and release them into the Inland Sea. A third passage is about six miles north, at Carry Bay, but it's less convenient and less used.

THE INLAND SEA

Chapter 1

THE BACKSTORY, 1972

Two boys are sailing in a nineteen-foot plywood sloop, heading north in a brisk breeze. The boat looks a little rough, but it's better than it looks. The boys, who are about seventeen, built it from scratch. It's a Lightning, a popular class of small racing sailboats.

The taller one, Freddy, is a little heavy, but fit. The shorter one, Luke, is quite slim, almost skinny, but wiry and strong. They're running parallel to North Hero Island at the northern end of Lake Champlain, a hundred yards offshore. They're approaching Carry Bay, which connects the main lake with the smaller Inland Sea. The opening into the bay is a narrow gap in an old stone railroad trestle, no longer in use. There used to be a drawbridge there.

The boat is heeled over in the south wind; the sails block the view of the gap. There's a lot of traffic here, with little room for error, and usually boats emerge from Carry Bay at five miles an hour, or ten if they're in a hurry. Boats could be coming from any direction. People fish off the rocks, increasing the confusion.

Though their view of the gap is blocked by the sail, the boys hear a speedboat screaming, heading their way. They expect the boat to veer off to their stern—sailboats have the right-of-way over power. But the rising roar of the motor tells a different story. Too late, the boater sees them, pulls back on the throttle, and spins his wheel right. The maneuver casts a huge sheet of spray over the sailboat. As the speedboat spins to a stop, its sharp rear corner slices into the sailboat's plywood hull.

Luke, at the back of the sailboat, has the tiller. He's thrown into the water by the blow. Freddy ends up in a pile on the deck. A couple of beer cans from the other boat fly into the Lightning. One lands right on his head then rolls into the bilge. From where Freddy sits, rubbing his bruises, he can see water coming into the hull along a two-inch crack at the waterline. Luke quickly pulls himself up and into the boat.

The boys see a heavy, black-and-red fiberglass speedboat bobbing in the water beside them. They know every make and model, and they recognize this one as a G3, a popular water-ski boat. It has an enormous black motor on the back shaped like a skyscraper. The ski boat's side in the back sticks out, low and sharp like a hatchet, perfect for scoring a slash in the sailboat's thin plywood skin. More beer cans rattle around on the ski boat's floor. There's nobody in the boat.

But a moment later, two big hands rise up from the water and grab the side, and a figure quickly heaves himself up and in. He's big, maybe six three, about their age. He's much broader than they are and very muscular in a quarterback sort of way. He has a red crew cut.

The redhead looks at the two sailors calmly and glances at the gash in the side of the sailboat. His boat is barely scratched. He opens another beer and, without a word, starts his engine and takes off at full throttle, curving in a short, dramatic arc toward the south.

The two boys have a little five-horse motor on the back, and as the boat fills with water, they're just able to limp through the causeway gap to a nearby marina. At the dock, the boat sinks to the gunwales.

Fred Davis's home is not far away. It's a dairy farm known as the Davis Farm on the western side of South Hero Island. The boys built the boat there in a barn they use as their shop. The Lightning is just the most recent of many such projects. Using a borrowed trailer, they get the boat to Davis Farm and put it on sawhorses in the barn. During the whole process, very little has been said. They are still a bit in shock, but it's obvious what they have to do. Though just boys, they have worked together for many years, and they understand each other. Often a gesture or a single word says enough.

Their boat is worse off than they thought. They'll need to repair two ribs as well as the skin. Though young, they have been working on boats since childhood; they are good at this. Luke is the mechanic. He can fix any machine or gadget. He likes to get his hands dirty. Freddy can work on motors if he has to, but he has a natural talent for the peculiar kind of woodworking used on boats. He's inventive, good with tools, and can picture things in three dimensions. He knows what a piece of wood wants to do.

As they get to work, they plan their revenge. Physical assault is dismissed after a short discussion. The redhead would make mincemeat of them and is also obviously comfortable with violence, a phenomenon they have no experience with whatsoever. Luke says, "Don't get mad, just get even."

They consider a couple of plans for the ski boat, if they can find it. One idea is to drag it out into the lake, drill a few large holes in the hull, fill it full of rocks, sink it, and then mark the spot with a buoy, on the idea that the boy will know who did it. But they eventually settle on a subtler scheme.

The next morning, in an old wooden motorboat they fixed up, they start the search for the red-and-black speedboat, bay by bay and dock by dock. On the evening of the second day, about twenty miles below South Hero Island on the New York side, they see it. It's on Brown Point, docked next to a big, brand-new cabin cruiser, maybe thirty-five feet long. The house above it looks new as well, a big, modern box in white stucco, more like a suburban home than a lake cottage. Phase one of the plan, find the boat, is complete.

They watch the weather reports. The forecast for three nights hence is rough, with two-foot waves from the south, and overcast. The weather will give them cover. They arrive by car, sneak down to the dock, untie the ski boat, and paddle it out a hundred feet, silently.

Luke starts the engine as quietly as he can. They point the boat toward the middle of the lake and secure the wheel with a piece of fish line. They remove the drain plug from the transom. Once the boat comes to a stop, it will slowly fill with water through this one-inch hole. Luke puts the boat in gear. They dive into the water and watch the boat slowly cruise eastward. They swim to shore and drive home, where they put the finishing touches on the Lightning and work their way through Fred's mother's deep-dish apple pie.

*   *   *

The next morning, the big, redheaded boy, whose name is Skip, looks out his bedroom window, as he always does when he wakes up. He has the coolest boat on the lake. He likes to admire it and imagine how other people must envy him. But the G3 is gone. Throwing on some shorts, he runs down to the dock. His heart is racing. There is no sign of the boat, or of its mooring lines. He scans the lake, hoping to catch a glimpse of red and black somewhere. He knows something funny has happened because he's certain he tied the boat up carefully the night before. He loves his boat. Someone must have stolen it.

His confusion turns to anger. There are three new Adirondack chairs on the dock, one red, one green, one blue. But he is a very strong boy. He picks up the red one, high above his head, and crashes it down on the dock. After three or four blows, it's reduced to splinters, which he pitches into the lake.

He does the same thing to the green one. He's breathing hard. Someone has hurt him, and he is desperate to hurt them back. It never occurs to him that the disappearance of his boat might have something to do with his crash into the sailboat. He's almost forgotten about that episode.

He turns and sees his father slowly walking toward the dock. His father looks like him but is a little shorter, a little heavier, and much stronger. For a moment, nothing is said.

Then his father speaks softly. "Skipper, do you know what I paid for that boat? For that matter, do you know what I paid for those chairs? Maybe next time, you'll tie up the boat like I showed you. And remember not to leave the key in the boat." His father turns and walks back inside the house.

Skip looks at the third Adirondack chair, the blue one. He desperately wants to destroy it, but he doesn't.

*   *   *

Two days later, a different boy, about the same age, is out in his aluminum boat at five in the morning. It was dark when he set out, and there is just a hint of daylight. The weather is calm, as it often is at that hour. He's fishing for bass on the outside or south side of what locals call the Fill. It's another stone causeway, part of the same defunct railroad line that encloses Carry Bay, where the boat crash took place. This section is a few miles south. It once brought trains from the Vermont mainland to South Hero Island. Now it's just a pile of huge boulders three miles long and twenty feet wide. A gap in the middle lets the boats through. It's about four miles from another causeway called the Sandbar, and the area between the two causeways creates a basin, a lake within a lake, called Malletts Bay.

The boy, whose name is Paul Brearley, has fished here many times and knows the prospects for bass are good, but nothing in fishing is guaranteed. He is slowly casting from the boat toward the causeway as a gentle breeze pushes his boat south. The sun is coming up, the world is turning red. He likes this time of day. In fact, he is almost always up at sunrise when he's

9

on the lake. He likes being by himself, having the lake to himself. This morning is particularly clear and calm. He works his way along the old stone railbed for over an hour.

His patience is rewarded as he approaches Colchester Point. After two hours of nothing, in the space of ten minutes almost every cast brings a strike. By the time things quiet down again, he has four large bass in his bucket and has thrown two others back. Then he notices the boat.

It's a red-and-black speedboat with a large black Mercury motor on the back, banging on the rocks at the base of the causeway, almost concealed by the weeds. Only the motor and the gunwales are visible above water. There's nobody anywhere around. A dozen beer cans are floating in the boat. Paul is very responsible by nature; he's a preacher's kid and does good deeds as a matter of course. It doesn't occur to him to just leave the boat where it is.

The boat seems intact, and he takes a bucket and starts bailing. After a half hour, it is as low in the water as before. He finally sees that the drain plug is gone. He whittles a temporary plug out of wood, inserts it, and starts bailing again. In an hour, he has the boat afloat, though a little water is seeping back in around the plug.

He ties the boat behind his little aluminum boat and tows it into Malletts Bay. He crosses the bay back to the Sandbar and beaches the boat safely at the state park. He tells the ranger, whom he knows slightly, what happened. He continues on his way home to Osprey Island, cleans the fish, sticks three in a freezer, and cooks the biggest one for breakfast. His family is not the least bit surprised to see him return with a batch of large bass, or to see him prepare a meal for everybody.

He says, "I found a boat on the rocks by the Fill around six."

His dad says, "Oh?"

"I dropped it off at Sand Bar."

That's the last mention anybody makes of the incident.

But a week later, the red-and-black boat cruises up to the main dock of Osprey Island, this time landing without crashing, without sinking, and with no beer cans in sight. The large, redheaded boy gets out, and so does an older man. The older man, the boy's father, isn't as huge as the boy but the resemblance is there, something in the face, but mainly in the walk, the lightness of movement. The dad seems determined, the son reluctant.

The island kids identify boats by sound. When the big Merc pulls in, they know it's somebody new, and they run down to check it out. The two men ask how to find Paul Brearley, and the kids point to a little house set back from the shore. Paul, his dad, and a pretty girl of about fifteen are on the porch, sitting in rocking chairs, reading their books with their feet on the railing.

The younger visitor has his speech prepared. "Paul Brearley? Hi. I'm Skip Tyler, and this is my dad, Travis Tyler."

Everyone shakes hands. Paul says, "Hi, I'm Paul. This is my dad, John Brearley, and my sister Helen. Your boat looks somewhat familiar."

Skip is warming to his part as his dad looks on. "I bet. I wanted to thank you for pulling it in. If you hadn't, it probably would have been pretty much of a wreck. I'm sorry to put you to all that trouble. The ranger told me where to find you. Somebody came to our place—" At this point, his dad gives him a very sharp look that says *don't*, and the boy starts over. "The boat got away two days ago. Anyway, you saved the day. We're over on the New York side. We have a new camp sort of near Port Kent."

It turns out Skip has a sister of the right age, Dara, also fifteen. The two families exchange visits. The Tylers invite the Brearleys down for a cookout. The kids water-ski behind the red-and-white boat and play Ping-Pong in the shiny new basement. The Tylers come out to Osprey Island for a cookout. They eat two more of Paul's big bass. After dinner, the four kids go to an outbuilding that serves as a rec room and play more Ping-Pong. Somewhere along the way, Skip has acquired a beer.

At first the games are casual. Everybody plays everybody. They attempt a game of round-robin. But after the girls leave, it starts to get serious. Paul and Skip trade games back and forth, but Paul quickly sees Skip's weakness—no backhand—and wins the last two games easily. Skip's muscles tense up; his face gets a little red. He doesn't like to lose.

*　　*　　*

A week later, Skip invites Paul to play tennis at the college courts in Burlington. Skip is a good athlete, very quick. He hits the ball with tremendous force, including the serve. But Paul has been taking tennis lessons since he was eight, and he plays on his high school team. The Ping-Pong has taught him all he needs to know: Skip's backhand is a little shaky.

During the first set, Paul hangs around the baseline and just returns Skip's shots. He's good at anticipating where Skip's balls will go; he's usually there ahead of time, in position to return. But Skip wins the first set 6–4. Paul isn't alarmed, but he starts to hit the ball a bit harder. Skip is energized. This time he wins the set 6–3. Skip thinks, *I'm much better than this pretty bozo.*

A tennis buff watching from the sideline would see that, in spite of the score, Skip has little chance of winning. He's athletic and agile, but self-taught. Paul has been schooled; he's had more tennis lessons than Skip has played matches. His movements are smooth, practiced, economical, unrushed. Each backhand traces the same graceful arc. He knows where Skip's return is going before Skip hits it. Skip is straining, playing in all-out-war mode, and Paul is still playing a friendly game. He knows he will probably win, but he doesn't really care; to him, it's not a real match.

At the beginning of the third set, Paul starts to hit mainly to Skip's backhand. At 5–5, Paul is serving. On the first point, he hits a hard backhand down the line, a perfect shot into the corner, out of reach. Skip calls it out.

In tennis games like this, the players are their own referees—anyone can call a ball out. There's an honor system understood among all players to never lie about a call. Some players interpret this to mean that if you think an opponent's ball *might* be out, but you're not certain, call it out. But Paul has been taught that if you think an opponent's ball might be in, or even almost in, call it in. That's the family creed, the cultural inheritance. In his family, making a bad call is a worse sin than stealing. You could go to hell for making a bad call. To be safe, call it in.

Though it could cost him the match, Paul thinks, *Anyone can make a mistake,* and he gets ready for his next serve. Skip positions himself way over, hoping to return the serve with his forehand. Paul serves down the middle, hard, a perfect serve, unhittable. But Skip calls it out.

Until now, Paul has been in "pleasant afternoon, friendly game" mindset, knowing he's the better player. He wants to hold back just a little, yet still win by a game or two. He imagines that, having had a pleasant outing, the two young men will shake hands at the net, congratulate each other, and go home, with Skip feeling good about his performance while conceding that Paul is a better player. But the second bad call changes everything. It's cheating, a violation of good form, of the nature of things, an insult to the social order. Though Paul is a very good high school player, he expects to lose occasionally to better players in school matches. But not here. Friendly-game mode is over, though it doesn't show yet in Paul's demeanor. Whatever he may be feeling, he almost always appears calm.

So far, Paul has been hitting firm, well-placed serves, but he hasn't brought out his big serve, his boomer, the serve he uses in school matches where playing all out is assumed. On the third point, he serves just to Skip's right. The ball is exactly in the middle of the service box and impossible to call out. Paul's serve is an above-average high school senior's hard serve. It will earn him a place on the Harvard tennis team next fall. Skip has never faced anything that fast, and the ball is past him before he reacts. Skip realizes something has changed. Paul would like to think this serve is just his way of saying "Skip, no more cheap calls, let's finish this the way we've started," and the friendly game will continue.

Paul wins the game with two more hard serves and one diabolical soft, spinning serve, which tails off into the next court. Skip is positioned way back to return the hard serves and can't get anywhere near the soft spinner.

In the next game, Skip serves even harder than usual. He gets an ace on the first point, but the next three points have a similar pattern. The first serve goes long. The second serve is a little softer, so Paul can place his return where Skip can't return it with force. Then Paul runs to the net and volleys Skip's ball out of reach to win the point.

Skip is up two sets to one, but the match is over. Both boys know this. Skip can't quite believe it. As the fourth set unwinds, Skip is hot, sweaty, hitting the ball harder and harder, running fast on every point. Paul has been cool up to now, but he's starting to sweat. Earlier he'd been roaming the backline of the court, hitting long, deep ground strokes. Now he's charging the net at times, running faster, making a few drop shots, dragging Skip around the court like a marionette.

Skip is getting mad. He's starting to talk to himself. When it's four games to one against him, and Paul has drawn Skip into the net with a little short, soft drop shot to win the point, Skip hits the top of the net hard with his racket, making a loud snapping noise.

Skip wins the next game with brilliant serves. But Paul serves the next game, and it's two sets each.

Though it's beginning to drizzle, neither boy considers stopping here and heading home, score tied. Paul is feeling a little uncomfortable with what's happened. He backs off his game a bit, puts the boomer back in its box. No more trick spin serves, either. *Give Skip a chance to win if he can,* he thinks. When Skip puts away an ace or a passing shot, he says "Nice shot," or gives a thumbs-up sign. Skip calms down a bit, and they play a dispirited, almost choreographed set, leading to a respectable 6–4 win for Paul.

They shake hands at the net, exchange some polite praise—Skip: "Those were some serves." Paul: "Thanks, I don't know where they came from."—and go home.

There's no return match, and the two boys don't see each other again for thirty-six years.

Paul heads home, brooding about the match. As he drives to the boat

14

launch and canoes across to the island, he's upset, and he doesn't quite know why. He doesn't like that his gentlemanly-tennis-player persona left the court. He wishes he had let the gentleman play on, with the boomer tucked safely away, win or lose, even if Skip's cheap calls had cost him the match. In a way, he'd have dominated Skip even more. But that wouldn't have been fair to Skip—it would be contemptuous, dismissive, to *let* him win. Would it have been more honest to play his hardest from the beginning? But that would have been mean. Maybe he should have refused the match, knowing that he and Skip were ill-matched. But that would have been arrogant. What would he have said? "Sorry, but I can see by how you move that you'll lose, so we can't play." Or "Sorry, I have a dentist appointment." That would be lying. Paul often has debates like this with himself without finding answers. He has a weakness for tormenting himself. But usually a vigorous paddle in his boat, into the wind, puts him in a good mood again. And when he gets home, the gentlemanly tennis player is back in charge.

"How was tennis?" his sister Helen asks.

"Great," he answers. "Good workout."

Chapter 2:

A KILLING—
WEDNESDAY, FEBRUARY 1, 2008

An old, battered, red Toyota pickup truck, with one black door on the driver's side, filed off the 8 A.M. Grand Isle ferry from Plattsburgh, New York. A tall man got out by a restaurant known as the Champ Diner. It was well below zero and the wind was blowing, but he was wearing only work pants and a red-check wool shirt. No gloves and no hat. His hair was brown, with white and gray here and there. He had a small, round beard in the same colors. He walked into the diner and reappeared two minutes later with a paper bag and a large, steaming coffee. Most of the cars turned right out of the parking lot, but the red truck turned left on West Shore Road. After about a mile, it turned east to cross the island and headed north on Route 2.

He drove a few miles and took a fork to the right. At a sign that said VERMONT FISHING ACCESS, he pulled in and parked. Though it was deep winter, there were two other trucks parked there. The state didn't plow out these boat launch areas, but the fishermen, most of whom had plows on the front of their trucks, did it for their own convenience.

He had made this journey quite a few times and he had his routine worked out. In the back of the Toyota was a snowmobile, which looked even older than the truck. He pulled out a couple of planks to make a little ramp, climbed onto the snow machine, started it up, and drove down his ramp. As the machine warmed up, he pulled on brown, insulated coveralls, some insulated boots, and a knit cap. Over that went an old, faded-green air force parka with a fur-lined hood. This outfit was good to about thirty degrees below zero. After eating one of the four breakfast sandwiches from the Champ Diner, he opened his large pack, rearranged some of the books and clothing, and made a warm little nest for the remaining three sandwiches. He closed the pack and flipped it easily up onto his back.

The first two years, he had made this trip on snowshoes. Though in his midfifties, he was fit. But a five-mile snowshoe hike was hard work, particularly with the backpack. And he figured that a lone man crossing the lake on foot, no fishing hut in sight, was more conspicuous than just another snow machine. The machine made a racket, but nobody would give it a second thought. Ten minutes after it passed, it would have vanished from any observer's mind. As if he had never been there.

He was headed to Osprey Island. When he was Reverend Paul Brearley, he had been one of the owners, and legally he still probably was. His family had a house there.

Everyone he knew from his previous life thought he was dead. In some sense, he did, too. He was a different person now.

He was now Paul Baer, who for eighteen years had been living a very low-profile life in far northern New York. He did some logging in winter. In winter he made a modest living, mostly as a guide or doing carpentry work. He led fishermen out onto the Saint Lawrence, took hunters out to

17

find big deer and moose in the Connecticut Lakes region, and in decent weather worked most of the successful back-woods guide resorts. In summer he made good money and saved up for the rest of the year. His favorite job was to lead canoe trips. He knew large sections of Algonquin Provincial Park and all of the Adirondack canoe wilderness, along with many other wild places, from memory.

Occasionally he would risk working out of Lake Champlain, really his home lake, but he was very careful. There were people who might recognize him; it could be awkward.

In deep winter, he holed up in Tupper Lake, a depressed town in the Adirondack Park. He lived in a rooming house. It was a backwater. Nobody could possibly know him, and the room was cheap. There had always been a lot of marginal people in the town, and nobody thought twice about one more. For three or four months, he read, walked, snowshoed, skied a little, and helped run a soup kitchen.

Though his ministerial side had, he thought, been left behind, he liked the soup kitchen. He liked being with the people who came there and had something in common with them, though he was never sure what it was. Working at the soup kitchen was a good way to help people a little, without drawing attention to himself. The main thing was to avoid any situation in which he was considered significant, special, or particularly virtuous.

Though he had no talent for it, he aspired to be ordinary. He was looking for his regular self. The men at the soup kitchen had nothing but their regular selves. Sometimes he saw them as his teachers.

He was good at solitude, but he was not reclusive. He'd had four serious relationships with women since he left his family and had a ten-year-old son, though he had no idea where the son, or the son's mother, was. Women loved him at first, but they drifted off after a year or so, and he could never figure out why.

Though Paul Brearley was supposed to be long gone, he sometimes missed his old life desperately.

He liked to go out to the island when the current owners weren't around, stay in his house for a week or two, read a few books, ice fish a little. He imagined his old life had worked out. He spent a lot of time walking about the island. He went into all the houses. They all used the same key, and he still had the copy he'd been given at age eight. It was worn and shiny; he loved to touch it. If he ever lost that key, he would grieve for weeks.

In his own house, he looked in every corner. He reread the books on the shelves. He looked at the pictures over and over, particularly those that included his wife and son. The pictures of his wife made him uncomfortable. They hadn't been getting along, but he knew his disappearance had been a cruel trick, no matter how he tried to explain it to himself, or, in his imagination, to her.

He was a woodsman, good at keeping a low profile, and he always planned to leave no trace of his visits. When he left, he wanted the dishes, the furniture, and the woodpile to look just as they had when the place was closed down in the fall. But usually he couldn't entirely help himself. He would leave a little coded message, a little bent twig, a clue that he might be alive and might have stopped by, checked in. He might move a book or turn a picture.

The trip across the lake took about twenty-five minutes. As he approached the cove, he saw a curl of smoke from the chimney of his house, and footprints in the snow leading from the waterside toward it. Next to the dock, sitting at an odd angle, was a huge, modern-looking black snowmobile, with a six-foot cargo sled hitched behind it. He knew immediately that if he were smart, he would turn around and head back to Tupper Lake. But coming here was always a bit of a game to him, putting himself in situations where he might see someone he recognized, or who recognized him. He couldn't imagine who would be here in January. Against his better judgment, he kept going. He shut down his machine and walked toward the house.

It was unlikely to be someone from one of the four island families.

19

His friend Pliny was too old, and in any case, if he were here, he'd be at his own house. He decided that whoever was using his house—it would always be *his* house—had no legitimate business here and he would make them leave, as if it were normal for him to be here. It would be like reclaiming his past for a moment, inhabiting his old identity.

He walked toward the house. The door was open and the doorjamb torn up.

He looked through the broken doorway and saw a large man, red hair going to gray, sitting on a couch, looking right at him. Though the big man looked familiar, Paul couldn't place him. Their last encounter, on the tennis court thirty-six years earlier, hadn't meant much to him; Paul had beaten lots of people on the court. But after a minute, as they looked at each other, he started to remember. Not the game itself, but how intense it had become. Then he remembered the whole thing: rescuing the boat, meeting Skip, playing ping-pong, and playing one of the weirder tennis matches he had ever played.

*   *   *

Skip recognized Paul instantly. To him it was as if they were seventeen, looking across the net at each other. His anger came back in full force. Skip had a pistol, a .32 revolver, in his left hand. It was match point again.

"Ah, Paul. Long time, no see. I never really figured you to be dead. I want you to know, this is my backhand. And thanks for bringing me a functional snow machine. You can have mine." He fired, point-blank, at Paul's chest. Paul collapsed in the doorway.

At first, Skip felt a surge of satisfaction as he looked at the body. Paul had humiliated him years earlier, and an opportunity to pay him back had fallen into his lap. But then he had second thoughts. Usually he stayed in control in every situation. Maybe this wasn't a decisive blow, discharged with a bit of wit, but more of a loss of control, an impulsive response where a rational one was called for. Maybe he had in this moment created a very difficult situation for himself. He had committed a careless crime, one that could be traced to him, one that gained him little beyond a momentary satisfaction. He had created a complicated situation that could get out of hand. Maybe he should have been patient, as he usually was, and figured out a response with more finesse.

But on reflection, he couldn't figure out what that might have been. Had Paul been allowed to live, or allowed to leave, it could only have led to trouble for him. And besides, he needed Paul's machine.

Skip had not planned to be on Osprey Island that day. He had been en route from Missisquoi Bay to St. Albans—where his truck was parked—and then to Burlington with a nice load of methamphetamine from Canada. There was a ready market for it in Boston, just four hours away. He had an appointment the next morning with a buyer who would take it there. He was not exactly doing it for the money. He'd inherited the white stucco house on the lake, and he had enough money to get by. But he enjoyed smuggling; it was another sport to master. Since he was a young man, he had been bringing cigarettes, liquor, marijuana, and prescription drugs down from Canada through the woods, by air, by car, and by boat. He knew every legal and illegal border crossing within one hundred miles. In recent years, he generally preferred to bring things down the Richelieu River on his big boat, and the boat had been adapted for that purpose. It was sort of a working vacation for him. His general philosophy was that if he appeared to be a somewhat rich, very conventional businessman or tourist, people would believe almost anything he said.

But since he had gotten involved in ice fishing—the perfect activity for the semiretired—he'd become interested in the possibilities in that direction. He liked the idea that he had smuggled things across the border by every possible means. His interests came together when he started thinking about Missisquoi Bay, a large, shallow bay that begins in Vermont and terminates in Quebec. There are very large northern pike in its shallow, weedy waters summer and winter.

He wasn't sure to what extent the border patrol cared about this area of the border, or how they policed it in winter. In his experience, drug runners were averse to discomfort and were looking for big profits. They tended to come across by road with large loads, using a variety of methods to hide their freight. The old favorite was to construct secret compartments in a car or truck. Not long ago, someone had been caught hiding their cargo of coke under a load of manure. His smuggling was more of a boutique operation, bringing in small quantities of high-quality product. He suspected that the big, shallow bay might provide another way to safely combine recreation with profit.

During the winter, he had researched the possibilities at length. He became a habitué of Missisquoi Bay. He would go there in his snow machine towing a cargo sled which held all his fishing gear—a folding ice fishing shelter, a portable heater for the shelter, food, and his GPS. And his pistol, tucked away.

He usually set up his fishing shelter just on the US side, in different spots on different days. His goal was to become a routine part of the view of anybody monitoring things. Often he just fished, and in fact he caught a lot of perch and a few large northern pike.

The idea was simple. Sometimes his Canadian partners would be fishing on the Canadian side of the line, maybe early in the morning when the light was poor. At some point, they would leave a package there, marked with an empty Molson Ale can, and go home for breakfast. Later that day, Skip would show up, fish for a while. Toward evening, as the light was beginning to fade, he'd pick up his package and head home.

Skip and his partners made two dry runs—no drugs—with no problems. They made two successful transfers. But having proved it could be done, he decided to abandon the idea. It was too exposed to view and too cold. The Canadian partners didn't like it. On one occasion a US helicopter flew over at an awkward moment.

But when he was returning from his final run, his machine broke down as he was winding his way through the islands off the town of St. Albans, and he found himself stranded at Osprey Island. When he realized where he was, he got a kick out of breaking into Paul Brearley's house, building a fire, warming up, and finding enough food to feed himself as he figured out what to do. On the second day, he heard an old snow machine arriving. *Sometimes patience pays off,* he thought. Even if he couldn't find a solution right away, a solution might come to him.

Skip stepped over Paul's body and dragged it outside. He went through every pocket and removed anything in the way of identification. He pocketed a cluster of keys. One was an old Yale, very worn, and on a hunch he tried it in the door and it fit as softly and smoothly as a hand sliding into a favorite glove. This key must be seventy-five years old. There were also a couple of padlock keys and a large car key marked Toyota. An old trifold wallet had an ID in the name of Paul Baer. Skip chuckled. *An alias, yet.*

He went out to Paul's machine and rifled through the pack. On top was a bag with three breakfast sandwiches, still a little warm, plus a substantial bag of other food. He went back into the house, threw a log on the fire, and sat down to think, chewing reflectively on the warm sandwiches. Paul had brought him two things he needed, but he also brought some problems. What would he do with the body? He didn't want Paul to have the satisfaction of being found dead on his own doorstep. It wasn't a bleak enough, lonely enough ending to suit Skip's tastes. Also, it made it too easy to identify the body. Another obvious idea would be to weight the body, perhaps with Skip's own snow machine, and sink him in the lake. But on the other hand, he wanted the body found. He wanted Paul's masquerade, whatever it was, exposed. So the body must go somewhere else. For the moment, he dragged it just inside the door.

Whether he sank Paul's body with it or not, he decided his own snow machine would have to be sunk in the lake. If he left it, it would be traced to him in minutes. But that was not as easy as it seemed. The ice was more than a foot thick. It would be a project to cut a big enough hole in it, and Skip had always been averse to physical labor. But it had to be done. If he did the work in darkness and dropped the snow machine where the water was deep enough, the likelihood of anybody finding it was nil. Then at dawn he would use Paul's machine to get back to his truck. He could ditch Paul's machine later.

Using his newly acquired skeleton key, he searched the island's outbuildings and found a big logger's handsaw and a five-foot-long crowbar. Waiting for dark, he prepared himself a good meal and stoked the fire some more.

Late that evening, he used Paul's machine to tow his own out into the little bay. He picked a spot he figured was at least twenty-five-feet deep. Using the ice drill from his ice fishing kit, he drilled four holes through the ice. It took an hour to connect the four holes with the handsaw. He pried out the resultant block of ice with the long crowbar. With a huge, grunting effort, he tipped the snow machine up and into the hole. With a few gurgles, it was gone. He slid the plug of ice back into its place and shoveled snow over it roughly. By morning the block would be frozen in place, and the next snowfall would conceal his work permanently.

Back on the island, he hooked his cargo sled up to Paul's machine and parked it outside the door. He tied Paul's body onto the trailer, lashed it down, and covered it with a tarp. Back inside the warm house, he wiped down every surface that might have his fingerprints. He ate the last breakfast sandwich, now cold and clammy. Then he went to bed on the couch in Paul's sleeping bag.

After a good night's sleep, he rose in the darkness. He jumped onto the snow machine. Fifteen minutes later he was at Burton Island, a state campground just a mile or so away. It was a simple matter to roll Paul's body off the cargo sled and wrestle it into one of the camping lean-tos. Twenty minutes after that, he was loading Paul's machine onto his pickup truck at a boat launch at the edge of St. Albans. As he drove toward home, the sun was just rising. He could make his ten o'clock appointment in Burlington, no problem.

Chapter 3

THE RED TRUCK

At two that afternoon, Skip was safe and warm, sitting in his house on Brown Point, in his favorite chair, looking out over the frozen lake, with a large cup of hot chocolate in his hand. It was snowing heavily. Soon his tracks and the hole in the ice would be completely covered. Except for the mess in the house on Osprey Island and the body in the lean-to, the day's events never happened. The meth was sold and already to market in Boston and Providence. None of it had stayed in Vermont, which was fine with him. Paul's snow machine was safely stowed in his garage next to Skip's old speedboat. Having it there didn't really put him at risk for the moment, but he'd like to get rid of it. Maybe sell it on eBay.

On a little table in front of him sat Paul's wallet. The ID inside gave his name as Paul Baer, with an address in Tupper Lake, and a truck registration at the same address. Next to the wallet was a cluster of keys. One, he knew, fit the house on Osprey Island. One went to the snow machine. There were several he couldn't identify. And there was the large, flat key marked Toyota. Logically, that had to fit a truck parked somewhere. Since he had heard the machine approaching from the west, there were only a few places where that truck could be.

Skip felt moving the body off Osprey Island had been worth it. He did not want Paul identified too soon. He wanted him to stay a lonely, unidentified vagrant for a few months. When they opened the camp and saw the mess, they would figure out who the body really had been.

He decided to find and move the truck. Why make it easy for the police? Let them work to figure it out.

He drank a beer, then another, then set out in his old, nondescript Subaru Outback. In the North Country, everybody drove these four-wheel-drive cars. They went anywhere, handled like sports cars, and never got stuck. The perfect drug dealer's car, almost invisible.

He took the ferry over to South Hero and started checking the public boat launch ramps. He found the truck at the second site he checked, covered with snow. The key fit, the truck started. He ran the truck for a few minutes to warm it up, then shut it down and locked it.

He made a plan as he drove home in the Subaru. In the morning he would drive to the park and ride on the New York side at Cumberland Head, near the ferry dock. He'd take the ferry to South Hero as a pedestrian. Then he would hitchhike, walk, or otherwise find his way to the boat launch, drive Paul's truck back across on the ferry, and park it at the parking lot on the New York side, leaving the keys in the ignition to make it as easy as possible to steal. He got home, had another beer, and went to bed. A long day.

*   *   *

At eight the next morning, he drove to the park and ride, then walked onto the 9 A.M. ferry. It was not odd for pedestrians to take the ferry at any time

26

of year. It cost over twenty dollars per day to take a car over and back, and many commuters found it was cheaper to keep a car on both sides.

On the way over, he chatted with the other passengers, and he got lucky right away. He found a French Canadian salesman returning home to Montreal. From his smuggling activities, Skip was fluent in Canadian French, and he talked the man into driving him up island to the side road that led to the boat launch. Skip thought, *This man will be across the border long before any policeman gets involved.* The man dropped him off on Route 2, and Skip walked the half mile to the boat launch.

The red Toyota was gone.

Skip stood there, stricken. A single set of tracks showed that someone had driven the little truck away. He couldn't imagine how this might have occurred, though he could tell from the paucity of tracks that it wasn't the police who had moved it. That was good because it meant the police hadn't found it and towed it away. Then he noticed a second set of tracks, boot prints plus a parallel track of bicycle wheels, also leading down toward where the truck had been.

*　　*　　*

The trip back to the ferry wasn't easy. He had to walk out to Route 2, and it was another mile before a man in a truck gave him a lift. By the time he had made his way on the back roads to the ferry, he had taken three short rides and walked two miles in the cold, worrying all the way. He couldn't imagine who had taken the truck. He had the key, and the truck wasn't really worth stealing. Nobody was likely to come to this boat launch except the occasional ice fisherman. All he could think was that there was somebody out there who knew as much as or more than he did about the situation, someone who was messing with his mind.

By the time he got back to the ferry, he was frozen and exhausted. Though as strong as ever, he was out of shape. The ferry had just left. The next one would come in twenty minutes. In the Champ Diner, he grabbed two egg-and-bacon sandwiches kept warm under a row of spotlights on the counter. He quickly had two cups of coffee, warming his hands on the mug. Then he walked down onto the ferry, huddling in the barely heated cabin. He still couldn't construct a story that explained the vanished truck.

When he got to the New York side, he walked up the ramp to the park and ride. There, right next to his Subaru, was the red Toyota. The window was half open and the cab still a little warm. The key was in the ignition. At first he panicked. He thought it must be the same key that was in his pocket two hours ago. But when he frantically checked his pocket, the cluster of keys was still exactly where he put it, clumped next to his own keys.

By now, he was imagining some diabolical force, someone who could read his mind, anticipate his plans, and knew what he was up to. But then he thought, *My goal was to get the Toyota to the park and ride and leave it to be stolen. That goal is accomplished. What's the problem?*

He got into his truck, cracked open a beer, and drove home.

Chapter 4

APRIL FOOL'S DAY

On April Fool's Day 2008, Detective Fred Davis decided to move out of his house in Burlington and live on the water. It was a decision slow in coming.

At one time or another, Davis had worked for every type of law enforcement agency in Vermont: town cops, sheriff's office as deputy, Coast Guard, Fish and Wildlife, and city police beat cop in Burlington. Now he was a state police detective, a sergeant, working out of St. Albans, a small city right on Lake Champlain not far from the Canadian border. He worked all sorts of cases, but sometimes his beat was the lake itself, which he knew as well as a person could in one lifetime. He was fifty-three, two years from mandatory retirement. He'd been thinking of "living aboard" for years. Maybe this was the time.

The closest thing to a real city in Vermont was Burlington, a university town also right on the lake. Davis's work had occasionally taken him down Starr Farm Road, near the Burlington bike path. He would see the boat sitting on a trailer in the driveway of a nondescript little colonial. It was basically a lobster boat with the rear deck mostly enclosed as a cabin. For boat lovers, style is everything. This boat had style. It was obvious, even under the blue tarps, just from the shape of the bow, rising in an elegant curve. The tarps obscured what might be inside. Dangling crookedly from the propellers was a For Sale sign with a phone number.

Eventually he started inventing excuses to drive down Starr Farm Road. This went on for two or three years. The For Sale sign was fading.

Davis knew that, for him, buying a new boat was a particularly effective strategy for evasion. When he wanted to avoid some major life question, he tended to get obsessed with some boat. By the time he had found it, researched it, bought it, and got it going properly, he would have totally forgotten the real issue at hand.

*   *   *

His life wasn't exactly in crisis, but he was having doubts about his work. He was also finally realizing that his relationship with his son and his family wasn't what it should be. It was cordial, but not close. The issue that threatened to bother him the most was his relationship with his ex-wife, Diane. The problem there was, he still loved her. None of these things were easy to fix. Better to buy a boat.

On April first, he called the owner of the lobster boat. He asked him if the boat was still on the market, and the owner replied, "Everything's for sale, at the right price."

Later that day, he inspected the boat up close. It was shaped like a Maine lobster boat. Under the front deck was a modest cabin where two nonclaustrophobic people could sleep, plus a tiny bathroom and a little closet. Behind that was the wheelhouse, which contained the helm, a little kitchen, a dining booth that turned into a bed, and a great many minuscule

30

storage areas. Behind that was a five-foot open deck, and behind that two luminous, fuel-efficient, silver Honda outboard motors.

With the economy in a slide, and gas at $3.60 and rising, boat prices were dropping. By dinner, the boat was his. By ten the next morning, he'd towed it to Bob's Boat Repair, where everything would be made "shipshape and Bristol fashion."

*   *   *

Later that day, Davis put his house in Burlington up for rent, May 1 to December 1, on Craigslist. Davis and Diane had bought the house in 1990 when they were both working in Burlington. When they split in 1996, he stayed on, mostly out of inertia. He wasn't particularly attached to the house or to Burlington. He just didn't want to move back home.

The Davis Farm, where he grew up, was on the west side of South Hero Island. In Fred's youth, it was a large dairy farm of 150 acres and 100 cows, its land sloping gently down to the lake, with a huge brick farmhouse surrounded by a long, languorous porch. Across the farmyard, stretching north along the road, was a massive barn, and beside it a trio of tall, metallic blue silos, with "Harvestore" lettered on the sides. Nearby were smaller barns and sheds. Beyond the barn to the north were three cottages with porches.

Like all successful farms, The Davis Farm was nothing like the simple dairy farm it had been fifty years ago. It was diversified. There were now only twenty cows. Though they made most of the work, they brought in little money. The farm now grew apples and vegetables of all sorts and made maple syrup in the spring. All of this was sold in the farm stand, along with hot dogs, pies, gifts, maple products, fruit, and ice cream made from their own cream. The farm was also a bit of a resort: families came back year after year to stay in one wing of the house or in the three cabins. When cash ran low every few years, Fred's father would sell a lakeside lot, and they would have a new neighbor.

31

Davis's parents were well into their eighties and still worked the farm. His mom made pies and ran the farm stand. She made jams and more jams from the berries and fruits they grew or bought from other farms nearby. His dad was a cow farmer and would die a cow farmer, even if it cost more to make milk than he could earn selling it. Of their six children, five, including Fred, had flown the coop. Hazel, the eldest at fifty-six, was the farm manager. She knew how to do everything. Fred and Diane's son, Andy, was twenty-six and the only grandchild working the farm. He also knew how to do everything. He had built a modern house, set back from the road, where he lived with his wife and two children.

Hazel was married to Luke. Luke was from North Hero and had been friends with Fred since the age of six. He had begun slowly adopting the farm, or being adopted by it, since he and Fred first played on the rocky beach after school. He fixed most of the Volvos on the islands and all the cars, trucks, tractors, and equipment on the farm. In winter, he repaired and restored boats in the far end of the big barn. Fred was a partner in this venture, but he made it to the boat barn only a couple of evenings per week and the occasional Saturday afternoon.

Fred had never taken to farming. Check that: Fred hated farming. There had been no childhood trauma; no cow had kicked him, he was not allergic to hay. He just hated farming. But he had taken to the water, to boats, fishing, and every other activity that can be done on a big lake. Over the years, he had owned, by himself or with Luke, twenty-seven boats. Until he bought the lobster boat, only four remained. One was an aluminum canoe, which lay upside down on the beach year-round and was occasionally used by summer guests. Another was an Adirondack Guideboat, an elegant, double-ended wooden rowboat made around 1900. When he was young, he particularly enjoyed taking it out when the wind was howling. He liked how alarmed his parents got, sitting on the porch and watching him disappear between the waves. Now they didn't look up from their novels when he went out there, no matter what the weather.

The third boat was a practical but unromantic Boston Whaler, your basic utility workboat, named *The Ute*.

The fourth boat was a Lyman Islander. When Luke and Fred were thirteen, a storm had dumped it on their beach. It had two basketball-sized holes in its hull and was sunk to the gunwales, flopping about in the waves like a dying fish. It was a twenty-one-foot inboard runabout made all of wood, with beautiful white lapstrake sides, an oak frame, and mahogany deck and trim. Afloat, it was one of the most stylish motorboats on the lake, excepting the Chris-Craft speedboats owned by wealthy families. Tom Burden in Plattsburgh, just across the lake in New York, owned the Islander, and he sold it to them for fifty bucks when they offered to repair it for $500.

When they found the Islander, dairy had already begun its long decline in Vermont. One end of the huge cow barn was empty. Luke and Fred used the tractor to drag the boat onto a farm trailer and towed it into the barn. Within six weeks, working nonstop, Fred had rebuilt the hull, painted it, and refinished the inside. Luke had dried out the engine and rebuilt it. The boat went back into the water, and the boys made a point of cruising past Tom Burden's dock on a daily basis. For several summers they spent at least one weekend cruising past all the marinas, showing people what a real boat should look like.

For Davis, his first sight of this old wooden boat, and the weeks of work that followed, were an awakening. He came to love the old boats, the ornery material they were built from, and the craft that went into them. They had a beauty that modern fiberglass boats never achieved. He wanted to know what the wooden boatbuilders knew, to be part of the conversation.

It was during this project that Fred discovered he had a gift for the boatbuilder's peculiar form of woodworking. He could visualize the complicated, curved shapes that went into wooden boats and figure out how to make straight pieces of lumber submit to them. He had a feel for what made a boat strong, and what left it vulnerable if the waves hit it the wrong way one day.

33

For the next forty years, some boat or other was always being made or remade in the boat barn. Some were restorations of beautiful but neglected old wooden boats, repaired for paying customers; others were boats they'd bought cheap, fixed up, and sold after a summer's use. A few Luke and Fred built from scratch. Working on these boats reached a part of him that his other activities never quite got to.

Davis's new lobster boat went into the water May first. South Hero is connected to the Vermont mainland by a causeway known as the Sand Bar. It forms the southern end of the Inland Sea. Apple Island Marina was tucked in a little cove at the island end of the Sand Bar and would be his home base until December 1. It was close to work by car or boat. The farm was a twenty-minute drive north. The Grand Isle ferry to New York was fifteen minutes away, on the west side of South Hero, not far from the farm. That evening, Fred took the new boat out in the bay to get a sense of how it handled. He slowed down to an idle and practiced landing it at an imaginary dock. Then he docked it at Apple Island about six times. Its dual engines made it possible to do acrobatic maneuvers, spins, and arabesques that at first seemed impossible.

The plan for the maiden voyage was for Davis to boat to Burlington early, grab a lunch, and meet Luke, who was delivering a Volvo to someone there. Then they would put the boat through its paces going back north on the Broad Lake up to the farm, where a section of dock was in place to receive it. Then dinner with the family, and home via the Gut, which was the gap that separated North from South Hero.

Davis made it down to Burlington uneventfully. The little harbor was just waking up for the season, but a space was waiting for him near the Burlington ferry. He met Luke at a sandwich shop. They bought lunch to go and set off again, with Luke at the helm. The wind was rising, the waves about three feet high. They were pleased that the boat was entirely happy in the rough water.

It was no speedboat. Lots of modern boats on the lake would go thirty, forty, fifty, or even sixty miles an hour. This one would top out at perhaps twenty-seven miles an hour, and cruised at about twenty. At that speed, the run to the farm was about two hours.

Davis was inordinately happy. The boat had all the attributes he liked. It was old-fashioned, it had workboat lineage in spades, it was sea-kindly, it was "salty." Its lines were much like the Islander's, high at the front, swooping low and wide at the back. At the same time, it was a modern, unsinkable boat, with the latest electronic bells and whistles. He wouldn't have to spend winter nights in the boat barn to keep it seaworthy. He had spent a lifetime tinkering with a succession of marine engines; he'd paddled home, or been towed home, many times when engines sputtered and died on the water. This boat had a pair of bombproof Honda outboards. If he didn't run out of gas, he would always get home. As Luke navigated, Fred sat in the passenger seat. He sat at his little restaurant booth and read the paper. He made a pot of coffee. He dusted every horizontal surface in the cabin.

Davis reclaimed the helm as they approached the single section of dock at the farm. It was an awkward landing with the waves so high. As he was approaching from the north side of the dock, his cell rang.

He could see it was Lt. Ethel Collings, barracks commander at St. Albans Barracks, known as A Troop. He said, "Hi, Ethel."

"We have a homicide, we think, up on Burton Island. We just got a call from a man named Perly Trimble, the maintenance chief there. They found a body in one of the lean-tos."

"I know Perly a little. I'm on the water now. I can be there in about forty-five minutes. I'll just go by boat."

Luke looked over at Fred. "Customers?"

"Yeah. A dead one. On Burton Island."

"Just drop me off and we'll talk later. Call if I can help."

It took Davis two tries to get close enough to the dock for Luke to hop off. He backed out quickly and gunned the engines. He went most of the way at top speed.

Davis was two miles from the Gut, a pond within a lake. It was the gateway to the Inland Sea. He went through a little too fast, just slowing down at the drawbridge connecting North and South Hero. Burton was about four miles from there, but hard to distinguish from the mainland. Yachters usually struck a compass reading to find it, but Davis had made this trip hundreds of times. The shape of the hills behind it gave him his direction.

There were many islands in the Inland Sea. A few were estates owned by wealthy families. A couple had been taken over by the cormorants. Several were state parks with a few designated tent sites, a couple of outhouses, and no other services. Burton Island, in St. Albans Bay, was an elaborate campground with dozens of tent sites, some lean-tos that made tents unnecessary, bathhouses with civilized, coin-operated showers, a nature center, open fields for volleyball, nature paths, and a little bistro that sold beer, insect repellent, chips, and delicious morning omelets. It also had the best yacht basin on the lake, with a totally protected inner harbor where dozens of small- and medium-sized cruisers could lay up for a week of socializing, or just shelter from a storm. Yacht clubs came here for their gatherings. Burton was very popular with French Canadian boaters from Montreal. There was usually an area where French was the first language.

On May 2, a small crew was just beginning to wake the place up for the summer. Most of the sections of dock were still piled up on the grass. Davis pulled in next to a Boston Whaler with a Vermont Forests, Parks and Recreation decal on the side.

A tall, young man in a green uniform was standing at the dock. The young man looked green around the gills himself. He helped Davis tie up the boat and introduced himself. "Hi, Detective Davis? I'm John Forest. We're down this way."

Davis grabbed a brown canvas bag, like a doctor's bag with a zipper top, and hopped out of the boat. They walked down a path through the woods toward the west shore of the island, past tent sites, lean-tos, and bathrooms.

Next to a lean-to marked APPLEWOOD, John Forest said, "We're here." An older man was standing next to a picnic table. He was maybe five feet nine and had a generous gut, what was known in Davis's family as a bay window. He was wearing the green parks department uniform. Vermont is a small state, and Davis, who once worked for Fish and Wildlife, recognized the man from a variety of interactions over the years.

"Hi, Perly. How are you?"

"Fine, though I won't say 'good to see you' under the circumstances." He pointed toward the lean-to. It was a log structure with three walls and a roof, open on the lake side. "He's in there," Trimble continued. "We were just working our way along, cleaning up. When we got here, well, this is what we found."

"How long have you been here?"

"This is our third day. We've just started cleaning, raking, getting ready to put in the docks, turning the water on, you know . . ."

John Forest looked uncomfortable. He was inching out toward the road as if to say, *This isn't what I signed up for.*

Davis said, "OK, just wait here for me, Perly. Mr. Forest? Go back to the dock. The crime scene people will be here in a bit. Bring them along. But don't hurry. I'd like maybe forty-five minutes with the place to myself."

He walked up to the open side of the lean-to and stepped up into it. He pulled a little digital camera out of his bag and started taking pictures. In the corner, just out of view, was a body, neatly sitting leaning against the wall, as if in thought. The man was large, perhaps a size bigger than Davis, maybe six feet two. He was wearing a brown insulated coverall, insulated Bean boots, and a hunter's red plaid hat. He wore bifocals with wire rims. His hair was brown going to gray, as was his small, round beard. He wore no gloves, and his hands were large and long-fingered. It was a peaceful scene. There were a few sticks on the floor and some windblown leaves, but no signs of a struggle. A small bloodstain on the man's chest looked like an entry wound.

Davis couldn't really see much of the body in all the thick clothes. The face looked dried out. It had been nibbled in a few places. At first, Davis thought the man might have been here a week or two. But then he realized it could have been much longer. The body would have been pretty much frozen until recently. It had been a cold winter.

Davis didn't move from where he stood. From there, the man's hands, crossed in his lap, looked as if they had done a lot of physical work. Davis took pictures from every angle. Perly stood nearby, watching.

In a half hour, John Forest arrived with the medical examiner and the scene-of-crime team. They put on suits and booties at the edge of the campsite.

Davis pulled Perly over toward the road that wound through the campsite. "They know what to do. What can you tell me?"

Perly liked to talk, but in fact he didn't have much to contribute. "We've been here three days, and we go home at night. I've been over most of the island. I haven't seen anything I can think of that looks funny. We've been up to the other end. None of the buildings have been broken into."

While the crew surveyed the campsite, Davis looked around nearby. The campsites were arranged along both sides of a winding dirt road that ran about one hundred feet from the water's edge. Little patches of scrubby woods gave each site an illusion of privacy. Campers had worn paths to the bathrooms, to the roads, and down to the rough, stone-covered bits of waterfront that served as beaches. Davis was trying to imagine where and how someone would have brought a body up to this particular lean-to. The ice had been out for a month but nights were often below freezing. The body could have come by boat, or over the ice. In either case, there were two pathways that seemed the most convenient routes from the lake to Applewood. One led along a little path through a piece of scrawny woods, through a campsite labeled CHERRYWOOD, and down to the rocky beach. It would be easy to land a boat or a snow machine here. A very similar route, just a little longer, went through the adjacent site, Birchwood. Almost any conveyance would work: dogsled, toboggan, snow machine, garden cart, or no conveyance at all. The distance was only about 250 feet.

Hoping to get lucky, Davis walked the Cherrywood route. There were no telltale beer cans, credit card receipts, or bullet cartridges. Where the patch went through the woods, though, there was possibly something of note. About five feet up, where the path narrowed, the lower branches seemed deformed, and a couple were broken. Davis snapped a couple of pictures, pulled some crime scene tape out of his bag, and marked off the area. He followed the path down past the lean-to and down to the water, seeing nothing else.

He pulled out his cellphone and speed-dialed Fish and Wildlife. "Henry Steinberg, please." Henry was a wildlife biologist, one of the people who made sure there were enough deer, moose, and various fish in the state, and not too many. He was one of the team of people who managed the deer herd, which he knew intimately out in the field. He surveyed their habits and habitat winter and summer. He also was a fanatical bow hunter. He knew as much about deer sign as anyone in Vermont.

He answered on the second ring. "Steinberg."

"Is this Henry 'Chingachgook' Steinberg?"

"Davis! How are you? What can I do for you?"

"I've got a crime scene here, on Burton Island. I'm hoping you can come out and look at some bent twigs for me. They might be evidence. Any chance you can come out tomorrow, say around 10 A.M.? Can I pick you up in St. Albans or at Hero's Welcome?" Hero's Welcome was a popular country store on North Hero, a meeting point for boaters, campers, and cyclists.

"It'll be more fun to boat out myself. It's kind of boring here, I could use a boat ride. I'll meet you at the island at ten."

*　　*　　*

The forensic team, the parkies, and the dead body had left the island. But Davis decided to stay over; he had his house with him. That evening, he shut his cabin door, opened a bottle of wine, and put a large pot of water to boil on his two-burner stove. He turned on the radio. The tech sector was in a slump, and somebody was stalking Uma Thurman. Gas prices were rising by the day.

He knew it was way too early to even think about what had happened at Burton Island, or why. He wouldn't have cause of death or victim ID for a day or so at best. But Davis was a chronic list-maker, and sometimes an item on one of his lists later proved important. It was also his way to suspend thinking about his cases and get some sleep, or to drop the current case sufficiently that he could pay attention to whoever he was with. He wasn't intentionally thinking about the case, but his mind was stewing, unbidden. He put a legal pad on the table with a pencil beside it. He knew some important point could vanish into the ether if he didn't write it down.

As he chopped the onions, he thought, *Well, there's a cadre of die-hard ice fishermen who waste their lives on the ice every day. Maybe they saw something.*

He wrote down: "ice fish."

As he diced the garlic, he thought of all the ways the body could have gotten there: *boat, truck over ice, dogsled, snow machine, helicopter, aliens from the sky. Maintenance crew brought him on the ferry yesterday in a golf cart.*

Davis crossed out "aliens, helicopter, and maintenance crew."

He thought, *What if we can't identify the man? Who could he be?* He wrote down: "drug runner, fisherman, mental patient."

He didn't look like a mental patient—some other sort of criminal, ordinary missing Vermont person, thought Davis.

As he stirred in the pesto, he thought of all the ways the body could have gotten into the lean-to from the lake: *truck on the road, carry from boat, straight in with the snow machine or dogsled, garden cart, plastic sled over snow.*

All of a sudden the game was over and he ate his dinner as NPR told of declining housing starts and the battle between Hillary and Barack.

*　　*　　*

40

It was not the first time Davis had lived aboard. For his first two years at Boston University, Davis stayed in the dorm like everybody else. He started reading books—English lit mostly, a little history—and rowed crew on the Charles River. But the summer after his sophomore year, he and Luke found and fixed up a very ugly, slightly misshapen thirty-four-foot cabin cruiser built in the forties. After a summer's work, it floated and the dual motors worked if tended properly. The kitchen functioned. They rigged up a tiny woodstove in the main cabin.

It was no luxury yacht. The woodwork was way past the point where it could be revarnished; there were no brasses to shine. They cruised down the lake, down the Champlain Canal, down the Hudson River, and up the coast to school. Luke hitchhiked back to Vermont. Davis docked it at various marinas, finally settling at the East Cambridge Yacht Club, where a very few die-hards kept their boats afloat all year long and an even smaller group lived on board. He lived there with two other rowers for two years, occasionally taking the boat out in the harbor, and once down to New York for a party. It was basically a floating dorm suite, with a pile of scrounged construction debris on the cabin roof for fuel, and heaps of laundry in every corner.

His first year at Suffolk Law, he cleaned up the boat and lived there by himself. He liked the solitude. He liked getting to know the other boaters. By then, Luke was taking ag courses at the University of Vermont, but without enthusiasm. On vacations, Luke would come down and they would explore the waters around Boston, getting as far as Portland Maine to the north and the second summer as far as Chesapeake Bay to the south. While Luke piloted, Davis kept track of the charts with one eye and read law with the other.

Then he was smitten by Diane. She was a tallish, slim, good-looking, brown-haired girl, a bit Irish and a bit Greek. He'd never really had a serious girlfriend. Diane was one year ahead of him at Suffolk Law, already wearing her good clothes to work at a local law firm.

At first he was wowed by how smart she was. He had never met anyone who read the *Boston Globe*, the *New York Times*, and the *Wall Street Journal* every day. She had long since read most of the books he had first encountered at BU and could quote from some of them. She was also funny in a quiet way.

She was much more focused than he was. She wanted to do public interest law, maybe family law, do some good in the world.

Her family lived in the working-class part of Cambridge and in Quincy, south of Boston at the end of the subway line. Her sisters and aunts were mostly housewives. A couple of them taught school until they got married, then again for a few years when their children started going to school, but they didn't really have careers. Her brothers and uncles worked in construction, or for the post office. Several were policemen. She made no secret of the fact that she wanted an entirely different life for herself.

She tended to wear very subdued, almost prissy outfits—woolen jumpers that attracted no attention and big glasses. But at a party one evening on the cruiser, Fred noticed her in a different way.

They started going out. He wasn't exactly sure why she liked him. But it made more sense when he heard more of her story. Her second week at law school, a tax law professor named Chadwick Ames plucked her out of the class. He was a charismatic, athletic guy about thirty years old with a prosperous, growing tax law practice. For the remainder of the year, they were an item. At first he was charming. He praised her intelligence, called on her in class. She moved into his condo overlooking Boston Harbor. But as their year together progressed, he became less supportive, more critical. He made fun of her values, and her desire to get into public interest law. He thought she was smart enough to make it in the business world, perhaps as a tax lawyer like himself. Why waste her talent doing good?

Around midyear, she learned she was but one of a string of student girlfriends, and that he usually made his pick during the second week of class. By spring break, she was back in her parents' East Cambridge house, in her old room, looking for her own apartment and a roommate to share the rent with.

Fred was the anti-Chad. His dwelling also looked out over Boston Harbor, but that was the only similarity. It never would have occurred to him, back then or later, to make judgments on her ambitions. He looked up to her, and let her know it. And he was loyal, no other girlfriends in the wings. He thought she might prefer a relationship where she was the more dominant half, the more together person. She might want to be with someone who treated her nicely all the time.

At that point, Fred was also planning on a law career, though he couldn't quite state what kind of law he would practice. It was only later, when he was working in a prosecutor's office, that he figured out why his career goals had been so vague. There was no sort of lawyer job that he wanted.

At first Diane was amused by the floating house. They cleaned and cleaned, repainted everything. Fred got the shower working. He rebuilt the galley so proper meals could be prepared. He built a closet, and they sewed new covers for the built-in seats. It was fun. It was playing house. The boat became a social center for their friends. Cruises into the harbor or up the Mystic River became the preferred party. For Diane it was a step toward a slightly grittier, more physical world, where things didn't happen if you didn't do them. The water or electricity or heat didn't just appear when you needed them; there was always a little task to do to make anything happen. For Fred, to whom these things were routine, the new things were reading, thinking, taking the Sunday *Times* and reading it all, having friends over to talk politics, learning to pronounce Camus and Sartre, beginning to be able to distinguish a bit of Bach from a bit of Beethoven. To him these were uncharted waters, a whole new Lake Champlain where he could spend years learning the winds, sounding the bottom, exploring the shorelines.

Their first summer together, they took a vacation run with Luke toward New York. For Diane, being at sea was new, fun, and sometimes scary. But it was very difficult for her to penetrate the unrelenting intimacy, boat chat, and unconscious, secret language that had grown up between the two men, who had spent most of their time together since the age of six. There were dozens of private jokes, little words or references that encapsulated a long joke or an important shared story. She could talk with Fred, she could talk a bit with Luke, but when the three of them sat on the back deck with a glass of beer, she might as well not have been there. The constancy of the boating tasks—piloting, navigating, fiddling with the engines, handling the changing weather—further isolated her. There was nothing for her to do but read and cook for the boys.

Diane became quieter and quieter as the trip progressed until she retreated with her book to the innermost cabin, shut the door, and didn't emerge for two days except to eat. As they got their first glimpse of Boston Harbor, she dragged Davis down into the little cabin. By that point, he was getting pretty shaky. He had no idea why she should be upset.

She looked right at him. "Fred, I love you. I'm willing to keep loving you. But you have to decide whether you are serious about me and whether you are serious about anything. You have a choice here. Perhaps you should marry Luke." The next day, Luke set off again, taking the cruiser back to Vermont. A week later, Fred and Diane rented a proper apartment in Cambridge. Grown-up life had begun.

*　　*　　*

That night at Burton Island, as Davis lay in his cabin under the old, frayed quilt with his book in his lap and his little reading light over his shoulder, he remembered that time with pleasure, in spite of how it ended.

He didn't know exactly why Diane left; there was no dramatic conflict. Fred read a lot of detective stories with detectives whose wives had left. One cliché was that the detective was emotionally crippled because of seeing such awful violence. He had slow-growing PTSD that left him unable to relate to wife and family; eventually the wife wouldn't be able to take it anymore. In another version of the story, the detective worked almost all the time. He'd stay out late, work weekends, cancel vacations to catch the bad guys. If he wasn't at work, he was thinking about the case. Eventually, the wife would seek consolation elsewhere.

Davis never found these story lines convincing. He worked in Vermont, and these scenarios, if they ever occurred, didn't apply. Most crime was ordinary. His weekly routine was ordinary, not so different from other people's. He was sure Diane left for ordinary reasons, too, even if he wasn't sure what they were.

He knew she had never liked Davis being any kind of policeman. She had an ambitious side. But he also thought they might have married too quickly. He had never really had a serious relationship before Diane. The one she'd had was a disaster. Neither of them had been out working in the world to any extent. Maybe that had something to do with it: Diane thought she might be missing something, doing the expected thing, like her mother and her various aunts back home. People sometimes think that by making a change, they'll feel better, their dissatisfaction will dispel.

After all, why would he want to leave a comfortable, fully fixed-up, heated house for a dwelling the size of a small trailer with a bedroom the size of a closet he couldn't stand up in? *I have no idea*, he said to himself, *except I sleep better here.*

He fell asleep, thinking of nothing, as the waves gently rocked the boat.

At exactly ten the next morning, Henry Steinberg approached the dock in an aluminum skiff at full throttle, heading right for Davis's new boat. At the last second, he cut the engine, the boat settled down abruptly, almost to a dead stop, and Steinberg pivoted into the dock. A moment later, it was all tied up.

"What is that thing?" he said, looking at Davis's pride and joy.

Steinberg was perhaps five-nine, slim and dapper, with a little, neatly trimmed mustache. He wore a Red Sox hat, a green Fish and Wildlife parka, and tall, green rubber boots.

"And you're supposed to be Chingachgook. Are you blind? That's my new house. What do you think it is? Admit it, you're impressed. You're actually green with envy."

"You never cease to amaze me. Will you ever grow up?"

The two men embraced. Though Paul had been on the enforcement side,

45

running down poachers and checking for fishing licenses, and Steinberg was on the scientific side, trying to keep the deer herd healthy, it was a small department. They knew each other well. They chatted about work and kids for a minute, then Steinberg cut to the chase.

"OK, let's see your bent twigs. While we're walking, tell me the story." They walked over to the campsite, and Davis told him what he had learned so far.

At the lean-to, now all cleaned up, Davis said, "I tried to figure out where someone might cut through to get a corpse up here. There are two obvious paths. One goes this way, through that campsite and down to the beach, and one over here. I'll show you what I found." They walked the path through the patch of woods to the spot Davis had taped off, where several twigs were broken off, about four feet up, on two small maple trees, right next to each other. Other branches were cracked and bent, all in the same direction, leading up from the lake.

Pointing to the broken branches, Davis asked, "What is that?"

"Well, a moose cuts a much bigger swath through the woods. You'd see bent *trees*. It's not moose. We don't see moose out here anyway, hardly ever. I don't see a lot of deer sign here. No scat, no branches eaten. I'm sure there are some deer on this island, but there's much more for them to eat on the south end. They might crash through the woods a bit, but the evidence would be lower to the ground. They move on established paths they keep open; they don't just bound through on top of the snow. When, supposedly, was the body placed?"

Davis answered, "I don't know, maybe six to eight weeks ago."

"Well, there was three feet of snow eight weeks ago. I'd say snow machine. It would be up on top of the snow, and not too graceful going, through an opening like this. It could also be somebody dragging something by hand or on a cargo sled. Sometimes I do see snow machine sign when I'm in the woods. You might look for oil drips, litter, snow sort of stained by the exhaust from the older machines. But actually, I can't tell much from this. Maybe a more modern snow machine would be distinguished by a lack of sign. Unless the oil pan leaks, there'd be no trace after the snow melted. Other than the old bent twigs."

They spent an hour looking for snow machine scat, if there was such a thing, but found nothing. Davis thought it might be time to start interviewing ice fishermen.

Davis ran into Perly Trimble at the dock.

"Mr. Trimble. We're gone for now, but I'm sure we'll be back. Who ice fishes here? I mean, who ice fishes a lot? Particularly on the west side of the island or here in the boat harbor."

"I'm not too sure. Frankly, when I'm out here checking in the winter, I'm mostly focused on looking around, staying warm, and going home as quick as possible, and I don't pay much attention. I'd say there are usually three or four permanent shanties, though. A couple of guys come out by truck, the others with snow machines. One of the shanties looks like it's made out of a truck cap. I seem to remember a black Dodge pickup. But I have no idea who's really out here."

"OK," Davis said. "Thanks."

Chapter 5

DINNER AT HOME

Three hours later, Davis's boat was back at Apple Island, and he had driven to the morgue. He and Dr. Andrew Kramer, the ME, were standing over the body. Without his many layers of winter garments, Davis could see the dead man was on the tall side, six two, lean, and muscled, particularly his shoulders, without being bulked up. Davis, who had spent a lot of time in school locker rooms, thought, *Swimmer, maybe rower.* The physique of a basketball player wouldn't necessarily look much different from that of a baseball or soccer player, but swimmers, rowers, wrestlers, and long-distance runners often had distinct body types.

As if he knew what Davis was thinking, Kramer said, "I know, he does look like a swimmer, but it's been a long time. This guy has been working outdoors. Look at his hands. They're heavily callused. So far, he seems healthy for his age, which I put at fifty to sixty. Of course, I'm just getting started here."

Davis drove north to St. Albans and went directly upstairs to a brown, nondescript room known as the squad room, where he would meet with the team working on the case. Detective Sgt. Bert Miller was already there. For the past few years, the two men had often worked together, particularly on murders and other difficult cases. They were the most experienced detectives in the troop. It was an odd partnership, not at all the TV version where two guys drive around in a car together, make clever banter, and roust out suspects. Bert and Fred usually worked separate threads of a case. Davis liked to be outside, running around, checking out a crime scene, driving or boating somewhere to gather evidence. Bert was more of an analyst and didn't like racing around. He was much happier indoors at his desk in their warm office, making calls, researching things, and putting together a narrative from the results, preferably a narrative that could be proven in court. He was happy to leave the sports activities to Fred. Davis was adept at finding excuses to investigate by boat. To Bert, any day where he could avoid a boat ride with Fred Davis was a good day.

Looking prim and fresh, Trooper Dick Fowler and Detective Trooper Janice Pearlstein came in on the stroke of four o'clock. This was their first time working on a murder case. Lt. Ethel Collings was right behind them. She ran the barracks and had her fingers on more useful information than any other single person in the state. She was about five feet tall, gray-haired, and slim. Though she rarely left the building on assignment, she always wore her uniform, but there were quite a few nonregulation rings and bracelets there, too, and her nails were a bright red. Her glasses, decorated with glitter, hung from a little chain. Her demeanor—raised eyebrows, often peering over her glasses—said *I'm watching. Let's get this right.* Everybody in the building depended on her skepticism to keep things on track.

She was followed by Sgt. Peter Dooley, the head of the scene-of-crime team, there to give a report. Everyone had a copy of a loose-leaf report, with photos of the scene and the victim, a preliminary autopsy, and various documents. The little book would get redone repeatedly as the investigation progressed. They each had copies of three eight-by-ten photos. One showed the body in situ, one the body at the morgue, and the third a touched-up version of the morgue picture to use with the public.

Normally investigations were organized using lead sheets. Every clue, tip, suggestion, rumor, or even suspicion got a lead sheet, giving the information needed to follow up on the lead. These would be divided among the members of the investigative team. But they didn't really have much in the way of leads, other than the body itself. They were still fishing for the leads that would get the investigation moving.

Davis went first with the preliminary pathology report. "The coroner says the victim was about fifty to sixty. He died of a gunshot to the heart, probably a handgun, maybe a .32 or 9 mil. No residue on the body. He wasn't shot at the scene, there was no blood there. The man was one hundred eighty pounds, very strong. He was a smoker now or at some time, and otherwise in good health. Not an office worker. He had a worker's hands. The pathologist says he had spent a lot of time outdoors."

Dooley was next. "Well, let's see. No ID. We found absolutely nothing in or around the lean-to. We'll be back today combing the island, including the entire shore, but we don't expect much. He was dressed very warmly in clothes that could be bought anywhere in the US or Canada. We're still working on the clothes—"

Bert cut in, "But don't expect much, I know. I'm looking for missing people who match the description, starting in Vermont and New York. I'm working back through the winter and branching out geographically, including Canada. A lot of people go missing in any given year, and a surprising number of them are tall, white men of this age. A next step will be sending out pictures to police organizations and hospitals."

Davis looked around the room from face to face. "Anybody?" Nobody said anything. "While we're waiting for more information, let's work on three fronts. Bert can continue looking wider and wider on missing people. Dick, you and I will start surveying the lake a bit; maybe we can come up with some ideas. Trooper Pearlstein, help Bert when he needs help, but also go out and try to find the ice fishermen who work that part of the lake. Look at the places that sell fishing licenses, talk to the bait places and country stores. We need to find the five guys who are always near Burton Island. We need to find the guy with the truck cap on his fishing shanty. They can't be hard to find; they've probably been fishing the same spots for twenty years. But take pictures along. You might get lucky."

*   *   *

Davis made it to dinner at the farm that evening. There were now three households living there. His parents lived at one end of the first floor of the farmhouse. Hazel and Luke had the north wing, which was as large as most houses. Fred's son, Andy, his wife, Jane, and their two kids lived in a new modern house they had built themselves at the edge of the field behind the farmhouse. A few other rooms were kept for occasional B and B customers. These rooms were in better shape than the rest of the house and had the best old furniture. Fred's upstairs room was still his room, though others used it at times.

The farm had always been an inn of some sort, going back to the early nineteenth century when sailing ships stopped there to pick up timber, produce, and livestock. There were three little cottages nearby, which were sometimes rented out for the summer but often ended up as storage for bicycles, broken furniture, or refrigerators too good to throw away.

The kitchen in the main house was much as it had been in 1850. It was a long, low-ceilinged room which occupied the center of the first floor, facing the lake. In the middle was a massive fireplace, where whole hogs were once roasted and enormous stews boiled. It now enclosed a large cast-iron, wood-fired cookstove used for cooking, heating, warming up plates, and heating water. The other kitchen equipment was not much newer. Down the middle of the room ran a huge trestle table, which could seat twenty people in a pinch. The table had been sitting there when they bought the farm in 1955, the year Fred was born. It had not moved an inch since. The floor was made from ancient pine planks, some of them two feet wide, unevenly worn to form a complex landscape, the softer areas abraded almost to nothing, the harder pine knots sticking up like hills on a model railroad. Toddlers explored its hills and valleys as they would later explore the land.

As long as Davis's parents, Hiram and Ruth, lived, the family gathered here most days for dinner. The family group was often supplemented by hired hands, the occasional neighbor, visiting kids, and sometimes B and B guests.

Tonight it was Hiram and Ruth, Hazel and Luke, Andy, Jane, their kids, and Davis. And Diane. Diane had an unusual relationship with her ex-husband's home. They had been divorced for twelve years, but she was still part of the family. She was very close to Hiram and Ruth, who had usually sided with her in her battles with Fred. They saw no reason to lose her as a daughter when the split occurred. Also, she enjoyed the farm in ways Fred never did. She liked to help with milking and weed the garden, and she filled in at the farm stand when asked. And of course, her son and his family lived there. Burlington, where she practiced family law, was only thirty-five minutes away. She was at the farm more than Fred.

Fred felt uncomfortable when she was there. He suspected that when they split, instead of her becoming less of a daughter-in-law, he'd become a bit less of a son. He tried to come when she wasn't around. But on Thanksgiving and Christmas, when everyone was there, you couldn't tell they had split up.

As usual, Ruth said grace efficiently but solemnly: "Bless this food to our use and us to thy service. Amen."

Hiram presided over the table from his armchair at the end. He was not a big man, but he seemed it. As usual he was wearing farm clothes: overalls, a flannel shirt, a brown and lined Carhartt vest, all of it frayed around the edges and well-stained. Like a lot of farmers, he had large, powerful, flattened hands, as if they had been rolled out and sanded down. Even at eighty-four, he was strong. His movements were slow but economical, languid. He usually sat with his hands on the chair's arms, not moving much when he wasn't eating. When he was still this way, his face had just the beginning of a smile. He was the last of the South Hero Quakers. Like a lot of birthright Quakers, he was determined to be virtuous; he had a mantle, an aura of rectitude, that was more powerful because it was rarely voiced or referred to. Beneath a benevolent surface of tolerance and affection was an undercurrent of judgment, which rarely bubbled up, but which everyone knew was there.

Fred hadn't been comfortable with his father since he was eight or so. He suspected that his dad, without having said anything about it, was disappointed that his talented, smart son had left the farm as soon as he could. Fred suspected his dad would never forgive him for this, that he thought his son was not quite serious, a little too flighty, that he had too much fun. Davis agreed with this assessment. He sometimes thought he had left the farm less from dislike of farming than from a feeling that he couldn't carry the weight of his father's expectations.

His mom always sat at the middle of the table, just a step from the cookstove and the big, old commercial range that sat beside it. Though arthritic and hobbled, she was constantly hopping up to stir a dish, check the oven, or bring the next course to the table. Like her husband, she wasn't a big talker. For that reason, she was considered wise.

Dinner was always a big production and something of a communal affair. Ruth, Andy, Jane, and Luke were all cooks and usually had some hand in things. Luke liked to bake bread, rolls, and sometimes pies. Few suppers were served that didn't end with a pie. The home and the farm stand were muddled together; things from the house might find their way to the counter by the register, and if a pie was needed, there was always a bunch of them just across the farmyard, made from whatever was in season, or on top of the pile in the freezer.

After dinner, Fred and Diane found themselves at the big double sink, washing and drying up as they had going back thirty years. At first, nothing was said. But as they finished up, Diane looked at him as she took off her apron.

"Walk?"

Fred never turned down an invitation from Diane. He suspected he might be in for some criticism of some sort, or maybe a grilling, but he liked being with her under any circumstances. He liked to look at her. To him, her graying hair and her slightly fuller shape didn't make her look older, just more beautiful, more sexy, sort of an updated, enhanced version of the girl he had fallen in love with a long time ago.

West Shore Road was right in front of the house. Just beyond it was their floating dock, always rattling about in the breeze. It was protected by the remains of an old breakwater. Beyond that was the Broad Lake. It was still early in the season, and they saw only one boat, a bass boat heading home at top speed, slapping across the top of the waves. Beyond the water were the Adirondack Mountains and the sunset, which Fred and Diane had shared countless times. They walked past a group of lakeside cottages from the forties. Then they walked past another big farmhouse, primly mowed and gardened, which was now someone's summer place.

"Have you really moved out of your house?"

"Well, it's an experiment, I guess. I'm thinking, when I retire, maybe do some cruising. I just like it on the water." He hesitated. He started to go into defensive mode, then realized the boat purchase couldn't be defended on any rational grounds. "There's nothing wrong with . . . I know it's nuts. I'm not completely crazy." The truth was, if Diane came back, he'd move back into the house, which had once been *their* house, in a minute. He'd even move back to the farm. Well, maybe not that. But he didn't say any of this.

The conversation was making him uncomfortable. He didn't really want Diane's insights into his life, mainly because they would probably be on target. He decided to change the subject. "Are you retiring anytime soon?"

Diane saw his diversionary tactic but answered his question anyway. "No. Why would I? I'm just getting good at this."

"Got any interesting cases?"

"A few. Actually, I have a lot of rather routine, boring cases. Divorces, custody agreements. Workers comp. But I have a few mediations I'm doing. That's what I like best, bringing people together who appear to be miles apart."

"Like?"

"Well, one is a group of teachers battling with their school. Another is two brothers who've inherited a business from their parents, and they are almost coming to blows. They've been fighting since they were five or six. I have to figure out what each of them is good at, some way for them to coexist. Or if not that, one could buy out the other one. Or split the business down the middle. That's more interesting than another nasty divorce, or even a nice, amicable one. Happy families are all alike, but so are unhappy ones.

"Freddy," she continued, "have you thought of going back into law? You know everybody in the state, and they know you. You know how everything works." His abrupt switch from practicing law to police work had been a bone of contention. She thought it was a comedown.

"Well, I think about it, of course. But, you know, it's the people, the convoluted situations that never get resolved. You thrive on all that, but it just gets me upset. It's too, I don't know, *intimate*."

Usually, when they had these talks, they were facing forward as they walked, or looking out toward a view. Too much eye contact made it harder to say important things. But she turned to him. "Freddy, it doesn't make sense. Every day you deal with crooks of all kinds, killers sometimes, irate citizens. Nutty cops, crazed witnesses."

"I don't know. Usually it's something simple, just a little greed, or somebody drinks a little too much and gets mad in a bar, or drives off the road. Small-time drug dealers. Simple crimes for simple Vermont crooks. Although the one we're on right now is a real three-piper."

He told her the story.

She asked, "Do you have some ideas?"

"Haven't a clue, really. We have no idea who this guy is, much less why he got himself murdered, much less why somebody bothered to stuff him into a lean-to on Burton Island." They walked on silently for a while. "What do you give that sunset?"

"Oh, maybe eight point two." It was an old joke. They walked without talking for a few minutes.

"Freddy, really—what's with the boat?"

"Well, I've been looking at it for five years, and finally I just couldn't help myself, to tell you the truth. An irresistible impulse. And I'm thinking about living aboard. I mean, you of all people know what— At the moment, I've spent so much money buying the boat that it's better to rent out the house. I sleep better on the water. Some people like the real world, the land world, and they step on a boat, and think, 'Whoa, a lot of things can go wrong here, I'm not sure this is a good idea. I hope the wind doesn't start to blow. What if the motor stops working?' I'm the reverse. On the water, I know nothing bad can happen I haven't dealt with a thousand times, and all the people I interact with are nice. On land, I'm not sure. Things go wrong all the time. You know, I'm really only completely comfortable when I'm in two places." As he said these things, he realized he was exaggerating, being overdramatic, off-key, a little false.

By now, they were back at Davis Farm. Diane said, "Let's go in." They put some dishes away, and Diane drove home to Burlington. Fred went out to the boat barn. Luke had a little fire going in a huge woodstove to take the chill off. The Guideboat was up high, hanging from a frame on pulleys. The Islander was on its trailer in the corner under a tarp. In the middle was an old Thompson sixteen-footer with no transom, and some serious holes along the side where planks had been removed. The paint was flaking off, and the varnish had turned an opaque yellow. Its vintage Evinrude 35 was on a rack beside a big wooden bench along the back wall with its red-and-white cover removed and an array of parts lined up neatly on the bench.

Luke was breaking down the engine. "People should take better care of these things. I think they forgot to read the maintenance schedule where it says 'Change the grease and repaint the hull every twenty years whether it needs it or not.'"

From a few cues, Luke could usually read what his friend was thinking. He said, "Turn you down again, did she?"

"I've stopped asking long ago." Fred knew that Luke wouldn't buy that answer. Luke could usually tell, just from the situation, and from Fred's facial expression, what Fred was feeling and what had transpired between Fred and Diane. He could probably reconstruct the conversation with fair accuracy. One of his major projects was to engineer a reconciliation. But Fred rarely wanted to talk about it.

"Now where is that stock for these planks?"

Chapter 6

TOURING THE INLAND SEA

At 8:30 the next morning, the squad room set aside for the lean-to case was beginning to get out of hand. The trash cans were full, and the floor needed to see a vacuum. Coffee cups covered most of the horizontal surfaces.

Davis was eager to get started and get the meeting over with. "We'll make this quick. Bert?"

"Well, no ID so far. We've looked at forty-seven missing persons in Vermont going back two years, and four hundred sixty-three in New York. So far, we don't see any matches. Our victim's fingerprints are not in the system. We're going to double-check these then go back another year and include New Hampshire and Quebec."

"Dooley?"

Dooley was a man of few words. "Zip. We still think the body's been there six weeks plus or minus, but it could be longer because of the temperature. We haven't found anything at all around the lean-to."

Davis, who had talked with the ME earlier, spoke next. "The interesting part is the stomach contents. He hadn't eaten much, but there were fragments of egg, muffin, bacon, and cheese. With the muffin, it looks like he'd been eating those breakfast sandwiches. Which every store now sells. However, the bacon was really thick, thicker than you'd get at McDonald's, and with a very high salt content. So if we find a place where they make their sandwiches with thick Canadian bacon, the sandwiches might have come from there.

"So keep your eye out for that. When you go into a store or restaurant, if you find some thick bacon, buy a sandwich and we'll have the lab look at it. Dick and I are going to go up to the islands and poke around. We'll take a boat ride and think about what might have happened, where the victim might have come from." The presumptive breakfast sandwich was one of the first real leads, but it wasn't something one person could follow up. Everyone would be on the lookout.

Detective Trooper Pearlstein said, "I will leave no fried egg unturned in St. Albans. Though this is an awfully cold trail. I'll mainly be looking for ice fishermen. In winter, a lot can happen out there with nobody noticing a thing."

* * *

Trooper Dick Fowler rarely spoke up in meetings. Eventually his supervisors noticed that when he did say something or asked a question, it was usually smart and to the point. However, his real value to the team lay in three virtues. The first was reliability. He was always on time, usually to the minute, and always prepared. Second, he was extremely thorough; when given an assignment, he would work it to death, however many hours or days it might take. Third and most important, he made life easier for everyone he worked with. He listened carefully, thought about what might be needed next, and quietly took care of it.

That morning, knowing he and Sgt. Davis would be searching by boat, he had come an hour early, determined which was the best boat available, requisitioned the boat and a truck to pull it, hooked the boat to the pickup, and parked it, headed in the right direction, just outside the barracks. The boat was a twenty-two-foot skiff with two huge Evinrude outboards, 150 horsepower each, on the back.

Fred Davis had also been thinking ahead and had a long list of tasks he wanted done right away. Lt. Collings had lined up a trooper named Danny Jones to do some of them. Jones was parked in a cruiser with the engine running, right behind the boat.

The plan was to put the boat in the water near the Davis Farm. This provided an excuse for breakfast at the Champ Diner.

The Grand Isle ferry connected South Hero Island to Cumberland Head on the New York side, just north of Plattsburgh. It was a major commuter link. Hundreds of people lived in Vermont and worked in New York and vice versa. The ferries ran like clockwork year-round. About five minutes before each departure, a horde of cars, pickups, and large trucks would jam the roads that converged on the ferry dock, like one continuous little train, intent on getting there at the last possible second. While they idled in line, another batch would debark the ferry and crowd the roads for another two minutes. Then the roads would revert to their usual backcountry silence. A lot of these people had left home in a rush and would run into the Champ Diner for a muffin or one of the breakfast sandwiches lined up in foil on the counter, waiting under a row of floodlights.

The restaurant was in an unpainted, shingled, one-story building that needed work; even the signs were flaking. The two men who ran it took their work seriously. In addition to the quick takeout food, they had a complete breakfast and dinner menu, fresh bread, and if you were lucky, some fish stew, with pike or bass right out of the lake. It was one of Davis's favorite spots, and having breakfast there had been his plan since dawn. The three men sat down at the table by the window and ate their number two specials with home fries, watching the lake, the cars and trucks getting on and off the ferry. This was a prime sailing day, but cold. One sailboat was out there and had the lake to itself. In August, there would be serious traffic there.

As he swallowed a large chunk of homemade toast, Trooper Fowler asked, "Sir, what are we doing, exactly, when we go out there? It's a big lake. I'm guessing the killer isn't standing on a rock waiting for us to pick him up."

Davis didn't answer right away. He liked to look out the window. Just outside was an old stone breakwater that been there since the days the ferry moved by sail and oar and carried men on horseback and loose livestock across to New York. The breakwater was slowly breaking down. The gull population was slowly being crowded off the rocks by the cormorants. When Davis was little, there was a red light there, and he could pull his boat up to a little dock.

"I have no idea what we're going to do out there. Well, I do have a couple ideas. First, we'll pretend we're the victim, and imagine how we might have gotten into this mess. What are all the reasons he might have been there, and in each case, where might he have come from, who might he have talked to or been seen by?

"Then we'll do the same for the killer. If you had a dead person and wanted to stash him on Burton Island, where might you have come from? Clearly if you were in Ticonderoga or Venise-en-Quebec, you would be unlikely to travel in plain sight for miles to get rid of your load. Why advertise? On the other hand, if you were on Knight Island and you had a body, you could zip over to Burton without necessarily being noticed. Can we narrow things down? Can we define an area that might be our search area? Here," he said, pulling a chart of the Inland Sea out of his parka. "The victim might have been fishing. Actually, let me make a call." He dialed Lt. Collings.

"Ethel? Davis. We should have somebody checking every place around here where they sell fishing licenses, and bring pictures of the body. Maybe he bought a license around the time we're talking about. We'll check out this way. Is there anyone available to concentrate on this?"

"Don't you listen to your messages? It's done already. But you check out that way, as you said." She hung up.

Davis turned back to Trooper Fowler. "Sorry. OK, he could have been fishing. Where? He was dressed for anything. What would have caused somebody else to shoot him? Had he seen something? Or maybe he was part of a larger crew, smuggling cigarettes or something, and there was some sort of falling-out. I don't know exactly what we're going to do, or where we'll go, but maybe we'll start at Burton, cruise around a bit, and just try to imagine. If we get a nice, strong 'hmm, maybe' signal, we can stop anywhere and poke around. But the big problem for me is that ninety percent of the people who use the lake in winter are ice fishing.

"Trooper Jones," Davis continued, "go to every place that sells fishing licenses. That will be convenience stores, sports stores, hardware stores, fishing stores, marinas. Go up to Alburgh. Go to Rouses Point. Take copies of the touched-up photo of the victim. Show them the picture. Keep it low-key. Go to all these places, wait a day or so, then do them all again. You might get them thinking about it the first time. Of course, keep a notebook on it. If you go by any other places somebody might have seen something, it's fine to stop there, too."

Jones left with a bunch of photos.

The cook loved to talk to his customers and had known Davis for a couple of years. Davis pulled out a photo. "Did this man ever come in here?"

The cook took the picture and looked hard at it for a minute. "Burton Island? I've seen the stories in the papers. I don't recognize the guy, but can I keep that?"

Davis nodded, grabbed four of the breakfast sandwiches, settled up, and they left.

The state boat launch was a mile north of the ferry. It was just a gravel parking lot, with an asphalted ramp into the water, and a blue Porta-

Potty off to the side. There were three pickups with empty boat trailers parked there. They had the boat running in the water in ten minutes. The skiff had two seats, with a little roof overhead which didn't provide much protection on a cold May 3. They brought along rain gear, sweaters, and knit hats, but they were beginning to get cold.

The police boat was very fast. Police boats have to be able to outrun most of the boats on the lake, and some of the fishing boats could go sixty miles an hour. This one could go almost eighty, though even Davis, who liked speed, found going anywhere near that speed terrifying. They headed out at a leisurely forty.

They passed the Davis Farm without comment, slid past the pair of islands known as the Sisters, shot through the Gut, and zipped over to Burton. They circled the island slowly, counterclockwise, starting at the campsites where Davis thought the body might have been brought in. When they got around to the boat landings, they tied up at the dock, and Davis showed Trooper Fowler the lean-to, the bent twigs, and the little stone beach. He described his inconclusive meeting with Henry Steinberg.

Though most people on the lake rather enjoyed being law-abiding and safe, crime beyond fishing without a license or boating under the influence wasn't unknown. Since long before Europeans came here, the lake, together with the Hudson River, has been one of the major transportation routes for native tribes. The northern tip of the lake, Missisquoi Bay, was Canadian water. During the Revolution, the lake was a major battleground. In 1776, a crucial battle happened at Valcour Island, almost visible from the ferry dock. Lake Champlain also had been a popular smuggling route for transporting whatever was illegal at the time: slaves headed north to freedom, hostages in various Indian wars, and products like cigarettes, bootleg whiskey, and drugs.

The two men walked quickly over the ground and back to the boat. If anything, the day was getting colder. The sandwiches had just a hint of warmth left. Davis pulled out two of them.

Trooper Dick Fowler was smiling. "Hmm. These are great, they hit the spot. A little salty, maybe. Good bacon." He didn't have to spell it out.

Davis looked at him. "Really?" He took the last piece, wrapped it up, and stuffed it in his pocket.

Then Davis pulled out the nautical chart of this section of the lake, and a pair of colored markers, and spread it on the little chart table.

He drew a big red circle including most of North and South Hero, the town of St. Albans, the eastern edge of the lake, the enclosed section of the lake, and a dozen islands. He marked the lean-to with an *X* and drew a dotted line down to the presumed beach. "I think for the moment this is our field. It's hard for me to think why someone from beyond here would go to the trouble to bring a body here."

He quickly marked all the stores in the area with *S*. The eight boat launches he marked *BL*.

Davis knew the lake by heart; it was his neighborhood. Above water, he knew the wrinkles of shoreline, the details of the islands, the characteristic wind and weather. He knew the landscape below the water almost as well. What the landforms didn't tell him, his fishing experience did: where it was deep, where shallow, where sandy, and where weedy. He could have drawn this map from memory.

As he sketched, he said, "Let's see. *S* for store, *BL* for boat launches. Bait places can be *B*." There were five of those. "Campsites, *C*. This one in St. Albans is where the ferry comes over to Burton. Knight and Woods Islands are primitive camping. Tent sites and outhouses, and no ferry. People canoe or kayak out here." He pointed to these spots as he talked.

"Butler is part of North Hero—it has maybe a hundred summer houses; it's like a small town. These others—Kellogg, Fish Bladder, Savage, and Osprey—are estates. I don't know too much about them, except Savage is, or was, owned by an old Vermont politician who was important in the sixties. It's one of the few islands occupied in the winter. They have sheep and goats. This down the middle is an airstrip. All these islands are big money; they take a lot to maintain, taxes are huge. Or they can be old family estates that go back to when land out here was cheap. Maybe those owners are just hanging on."

Davis backed out the boat, turned it around, and found a speed of about twenty miles an hour where the motors were relatively quiet and the two men could talk over them without shouting. He drove through the narrow channel into St. Albans Bay. They didn't talk a lot. "Just mark a green dot at any spot that seems interesting." Dick didn't need much prompting. Occasionally Davis would point to a spot on the shore.

They continued along the Vermont shore headed south, almost as far as the Sandbar, then cruised into the middle of the lake. At high water, Fish Bladder looked like two islands. The northern end was much smaller. The southern bit looked like an estate, which it was, but the northern piece looked like a wasteland. It was one of the islands where the cormorants nested, gradually killing off all the trees and underbrush with their leavings.

The southern part was larger and had a small cottage on it, lawns, a little boathouse. A pseudo-Adirondack mansion was under construction, with two huge stone chimneys rising up. The beginnings of a timber frame were in place. Near the dock was a pickup truck, and next to it a large excavator. A temporary plastic-arched building held piles of plywood and framing lumber. Two men were transferring lumber into the truck. They had a bonfire going on the rocky beach. Davis pulled up to the dock and they tied off the boat. The carpenters were happy to stop for a minute. They were midtwenties, hirsute, athletic looking, wearing coveralls. They had a coffeepot going, and they traded some uncharacteristically delicious coffee for the last two breakfast sandwiches.

The men had been working on the island for three weeks, having resumed construction when the ice went out. They worked for a construction company from New Hampshire and didn't have a lot of local knowledge. They had seen nothing but would keep an eye out.

Savage was the most impressive island in the Inland Sea, other than Butler. It contained over a hundred acres. At the north end, a rocky point stretched westward out into the lake. At high water, this was submerged,

65

and many boats had found it with their propellers or keels. By summer it would be visible, and there would almost always be a couple of boats fishing here, day and night. Davis had fished this island for fifty years and knew everything there was to know about the bottom. The rocky point created a bit of a breakwater. When the wind blew from the south, cruising boats often lay at anchor overnight under its protection. The western side, by the point, always seemed uninhabited. But from the east it looked like what it was: a farm estate. They cruised up the east shore. Davis drove close to the shore, past a beach with a small barn. A pickup was parked there. A bit farther north loomed a large, new-looking modern barn, with a beautiful clerestory along its ridge. A few dozen sheep and goats were milling about. A man and a dog, who seemed to know what they were doing, were herding them into the barn.

The dock was farther down, below an enormous house that looked like a modernist wedding cake, each story stepped in from the one below, a small cupola at the top. The house had an unobstructed view of Burton Island, but it was probably four miles away. At the dock was a large square boat, a sort of minibarge. They tied up on the opposite side.

Walking toward them was a large, redheaded woman in jeans and a flannel shirt with the sleeves rolled up. She had a toddler on her hip, dressed about the same way. She looked about thirty, healthy-looking but tired, also.

The two men were obviously police—all the official boats had a distinctive, nonrecreational look—which didn't seem to bother her at all.

"Hi. I'm Sarah, and this is William. My husband is down at the barn. We're the caretakers here. What's up?"

Davis briefly outlined the situation. "We found a body on Burton Island. We think he might have been put there around six weeks ago, and we're hoping you've seen something."

"Like what? Let's go see Earl."

A few minutes later, the two policemen and the couple were in the house. As the little boy played in the kitchen, they looked around. There were windows on all sides. The house was on a little rise and had a good view in all directions. On the porch was a long birdwatcher's scope on a tripod. Burton was clear, but distant.

Davis spoke, pointing in an imaginary line toward the Davis Farm. "You know, I grew up on a farm on the Broad Lake, and I spent a lot of time on the porch, or doing stuff outside, or looking out the window. Without really thinking about it, I became very familiar with everything on the lake: boats and their sounds, the houses, wildlife. I often noticed if anything unusual was happening, anything out of the regular rhythm of things.

"I'm hoping you're a bit like that," he continued, "and might have seen something that didn't belong there. We're talking about a time period of four to twelve weeks ago. This would encompass the hard ice, and the process of ice-out, and the beginning of the lake being navigable by boats. So we could be talking about snow machines, boats, or something else. We need to find some sort of witness."

The sheepdog was on the porch, nervously wagging its tail, tapping it on the floor. Earl was tapping his foot, looking at the door. He was smiling, but he seemed eager to get back to work. "I'll think about it. I've got a lot of sheep down there I've got to deal with. I'll be back in a bit."

They watched him leave. As he rose, the dog scampered after him. Sarah was sitting in a huge wooden rocker. William crawled up beside her, and she dragged him up into her lap. The little boy was fumbling with her shirt.

"Actually, I'm the watcher. Earl wouldn't necessarily notice much when he's working. There's a lot to do here, and just us to do it. Mostly William and I are in here, particularly in the winter, and we follow the sunlight. We're also down by the dock a lot, though that doesn't directly face Burton Island. Sometimes we play up on the landing strip, which has a good view; it points right toward Burton. I'd say between reading and nursing and taking care of this house, I'm glancing out these windows half the time, and I do pay attention. We watch the sun rise, and we watch it set. Burton is part of the sunrise view.

"I'm a photographer. At least I used to be, and would like to be again if

I ever get off this island. Also, I'm a birder; I'm always looking to see some unusual bird, and I like to see how the common birds are doing, too." She stood up. "Watch this."

She unceremoniously put William down on the floor, grabbed a camera with a very long lens from the desk, walked out onto the porch, and clicked it right onto the end of the scope. She swung it around toward Burton, focused, and shot. Coming back in, she connected the camera to a large desktop computer. A few seconds later, a printer next to it started clacking.

A minute after that, she handed them a printout of the photo. "I think I have about five hundred photos from this winter, in all directions. I can't think of anywhere I thought, *Hm, could be some murderers, maybe I'd better keep it in case a couple of cops come by someday.* But there are lots of pictures. You can look through them here, or I can just copy them off for you." She slipped a CD in the computer and pressed a few keys. The machine whirred.

"The all-winter-long ice fishing shanties are here, here, here, and over there," she said, pointing in every direction except toward Burton Island. "I guess there were a couple of shacks over by Ball Island." Ball was just south of Burton. "There are usually two shacks there. Hmm. Let's see, I may have something." She scrolled through the pictures as the machine was copying.

William climbed into Davis's lap, and Trooper Fowler walked around the kitchen.

She said, "Well, this doesn't show much." It was a photo off toward Burton across the frozen lake. It showed the two fishing shanties by Ball Island. These would be in view of the little beach. But they were just tiny black-and-white spots on the photo at this distance.

"I'm going to need to think about this some more, but I'm not sure I have anything else for you. William and I have spent a lot of time staring out these windows." William was back clawing at her shirt again.

The computer had stopped whirring. "This is the whole set. I hope it helps."

*   *   *

From Savage Island, they moved southwest toward Kellogg Island, right in the mouth of Keeler Bay.

Kellogg was a tiny island, maybe ten or twelve acres. A big white Victorian mansion was at the top, with a lawn before it. A shingle cottage with a nice porch and eyebrow dormers sat down at the water on the northern corner. It needed a coat of stain badly. A charming little red-roofed boathouse perched over the water on the west, in a tiny harbor. There were two log cabins tucked up in the pine woods. They drove slowly around the island twice. No one was home. It looked like a camp that had been completely closed up and battened down; there was nothing obvious to indicate anybody had been about since the previous October.

Davis then followed the shore from south to north along Kibbe Point down into Keeler Bay, past the boat launch there, past lake cottages, past another state camping area with another boat launch, past more cottages.

"Dick, I want you to go to every one of these boat launches, starting down at the Sand Bar, and talk to everybody you can find. Take your photos; paint them a nice picture of what we're looking for. Somebody must have seen something."

There were a lot of cottages, and most of them were nondescript, recently built. Most had aluminum or wooden dock sections piled on the lawn. A few looked like their owners were opening up. Another group of mostly larger houses were obviously year-round homes. Though most of the shoreline had been sold off, Davis and Dick passed three farms that still ran right down to the water.

Davis continued his thought. "Then do the farms. Some of these farmers have been here a long time. They are sure to have noticed anything strange, though they might not remember it now."

They passed the Gut and crossed over to the North Hero shore. They followed the shoreline up to City Bay. This was a well-known fishing area because of a reef popular with the bass. City Bay was the heart of North

Hero. A famous country store was there, which sold everything, including most of the things boaters needed. They pulled up to the dock, bought some gas, and warmed up inside the store as they drank coffee. Nobody there remembered anything useful.

Back in the boat, they crossed toward the Vermont shore and circled Knight and Woods Islands. These were state-owned islands with public campsites, but few amenities beyond outhouses. There was nothing obvious there that they could think of. Though they were near Burton Island, Dick didn't mark any green dots on the map.

Tucked between Knight Island to the west and Woods Island to the east was Osprey Island.

Osprey was a large island, about thirty acres. It was an oval, oriented east to west, with two coves facing north, little harbors. At the first cove, there were two shingled cottages with green trim and a third house, more of a Victorian, behind them. Between the cottages was a large dock. Most of the docks on the lake were removed each winter. The few permanent docks had mostly been torn up by the ice, long ago. But this one was surrounded by a double-strand necklace of huge logs chained together to form a boom to protect it from the ice. Next to the dock, and within the log boom, was a large shingled boathouse with two boat slips, and what looked like a rec room or guest room upstairs.

Behind the houses were some smaller buildings and a few clusters of birches, large white bouquets. Behind that were huge pines on the hill that formed the center of the island. There was no visible evidence that the place had begun to awaken to the spring warmth. Every window was covered with wooden shutters.

Davis idled slowly along the shore. Dick was drawing a distinct green question mark on the chart. The little cove faced Butler Island three miles distant, a large island with hundreds of summer residents, but empty in winter. Dick said, "Even in summer, this place is pretty protected. But in winter, you could have a party here and nobody would know. Unless people ice fish out here."

Davis had been here visiting once or twice over the years. He pulled his phone out of his pocket and flipped it open.

"Ethel? Hi. Could you give somebody a little project? Find out who owns all these estate islands in the Inland Sea. Yeah: Kellogg, Fish Bladder, Savage, and Osprey. Start with Osprey. See if you can get phone numbers, and I'll call the people myself tomorrow."

They continued. Past a little point was a deeper but smaller cove, and next to it a much larger house with its own small boathouse and dock. The house was one story in the Adirondack style, with log rafter ends, fanciful rustic railings, eyebrow dormers, and a red asphalt shingle roof, the worse for wear. Unlike the other houses, the old pile was in sad shape; the roof was sagging in a couple of places. It hadn't seen a paintbrush recently. The boathouse was at a tilt.

They circled the end of the island without comment. The back, southern side of the island was undeveloped, nothing but tall pines and cedars. A few of the pines had been upended by storms. From the water, their exposed root balls looked like huge mushrooms.

"Dick, you better roll up that map. Here we go." They buttoned up their parkas. Davis pushed the two throttles forward evenly, and the boat took off. Dick grabbed the arm of his seat, his knuckles turning a shade whiter. In a moment, the boat was going fifty miles an hour, up the east side of North Hero Island. He circled around the tip, then back down the west side through a narrow channel between North Hero and a peninsula called the Alburgh Tongue. As he entered Carry Bay, he slowed to twenty, then ten miles an hour, and idled through the gap in the railroad causeway and back out into the Broad Lake. This was the spot where, as a boy, Davis's sailboat had been gashed, but he didn't think back to that day.

The waves were much bigger here, but Davis pushed the levers forward anyway, and in ten minutes they were back at the boat launch, shivering. Trooper Dick Fowler jumped out and backed up the trailer. Davis drove the boat onto the trailer. Fifteen minutes later, they were at the Champ Diner with two large bowls of pike-bass-sausage stew before them. Looking out

71

the window, they watched forty cars and trucks stream off the ferry, like schoolchildren being let out for recess. Another forty filed on.

The owner was standing over them. Closing time, five o'clock.

Davis said, "Can we have ten minutes? And give me a quart of that soup to go, and some of that white bread if you have any extra." The owner shrugged and walked away.

Davis turned back to Dick Fowler. "I'm having a hard time putting a story line to this map. Why would any of these people be here at all? Mainly I want to keep talking to people. I want to talk to the owners of these islands. Osprey seems worth a look; it's so close to Burton and also so hidden. If you were careful, you could live there all winter and nobody would know. Dick, I want you to drop me at my family's farm. I can get a ride home somehow. Then I want you to visit every sheriff station, forest ranger, and firehouse on the islands and see if anybody saw anything, received any reports that might bear on this. Stolen or missing vehicles. You'll do better if you go there than if you call. Try to get them interested. Intrigue them. Who knows, this could be the most interesting thing that's happened around here in months. I'll see you in the morning. I guess just take the boat with you."

Fowler asked, "How much do I tell them? How long do you want me to spend on this?"

"You'll have to figure that out. Whatever it takes."

As they pulled into the farmyard, Davis said, "Actually, why don't you just go home, put the boat away, and do it all tomorrow? And go to Rouses Point, too." Rouses Point was right up by the Canadian border, on the New York side.

Davis found Luke in the boat shed. They worked on the Thompson until nine. Then Luke took Davis back to his still-unnamed lobster boat. In a few minutes, the little heater had been lit and the quart of soup was being warmed. He opened a bottle of wine. The chart was spread out on the little table. Davis briefly described his boat ride with Trooper Fowler. Luke still did some fishing and knew some of the spots even better than his friend.

A lot of law enforcement officers didn't like to talk about their cases after work. But Luke was Fred Davis's lifetime best friend. Confidentiality rules had never applied. Talking things over was part of Fred's way of winding down. Sometimes Luke made a useful comment or asked a smart question that turned the investigation a few degrees. Usually he just listened.

Davis said, "My problem is, I'm having trouble visualizing what might have gone down. Maybe the killer and the victim were involved in something together and fell out. That's probably the most likely. But it's hard to imagine a crime on Lake Champlain in winter that wouldn't be easier and more comfortable to do somewhere else. Crooks don't generally like to be that uncomfortable."

Luke responded, "Well, you do have privacy out on this part of the lake, I suppose. But if you want to break down drugs or something, wouldn't a cheap motel be almost as private? And you'd have cable TV. Maybe it was very local, something right out of St. Albans or Alburgh that had almost nothing to do with the lake. You have your gang of, say, bank robbers—or internet something—and they decide to get rid of this guy. Burton's a mile away. They rent a nice, quiet Japanese snow machine. In the night, they zip across the harbor, nobody gives it a moment's thought. Nobody's going to find the body for a while, and they're off to Florida, or back to NYC. That's the simplest option."

Luke was quiet for a minute. He was taking a mental tour of the part of the lake that was near Burton Island. He asked, "What about Butler?" Butler was a big island with lots of summer houses, empty in winter. "You could go from there to Burton and be out of sight almost the whole way."

Fred thought, *Something to do tomorrow, a close run around Butler Island.*

Standing up, Luke said, "Listen, thanks for the soup. I'm headed home. We've got a peach pie I've been thinking about. When are you going to give this tub a name, anyway? Or maybe if it's just going to sit here, it doesn't need a name."

Chapter 7

POWERS OF EVIL EXALTED

The next day, Trooper Dick Fowler worked his way slowly up the islands from south to north, all the way up to Rouses Point, New York, and Swanton, Vermont. He stopped at police and sheriff stations, fire stations, and marinas. At first he thought that if he went to the trouble of looking for clues, some clues would be there to be unearthed. Someone would remember something. By the end of the day, he understood that the chances of a hit were slim. As he drove along Route 2, he thought about it statistically. He had talked to forty people. While a few of them gave him close attention, most of them were naturally distracted by their current work. They were just waiting for him to go away. Another forty people were out doing their work, and unavailable. Maybe lodged in the brain of one of them was a single fact that might be relevant.

Detective Sgt. Davis had suggested that many people don't remember things the first time they're questioned. At the same time, he might not know what question to ask. An important fact might be right in front of him without him knowing it. Maybe he'd have to stare at that fact three times before it dawned on him that it was a clue. A lot of chance was involved. If the subject of thick Canadian bacon hadn't been discussed in the meeting the day before, he wouldn't have known the sandwich in his hand during the boat ride might be significant. Taking that thought a bit further, suppose there were two shops that used Canadian bacon. Then it wouldn't be a clue as much as a red herring.

What all this meant was that to find the one or two useful bits of information, he might have to go back several times, talking to different people, hopefully without annoying anyone so much that they clammed up or threw him out. When he did this, he also had to pay the closest attention. He found this way of thinking of things comforting. Fowler might not be particularly good at intuiting things or making clever deductions. But he was very good at going back again and again.

Meanwhile, Trooper Danny Jones was going to every bait shop and corner store on the islands, hoping someone might remember something just a little bit odd that had happened months before. Many of the people he quizzed were happy to talk. Most had no trouble remembering odd things and strange people who had been in their stores in the past few months. After all, the percentage of odd people in the world was fairly high. Jones took a lot of notes. As he did this, he was sure all the information he was writing down was completely useless.

At the state police barracks in St. Albans, Bert was expanding his search to identify the victim. He went further back in time five years and moved out to databases for Massachusetts and Connecticut. Some of the men could be eliminated as too old, too young, or too short. But a lot of the descriptions were close enough to the victim's that he had to dig a little to check them off. He had a small pile of "possibles," but none of them were "likelies."

Janice was concentrating on St. Albans, checking stores that sold bait

75

or fishing licenses. She checked the two places that rented snow machines. She spent a lot of time around boat launch ramps. Her experience was a lot like Trooper Jones's, except she didn't bother to take notes. She could see that none of the people she talked to had any useful information.

Davis spent the morning looking at all of Sarah's five hundred photographs. There were dozens of pictures of cormorants, gulls, hawks, and Canada geese. There were photos of seven different species of ducks; Davis was pleased that he could recognize six of them. Another series focused on small birds photographed on Savage Island. He could name most of these, but there were four he couldn't remember seeing before. He had no idea what they were. Among the photos was a small number of shots she had taken of life on the lake in late winter and spring. She seemed particularly interested in the ice, how it breaks up, moves around, and dissipates. It had a life of its own. There was one time-lapse series showing cracks appearing in the ice, widening, the snow breaking up, the ice resolving into large chunks, and then melting away.

Several of these photos depicted activity on the lake. A couple showed intrepid ice fishermen with elaborate fishing shanties, their large Chevy Silverados and Ford F-150s parked next to them. Sometimes a fisherman or two were shown hunched over a hole in the ice. One dimly showed one of these people hauling out a large northern pike. The shots toward Ball and Burton were more obscure because they were four miles distant. But a pair of shanties could be vaguely seen off Ball Island. Next to one was a big pickup, and next to the other, a snow machine. Another was even farther away, near Woods Island. He wasn't sure, but it was an odd shape. It might have been made out of a truck cap with plywood sides added. There were no trucks here. The fishermen had come by snow machine or walked out onto the ice.

He called the police lab and asked for June McDonald. She was a good photographer herself and had been trained to work with photos. "June, it's Fred Davis. I'm going to email you a few photos. Can you see what you can do with them? I'm interested in the fishermen, their vehicles, and the fishing huts." He emailed the most promising shots to her. Then he called Ethel to get the list of phone numbers of the island owners.

One by one, he called them. Before each call, he googled the owner and the island itself. The first two islands, Fish Bladder and Kellogg, didn't show up on the web, but one of the owners did, a famous surgeon in Providence. Savage Island had quite a web presence—it had been a resort for a while, and the owner had been in Vermont politics in the 1960s and 1970s. But when he caught the owners on their cell phones, they all told the same story: None of them were anywhere near the lake in winter. None of them had seen anything. None of them had any suggestions for other people to call who might have been in a position to see something.

The next island on the list was Osprey, which was shared by four owners. The first two didn't answer at the numbers given, and Davis left messages. The third owner picked up on the first ring. His name was Pliny Winthrop, eighty-five years old, retired minister. Davis's Google search listed a variety of articles on religious topics that Winthrop had authored, plus four hymns and one small book titled *The Gospel of Luke*. Davis imagined him comfortably sitting before the fire in an old farmhouse somewhere, in his Morris chair, a wool blanket over his legs, reading an uplifting book.

"You'll have to speak up, I'm afraid. This is Pliny Winthrop."

Davis explained who he was and told the story once again about the killing. "Reverend, I'm wondering if anybody from Osprey Island might have seen something. We're talking about the winter, I'm pretty sure. We're just casting a wide net and hoping to catch something we can use. I'd like your permission to walk around the island a bit and see if there's anything that might be relevant."

"Mr. Davis, actually, just Pliny will do. We close up on Columbus Day weekend. We don't have much money, there's no caretakers or anything. Usually we open up June first or thereabouts, though I've been known to come out sooner. You are welcome to walk around as far as I'm concerned, but I should check with the other owners. I can do that tonight."

Davis said, "I can call them; that's no trouble."

"Well, if you don't mind, I'd prefer to check around first if that's OK with you. I can call you in the morning."

As he left his office, Davis called the new Vietnamese place in Winooski and ordered a #25. Any day that ended with a #25 was a good day. It was only fifteen minutes from there to his boat, and the food was still hot. As he ate, he watched the news. Obama was fighting Hillary's negative ads with one of his own, and a sea lion had been "shot dead" in Oregon.

Later, he set up his nest in the forward cabin. He had a new copy of *Wooden Boat* magazine, and he slid *The Hound of the Baskervilles* into his VCR. It was the version with Nigel Bruce and Basil Rathbone, from 1939. He knew the story inside out, but he found Rathbone's voice soothing. In the film, Dr. Watson is upstairs at Baskerville Hall, looking out the window. He sees a light in the distance, out upon the moor. He thinks Holmes is back in London doing something, but in fact Holmes is camping out on Dartmoor, living in a shepherd's hut at the edge of Grimpen Mire, unswayed by the warning "As you value your life, do not go out upon the moor when the powers of evil are exalted." Fred knew all the lines.

He leafed through his magazine while the story unfolded. He was dozing when his cellphone rang. He paused the movie with a very tweedy Dr. Watson looking confused in the upstairs hall. It was as if Watson were listening to Davis's phone call, wondering what was up.

"It's Pliny. I've been lying here, trying to sleep, thinking about your story. A couple of pennies dropped."

"What are you talking about, Reverend?" Davis put down his magazine and paid attention.

"I've got an idea about who your guy is, I'm sorry to say. Do you want to go out to Osprey with me tomorrow? Can you hear me? The signal is a little weak." Pliny Winthrop spoke softly, but even over the phone, his voice was unusually clear and resonant. The voice reminded Davis of a minister he'd known years ago who would deliver his sermons without a microphone, in a quiet voice. Sitting in the back row, he could hear every word.

"I can hear you, sir, just fine."

"I can be there about ten thirty. And bring a picture of that corpse. I want to show you a picture I've got in my cottage."

"Do you know who it is?"

"I really can't talk about it over the phone. I don't know whether I'm hoping I'm right or wrong. But if you'll meet me, either we'll have figured out something, or we will have had a nice boat ride. Where can I meet you?"

"I'm at Apple Island. I'll be at the dock."

"What am I looking for?"

"Well, it's almost the only boat here—it looks like a lobster boat. Wear your warm outfit, it's going to be pretty rough tomorrow."

"I always do, winter and summer."

*   *   *

The third team meeting was early the next day, 8 A.M. The squad room had been tidied, the coffee cups cleared away, but the brown rings from the cups were still there, and they were now coated in dust. Ethel Collings was going around with a damp cloth. She thought the detectives could think more clearly if the tables and windowsills were clean. She knew *she* could.

The bulletin board was beginning to fill up with images and information. In one corner was a copy of Davis's chart. Next to it was a gauzy blowup of the best of the photos of the fishing shacks near Ball Island, dark blobs against the snowy background.

Davis began, "I'd like to keep this short. Just new information."

Bert started. "No progress on identifying the body. I'm still at it, though. We're also looking into missing vehicles, stolen snow machines, or any other items that might show up on the police blotters and might have some bearing on our case."

Trooper Dick Fowler went next. "I'm checking with sheriff and police stations, firehouses, and marinas on the islands and up to Swanton and Rouses Point to see if anyone has seen anything out of the ordinary. After that, we'll poke around at boat launches, talk to people there, and talk to the farmers that face the lake. There are lots of places to check."

Davis said, "June, tell us what you can about the photo."

June McDonald, the photo expert, had a completely no-nonsense look. Medium height, straight brown hair cut short, she looked like she spent a lot of time in the gym. She moved around like an athlete. Davis thought she might be a skier, in balance at any speed and angle. His realization that he was way too old for her didn't stop him from having a fleeting thought of dating her. She got up and stood by the extremely grainy photo on the bulletin board. The two shanties by Ball Island, with the truck and snow machine, were barely visible.

"Well, you have copies of this. This is from over three miles away, but with a very long lens. I've done everything I can to enhance it. Fortunately, the woman who took this picture knew what she was doing and had the very best lenses. The truck is a Ford F-150, about 2003. A friend of mine who sells snow machines says the snow machine is probably a nearly new Yamaha. I can't see anything more than you can about the shanties. The one farther away, that looks like a truck cap to me. The date on the photo is February sixth."

Davis cut in. "If I were fishing there, I might put in at the boat launch at Hathaway Point." This point was on the peninsula that enclosed St. Albans Bay and was the boat launch nearest to the fishing site.

After a moment, Bert glanced toward Davis, who returned an almost imperceptible nod. Bert said, "That's not much, but Janice and I can work on that. Actually, there are several places along the shore near Melville Landing that could work, at least for the snow machine. There's a VAST trail through there." VAST was the Vermont Association of Snow Travelers, which operated a huge network of snowmobile trails, one of which ran close to the shore to the east of Ball Island.

At this point, any breakthrough was welcome—the mood of the group was rising. Then Peter Dooley, head of the scene-of-crime team, spoke up. He liked to make an impact.

"We think we've identified the sandwiches from the stomach contents. Do you remember we thought the bacon was on the thick side? It's Canadian bacon we found in the stomach. It's basically thicker and has a higher salt content than regular bacon, and costs about twice as much. A chain restaurant or convenience store wouldn't bother with it. Last night, Detective Davis handed me some leftovers from the restaurant at the Grand Isle ferry, and I think it's a match. I've called around, and they may be about the only ones who use that quality of bacon. It's not proof, but I think the sandwich in the victim's stomach could have come from there."

Though Dooley didn't say it, Dick Fowler had first made the connection. It was his first career clue. He wanted to follow it up. "Should Trooper Jones and I go talk to people there?"

Davis was making notes on the large piece of paper. They were almost legible. "Yes, go out there, but try to get people talking unprompted before you give them any hints. Talk to everyone who works there or was working there earlier. The people who herd the cars onto the boats or the ticket people might have remembered something."

Davis continued, "OK, I'll go next. Dick and I took a boat ride." He pulled a little laser pointer out of his doctor bag and traced their route on the chart. "These green marks are our question marks—places that might have something to do with the story. But we have no actual information. Of course, most of the summer people aren't there yet. There were people working on Savage and on Cedar. The caretaker on Savage took that picture. But none of these people saw anything other than what's in that one photo. Actually, now that I think about it, the woman who took these photos was very observant, a trained observer. Maybe she's worth visiting again." Davis was mostly saying this to himself, and made a note in a small notebook he always carried in his back pocket. Then he continued with his comments.

"I've talked to the owners of most of the private islands, and nobody has

81

seen anything. Nobody was up there this winter, either. Both Dick and I were most interested in Osprey Island, not because we saw anything, but because it's so private and protected. But there's a lot of nature reserve and other areas around here that are very protected."

"I got a call late last night," he continued, wrapping it up, "from a man named Pliny Winthrop. He's one of the owners at Osprey. I'm not sure there's anything to it, but he has a theory about our body and is driving up here this morning to tell me about it. We're going out to Osprey Island to compare our corpse with a photo he has out there. I have to meet him at ten thirty. OK. Thanks, we're moving a little. Let's go. Call me if anything earthshaking comes up, and we'll meet tomorrow morning, unless we have nothing to talk about."

Chapter 8

TRAVELS WITH PLINY

Davis pulled into Apple Island Marina at ten fifteen next to an ancient black Volvo, the old rounded-over kind. It was probably thirty years old, but impeccable. It had dark red leather seats. A tallish, slim, slightly hunched figure was standing peacefully at the dock looking out toward the lake, hands in his pockets. From the road, he looked like Rathbone's Holmes: he was wearing much the same tweedy outfit, but with a baseball cap in place of Holmes's deerstalker. Up close, his face was narrow, with a beaky, long nose, also a bit like Rathbone. He turned as Davis walked down.

"I'm early. I really couldn't sleep; I left Boston about five."

"Well, I'm all ears. But I'm going to make some coffee before we take off. I like your car, by the way."

"Tea for me, if you have it. When they make a better car, I'll buy it."

While the water was heating, the two men cast off the boat. Pliny had spent a lot of time on boats and knew just what to do. He moved about with surprising agility for eighty-five. It wasn't so much that he moved quickly, but in a practiced way. Usually, on a boat, there's an awkward discussion about who does what. Pliny just did the obvious things while Davis started the engines. They pushed off gently, filled their cups, and headed out. The waves greeted them about a hundred yards out. Following them from the south, the waves got bigger as they proceeded north. It was cold outside, but cozy as could be in the pilothouse. Davis was congratulating himself on the boat, a floating old-folks home. With the door closed, the motors were almost silent, but the waves made slapping noises against the bow as they argued with the boat. Pliny sat beside Davis and watched the lake as he sipped his tea. In the rough seas, the ride would take an hour at least.

After a while, Pliny pulled out a *New York Times* and sat down in the booth. He nodded off with the paper on the table, oblivious to the boat's bouncing. When they neared Osprey, he came to.

"Go around the right side, it'll be faster. When we get close, go where I point. There are some nice rocks just below the surface that you don't want to find this morning. Basically we stay close to the island. My place is just around the corner." As instructed, Davis slowed down and cut inside the invisible rocks. A lot of boats on the lake came to grief in the spring, when rocks that were exposed in summer were lurking just below the surface.

As they maneuvered around the point, a large house came into view. It wasn't really a cottage, but a big one-story bungalow surrounded on three sides by a covered porch. It seemed to have grown out of the rock. The windows were covered with shutters made of beaded boards.

Pliny said, "Just pull up against the boathouse. At this time of year, we can dock there." They docked the boat, wordlessly as before. Davis grabbed his doctor's bag. They walked up the stairs from the boathouse and onto the porch.

"Wait here." Pliny unlocked the door and went in. In a couple of minutes he reappeared. "Let's just pull these two shutters off. It's depressing in there with no light at all." They entered a parlor dominated by a huge stone fireplace. A very large lake trout, a bit moth-eaten, looked down dolefully from above the mantle. The room was about twenty by thirty feet, finished entirely in varnished paneling, nailed outside the varnished wall posts. The furniture ran to overstuffed and wicker. Beside the couch was a side table with a birch bark top. As they walked past it, Pliny grabbed a framed picture.

The next room was the dining room, in the same décor but with a vaulted ceiling framed with log trusses. After that was a butler's pantry, with beautiful glass door cabinets which held several sets of dishes—a history of the family in pottery.

After that came a kitchen. This large room was gaily painted in off white, gray, and green, the windows unshuttered. Pliny had already fired up a little gas fireplace. The room had an old cookstove, an icebox, and a wall-hung sink that must have been there from the beginning. But a group of more modern cabinets was there, too. In the middle was a huge table where ten or a dozen people could easily sit. Off on one side was an old daybed with a row of thick cushions against the wall.

"This is really where we live. When I come up here in the off-season, I just use this room. Sometimes I think I should just tear down the rest of it. It's a life's work to keep this place upright." Pliny had a nice, ironic smile. His eyes conveyed sadness and amusement at the same time. He turned the light on over the table. "OK, let's see your picture."

Davis had two photos. The first was a shot from the morgue with the face tidied up a bit, composed. But the face was withered and had been nibbled in places. In the second, the image had been Photoshopped. This was another of June McDonald's skills. Under the directions of the ME, she had tried to represent what the victim would have looked like alive, or more alive. Handing this second version to Pliny, Davis said, "This is what we think he really looked like, more or less."

Pliny's framed picture showed a group of six men, men and boys, standing on a large, square dock. Davis recognized it as the large swimming dock on the other side of the island that he had seen on his boat trip with Trooper Fowler. In the background, Davis could see the Victorian house. Four men and two boys were in their bathing suits posing with hammers, big wrecking bars, and large paintbrushes. They seemed proud of themselves. Two sixtyish men framed the grouping. The one on the left was obviously a younger Pliny. Opposite him was a slighter, shorter man. Next to Pliny was a larger and younger version of himself, obviously the second generation. Beside this man was another man of the same age, but taller. He seemed long and lean, big through the shoulders and arms like a rower, which in fact he was. Davis was beginning to get the picture. He'd seen this body before—on a stainless steel table.

Before them, kneeling on one knee dramatically, were two boys. On Pliny's side was a boy of about thirteen and on the right side a boy a few years older. Each held one end of a huge, five-foot-long, two-man saw, and were adopting very serious, mock-manly expressions. They were looking right into the camera.

Pliny said, "Well, this is me, obviously, here. That's Pliny V, or Junior. And in the front is VI, who we call Timmy. This guy here is John Brearley, the best friend of my life. That's his son Paul, and that's Paul's son, John, who we call JB."

Pliny looked right at Fred Davis as he tapped Paul's figure in the photo.

Davis pulled a magnifying glass out of his bag and looked closely. People change in twenty years, and the beard made it harder to compare. He was just a little heavier. But the likeness was obvious.

They said it at the same time. "Same guy."

Pliny said, "You know, Paul had a little scar right under his chin, from some dental work." Pliny was starting to tear up. "I'm sorry, I'll be back in a bit." He walked out the kitchen door into a little yard where a bunch of kayaks and canoes were stacked three high on a wooden rack. Some were newish. Two of the canoes looked a hundred years old.

The old man was walking slowly out onto the dock, down the path, up onto the porch, and back. He looked very old, as if the litheness had bled out of him. Paul placed the dead man's face next to the living and moved his magnifying glass back and forth. Then he called the morgue on his cell phone.

"Kramer."

"Doctor, this is Detective Sgt. Davis. If there's a little scar under that beard, just under the chin, right side, I think I have a positive ID for you."

A minute later, the doctor came back to the phone. "OK, who is it?"

"His name is Paul Brearley. About whom I know nothing, but I think I'm about to learn a lot about him. I'll talk to you in a bit. Would you call Ethel and Bert and tell them we've ID'd our guy almost certainly?"

Pliny walked back in the kitchen, largely recovered, or at least composed. "I'm sorry. Paul was—is—one of the most important people in my life. I don't know whether to feel glad that in fact he was alive or grieve for him. I sort of knew it was going to be him, though I don't know how I knew. I'm afraid I'm going to make you listen to a fairly long story.

"I met John Brearley at Harvard." He pointed to the other sixtyish man in the photo. "We were roommates. Then we went to Union Seminary together. We were the closest of friends. I can't tell you how many adventures we shared, hikes, boat trips, hitchhiking. But mostly we talked about things, politics, religious questions, what you should do with your life, you know. Meaning of life.

"In those days, young ministers usually got small churches, young churches just getting going or often little old congregations that were dying off. We both had a bunch of churches in this part of the world. But we always found time to do something together, often canoe trips, or fishing. We had a lot of conversations about someday getting a place somewhere on the water.

"One year we both had churches in Western Mass, a few miles apart," Pliny continued. "We were both married by then, starting families. One evening he stopped by—it was nothing unusual for him to show up unannounced—and slapped a picture down on the table, actually sort of a collage of three pictures, in a little real estate magazine ad for summer houses. This was about 1955. One picture showed this house, and one showed that front dock, with the houses behind it, shot from the lake. He said, 'We can have this whole thing for twenty-seven thousand dollars. If we can find two other families, we can each pay about six thousand dollars. Even I can afford that.' At that time, there were a lot of old estates up here going begging. They weren't in fashion. This one had been unoccupied since the Depression. The attics were full of bats.

"Anyway, he wasn't about to take no for an answer. We found the other families, the Dawses and the Roses. The Roses sold out a few years ago, but the rest of us are still here, at least those of us who are still alive. My wife, Mary, died fifteen years ago. John's wife, Ann, is going strong. She still comes up for the whole summer. My family had a little money, and to my regret at times, I got the big house we're now in. What a trial! It's a life work, this place, to tell you the truth. For all of us, this island has been our real home as we've moved about the world. It was great for kids. In the early days, there was always a gang of kids, and they spent most of their time in or on the water."

Pliny stood up and walked over to the window. The sky was clouding over; the kitchen was suddenly darkened. But it was still cozy with the gas fire going. The old man seemed to be looking at something in the yard.

"As a kid, Paul was often a leader, organizing games, getting out the water skis, teaching the younger kids how to do stuff. He particularly loved canoeing and camping. Starting as a young boy, he took longer and longer trips. By his teens, he would go out for a week or two in June before anybody else showed up. If no one wanted to go along, he'd go by himself. Of course, they all swam, fished, played games in the evening, as you can imagine.

"He was a thoughtful kid; he read serious books even when he was ten or twelve. When he grew up, he became a minister, like his father and me. He was a bit of a star at that, too, very popular in the pulpit. People liked to hear him preach. But still, he was always doing things with the kids, all sorts of projects and trips, much more so than the other adults."

Pliny walked back to the table and picked up the photo of the scene on the dock. He said, "This picture is typical. These docks get torn up terribly by the ice. He organized this, and we all had fun working on it. He and I were quite close. We shared the same interests. Meaning of life, as I said.

"About two years after this picture was taken, in 1990, he disappeared. It was in July. He was going to camp out on Valcour Island. The weather had been harsh, cold and windy. They found his canoe on the rocks down around Burlington, with a big backpack lashed to the thwarts. There was no sign of a body.

"We could only think that he had drowned. He seemed the last person to kill himself, really, but we thought about that, too. There was a big Coast Guard search. Volunteers went out.

"His dad and his sister spent two weeks in their boat, combing the shorelines, looking under docks and in boathouses, under bridges, searching for his body. They thought, maybe he was injured, stranded somewhere. They looked in unopened camps, in case he had found his way into one of them. It's unusual in a drowning here to not find the body.

"But I couldn't entirely buy the idea that he'd drowned. He was a skilled canoeist on the lake, and a powerful swimmer. We had all learned how to deal with capsizing a canoe; in fact, Paul taught us what to do, how to climb back into the boat over the end and bail out the boat by hand.

"Eventually," said Pliny, "we had a memorial service and tried to move on. We had the service right here on the island. His wife, Cassandra, left the next day with their son. She's never come back here, though her son comes with his family. This place has never been quite the same."

Davis cut in. "You know, I think I met him a couple of times on the lake. I liked to go out in my Guideboat in rough water, and once or twice I'd meet him battling the waves in his canoe just for sport. We'd talk, or just wave. We might have water-skied over here from your dock once or twice. But I don't understand why, when I asked you about a killing on Burton Island, you thought of Paul Brearley. That seems like a pretty improbable connection after all these years."

Pliny sat quietly for a long time, and Davis knew enough to keep silent. Pliny looked right at Davis, very intent, ardent. "It goes back to *doubt*. Forgive me, I've been thinking about this for eighteen years. First, I never completely bought the drowned-at-sea idea. I was always looking for other explanations.

"John and I were ministers. Our job was to be *good*—by some light— in spite of our doubts, our sufferings, our struggles. And the other part of our job was to witness the sufferings and doubt of others, share in it, maybe help carry a little of it. None of this came easy to either of us. Our friendship was a great support.

"Paul was a preacher, too, but he sort of cruised over everything. He didn't seem to struggle much, things came easily to him. He was very empathetic with other people, but unruffled himself. For years I admired this steadiness as a sign of great faith.

"But later, after his death, if that's the word for it, I realized this was probably wrong. Nobody is exempt from suffering. There probably was some deep water there; we just didn't see it. As his dad and I talked about it, and we talked about it a lot, we started to think about his death differently. We didn't think that he did kill himself that day, but that it was conceivable that he could have. It was possible."

The old man was silent for a minute, then continued his story. "Then, after John died a few years later, I thought, maybe he checked out another way. Maybe he left."

Pliny stood up, walked over to the window, looked out at the lake. He walked over to the gas fireplace and turn down the flame.

"There was something else. After John's death, I always helped close up their house on Columbus Day and open it on Memorial Day. Sometimes I would come up in late May and start to open things up, and sometimes I would see things, little things, that seemed a bit off, a little odd. A picture in the wrong position. Sometimes the woodpile looked a little lower than I remembered. Once there was a coffee cup in the sink that should have been on the shelf, and it was Paul's favorite cup. I didn't make much of these things. They could have been tricks of the mind. But still . . ." His voice trailed off. After a pause, he continued. "Still, it opened my mind to the idea that there was something missing in him, and maybe he went looking for it, either at the bottom of the lake or somewhere else."

The old man stood up. "These were mostly vague feelings, flitting images. But when you called, they took shape for me. I can't say I knew it was Paul you found, but I was ready to believe it." Pliny was composed again, firming up. "Let's go look at the house. It's only a short walk."

They walked along the shore. As they approached the little Victorian house, it didn't look right. There was some litter on the ground, and as they came around the building, the door was open.   The nice, clean house Pliny had left in October was a mess. Food packages were all over, and the sink was full of dishes. There was a little blood on the doorstep, or some stains the two men were prepared to think of as blood.

Pliny groaned and started to walk in. But Davis held him back. "We can't go in there. It's a crime scene."

Pliny turned away. "You'll have to excuse me for a bit." As he had before, the old man walked down toward the lake on the pathways among the buildings, and as he walked, he seemed to get older.

Davis pulled some surgical booties out of his bag and walked into the house. He took pictures from just inside the door, all around. To the left was a living area with a large fireplace, a huge old couch facing it. In front of him was another couch against the far wall, and just to the right, a large, painted table. The remains of a meal—seemingly a meal for one—were on the table. A big cast-iron griddle was in the center, where it had scorched the paint. To the right was the kitchen, with more mess in the sink and on the stove. He took pictures and spent several minutes just looking.

"Bert?" Davis had called Bert's cell phone. "I'm on Osprey Island. I think this could be our murder scene." He gave his partner a précis of the situation. "I'd like to get a full workup on this, but not tonight. I'll call Ethel and set it up for tomorrow morning."

He called Ethel and repeated the news. "If you could have them come

91

out fresh in the morning, that would be best. Can you set up a search warrant for us? It could be for the Brearley house, Osprey Island, and outbuildings. I'll stay here and mind the fort. And I'd like a team meeting, say at 4 P.M. tomorrow. Thanks."

As he walked out the door, Pliny approached from the lake, looking as if he'd been up all night. He said, "You know, I don't know which is worse. Knowing he was alive and I didn't get to see him and talk to him, or knowing he's dead now. Listen. I have to call four families, and it's not going to be easy. I'm going to stay here, at my house, for a few days at least. I know enough to stay out of the way of the police. But I'm hoping you could help me put in my boat. It won't take long. Otherwise I'm stuck here."

"Sure. I'm going to stay here tonight, too, on my boat. I'm going to park it right at the dock out here, and then in the morning the scene-of-crime people will come out and make even more of a mess than there already is."

"Let's do the boat, then I can start making calls. It's going to take quite a while."

The two men walked back to Pliny's house. He had a small aluminum boat blocked up on timbers in his boathouse. In a few minutes, they had lowered it into the water, and Pliny was charging up the battery.

"Pliny, when you're done calling, how about come tell me what you've learned that I might need to know, and I'll find some dinner for us."

Chapter 9

PLINY'S PHONE CALLS

Pliny had six phone calls to make, at a minimum. Everyone in the two families would be upset, but Helen, Paul's sister, would be the most shaken. He decided to call her first. He had spoken to her briefly the night before. She knew what he was thinking, and that he was headed to Vermont in the morning. She didn't believe for a minute that the body was Paul's. Pliny thought it would be difficult for her to accept what had happened.

He felt Helen had a slightly skewed idea about the Brearley and Winthrop families. She thought they were special, a bit blessed. Not exactly better than other people—it would be wrong to think that—but maybe just a little more focused on being virtuous. Never stated, but assumed, was the notion that if you did the right thing, every day, and thought the right thoughts, things would work out. Enough money would be there, you'd have a bit of good fortune because you weren't looking for it. She never said such things out loud. If she did, the spell would be broken. It would be a fall from grace. Her brother Paul, his ease of living, his goodness, had personified this ideal to her. That's why she could never accept that he would have run away or killed himself.

To Pliny, this was a cartoon version of what he, his friend John, and Paul believed. It was a misunderstanding about how they lived their lives. He saw Helen's attempts to be virtuous as a little forced. Sometimes they seemed phony or silly.

The key point to him was to be good for no particular reason, certainly with no expectation of getting any sort of return on investment. He had spent a lifetime learning how this might work.

What worried him was the thought that perhaps Helen's phoniness, and her vision of the two families, wasn't all that different from what he thought or felt at times. Maybe underneath his calmness, dignity, and quiet humor, he was expecting something in return for his virtue. Maybe underneath his tweedy exterior was a core that was a little silly. Maybe he was the phony and she was the honest one. That was why he often became angry or annoyed when he had to deal with her. That was why he could rarely acknowledge her basic warmth, sincerity, and intelligence.

He held the phone in his hands for several minutes before he dialed. "Helen. It's me. I was right. It *was* Paul."

Long silence. "Can you tell me how you figured this out?"

"Well, I compared a photo of Paul back then with a picture of the corpse."

"No, I'm not sure I'm ready for that part. I mean, can you tell me why it occurred to you that when a cop called you about a homicide that didn't seem to have anything to do with us, you thought it might be Paul."

Pliny paused. "Not really, except I'd been halfway expecting him to turn up someday. I didn't know it, but I've been waiting. I've been imagining I would see him on the street. Though I never thought his return would be like this. The police don't know what happened in detail. But something happened in your house; someone other than Paul was staying there. He may have been shot there. The house is a mess, and the police are going over it tomorrow. I don't know how much more of a mess that will make. I don't think we'll be allowed in the house for a while, but I'm going to stay here at my house for a few days."

Helen didn't say anything for a full minute.

Pliny said, "Helen, are you there?"

Helen finally spoke, her voice rising. "I'm coming up there tomorrow. I want to see the body. I'm sure there's some explanation for all this." There was a panicky note in her voice.

He wanted to calm her down. He didn't want her anxiety to get to him more than it had already. "I know there is an explanation, but we may never know what it is. You don't have to come up. Where will you stay? The police have your house tied up, it's a crime scene. My house isn't open really." Pliny had plenty to think about without having to take care of Helen. He couldn't really deal with what she must be thinking. It was all he could do to manage his own thoughts. He didn't want anything to distract him from that. He had a lot of thinking to do.

She was barely audible over the phone. "I don't know. I'll stay in a motel." She hung up.

Pliny fixed himself a cup of coffee to break the mood Helen had cast over him. As he did, he realized that her panic and consternation weren't that inappropriate under the circumstances. Maybe he should give her some credit for being honest, present.

Next, Pliny called his daughter, Abby. She and her husband were schoolteachers in Virginia. They spent most of the summer on Osprey Island. Abby knew of Pliny's suspicions, and, like Helen, she hadn't taken them seriously. She thought her father was prone to reveries; he spent too much time thinking.

Pliny knew what she thought, and didn't mind. Since his wife's death, he liked the idea that his daughter would intervene when he needed sorting out. Abby was the anchor of the family, the truth teller. She could be a little fierce when the occasion called for it. He depended on her for that. However serious the topic, he always enjoyed talking to her.

"Abby, it's me. It's definitely Paul, not a shadow of a doubt about it. I saw a photo of the body."

"OK, Dad, what happened? Tell me exactly what's going on up there."

Pliny told her about the photographs, about telling the story to Davis, and about seeing the Brearleys' house in a shambles. "He looked the same in the photo, really, just a little bigger, a lot more worn of course. But the most disconcerting thing, he had this funny little beard. Somehow that bothered me. Right now I don't know how Paul got there, who else was there, who shot him, or why. They don't really know that he was shot on Osprey Island. That's just a surmise."

"Dad, tell me—what do you feel about it?"

"When I figure it out, I'll let you know. I'm wandering around in a fog. My assumptions are all tossed up in the air. I missed him before, then it turns out he's alive, then he isn't, and he's killed in this horrible way. What does it mean for us? How does it change how we think about things?"

He could sense Abby getting a bit angry but controlling it in an almost parental way, as if she were looking at him sternly through the phone wires. "Dad, I want you to listen to me. I know I'm wasting my time saying this, but please listen. I'm sorry this all happened, though not altogether surprised. I loved him, too. But the Paul you mourn died a long time ago, if he ever existed.

"Paul wasn't the saintly guy, the steady guy you remember. We kids knew him in a different way than you did. We didn't really like the perfect-boy thing. It was a little put-on, a little much, a bit contrived. It's annoying to be around somebody who's always nice, always helpful, but who also always wins the games. We were angry at him a lot."

Abby paused. Pliny could tell she was upset. He could hear her breathing into the phone.

"For a while, when I was about fifteen or sixteen, I was enamored of Paul. One summer we explored being a couple. We spent a lot of time upstairs in the boathouse in the late evenings. But I found it's heavy lifting being with someone who's trying to be good all the time. It's not that satisfying. I just wanted a boyfriend. For a brilliant guy, he was one of the most clueless people.

"There was something a little funny about his relationships with girls. He tormented himself more than was absolutely necessary. It was a great relief when I figured out that he might seem like the big prize, but he really didn't have much to give me."

Pliny interrupted, "I'm not talking about him as a boy, really, but later—"

Abby cut him off. "Dad, you really are hopeless. Here's what I want to say. Junior or Timmy or JB—or me, for that matter—are real. We're much more solid than Paul ever was and we're here, every day. Paul left. Let him go."

She paused again. Pliny didn't know what to say. She said, "Dad, I have to go think about this. I'll talk to you later." She hung up.

Next on his list was Cass, Paul's wife, or perhaps former wife. He hadn't talked to her in several years. She had left Vermont right after her husband's memorial service in 1990 and never set foot on Osprey Island again. She lived in New York and was married to someone named Charles O'Reardon, but they'd been separated for a couple of years. He knew Cass had gotten an MBA, but couldn't remember where she worked. Whatever she was doing, it was the opposite of her life with Paul.

He didn't particularly want to talk to her, but it wasn't fair to make anybody else, particularly her son JB, break the news. When he called, she was home.

"Cass, it's Pliny."

"Pliny, good grief. How are you? What can I do for you? Where are you?"

"Well, I'm at the island in my house, and I'm fine. But I have to tell you something, and there's no easy way to do it."

"OK. I'm sitting down," she joked, but sounded uneasy. Pliny wouldn't call her just to chat.

"Well, here it is. Paul wasn't dead all these years. I'm not sure where he was, but he definitely was alive. But he's dead now. He was killed up here this winter. He was shot." Pliny didn't think it was necessary to get into the details unless they were asked for. "None of us knew he was living. I just found out today."

Long silence.

"Pliny, I guess thanks for letting me know. You know, I'm a different person now. But he was JB's father, I loved him once, and I think he loved me, too." Pliny could almost hear the wheels turning as Cass started to realize the ramifications of this news. "Do you know where he was, what he was doing?"

He was expecting this question. He answered, "I know not one single thing about where he was or what he was doing. Except it's possible he had been to the island before when nobody else was there."

Cass said, "You know, what used to make me mad was that however considerate he always seemed, however affectionate, it was always about him in some way. When he died, it just seemed so selfish and stupid of him. Even if it was an accident, it was a useless, unnecessary one. Whatever happened, even though we had no idea what that was, it had to be selfish and stupid. Think of leaving me like that, leaving JB, for heaven's sake, over a weekend canoe trip! And if he was alive, that's even more selfish." She was almost shouting.

"And now he's made me a bigamist! I've been a bigamist for fifteen years, can you believe that? I collected double indemnity insurance. He made a crook out of me. I really can't believe it. Are you sure you didn't know something about this?"

Pliny didn't answer. Though he hadn't seen her in years, he could picture her expression as she accused him of not coming clean with the whole story.

Cass paused, and Pliny filled the space by walking over to his gas fireplace and turning the dial up to nine. He couldn't erase the winter chill in the house.

She started up again. "Then coming back to life, really, that's even more self-centered. Can you imagine anything more egotistical than that?

Running away, then coming back, then getting killed. Making himself the center of attention again. It's really typical, if you think about it. And now I'm going to have to clean up after him one more time, and get no credit for it as usual."

Pliny, alone in the huge kitchen, looked out the window. He remembered the days when the kitchen was noisy, full of people reading, making snacks, talking, getting ready for the day's adventures. In his mind, that all ended the day Paul left. He put on the kettle.

"Pliny, thanks for letting me know, but I'm going to check with my lawyer and stay as far away from this as I possibly can. I don't really want to hear from anybody if it can be avoided. As it is, I'll have to deal with JB, with my real husband, and with my daughter, and I hope that's all. This could be in the fucking newspapers! Good grief. My friends will read about it, I'll have to talk about it. Pliny, who talks to JB? I think you should call him first. He'll want to know all about it, and probably he'll come up there. Listen, Pliny, thanks for calling, I guess you had to, but goodbye. You know, I have a nice life here, and I hope it survives this in one piece." She hung up.

Pliny made some tea and sat by the fire for a few minutes. He was expecting it to be difficult to tell these three women what had happened. But he wasn't expecting they would challenge him personally, and what he thought about the situation and its history. He had a lot of thinking to do. Anything that helped him understand things better was a good thing; that was his job in the world.

Pliny's next call was to Paul's son, John, known as JB, who was thirty-four, almost the same age his dad had been when he had disappeared. JB lived in the Catskills with his wife and two daughters. He was a mechanic with a small, three-person shop. He had never had the slightest temptation to follow his father and grandfather into the church. His good deeds were of the ordinary type: keeping someone's old car alive for one more year, earning an honest living, reading to his kids at bedtime, showing up on time.

Pliny and JB had always worked together on group projects, going back before the dock project in the photo. When Paul left, more of the responsibilities fell to Pliny and JB, and they found it comforting to work on various chores and repairs together. They became friends. In later years, they often went fishing and put in lots of porch time together. They worked on the walking trails that laced through the island. They often closed up the island together in the fall or opened it in spring.

Their intimacy was one of things: JB knew where the keys to Pliny's boat were tucked behind the beam, and as a matter of course was thinking ahead to the summer, coming soon, when they'd have to jack up Pliny's boathouse. Pliny knew that to light JB's water heater in the spring, you had to tap a few times on the side of the gas valve. He knew the origins of most of the treasures in JB's house, and of the junk in the toolshed. Pliny was closer to JB than to his own son and grandson. Pliny sometimes thought that JB just naturally had the wisdom that he had spent so many years thinking his way toward.

Like his Aunt Helen, JB had admired his father, but perhaps in a less complicated way: a son, loving his dad, missing him.

Pliny called JB at work, and at first JB wasn't surprised to hear from him. But after greetings and pleasantries, it was obvious more was afoot. The cellphone connection was a little weak. JB found a landline and called him back.

"JB. Your father has been alive all these years, I don't know where. But he was up here, at the island, this winter, and managed to get himself shot. He's dead now. He may have been shot in your house. The police are going to go through it tomorrow. I've spoken to your mother, to Helen, and to Abby. I haven't called anybody else, though the word may be spreading by now. It wouldn't surprise me if this ended up in the *Burlington Free Press* before long. I'm at my house, I have my little boat in the water. I don't really know what's going to happen, but I'm here at the moment."

"You've seen the body?"

"A picture of it."

JB was thinking less about the meaning of all this, and more about what had to be done. "Well, you know, I really thought he had died, and now he has. I'll come up in the morning and go directly to the morgue. I can formally identify the body, at least. Then I'll come out there. We'll see. Is there anything else I can do?"

Pliny had been planning to inform allthe families himself—make all the calls and have all the difficult conversations. But with JB's offer, he realized that making all the calls himself was both self-indulgent and unnecessary. Also, it was exhausting.

"Well, actually, yes. Could you call the other families and get the word out as best you can? If anybody wants to call me, they can. I'll call Pliny and Timmy." He meant his son, Pliny V, and his grandson.

"OK. I'll call you tomorrow when I'm ready to be picked up. Thanks, Pliny."

Finally, Pliny, already drained, called Pliny V and Pliny VI—Junior and Timmy—and in rather perfunctory calls, told them what had occurred. Timmy was the most upset. For a period—represented in the dock repair photo—they had all been very close, had spent most of their time together in summer. The best of times.

*   *   *

Pliny sat in his rocker for a while. He stared at the fire. He couldn't make any sense of what was happening and stopped trying. He couldn't figure out how or what he should be feeling. He was numb.

He decided to do some housekeeping, some chores. He plugged in the fridge. He didn't really want Paul's sister Helen to move in, but she might do it anyway, so he took down the shutters on the bedroom by the living room and took sheets and blankets out of the cedar trunk, just in case. It occurred to him that any number of islanders could show up; he took down some more shutters on some more bedrooms. Pliny had a lot of bedrooms, lined up along the porch. He would camp out in the kitchen. Just in case, he brought in a load of wood and put it near the big fireplace.

Then he started looking for food. He found a remnant bag of coffee beans and a can of cocoa powder. He could live on that in a pinch. There was a cardboard can of oatmeal, but some mice had been working on it. Some intact bags of ramen noodles, probably as good as new. A bottle of corn oil. That was it. Fortunately he wouldn't starve quite yet; Davis had invited him to eat something or other on his boat, now parked at the main dock by the crime scene house.

He was exhausted. "I'm a little old for this," he said, and chuckled. It was hard, but he realized he was having fun, too, a new project to work on, a mystery.

It was getting dark. He got into his boat, said his annual boat-starting prayer. Lo and behold, the outboard engine hesitated, coughed a few times, spewed out blue-black smoke, then started. It sputtered to a stop, but on the next try, it agreed to cooperate. Soon it was purring as if it hadn't been hibernating for six months. The running lights worked also, which was good, though the likelihood of meeting another boat was nil. He cast off and slowly drove around the back side of the island. Everything was just as it had been for fifty years. The trees, the waves, were as they always were. The little aluminum boat was the same one he'd bought their first summer. He had made this trip, in this boat, a thousand times.

At the front dock sat Davis's lobster boat, lit up like a cottage come upon in the woods. But next to it was a second boat, a long, low, white, lapstrake wooden inboard. Puzzled at first, he soon realized he'd seen it before.

It was Luke and Fred's twenty-one-foot Lyman Islander. Davis had called Luke and asked him to bring out supplies for Pliny. Luke had made a raid on the farm stand, stopped by the Grand Isle market, and then come out in the Lyman. There was rarely a need to take the old boat out, but an excuse was always welcome. Its beautiful throaty rumbling voice always cheered Luke up. Luke had rebuilt the engine more than once; it was almost part of him.

The Islander was one of the few remaining old wooden boats still in use on the lake. Pliny remembered seeing it occasionally over the years. As he thought back, he remembered it bobbing in the waves at this same dock long ago, and he also remembered one weekend when Paul was a teenager, when they had all water-skied behind it, including Pliny himself.

Inside, Davis's new cruiser was a little hobbit house. It had curtains on the windows. There were even a couple of little pictures hung on the wall. Davis had his apron on and was stirring something on the stove. A warm, yeasty smell emanated from the oven. Davis had put a checkered tablecloth on the little Formica-topped booth table. Davis liked housekeeping on this minute scale.

Davis turned around. "Pliny, this is my friend Luke Walker. He's brought us dinner, and a bag of groceries for you." The two men shook hands.

Pliny looked at the small, slim man before him. "I think the last time we met, you were right here at this dock. You took us all skiing."

Luke smiled at the old man. "I remember it very well. We were always looking for flat water. The skiing was always god-awful by our farm, and sometimes we could find some decent flat water in among these islands. As I remember it, you were a pretty decent skier. I have a very clear memory of you making a jump start on one ski off this dock. Perhaps we should have a run after dinner," he teased.

Pliny smiled. "Maybe we shouldn't. I don't think my insurance covers water-skiing accidents."

In early May, the evenings were cold on the lake, even after a hot day. But Davis's boat was toasty. Davis pulled a loaf of Luke's bread out of the oven. On the tiny stove, he was tending the last of the sausage-and-pike stew and was cooking a steak, with a liberal heap of garlic and onions around the edges. Luke set the table and opened a bottle of wine. He used the same brown plastic dishes the two men had had on their first big boat, the cruiser Davis had taken to Boston in his college years.

103

They were all hungry. They couldn't see the sunset from their position, but they could see its glow on the water. As they were opening the second bottle of wine, Davis asked, "How did your phone calls go?"

Pliny didn't know how much to say. He thought about it before speaking. "I've spoken to my daughter, to Paul's ex-wife and their son, and to his sister. Frankly, I don't really want to reprise everything that was said. But there were some sides of Paul's personality I had no idea about, or only an inkling. My daughter in particular was not in the least surprised that he'd taken off. Cassandra, Paul's wife at the time—she's married, sort of, to someone else now—was steaming about the whole thing. She may have been on a low boil for the whole eighteen years since his disappearance."

Pliny had a few sips of wine before continuing. "I don't know if you'll want to talk to any of them yourself, but as far as I can see, none of them know much that will help you. At least, I don't think they know any *facts*. Paul's son is coming up tomorrow—he wants to identify the body, then he'll come out here. And I think Paul's sister will show up also. She says she wants to see the body. For all I know, all the people who come to this island may show up tomorrow. Something like this doesn't happen every day."

Davis said, "Well, they'll have to stay out of our way. I don't know who I want to talk to, but perhaps you could give me the phone numbers just in case. We'll have to get everyone's fingerprints, too." He walked two steps over to the little galley, and served himself the last of the stew. "Where would Paul have gone? How come no one ever ran into him in eighteen years?"

Luke put in, "How could someone leave like that, and then keep living and working without ever running afoul of the system? What did he use for a Social Security number? Did he pay taxes? How could he collect wages without causing a hiccup in a computer somewhere?"

Pliny looked up at the two men. "I don't know. I wouldn't have lasted a week. I'd have run back home no matter what the circumstances. But Paul was very resourceful. How would you have done it, if you were him?"

Luke said, "That's what we were talking about while we were waiting for you. Where would you hide? Canada? Today it's hard to get back and forth without the right ID, but it wasn't so hard even ten years ago. Any old driver's license was good enough. Could he have used his real ID? What happened to his passport back then? If you're missing or presumed dead, and you cross the border, what happens when you present your ID? Can you renew your license by mail? How does that work? I'd think eventually you'd get found out."

An hour later, they sent Pliny off with his bags of groceries.

Then the two men got down to serious business: planning their summer trip. Davis had a short bookshelf in the cabin with a nice collection of navigation charts, regional maps, and copies of the two guidebooks that covered the lake and the waterways it connected north to south. They could go north, through the Richelieu, and up to Montreal. Or they could go south, through the Champlain Canal, then down the Hudson River, reprising their trip from Davis's college days. Or they could turn right and go up the Erie Canal. They had never done that. The ultimate trip was to go "around the block," meaning leaving the farm dock headed south and returning from the north, having done the Champlain Canal, the Hudson River, the Erie Canal, Lake Ontario, the St. Lawrence River, and then returning through the Richelieu.

That was for the future. The most time Davis could take was two weeks, and that was pushing it. And there was no day, no moment, when Luke was not needed at the farm. They settled on ten days. The next issue was whether it would be one way or round trip. If they had to return by water, they could get five days out and then have to turn around. But if they could get the boat trailer and plant a nice, big pickup truck ten days away by boat, they could double their range.

This was the kind of conversation that could go on a long time. Around ten, they had a plan: south, Erie Canal, one-way, August 15 start. Family invited, but not required to show up. Hopefully, hay would be in, crimes would be solved, and all the vehicles at the Davis Farm would be working like new. And no one would miss them.

Luke, refreshed with two cups of coffee, took off in the Islander, near full speed. If it wasn't raining hard, almost any boat trip was enjoyable. In a dead-calm lake, a boat was smoother than any car. It could go all out. Whatever you tell the boat to do, it does without argument. But in rough water, the lake was in charge. You had to pay attention to each individual wave. It was just as much fun, but an entirely different experience. Boating in the dark was a third pleasure, a more solitary feeling. Few other boats about, and you had to watch for their lights. Without their lights on, boats were invisible at night.

It was in fact dead calm, and the moon was out. Though the shore was just an outline, Luke could tell exactly where he was and knew every rock to avoid, every buoy to skirt port or starboard of. The cold wind felt good.

Davis stood on his little deck for ten minutes, the rumble of the Islander slowly dissipating. He heard the boat slow down, which meant Luke was approaching the drawbridge at the Gut. He would be home in ten or fifteen minutes.

Chapter 10

JB AT THE MORGUE

The four members of the scene-of-crime team arrived at nine the next morning. None of them had dressed for a chilly boat ride, and they were shivering. Davis gave them hot coffee and went over what was known so far. He had already drawn his own conclusions and was often tempted to point them in that direction. But he'd learned that his theories were often wrong. Left to their own methods, the experts discovered things he might miss. They talked for a few minutes at the doorway to the house. With the door open, the basic situation was obvious.

Fred Davis liked Pliny, his cast of characters, and their island. He didn't want more damage and mess than was absolutely necessary, and he told them to work with Pliny. As he was making this speech, Pliny himself arrived, looking slightly improved. He said, "I've checked through all the other houses, and I don't think anything has been disturbed in any of them. They were all nicely locked up. A couple of the outbuildings were open, broken into. But if you need to go into any houses, I'll let you in myself. I've unlocked all the boathouses and outbuildings if you need to look there. Also, there's a whole reef just underwater down on that end of the island," he said, pointing toward the east. Come around the west and you'll have no problem."

It was eleven before Davis made it to the morgue in Burlington, where he was to meet Paul's son JB. JB sat quietly on a bench in the waiting room. He was reading a tattered paperback mystery. It was an old Martin Beck story, "The Locked Room," the one where Beck is recovering from terrible injuries and finds true love with Rhea Nielsen. Davis had a copy on his boat.

JB wore jeans, a flannel shirt, and a baseball cap. To Davis, he looked like his dad, but shorter and chunkier, a pleasant-looking man but not a particularly handsome one.

"Mr. Brearley? I'm Detective Sgt. Davis. I'm in charge of the case."

JB said, "If you call me 'mister,' I won't know who you're referring to. Just JB will do it."

"OK. I want to have a long talk, if possible. Do you want to identify the body first, or after we talk?"

"Let's do it."

They went downstairs to the morgue, and JB made the identification with no hesitation. The resemblance between the two men was even more obvious to Davis here, even though the body was the worse for wear. JB was just barely holding it together and was happy to cut it short.

Both men were eager to leave the building. It was sunny as they walked out the door, but some clouds were coming in across the lake to the south. They walked down toward the waterfront and into a seafood place and grabbed a table by the window. There were only two or three other customers. Davis got a sandwich to go with his coffee. JB couldn't eat anything and ordered tea. While JB calmed himself, Davis pulled out a copy of the photo of the dock project many years ago, the photo they had used to make the identification. JB picked it up.

"Tell me about your dad."

"Well, he left when I was only sixteen. At the time, I totally believed that he was dead. In some sense, I still think he drowned then, in spite of that corpse down there. I loved him. We were very close. We did a lot of things together. We climbed most of the High Peaks in the Adirondacks. We built things. We did a lot of fishing. We went hunting sometimes in the fall. He was always very warm and loving to me." As the men looked out over the lake toward New York, the sky turned black.

JB looked at the darkening sky and said, "Here it comes." Hard rain hammered the water noisily. A bass boat raced in and banged roughly against the gas dock. Two men tied up and dove into a little shack on the dock.

JB turned to face Davis. "I wasn't really like my dad. He and my grandfather and Pliny were very serious. They were theologians; they liked to think about things. They were always writing things—sermons, poems, books. They could talk about important subjects endlessly. It was fun for them. I wasn't like that at all. I was a good student, a reader. I could understand their conversations. But I was never tempted for a moment to go into the church or anything like that. I like to *do* things. The only time I go into a church is to do the repairs, or attend weddings when I can't avoid it.

"But my father never pushed me. He was totally supportive of whatever I wanted to do. That meant a lot to me. For that matter, so was my mother. To tell you the truth, when he disappeared, I cried for a week, and I've never really gotten over it. I miss him all the time. I don't know where he was for these years, but I wish I had been with him."

Fred was moved by this story. He almost envied JB. Though his own son and his own father lived just around the corner, he'd never felt that close to his son, or that supported by his father. He said, "JB, I have a sense that he was in some sort of crisis when he left. He must have been, isn't that so? Do you remember that? Do you know what might have been bothering him?"

"I've thought about that all the way driving up here. I never actually saw anything like that. We had a warm relationship, but I can't imagine him sharing his feelings with me. I think that's a question for Pliny. He had those kinds of conversations with Pliny."

"I can't believe there was really no warning."

"Well, maybe. I was off working, not on the island much. I could believe there was some kind of crisis with my mother. If so, I never saw it. Of course, I wasn't looking. And I could just as well believe it had nothing to do with her. In fact, I was clueless then, and I'm clueless now!"

JB stood up. "Listen, I have to go out to the island and help Pliny. Thanks for the coffee." He gave Davis a card with his cell phone number and started walking out. But then he turned back, a little teary. "I think I actually saw him. Twice."

Davis looked up.

"Once I was out on the lake, and I saw someone a ways off, paddling. Probably half a mile away, or almost. It just looked like him. A person has a definite posture paddling, just as you recognize someone by their walk from a distance. At the time, I dismissed it as an illusion. But now I think it was him. That was maybe five years after he left."

The rain stopped abruptly, like a curtain being raised. The two fishermen emerged from the shack, cast off, and raced back cross the lake.

JB continued his story. "Then a couple of years ago, I was out hiking with my kids on Mount Marcy on Labor Day weekend. My dad often took a bunch of us up there on Labor Day, sort of a family tradition. It was my biggest hike so far with the kids. We had the camping gear and all that. There's a big campsite maybe two hours from the lodge, and we were setting up there, putting up our tent, hanging our food bag. And he walked past, or someone who looked like him—tall, same walk. It had been one of my dad's favorite hikes. We'd done it together two or three times. He was maybe two hundred feet away, heading downhill. It was the strangest thing. I looked right at him, and I think he looked at me. But it was more than fifteen years since I'd seen him. I dismissed it. He walked down. Now I'm sure it was him, particularly after seeing what he looks like now.

"To tell you the truth, if it was him, and we had talked, I would have accepted his explanation, and continued our relationship from that moment. But with my kids there, I let it go and pushed aside the idea that it actually was him. I'm sure he had a good reason for whatever he did. I'm sure of it. I'm sorry, I have to go now." JB put a couple of dollars on the table and walked out.

*   *   *

Davis bought a *Burlington Free Press*, got himself another cup of coffee, and sat back down. It was a small paper, and he read it cover to cover, except the recipes. Reverend Wright was acting up, but Obama's numbers were holding. The Clinton camp couldn't quite believe it. He was pleasantly surprised to see no stories about his case, which had been featured for two days.

Vermonters like a good crime story, but crime was in relatively short supply. As a result, almost any crime made the papers. Any car crash above a fender bender, arrested drunk driver, or minor robbery stood a good chance of getting coverage. A distraught man in a Montpelier bar had pulled a gun and been gently guided to the door and into the arms of a waiting police officer. No one was hurt, no shot was fired. But the story was front-page for two days. Any sort of killing got lots of attention, though most of them were routine: a hunting accident, friends shooting each other while inebriated. Half were domestic violence. Finding a body at a campground qualified as unusually interesting news, particularly as the body was unidentified. Davis knew that when the word got out that the body had been identified, and had belonged to a man who had been presumed drowned eighteen years previously, it would be a big story. Maybe the reading public would come up with some useful information—

perhaps the fabled ice fishing witness—along with the misleading and false information sure to arrive.

As if to confirm these thoughts, when he looked up, Elaine Drew was walking toward him. She had a lot of food on her tray and an amused smile on her face. "I can see you're thinking hard." Elaine was a particularly well-connected veteran reporter for the *Burlington Free Press* who sometimes appeared on evening TV news shows. She often knew what was happening before Davis did. "So, I hear you've identified your campsite victim. Can you talk about it?"

"A little, if you don't quote me by name. His name is, or was, Paul Brearley, age fifty-five. His son identified him this morning. He may have been killed on Osprey Island. Mr. Brearley disappeared on the lake back in 1990. His family is one of the owners of Osprey. We're pursuing a lot of leads, but in fact we don't know why he was killed, or by whom. We have no suspects of any kind. We don't know what Mr. Brearley was doing, or where he was between the date he disappeared and the moment we found his body. We're really just getting started."

Elaine Drew made an entry in a little notebook. "That's it? That can't be everything."

"I wish it weren't."

Chapter 11

WHAT REALLY HAPPENED

A year and a half earlier, JB had run into his dad on Labor Day on Mount Marcy. The mountain was the tallest peak in the Adirondacks, and before Paul's disappearance, it had been a family tradition to climb it on Labor Day. This was the first time JB had taken his kids up the mountain. Since his father was also sentimental, it wasn't that much of stretch that Paul would be up there on the same day. It was a popular climb, and there were often a lot of other hikers around.

When JB described this encounter to Detective Sgt. Davis, he left out the part where, after his kids were tucked into their sleeping bags, he had a two-hour conversation with his father, and heard his story.

They had been meeting every few months since. They communicated the modern way, by email. They met at diners here and there. Twice JB had gone up to Tupper Lake, where his father lived under the name Paul

Baer. JB had been introduced around as Paul's son.

His father didn't want to go back to his old life, and even if he had wanted to, he couldn't. He'd betrayed too many people. There were the legal issues. He wanted to stay Paul Baer. He had to stay Paul Baer.

JB had no talent for deception and little experience at it, but at Paul's insistence, he kept these meetings secret. JB felt like a man having an affair. He had to concoct stories to explain his absences. Over time, he got used to lying, and he got better at it. He'd always been a simple person who did what was in front of him. Now he'd been drawn into the complexity and self-examination he'd run away from his whole life.

On the other hand, he loved being with his father, and he loved having him to himself for a few hours at a time. In a way, he liked his father better as Paul Baer. No more confusing discussions about theology with his father, grandfather, and all the Plinys sitting together around the fire of an evening, leaving him out.

The plan had been for JB to join Paul at Osprey Island for the day. He would park his truck on Shantee Point, and depending on conditions, snowshoe or ski out to the island. JB would make a little adventure out of it and get some exercise at the same time. He could use a little exercise. As it turned out, the snow was skiable, particularly since fishermen had created snow machine tracks for him to follow. But as he passed the end of Woods Island, he saw his father's antiquated snow machine flying south, towing a cargo sled, heading toward Burton Island. JB knew something was wrong, and he followed along behind as fast as he could go. He was certain it was his dad's machine. He'd rebuilt it himself, and there were few that looked and sounded like it. The snowmobile was small by modern standards. By comparison, the man astride it looked enormous. It was clearly not his father.

By the time JB was in view of Burton Island, the machine was leaving the island and heading through the gap that leads toward St. Albans Bay. But he also saw a track leading onto the island, and he followed it.

He found his father's corpse in the middle of the lean-to. The body had been cast aside like a child's doll, arms and legs in every direction. His dad was dead again, just when he was getting to know him. It hurt even more the second time. He sat next to the body and wept for a long time.

He couldn't stand seeing his father tossed aside that way. He dragged the body to the corner of the lean-to and propped it up against the wall. He placed the hands in a normal position in his lap. His father's body looked as if he might have just put his book down, or as if he were sitting there thinking. His father was capable of sitting and thinking about something, hardly moving, for long periods. *It's not much of a funeral*, JB thought, but one his dad might appreciate. Maybe his father's spirit was still hovering around and saw him do this. JB had heard of such things.

As he sat there looking at the body, he realized he had landed himself in just the sort of muddle he had managed to avoid his whole life. His family, his wife, would find out that not only had Paul been alive all these years, but that he, JB, was complicit in it. Everybody would be mad at him. His wife would be just as upset as if he were having an affair.

Cringing and crying at the same time, he fished through the pockets of his father's coveralls, looking to one side, trying not to look into his father's dead eyes. There was no wallet or other ID.

He drove to Burlington and wandered around for hours. He walked down to the lake and along the bike path as the snow began to fall. He passed young couples towing their little kids in plastic sleds. Skiers slid by almost silently in the new snow. A few determined cyclists passed, grinding their way through the snow. He walked up to the mall, the streets where the cars had been banished and pedestrians walked from trendy shop to trendy shop. On one corner, a busker was singing Dylan songs, and on the next, a trio with guitar and fiddle was singing country songs under the awning of a furniture store. JB wasn't much of a drinker, but he went into a bar and had a few beers.

Perhaps if Paul Brearley was the Paul that was found, and nobody made a connection to Paul Baer, he could avoid a nightmare. He knew where Paul's truck was. The one thing he could do was to move the truck

115

far enough away so it wouldn't be linked to the body on the island.

He drove out toward the airport and rented a room for the night. The next morning, he drove to the park and ride on the New York side of the ferry, not exactly knowing how he would get to the boat launch. He had a set of tools in his truck, and he threw a few key items in a daypack.

He was in luck. There was an old, battered mountain bike leaning up against a tree, and it didn't look like it had been used for a while. After spraying some oil on the chain, he walked the bike onto the eight o'clock ferry, looking as casual as he could. As long as no one on the boat recognized the bike, he should be OK.

The bike was marginal, but JB was an old mountain biker and a skilled mechanic. He stopped to oil it some more and make a few minor adjustments. When he got to the boat launch, he pulled a flat iron tool out of his bag. It had various notches and hooks along its edges. It was the tool mechanics use to unlock cars when their owners have locked their keys inside. He opened the door, rooted around, and found a spare key in the ashtray—he thought there might be one there. The truck started right up. He threw the bike in the back, and the four-wheel-drive Toyota had no trouble climbing through the eight inches of new snow and up onto the plowed road.

He drove to the ferry dock, bought his ticket, and was just on time to drive right onto the ferry. He was shivering. As the ferry crossed, he turned up the heat in the little truck. At this time of year, the lake was trying to freeze over solid. The constant transit of the ferries kept the travel lane open. The boat's path looked like a river, one hundred feet wide, cut through the iced-over lake. On the New York side, he parked in the park and ride and left the key in the ignition with the window half open, in the hopes that some young person would oblige him by stealing the car and driving it far away. He leaned the bike back up against the same tree where he'd found it.

He thought, *Whoever owns this thing will be surprised their bike is all of a sudden running and shifting like it's supposed to.*

Chapter 12

THE WRAPUP

The team arrived at the meeting at eight thirty. Several people were carrying copies of the morning *Free Press*. Davis was making a pot of coffee with French roast grounds, the same stuff he made at home.

A row of eight-by-ten photos was posted on one wall showing the body, the Photoshopped version of the body, the lean-to, and the house. There were two schoolhouse easels with newsprint pads and some markers in the crayon tray. The marked-up chart of the Inland Sea, with various color-coded marks on it, was also posted. Certain sites on the lake were marked with green numbers in little green circles. Other green numbers were circled in red.

Ethel was perky in her fresh uniform, as always. The younger officers were at the conference table, sitting up straight. Bert had pulled his chair toward the wall and tipped it back. He was wearing a huge, shapeless brown sweater, but he seemed to be shivering a bit anyway. He had both hands around his coffee cup.

There were several copies of the morning's *Free Press* on the table, but Bert read Elaine Drew's article out loud.

" 'Police have identified the body found at Burton Island Campground as the Reverend Paul Brearley, age fifty-five. Brearley, whose family is part owner of Osprey Island, near Burton Island, disappeared eighteen years ago under somewhat mysterious circumstances. He left for a solo canoe camping trip on July 11, 1990, in rough weather. His canoe and gear were found in the weeds near Colchester Point, but a body was never found. A year later, Brearley was declared dead. State Police Detective Sgt. Fred Davis said that although they are pursuing various leads, they do not know who killed Brearley or why. Davis also said they know nothing so far about where Brearley spent his last eighteen years.' "

The article went on to give a detailed bio with Brearley's work history, a mention of his two, not-widely-read books, and a garbled description of the ownership of Osprey Island. Around the article were three pictures. One showed the sanitized version of the body. Another, used at the time of the original search for the missing canoeist, showed his appearance in 1987, clean-shaven. A third, very grainy black-and-white shot showed the Harvard tennis team the year Brearley was captain. It was a classic shot, a row of tall men wearing white pants and white sweaters, holding their rackets. The coach was kneeling in front. Brearley was on the left end of the line, second tallest.

After reading the article, Bert started the discussion. "We need to regroup here. We've gathered a lot of information, only some of which helps us, but there are huge areas about which we know nothing. I'd like to go over what we know, what we don't know, what we need to know and don't, and what we can do. I'd like to start with Peter's summary of what they found at the crime scene, and then do a little exercise."

Peter Dooley got up, and while he talked, Davis took notes on an easel board. "Well, we know that someone else was staying in the house before

Brearley got there. We know what that person was eating. We think, from looking at the bed there, that it was just one person, who was there about a day. The water was off, and he, if it was a he, didn't bother to wash any dishes. Or flush the toilet, which was well used.

"We probably do not have the killer's prints. Whoever did this either wore gloves or was meticulous about wiping down. There was a fire in the fireplace. The person tried to use the gas space heater, but seems to have given up on lighting it."

Davis thought, *If it was Paul, he'd have known to tap the burner on the side a few times to get it going. That means Paul got there after the other person had moved in.*

Dooley continued, "I think Brearley was shot while standing at the door, by someone sitting on the couch opposite." He pointed to a floor plan of the house. "There was one shot from a handgun, a thirty-two. We have the bullet and are working on it now. We don't expect much. The body—if he was already dead—fell right in the doorway, in all likelihood. There was a lot of Brearley's blood on the doorsill and the doorpost. He wouldn't have stayed alive for long; he was shot right in the heart. Maybe ten or twenty seconds. Paul's prints were on the doorpost.

"We're still working on fingerprints. We've looked through the house of course, but also outbuildings, the docks, boathouses, some of the tools. But a lot of people live here in summer, so we have to eliminate all the owners. There are a lot of nooks and corners to check out. We don't have all the prints of the regular occupants of the island yet.

"So far," continued Dooley, "we've found virtually nothing on the grounds around the docks or paths. But we're still sifting through the garbage; we might get lucky.

"Our reconstruction, based on the geometry of the site and the wound, is that Brearley went in the door and was shot from the couch while in a standing position. He sagged down right in the doorway. Then the body was dragged outside. Since the shooter was seated, we can't tell anything about his size.

119

"We *think* the shot was made from the couch because we found residue on the couch, just as you would find it on the clothing of a person who had fired a gun. Or at least, *a* shot was fired from that position recently."

Davis said, "I want to add a funny thought here that may be misleading. Pliny told me that to get the gas heater in that house working after the winter, you had to tap on the burner. It's been like that for decades. Paul would know that. You could argue that the fact that somebody tried to light it, and failed, suggests that the somebody got there first, and didn't know about tapping the burner. Then Paul arrived later. Just a thought." Davis believed in random thoughts and tried to catch them in his own musings about cases. Reality wasn't always logical.

He continued, "Before we move into what else we know, I'd like everybody here to just write down at least three ideas about what the person on the couch was doing there. And pass them up here. We'll look at them a bit later. Three ideas, and they don't have to make a lot of sense at first glance. Don't think too much. It's not that easy to figure out what someone would be doing there in February."

While everybody was doing this, Davis wrote down his own list: "smuggler, stranded fisherman, filmmaker, naturalist à la Thoreau, legitimate island member who is there for some reason he or she doesn't want others to know about. There to meet Paul by prior arrangement. With intent to kill. Or an argument later. Someone who Paul asked to come there for some reason and something went wrong having nothing to do with a crime. A lover."

A little pile of miscellaneous papers grew on the table. "Janice, while we're talking, go through these and make a new list, please. You can mark the most popular ones, you know, 'Survey says, smuggler!'"

While she was making her list, Paul posted the forensic list on the wall and started another labeled "What we know about Paul." Davis now referred to him as Paul, as if they'd been on a first-name basis.

The list started with a few biographical facts.

Name, Paul Brearley
Born, 1953
Disappeared 1990 – canoe accident – no body found
Minister, written some books
One son, JB, lives in Poughkeepsie, NY, Mechanic
Wife Cassandra, remarried, lives NYC

Then people called out other key items as he wrote them down. Everyone was familiar with them.

Big canoeist
Family-owned house on Osprey
Identified by: Rev. Pliny Winthrop, 85, another owner at Osprey, from photo
Shot once
Athletic, healthy, strong, spent a lot of time outdoors
May have been sighted by son
Bought sandwiches at Champ Diner (at Ferry landing), possibly crossed from NY on ferry
On a second easel, he put another sheet titled "What we don't know."
What he was doing for the last 18 years
How he survived
Where he lived, how he made a living
What he was doing on the island
If he came alone
Why he came to Osprey at that particular time

Davis added, "We know very little about him as a person. And we don't really know much about the community of people on that island. What else?"

He added two items to the list:

Paul as a person, before or after disappearance
Community – the real skinny

Bert uncurled himself and stood up, seeming to come alive all of a sudden. "I think a key question is whether or not he had a relationship of some sort with the shooter. If we can figure that out, we'll be close to a solution. We also don't really know exactly when these things took place."

Fred wrote:

Relationship with shooter?
Time line of killing

"Anything else?" he asked.

After a minute, Janice got up and posted the list she had put together. The wall was getting covered with lists, each two feet wide and two and a half feet high.

What was couch-guy doing?
Smuggling (all mention this)
No connection with Victim (4)
Connected somehow to Victim (4)
Criminal activity connected to Paul (3)
Criminal activity unconnected to Paul (4)
Lovers quarrel (2)
Killer lured Paul to Island (1)
Gang falling-out (2)
There to meet Paul by prior arrangement (2)
Island Owner who happened to be there, in conflict with Paul (1)

Davis interjected, "I see some of my cleverest ideas have been deleted. Is there any reason to like one of these ideas more than another?"

Janice said, "If you want me to put 'returned from the dead' on the list, I'd be happy to. Well, it's actually fairly preposterous that anybody would want to be on that island at all in midwinter, and statistically very unlikely that two unrelated people would show up at the same time. I think they came together, or met there by prior arrangement."

Bert responded, "I don't make out Paul so far as minister turned gangster. That doesn't work for me."

Dick Fowler went next. "Well, if I were setting up a lover's tryst, I'd pick a place with heat. I think we can eliminate that one. A former lover, from the island, maybe, if they just happened to be there at the same time."

Davis flipped another sheet over on the easel, and marked it "What we know about the killer."

He asked, "Anything to write here?"

Bert spoke up, "Actually, yes. Almost certainly male, good shot, familiar with guns, owns a gun. Up to no good; there is no sportsman's use for a handgun at that time and place. Unless, of course, the gun was already at the house. Strong enough, young enough, to survive in a frigid house for a while." He fell silent and seemed to be struggling for an idea.

"He might not have meant to be there. What about that? Does the food there, or the mess, tell us anything about that? If I were holing up there in the winter, I'm not sure what I'd bring. But I'd bring some food, and I'd want to stay warm above all. I'd shit outside, or get the toilet working."

No one had any answers to these queries. Davis let the question hang there.

Bert took over the meeting again. "OK, let's move on to our house-to-house, or dock-to-dock, search." He took a sip of coffee and walked over to his map.

Sifting through data, connecting seemingly unrelated facts, was Bert's specialty. It could be done indoors, at a desk, without getting cold or wet. To Bert, this was the fun part. Davis was always impatient to get out the door.

First, Bert passed out copies of a list, several pages long. He began, "This is a list of most everything we've done so far, with dates and other notes.

I've also included the Savage Island photos and Perly Trimble's possible observation of fishing shanties."

Then he handed out copies of a map, well marked up. The map showed the entire Inland Sea on one large page, along with the islands and the Vermont mainland. "This map has all the notes that Fred and Dick made on their tour. But I've added a lot of notes from our investigation so far. The items on your list are keyed to the map. The green numbers circled in red indicate our interviews that came up empty. These are the ones where there was actually someone there that didn't see anything or hasn't remembered yet what they saw. The 'nobody home' cases aren't listed. There are a hundred and sixty items indicating interviews that came up absolutely empty. Some of these were fishermen, walkers, skiers. Others were people who lived near boat launches, or farmers, or homeowners with a good view of the lake. We got no results from bait shops or any of the places that sell licenses. The open green circles are places we should try again."

He continued, "So far, the only thing definitely linked to the killing are the breakfast sandwiches that conceivably are from the Champ Diner. We don't really have a date for those, though.

"You also have there a list, also coded to the map, of police reports of suspicious events in and around this part of the Inland Sea. We left out domestic disturbances and bar fights, fender benders, and criminal cases with solid arrests."

"Starting December fifteenth and ending April fifteenth, we have eleven stolen cars and seventeen DWIs and other serious traffic infractions. Some guns stolen in Rouses Point, but no handguns. Fourteen burglaries, including nine summer houses, four stores, and a rental storage place. A stolen bicycle at the ferry dock on the New York side reported, then found in the same spot. Forty-one arrests at the border, but none with obvious connection to our case. None of this may have anything to do with our case."

"We've found four ice fishermen who habitually fish around Burton. One was in the hospital the whole time. One is an alcoholic who didn't remember much. The other two said there was a fifth fisherman. This is the one with the snow machine, who sets up around Ball Island. This is the guy who we think had a new Yamaha machine, and who had a truck cap set up on plywood as a hut. One of us will be calling every registered Yamaha owner til we find this person. Let's hope he's from Vermont."

Bert then handed out lead sheets, basically to-do lists for each investigator.

"OK. We have incredibly little to work with here. But somebody must have seen something. We're going to have to slog on til we find some witnesses. Janice, see if you can figure out if anybody was out on Butler Island at the right time. Troopers Fowler and Jones, go to every one of those green circles on the map and find people to talk to. Find somebody who saw something, or thinks they saw something. Go back to all the police and fire stations and try again. Maybe somebody remembers a crank call of some sort. I'll be here, going through all these lists over and over and updating them. Report everything to me. And don't give away any information. We don't know much detail, but let's keep it to ourselves."

Davis, who'd been sitting in the corner working on a donut, stood up. "I'm going to concentrate on the island and its people. I want to learn more about Paul. Those people must be able to tell me something that will give a little insight into Paul's missing years. I'm not sure I believe that they are really outside the story. I'm also going back to Savage Island again. The woman there is a great observer; maybe she's thought of something."

Chapter 13

A DAY ON THE LAKE

D avis wanted to solve the case, find the killer, and bring him in. But he
suspected that when they finally sat the killer down in the interrogation
room and hammered him mercilessly with questions, the story would be
very ordinary. That was true of most murders.

In fact, he found the other mystery more compelling: why Paul had left,
what he'd been doing, why he'd returned. It had come to matter to him.
The little community at the island interested him, too. It was about as
insular and minute as a community could be. Perhaps the meaning of what
happened resided there. Of course, it could just as well turn out that Paul's
story and the island story would prove to be mundane and tawdry, too.

Davis was planning to take a boat, maybe the police boat, out to Osprey
Island, but when he called, Pliny insisted on picking him up.

"I'm desperate to get off island. The whole crew is here, and they're all

126

staying in my house. I'm ready to move to a motel. Let me meet you at the Sand Bar. I'll buy you lunch and bring you out here later."

It was a sunny, calm day, and Pliny's little boat was happy to get out. They met at the Sand Bar and went for lunch at the Blue Paddle, the nicest restaurant on that part of South Hero, where they could have a beer and a quiet conversation. The Paddle had an exceptional Caesar salad and first-rate sandwiches.

"My son is here; he came up from Baltimore. He's difficult to be around—he tries to take over. But he knows how to put our big boat in, that's something. His son Timmy is coming tonight. My daughter Abby, praise be, is staying home; she trusts me to take care of things. She thinks he's really been dead all along, so all of this isn't that important, except as 'pornography' as she put it, titillation. Actually, she's one of the more sensible people here."

The waitress, who was also the owner, brought the salads.

Pliny continued, "Helen, Paul's sister, got in last night, after stopping by the morgue to torment herself. That's what I was most worried about. She said she was going to stay in a motel, but that was never going to happen. She's at my house, of course. She can't stay at her place. It's shaken her up, but she's trying to put on her nice, cheery, look-on-the-bright-side face. She says, 'Oh, I'm so *glad* he's been alive, I'm sure he had his reasons, I'm sure he's been doing something useful and important with his life,' stuff like that. It makes me want to leave the church. It's exhausting being with her under normal circumstances. She's started cooking. In my kitchen!"

Davis took a bite of his salad and looked at Pliny, who wasn't eating a thing.

Pliny was enjoying delivering his monologue. "Then the other two families—the husbands and a couple of grown-up kids—are here, too. The Daweses and the Blacks. At least they'll move to their own houses tomorrow."

Pliny munched on his salad for a minute. "I'm being so unkind. These are wonderful people, all of them. It's just, I'm eighty-five. It's great being

127

on the island in my little kitchen by myself and having the occasional interesting conversation with you. Or with these islanders. But taking care of them is something different. Even worse is being taken care of by them! If Helen and Junior take any better care of me . . . Well, I suppose, it's good for me, not being in control."

The waitress brought their sandwiches. The restaurant was usually busy, but they had the place to themselves. Davis could see that even though Pliny was complaining, it wasn't that serious, it was mostly for fun, an indirect way of describing what was going on at the island.

Pliny continued, "Junior loves to take charge. I can't boss him around anymore. After all, he's sixty-two himself. Actually, later today we'll put the big boat in—we've got a twenty-four-foot inboard/outboard with a little cabin—and he's already brought in more groceries. He's really a big help. You know, it's funny. Of all these people I've known so long, I'm most at home with JB. It's a good thing he's here. He just does one thing, then he does the next thing, and doesn't say much. It's so soothing. He doesn't talk philosophy, but he embodies it somehow. Maybe we'll do a little fishing this evening.

"Well, I feel a little better venting. I won't really get a motel room. Everybody's doing their best. As long as Cass doesn't show up."

Davis was surprised. Pliny's speech expressed a side of his personality he hadn't seen before: less in control, more emotional, peevish. On the one hand, he liked Pliny, identified with his dilemma, wanted him to be happy, liked the way Pliny had helped figure things out. Pliny was observant, had a good intuitive mind and a lot of insight into people. Davis was happy to be his lunch companion and a sounding board. But the old man's comments were also evidence of a kind. He'd learned a bit about the people on the island and wanted to talk to them. Though he couldn't quite figure out a good way of doing it. Perhaps he could sit on the huge porch with them, one at a time. Maybe looking out over the lake, in a comfortable rocking chair, would make them more able to open up to him. He thought, *There are worse things than spending a few hours on the island. Maybe I'll learn something. I'll soak up the atmosphere, like Hercule Poirot.*

Davis's mind didn't work like Hercule's or Sherlock's. It was more haphazard. He just kept looking around, talking to people, sometimes trying to identify with them a bit, asking a lot of questions. Then he would either stumble on a solution or occasionally have some little thought that was useful. He did have an ability to pay attention when some tidbit of information came into his peripheral vision. He could notice it and capture it before it drifted off. He also was able to hear what his colleagues thought—he wasn't attached to his own ideas or theories. That was a strength.

Sometimes he wasn't sure he was a particularly good detective. Bert was brilliant in his way, made clever, nonobvious connections. Davis's strength was just being interested in the problem, fairly dogged, a good listener who knew when to shut up. Sometimes he seemed clever to others, but usually that was in cases where his specialized knowledge helped him out, particularly his knowledge of the lake, its people, and their ways.

As they had their coffee, Pliny asked, "What have you learned?"

Davis would have liked to share it all with Pliny, mainly because it would be fun to discuss it with him. But he knew he wasn't supposed to. If somebody on the island was involved, they would hear about it. "Nothing you don't know already. He was shot at the house and left at Burton. We don't know who did it or why. We don't know when it happened."

They drove back to Davis's dock and spent an hour getting to Osprey. On the way, Davis realized he might get stranded, and he didn't want to be yet another guest for Pliny. He called Luke and set up a rescue mission, should it be necessary.

Davis and Pliny tied up and climbed the rickety steps to greet Helen. She was a tall, rangy, almost lanky woman, with neat, short gray hair. As she walked toward them, Davis could see that she was graceful in a way.

129

She reminded him of Katharine Hepburn in one of her sporting movies. He wondered if he was seeing another version of Paul in the flesh. She wore jeans and a baggy sweater.

They introduced themselves at the porch. Helen, though she had been married a couple of times, always used Brearley as her surname.

"Come in," she said, and they walked onto the screened porch. On a round table was a huge, silver tray with cold cuts, cut-up vegetables, egg salad, stacks of various breads, and spreads in little bowls. A pot of coffee had a quilted cover that said *Osprey Island*. "Everybody else is off working; I hope you'll have some lunch." Helen's default presentation was a slightly placating smile. Under the circumstances, she was having trouble holding it. After all, she'd seen her missing brother dead on a stainless steel slab not many hours ago.

Pliny was eager to be somewhere else. "Helen, I promised to help Junior with the boat, and we just ate. I'll see you later." He bolted off the porch and down the path without ceremony. Davis thought how Pliny could be the soul of grace one minute and bumbling, even a bit boorish, the next. His elegance was real in one way and a pose in another.

Davis said, "Helen, it would be great if we could sit and talk for a while. I could really use your help. And I would nibble a bit, but mainly a cup of that coffee would be great."

They sat in tall green rockers with rush seats. There was a row of seven of them facing the lake. They needed new paint, and Fred could see a couple of them needed new seats woven. The chairs were the type now known as Kennedy rockers, but these had been here since long before JFK was president.

Davis admired the view for a minute. Helen handed him a cup of coffee on a saucer. Fred said, "We don't know much about the killing. We know so little about Paul. I'm hoping that if I learn more about him, I might get closer to figuring out what happened. Even if nobody here on the island has any clues, I think somehow the solution may be here among this group. Can I just ask you some questions about this place?"

"Of course, I'll answer anything I can. Or almost anything." Davis noticed that once he had her attention, the mask fell away and a natural warmth took its place.

"Well, perhaps just tell me about what Paul was like in 1990, the summer he left. What was going on here?"

"Well, let's see." Helen gathered her thoughts for a minute. "He was an unusually active person. A typical day for him would be to get up very early and do something vigorous. Sometimes he would run here on the island, but I think he preferred to take out his canoe. Sometimes he would go to the mainland and go out on his bike for a couple of hours. Actually, we went biking together quite a bit. We'd go out for twenty or thirty miles in the hills. The roads along the Vermont side are quite lovely. The islands are flat, but lovely, too. He also had a tennis game lined up a couple of times a week.

"He usually had some sort of project going, either by himself or with others, repairing something. These docks and boathouses need a lot of attention. That year they were shoring up Pliny's porches. Also, I think that summer he was teaching a course at UVM a couple of days a week. He was also always writing something, sermons, but also poems, or working on some book. He'd usually write a bit in the afternoons.

"Did you see that little outbuilding in the cove there? It's part of Pliny's property. Pliny, our dad John, and Paul used it for their writing study, a little clubhouse. They had it all set up with a library, some old oak desks. They got some worn leather club chairs. It was like a British gentleman's club in miniature. They even had little snifters of brandy. That's where the best scotch tended to be. Anyway, Paul usually spent some time there writing, and sometimes the three of them would disappear in there to discuss things. It was great for us; we didn't have to listen to their theories. Pliny still uses it. It's a little bit of a shrine, maybe."

Davis asked, "Can I see it?"

"The key's over the door."

"The three men were very close?"

131

"The three men were joined at the hip," replied Helen. They had a lifelong conversation going. I'm sure Pliny misses it every day. Their conversations and debates were a chorus that framed our life here. Of course, not all of us were much a part of it. JB always left the room when the theological discussions began. Actually, it was more philosophy than just theology, maybe."

"Was Paul close to JB?"

"I think so. They loved to do things together. But that year JB was off working, living in Burlington, and not out here that much. He'd come out in the evening or weekends. JB loved machines, and had a job working on sports cars at a small auto place."

"And you? How about you?"

"I always felt very close to my brother; he took care of me in lots of ways, taught me things. I was still married then. We were living in Connecticut. My husband was a lawyer. I was working in a hospital—I'm a nurse. So we usually got up here on a couple of long weekends, and maybe one or two full weeks. That year we were up for the Fourth of July. There was a huge party here. There were a lot of kids around the island at that point.

"Actually, Paul and I spent two days out on our bikes. He liked to organize excursions. We called him the Recreation Director. We went out one day on the islands with a bunch of kids and once on the Vermont side with just him, me, and my husband. Those were two of the nicest days I spent with him. Then he left, and I never saw him again."

"Was Cass on those trips?"

"No, that wasn't her kind of thing at all."

"What was Paul and Cass's relationship like?"

Helen was silent for a full minute, looking out over the lake. "They were a great team. They always got a lot done together, all kinds of things in their lives. He tended to go overboard about things, including money things, where she tended to hold back. I think he could promote most anything in the safe knowledge that she would put a stop to it if need be. In the family, in our family, at the table, sitting around on the porch, going on a trip, things always seemed really nice, no shouting, no bossing, no smoldering resentments I knew about."

"But what was their relationship like?"

Long silence. "I'm hesitating. They seemed very warm; there was a friendly banter there. He tended to be a bit solicitous of her. She was a bit bemused, tolerant, maybe a little parental toward him. But I hesitate because I don't know anything about their intimate life. I'm not sure people outside a relationship can see inside very much."

Davis said, "Hmm. I think with lots of couples the inside is hard to miss. It comes out in looks, comments, little digs. I don't know—affectionate pats, hugs, smiles. Or the lack of them."

"Well, maybe in some couples. But I wouldn't venture much about their personal life."

"Do you think he could have been seeing someone?"

Another long silence. "Your asking that makes me think you might not have seen Cass in 1990. She was a very beautiful woman. Sexy, too, in a warm, casual way. As Paul Newman said, 'Why go out for hamburger when you have steak at home?' How do I know? I don't, but I doubt if he was involved with anyone."

"Could *she* have been seeing someone? I'm grasping at straws here, but I'm having a lot of trouble figuring out why he would have left—things seemed to be going well for him."

Another long silence. As he was waiting, Davis thought, *I should ask Cass these questions.*

They had mostly been gazing across the bit of lake, off toward Butler Island, as they talked. But now she turned toward him. "Maybe."

*   *   *

A few minutes later, Davis walked down a path to reach the cabin that served as Pliny's study, the clubhouse. On the outside, the shingles had once been stained brown, but there was little color left. Now, in places,

133

they were worn thin as paper, curled up by decades of weathering. The trim had a few remaining flecks of green paint. The building was so fully enclosed by trees that it would be barely visible from the water. It looked like a neglected old storage shed, which in fact it had once been. He found the key over the door, but the building wasn't locked.

The interior was one large room, in the Adirondack mode. The walls were fitted out in dark-stained paneling. The vaulted ceiling had once been white. An eyebrow dormer let in a little light, a glow from above. An Oriental rug covered much of the floor. The rug was worn, but it was probably still valuable. French doors led out to a porch, ten feet above the water. It had a pair of the same big, high-backed rockers, but these were newly painted. There were built-in bookcases all around, about six feet high, stuffed with books and papers. There were a few photos on top of the bookcases, and four amateur watercolors of Lake Champlain. In the middle of the room was a large, dark oak table with three enveloping green leather wing chairs. They were worn, the leather cracked but intact. Off to the right was a smaller table. On it was a huge, black Royal office typewriter, the kind where you could see the letters popping up and retreating with a clatter as you typed.

Davis found the space mesmerizing. He could imagine himself here, reading difficult books, thinking complicated thoughts. He could picture Pliny, his friend John, and the younger Paul in their wing chairs, talking late at night, as slapping noises came from the lake when boat wakes dissipated against the rocks. He could almost hear Paul pounding out a pithy sermon on the old Royal.

Davis was tempted to start opening books, looking through files. He wondered if the clues to Paul Brearley's disappearance were here, in this room, in this typewriter. But if so, he had no idea how to coax them out. Even if there were actual clues here, he wouldn't look for them without Pliny. He'd never let the crime scene people in the door. They were trained to uncover secrets, but not this kind. He walked out.

He took the path to the other end of the island, choosing the long way that led around the back, uninhabited side. The path was used every day in the summer and was easy to follow. Over the afternoon, he talked to almost everyone on the island. Pliny's son was grumpy and wanted to get back to his spring projects. Timmy, Pliny's grandson, was off fishing. The other families hadn't arrived yet, except for a man named Todd Black, who was unscrewing the shutters on the windows of his cabin. He was a tall, stout man in his early forties.

He said, "Look, I just came out here to make sure nobody was messing with my house. We only bought this place about fifteen years ago, and I only met Paul a couple of times before he left, before we bought this place. I'm really an outsider here. I'm friendly with the Winthrops and Brearleys, but we're not close at all. Come to think of it, I'm not sure it's possible to get close to them. They're a little clubby. We just live our life and help with the group projects and go to the island picnics a few times a summer. I don't know anything, and actually, I have to get out of here as soon as I'm done with this. I have to drive all the way to Boston tonight."

Around six o'clock, Davis was at the front dock, standing with Pliny. He heard the Lyman Islander approaching. It hadn't quite hove into view. He said, "Pliny, I like your study. I don't suppose there are old journals of Paul's, letters, any kind of notes or anything?"

"Don't you think I've looked? There are probably a thousand pages written by Paul, all neatly filed away. But as far as anything that explains why he left, or what was happening in his life at that time, I don't think so."

As it turned out, it wasn't Luke at the helm, but Davis's son Andy in his overalls. Andy, at twenty-six, had already acquired the look of a farmer. Strong, a little heavy. Big through the shoulders and arms. His strength, and the way he moved even just getting out of the boat, looked like it had been acquired the old-fashioned way: by working outdoors, all day long, doing difficult things in awkward positions. Andy moved gracefully, but it was not the grace of an athlete. His movements were economical, those of a person who knows that it may be six o'clock now, but he has hours of work ahead of him.

On the ride back, they didn't talk much. The old engine had a beautiful voice, but a loud one; you had to shout to be heard. Davis was a little thrown by seeing Andy there. Over the past week, he'd been lost in a world of immensely complex, powerful relationships between men and their sons, men and their friends, relationships freighted with many layers of meaning. His relationship with his own father was a bit like that. There was no actual conflict, but there were few things he did with his life that didn't refer in some way to Hiram.

Davis zipped up his parka. It was still just early May, it cooled off quickly toward evening, and it was always colder on the water. As the boat banged through the waves, he grabbed one of those fleeting thoughts that sometimes pried open a case. But this thought was about Andy. He loved Andy. He liked to look at him. He was amazed at his capacity for work, his enjoyment of his work no matter how difficult or tedious it might be. He envied him, too, the solidity of his family. It was obvious when he saw him with Jane, or together with their kids, that they were in it for the duration. He knew it couldn't be true, really, but they seemed to have an uncomplicated relationship.

The thought he snagged out of the air, as the boat slapped across the waves, was this: What was different and a bit odd about his relationship with Andy was what wasn't there. There was none of the anguish of his own relationship with Hiram, but none of the closeness, either. He and Andy could help each other do things. They could give a sincere hug when parting. He could hang out comfortably in the family circle and interact with Andy's children. But there was no point of contact or real impact. The fact that they were so cordial and unconflicted obscured the distance between them. He'd like to bridge the chasm, but he had no idea how to do it. The most obvious things to do would have happened long ago.

*   *   *

Supper at the farm turned out to be more of a family reunion than anyone had planned or expected. The menu was the start of it. Ruth had thawed a huge roast from one of their beef cows and was planning a Yorkshire pudding. From there, things had gotten a bit out of hand. In addition to the usual potatoes, salad, and beans from last year's garden, Luke was baking dinner rolls and garlic bread, and Jane was working on the family recipe for peach pie, which, for reasons shrouded in mystery, was known as Siberian peach pie. Then there was ice cream and whipped cream, from their own cows.

Alcohol wasn't usually served at dinner, it being, historically at least, a Quaker household. But Luke was testing out this year's chokecherry wine; two or three bottles were already on the table. Andy had purchased something he called a growler. This was an enormous jug of local, unpasteurized beer, which, once opened, had to be consumed or wasted. And waste was frowned upon. Diane, out for her weekly fix of contact with her grandchildren, had brought a bottle of white wine.

The wind had died down. It was also an exceptionally lovely, warm, clear evening, and the lake was calm, a rare blessing on this side of the island.

Hiram could normally sit through an entire dinner uttering hardly a word, limiting himself to "pass the butter," appreciative slurping noises, and beatific smiles. But the chokecherry wine loosened his tongue. Once it was uncorked, he was a good storyteller. He told the story of his grandfather and the cow. He told of his memories of the last few Quakers on South Hero, who drifted off to Ohio and Indiana when he was young. The most romantic story was about the day Hiram and Ruth met in the cow barn at the University of Vermont Ag School. She had been walking down a row of cows standing placidly in line. Her job was to clean the udders and attach the milking machines. She was just learning to do this, but confident in her awkwardness. She wasn't afraid to get her hands dirty. She was a pretty girl, but he mainly liked the way she handled herself. He fell in love then and there.

Davis liked to hear this story. His parents were old, work-focused, and straitlaced, but there was always an erotic element in the way they talked about each other. And to each other. Many of the other couples he knew, including many his own age, had little hint of that. Their relationships were complex, but not that sexy. He sometimes wondered how these people had managed to reproduce themselves. The buzz in Hiram and Ruth's interactions gave Davis hope.

The grown-ups at the table had heard the story of the meeting in the UVM barn, but to the two great-grandchildren, it was new information. By this point, the growler was half gone, as was a bottle of the chokecherry wine.

As the sun was setting over the Adirondacks, Fred and Diane took the children on a walk along the road. At this time of year, few cars came by; the road was a country lane. Fred liked these walks. To the grandchildren, they were Grandma and Grandpa, and anyone driving by would think Fred and Diane were still a couple. These walks were his best opportunity to look at Diane these days. When he first saw her, years ago, she had been quite skinny, with straight, dark brown hair. She wore glasses—they were granny glasses in those days—and she favored severe outfits, woolen skirts, and crisp white blouses. She was quiet, seemingly a little prim. But he also saw a very lovely face behind the stillness, almost hiding there. It wasn't as if she were shy. It was more that she seemed to be saying 'If you can't see who I am, I don't need to talk to you.' He also noticed that beneath her woolens she had a very narrow waist and a very round rear. Fred had never really gotten over the combination of the prim demeanor and the sexy shape, and the walks gave him a chance to look at her again. He took careful note of every change in her. After all, it had been almost thirty years. She looked basically the same to him; she was the same girl, if a little less skinny and a little grayer.

When they came back, everyone was on the porch, where the pie and whipped cream and ice cream were set out. Luke had lined up some clean glasses and opened the white wine. In a while, Jane and Andy led the children off, and the grown-ups sat on the porch watching the last of the sunset shut down. A few minutes after that, only Davis and Diane remained. The chill was falling, and Davis got an old bedraggled quilt from a chest and threw it over them on the equally bedraggled couch that lived on the porch year-round. That was as close as he could come to making a pass.

Diane and Fred had lived on the farm when they first moved back to Vermont in 1982, when Andy was born. They lived mostly in Fred's big, old room, which was still known as Fred's Room years after he'd moved out. Diane and Fred used it still on the rare occasions when either of them stayed over, and it was sometimes used for the B and B. On the even more rare times when they both were staying over, things got a bit awkward.

Davis said, "You know, I'm an officer of the court. I can't really drive home."

Diane answered, "Well, I am, too. It wouldn't do for me to get a DWI." Davis suspected Luke may have had this outcome in mind when he opened the last bottle of wine. There may have been other conspirators. Usually Luke was available to take Davis back to his boat, but tonight he was nowhere to be found. Davis was always ready to get together with Diane, but for that very reason, he would never make a move; he didn't want to get shot down. Diane got up and gave him a tug by the hand.

"Come on, Freddy, come meet your fate. It's not your fault."

The room was pretty much as it had been when they had lived there. It was shabby, with wallpaper that had been there since 1930 or 1940—a floral pattern almost completely faded out. In places it had worn away, and the previous pattern, also floral, peeked through. The plaster on the ceiling was intact but cracked. Chunks could fall down at any time, but didn't. Two windows looked eastward over the fields. Long ago, Davis had put in a gas space heater, which was running now. Next to the room was an old bathroom, the first indoor bathroom built in the house. It was really a converted closet, with the original wooden toilet tank hanging from the wall. Beyond the bathroom was a little room where Andy had lived as a baby.

The big bed, where they now lay, had a huge woolen quilt, which had

139

come down from Hiram's aunt Esther, known as Essie. It was made of remnants of old men's suits, and in the corner was marked *Esther, 1908*. The quilting threads had rotted away along certain meridians, and the white stuffing was peeking out. Some of the quilted pieces were gone. But it was warm under there, in any season.

Sex had never been the issue with them; they knew what to do. Since they had separated, they had gotten together like this several times, maybe once a year or so, except when one of them was involved with somebody else. Neither of them had remarried or had the knack of keeping a casual relationship going for very long.

For Fred, lying like this, under the old quilt, naked with Diane after sex, was pretty much his favorite thing. The sexual experience was a bit sharper for him because of the infrequency, sort of a two-for-one special. On the one hand, he was a fifty-three-year-old man making love with a fifty-three-year-old woman, nice-looking, both of them, but a little worse for wear. Not as worn as the old quilt, but frayed at the corners. But at the same time, it was also their youthful, perfect selves making love there, too, all the times blurring together. Each encounter recapitulating those before, going back to day one in the battered cruiser in Boston. Those early experiences came alive in the new ones.

Davis often fell asleep quickly in situations like this. He couldn't tell for sure whether Diane was awake, dozing, or asleep. But this time he was wide awake, thinking. He was thinking about his boat ride with Andy, being both close to him and estranged at the same time. He was thinking about his gnawing relationship with his father—probably nothing to do about that. But mainly he was thinking he didn't want to end up like Paul Brearley, wandering around looking for hamburger when he had steak at home.

He didn't say anything about any of it to Diane but was getting just a little closer to it. She was asleep anyway.

Chapter 14

INFO TRICKLES IN

Davis and Bert sat in the squad room, with its lists and photos on the wall. The rest of the team was off looking for information, going door-to-door, dock to dock, farm to farm.

Davis told Bert what he had learned at Osprey Island. But then he said, "I don't know whether learning more about the people on the island, or about Paul's personality or life, really tells me anything. Maybe all I really need to know is that he lived there, he left, he came back and was shot, and it may be that none of his personal adventures provide the slightest clue to his killing. But I'm going to pursue that line for a while longer, talk to some of the people again, and try to talk to his ex-wife."

Bert said, "It's funny that on a lake, where you can literally see for miles, nobody has seen a damn thing. It's easy to imagine why in a city or a town, with lots of dark corners, you could do something without anybody noticing. But you'd think a person against a vast white background of snow would be seen." He walked around the room a little and stared up at his beloved lists. "I think some people saw something, and we'll find them if we keep looking."

*   *   *

Over the next two weeks, the case slowed down. Troopers Dick Fowler and Janice Pearlstein were grinding, knocking on doors. Bert was working through the information that came in, as well as keeping track of other cases.

Davis had another long talk with Pliny. They met at the Paddle for lunch as they had before. But nothing new came of it. Then he went to see Sarah, the amateur photographer at Savage Island, for a second time. She was smart and observant; perhaps she saw something after all. It was pleasant going out there, he liked talking to the young woman and her grumpy husband, but there was no other result.

He wanted a meeting with Cassandra Brearley, Paul's former wife. If anyone would have some insight into Paul's mind at the time of his disappearance, or perhaps some ideas about what he might have done with himself, it would be her. He called to set up a meeting. He offered to go to New York to talk to her. But this idea didn't seem to be panning out.

When he got through to her on the phone, she said, "Officer Davis, I will not answer questions. I will not talk to you. If you show up at my door here, I still will not talk to you. Please leave me alone. This situation is creating some problems for me, and I'm not going to compound them by talking to you. I'm sorry. Actually, I'm not really sorry. Just don't call."

He spent some time cruising slowly around the Inland Sea near Osprey Island, trying to re-create the situation in his mind. He spent a quiet night anchored off the island, imagining scenarios. The next day, he interviewed more of the Osprey Islanders. He reinterviewed JB. He liked

JB but was conscious of a little nervousness in his speech. But that could be that JB himself was struggling to sort things out.

Making little headway, Davis spent more of his time on other projects, other cases, and old paperwork. He knew something would probably break eventually, but decided for the time being to lead a normal life. He came and left work at normal hours.

He took some of the dozens of vacation days he had accumulated. His impulse was to spend more time with Andy and Hiram. He helped Andy with some of the planting. He weeded lettuce in the greenhouse and set out plants in the three acres of vegetables Andy raised. He helped his father some with the evening milking. Both son and father were cordial, but a little perplexed as to why Fred was volunteering when for forty years he had to be drafted to touch soil or handle animals, though he knew how to do both things. In the end, Davis spent most of his time in the boat barn, by himself or with Luke, working on the Thompson. Each evening, he drove back to his boat, or if weather permitted, docked at the farm dock.

He decided to take a three-day cruise north, up the Richelieu, into Canada. It was a way to spend time on the new boat, which he had used a large chunk of his savings to buy. He hadn't been over the border by boat since a brief trip in his youth, with Luke. But he didn't crave a real adventure and was content to just cruise along slowly. He didn't try to go a long way each day; he'd find a place to anchor well before dark. He spent a lot of time reading, or just sitting thinking with his book in his hands. He left his cellphone off.

*   *   *

Meanwhile, Bert was at headquarters. He experienced the same two-week period very differently. To him, this was the fun part. He was like a great blue heron, standing absolutely still at the edge of the water. He knows if he waits long enough, an unsuspecting fish will swim past for him to spear.

He pored over all his lists, secret manuscripts to decode. Sometimes, as he read through lists of stolen cars or talked again to the medical examiner, he got an idea for further research, a new database to comb through. With his feet on his desk, he liked to picture who the murderer might be, and why he would be at Osprey. It boiled down to four plausible ideas. The killer could be a drug dealer of some sort. He could be a fugitive hiding out, though in that case, there should have been some police agency who was looking for him. He could have been someone who knew Paul was going out there and wanted to kill him. Or he could be someone who met Paul out there on purpose and *then* decided to kill him. The mess at the house, in Bert's mind, made option four unlikely.

With option three or four, he would have expected to see evidence that the person came after Paul's arrival. The place might not have been a mess. The shooter might be in the door and Paul on the couch, for example.

Bert had other projects and cases, but he spent a chunk of most days on these musings.

Janice Pearlstein and Dick Fowler, whenever free, went wandering around asking questions, Dick on the islands, Janice on the mainland near St. Albans. They also followed up on crank calls and false confessions, but those tailed off after the story tumbled off the front page. Janice was beginning to wonder if the case might be one of those that was never solved.

*   *   *

But on May 23, Janice called Bert around noon. "I found the missing ice fisherman, the one with the truck-cap fishing shanty."

"Where did you find him?"

"It was by accident. I was driving down a back street in St. Albans, and I saw the shanty in a driveway, tied down to a boat trailer. It's a professor from UVM, and he'd like to come in to talk about it."

"Come on in. I won't go anywhere." As soon as Bert hung up, the phone rang again. It was Dick Fowler.

"Sgt. Miller, it's Dick Fowler. I think I may have something here, at least something a little odd."

"Go on."

"Well, there's a boat launch near a campground north of North Hero Village. It's the one nearest to Osprey Island, and also sort of out of the way. I've been talking to everybody who lives on the road, one at a time. They're not usually there when I knock. There are about twenty houses between the boat launch and Route 2. I started from the launch and worked back toward Route 2. Anyway, at the eighteenth house back, I found a woman who saw something that struck her as funny around the time we're talking about, early February. It might be important.

"She saw somebody go by toward the campground riding a mountain bike. She noticed it because it was very snowy and bitter cold, the worst time to bike anywhere. Then a few minutes later, she saw an old red Toyota pickup driving toward Route 2, covered in snow, she thinks with a bike in the back."

Bert knew these things were on his lists somewhere. In a moment he would have it figured out. This was important. "Dick, good work. Have her show you exactly where she saw things, and see if she's willing to come in. If she won't come in, let me know, and I'll come out there. But I've got another witness coming in already today."

He called Davis's cell but got no answer. He left a message.

*　　　*　　　*

Janice, Bert, and Professor Tom Tower sat down in the little office Bert and Davis shared. It was more friendly than the interview rooms and less chaotic than the squad room the team had been using for the case. Janice made the introductions. She had also brought coffee and pastries. It was an article of faith in law enforcement that pastries begat information. Studies had proved it.

Bert said, "Thanks for coming in. Please tell us what you know." Janice had her notebook out but had written most of the information down once already.

"No problem, I have to teach a class later anyway. I had my fishing shack on the Vermont side of Woods Island. I can walk right out there. Actually, I just bought it this winter; it was already sitting there. What I saw was around dawn on February second. It was a Thursday, pretty early, probably around seven thirty or eight. I know the date because I went to a memorial service for a colleague later in the day. I've checked my datebook. Anyway, I wasn't sleeping very well. I went out there maybe around 6 A.M. or so. It has a little heater, it's quite civilized. I was walking my dog as much as anything.

"Anyway," continued Tom Tower, "first I saw someone skiing west from Shantee Point. That's odd in itself, but I didn't think about it too much. Then about fifteen minutes later I heard a snow machine outside, very loud, and when I went out to look, I saw it towing a cargo sled, flying out from behind the far side of Woods Island, headed toward Burton. About fifteen minutes after that, the skier went by, following in the track of the cargo sled. Around that time I was getting cold, and started to walk back to my car. I heard some more noise from the machine, but I wasn't paying attention anymore."

Janice wanted to keep him talking; maybe he could remember more details. "What did either person look like? Can you describe them? What about the cargo sled?"

"It was pretty dark. There could have been some yellow on it. Mainly it was noticeably louder than most of them are these days."

Ethel stuck her head in the door. "Dick Fowler is downstairs with somebody else to see you."

"Give me another ten minutes."

They continued talking for a few minutes and then the professor left, encouraged to continue to work his memory. Janice stayed to hear the next witness, if it in fact turned out to be legitimate.

Trooper Fowler knocked and walked into the office. It was getting a little tight in the small room.

"Mrs. Lane, this is Detective Sgt. Bert Miller and Detective Trooper Janice Pearlstein. This is Mrs. Betty Lane. She lives year-round on that road that goes down to the boat launch." Mrs. Lane was fiftyish, a little stout, wearing jeans, a wool shirt, and Bean boots. She seemed eager to talk, happy for some attention.

Janice was official hostess. "Mrs. Lane, I've got some donuts and stuff here. Can I get you something, a coffee maybe?"

Mrs. Lane was looking around the room. "A doughnut would be nice. Got some tea? Actually, can I smoke in here?"

"They won't let us smoke in here, but I'll make some tea. I could use a cup myself." The corollary of the doughnut theory was that hot beverages calmed witnesses down. Janice used Davis's little gourmet coffee setup to get some tea going.

Fowler set up the conversation. "She saw a cyclist on her road around the right time. Mrs. Lane, if you could just tell us again what you saw."

"Well, in winter, basically nobody goes down that road. There are just a few of us who live there year-round. It's a damn cold place. Of course, I know everybody's cars—mostly pickups. If I'm home, I watch every car that goes by. I don't mean to, I just can't help it. So I see residents go by. There are a few people who walk their dogs on the road. One or two locals who park at the boat launch and go fishing. Sometimes the Parks people will go out to the campground in winter for something.

"Well, I saw a guy riding a bike. All bundled up, sort of trudging along, very slow. Right after the plow made its first pass on the road. We'd had a pretty good snowfall the night before. At first I didn't think that much about it. The islands attract a lot of nutty people who do crazy sports, sailing on the ice, whatever—I wrote it off to that. After all, people come from around the world to go biking here. Maybe this guy got his seasons mixed up.

"Then maybe a half hour later, I see him coming out—at least I think it was the same guy—driving an old red Toyota pickup. I know that's what it was because my husband—he's dead now—he had one from the eighties. He drove it for years, and I drove it a lot, too. It was the same model, long-bed four-by-four, and the same color. Eventually, the doors on those rot out. This one had, and they'd put a new door on it, blue or black, I think. Maybe gray. Not sure about that. Anyway, I could see the bike sitting on the snow in the bed of the truck."

Janice served up the tea. Mrs. Lane worked her way through the box of doughnuts. But after a half hour, she couldn't remember anything else about it, except it was right after a storm the night before, in the dead of winter, and she hadn't been feeling that well. The clearest idea she could add was, "It might have been late morning or early afternoon. It was light anyway, not early and not late."

Dick Fowler drove Betty Lane home, trying to get her to remember more things about the day. Dick didn't really know why this information was important, and Bert hadn't had time to explain. But he could tell it was a breakthrough from Bert's tone of voice. His usual uninflected, slow bass was up a half scale, and Bert was talking a little faster, slouching less than usual.

When he left, Bert flipped open his notebook, his updated book of lists. Janice did the same. "The Case of the Borrowed Bike," he said out loud. He was remembering an odd little point on one of his lists, that a bike had been reported stolen at the park and ride on the New York side of the ferry run, and then whoever called it in had called back a few hours later to report that the bike was back, exactly in the same spot, having been oiled and tuned up in the meantime.

Janice said, "Wait, let me call the weather service about that snow." While she was on the phone, Bert sat silently, hardly moving, with a calm smile, his old oak office chair tilted back as usual. This was a key part of dating events, making a narrative out of their little collection of information. He'd been waiting for two weeks. He could wait a little longer.

Janice said, "Six inches the evening of the first and another four on the morning of the second, the day we think the body was placed on Burton."

A lot of random things came together. Janice wrote them down. She was having a lot of fun. She'd been asking questions with no purpose for weeks. Now they were moving, or she thought they were. She had begun to think that "police investigation" was another term for aimless wandering. Actually, it was the aimless wandering that had brought her to the professor's door.

On a piece of paper, she wrote:

Killing: on or before 2/2 – if the shooting was that morning, the Professor could have heard a shot.
Transport to Burton, roughly 7 AM 2/2
6" snow, evening of 2/1, 4" morning of 2/2
2/3, 10 a.m. bike reported stolen at park and ride by the ferry dock in NY.
Same day around 12, Mrs. Lane sees the cyclist, then the red truck
At 3 PM, bike owner calls in and says the bike is back

She slid the paper across the desk. They both said, "Talk to the bike owner."

Bert changed the subject. "Let's talk about the Toyota." He leafed through his notes to the list of car thefts, car arrests, and car accidents. The list named thirteen Toyota pickups, of which three were old red ones, of which one was a long bed with a repaired door. It was found wrapped around a tree in Malone, New York, February 28. It had not been claimed. Plates were on it. His list didn't say who the owner was.

Bert interjected, "If the plates were on it, it probably wasn't the owner who cracked it up."

Bert immediately called the Malone Police. He told an Officer O'Malley that he was interested in the truck, that it might be connected to a Vermont case. O'Malley was busy but would get back to him shortly.

While they waited, Janice said, "Well, let's see. Maybe Wednesday or early Thursday, Paul Brearley is shot. We still know nothing about who did it, except that they can drive a snow machine. We don't know how they got to Osprey."

Bert put in, "We don't know if he arrived with Paul. We don't know who the skier is."

Janice added, "If the snowmobile run the professor saw was to dump the body at Burton, then there's no reason to think the skier was the killer."

Bert said, "But we must assume the skier had something to do either with Paul or with the shooter. Otherwise, why would he follow the snow machine?"

Janice asked, "Could he have just been out for a ski? Maybe followed a nice, new track conveniently laid down by the snow machine?"

Bert called the weather service back. It was about fifteen degrees on the lake at 7 A.M. on that day with a ten-mile-an-hour wind. He said, "It was plus fifteen degrees and windy. A little cold for recreational skiing in the dark. He could have, but I think he was going somewhere. Anybody I know who skis for fun goes out when the sun shines."

He thought for a minute, then continued, "If the skier was headed to, say, Burton or Woods, he probably wouldn't have passed to the north of Woods. He'd have come straight south. That means he was headed to Osprey. Or possibly Butler or Knight Island."

After a quick rap on the door, Fred Davis walked in. "I got your message. What's up?"

It took them a half hour to review the new information and outline the conclusions they were coming to. Davis, as usual, was a good listener. He remembered everything they told him as if he'd been there himself to hear it.

Then O'Malley called back.

"OK, this is O'Malley. I have the truck here in my pound. Nobody has asked for it. It's registered to a Paul Baer, age fifty-eight, residing in Tupper Lake. The Tupper police up there say it's a boardinghouse, and Paul Baer hasn't been around for a while. But we haven't followed it up, and neither have they. Anything else? I've got a situation here."

"Can I have the truck? I think it's evidence in a murder case over here."

"Take it, please. We've got all the junk cars we need at the moment. Just let me know when you're coming. If you learn anything exciting, tell me."

Bert hung up and shared the news, adding, "Of course, we don't really have any evidence that the truck or the bike have anything to do with Paul Brearley. But I'm liking Paul Baer for Paul Brearley at the moment."

Davis said, "Remember the breakfast sandwiches from the Champ Diner? If it's a New York truck, and our victim ate at the diner, it's not hard to imagine him coming over on the ferry, getting his bag of sandwiches, parking at the boat launch, going out to Osprey, and then . . . then something . . ."

Bert wanted to pursue one other line of thought. "The bike. The weather pattern, plus what Mrs. Lane says, suggests the cyclist came and got the truck the day after the killing, after the six inches of snow. The stolen and unstolen bike suggests pretty strongly that the bike and the truck went back across to New York. Why would somebody bother, after a murder, to take the truck—if it's really Paul's truck—back to New York? Why not leave it where it was?"

They all thought about it for several minutes. They polished off the remaining pastries.

Janice spoke first. "Well, they moved it for our benefit. Because the killer doesn't want us to figure out that Paul Brearley is Paul Baer."

Both men looked at her. In a way, it was the key to the case. Davis said, "Exactly." He thought, *She's smart. Smarter than either of us.*

Bert said, "I agree. But why? We're obviously clueless about who did this. Why would they care if we make the connection?"

Davis said, "I think this has to mean that our killer knew about the two Pauls on some level. Actually, I think we do know something about our killer. He's a complicated person, someone who thinks in convoluted ways. He doesn't like to do things the obvious way. Maybe he overthinks things."

Janice added, "Well, if he knew Paul Brearley had died or disappeared, and somehow figured out who the person was when they met at the island,

151

he wouldn't really have to know who Brearley had been, just that he was alive and out of circulation."

Davis said, "If it isn't obvious, I think they knew each other. I don't know if we can say much more than that."

The next moves were clear.

Janice and Dick would start asking questions yet again, beginning at the ferry landing, with the idea of a bike, a red truck with a black or gray door, and something happening around February first and second. People who had already been interviewed once might remember something with specific cues to work from.

Fred would go to Tupper the next morning. It was about two hours away, once he was on the New York side of Lake Champlain.

Bert would arrange to get the red Toyota brought back. Then he would sit in his office, read his notes over and over, tilt back his old office chair, and await developments.

*   *   *

Davis was familiar with the Adirondack region, often known just as "the Park." He could see the foothills from the front porch at the farm. Wherever you were on the lake, you could look west and see a beautiful view of the Adirondacks. He had climbed many of the forty-six peaks over four thousand feet with his dad, with his kids, with Diane, with Luke, and once or twice with all of them at once.

But he knew the watery part of the region best. There were a lot of lakes and rivers there, some of them remote. It was one of the best areas for extended canoe trips. His first big adventure had been a two-week trip there by canoe and Guideboat. The Adirondack Guideboat had once been a primary means of transport in the mountains. It was fast in the lakes and rivers, and relatively easy to carry when a portage—known locally as a carry—couldn't be avoided. When he was fourteen, Hiram had taken him, his older sister Hazel, Luke, and one of Hazel's friends on a canoe trip.

They took turns paddling the canoes and rowing the Guideboat. After five days, Hiram went back to his cows, and the four young people kept going for another week This was the beginning of the romance between Luke and Hazel.

Though just a few miles distant, the Park could have been another country. In Vermont, you could drive all day and see almost nothing but a bucolic, largely cultivated rural landscape, punctuated every few miles with a charming village chartered around 1800. There was poverty in Vermont, but it was mostly tucked away in the hills, on little dirt roads, or in the big towns. There might be poorly fed people in houses that were frigid all winter long, but they were well-proportioned houses with artfully sagging barns.

In the Park, the poverty was right out there, and the villages weren't charming. As you drove through, there were moments of splendor, but most of the beauty was off-road. You had to walk to see the mountains or paddle to see the dozens of beautiful lakes, with their rustic Great Camps. From the road, you were more likely to pass through miles of barely inhabited forest lined with swamps that looked like an extended Smokey the Bear poster: "Remember, only you can prevent forest fires!" Some parts of the Park had started to come back. Towns like Saranac Lake had gotten more prosperous, had more going on. But he thought Tupper might still be a bit down-at-heel.

He liked the route to Tupper. Once you got out of Plattsburgh, it followed along the Saranac River, then wound its way toward Upper Saranac Lake. There were stretches of bleak swamp country, but some of it was pretty, too, particularly along the rivers and lakes.

Main Street in Tupper was a mixed message. Some prosperous older businesses, some optimistic new ventures. But a lot of For Sale signs, too. Davis stopped by the police station and told them what he was up to. They had no information on Paul Baer's whereabouts, but they said he was welcome to go looking. Paul's address was really a boardinghouse. It was a big, shabby clapboard building with a wide sagging porch and a flat roof.

It needed paint. There was no sign outside, but it looked as if it had been a hotel at one time. It was between a little convenience store and a hardware.

He went into the lobby with a desk clerk setup, like a real hotel, but nobody was there. He rang the bell, but nobody responded. He went to a little store next door to pick up a paper. A young woman was behind the counter. While he paid, he showed her the sanitized version of Paul's picture.

"Hi. Could you look at this picture for me? Do you recognize this man?"

She looked, and her eyes widened. "He looks dead."

"He is."

She was upset. "Well, that's Paul. He lived next door. When he was here, he came in every day for something or other. Such a nice man. What happened?"

"Well, we're not exactly sure, but he was killed over in Vermont sometime in the winter. Could you tell me who knew him best around here?"

"I'm not sure. He was mostly here in the winters, like a lot of the men. All the men next door will know him. But they won't be here now. They'll be at the soup kitchen."

The soup kitchen was in a church basement down the block. It was a large white room, with worn tile squares on the floor and six-inch round iron columns every twenty feet holding up the sanctuary above. A row of squat, high windows let in a bit of natural light. About twenty people, mostly men, were finishing up their lunch, and a trio of women were behind a counter, serving.

Davis spoke up loud enough so everyone could hear. "Excuse me. Does anybody here know Paul Baer?"

A few people ignored him, but most of the people walked right over to him, including the three women who were cleaning up. A lot of people knew Paul Baer and didn't know where he had disappeared to. Davis told the group the basic facts about Paul's death. Over the next hour, they told him about his life as Paul Baer.

Paul had been wintering in Tupper for around ten years. They didn't know anything about his life before that. He had arrived with a woman who had a little kid, a baby maybe a year old. She left with the baby soon after they arrived. After she left, Paul moved into the rooming house. In warm weather, he was usually off working as a logger, carpenter, or guide. He was often in Tupper from December to about April. When his guide work was local, they would see more of him. He worked as a hunting guide, but his main skills were in canoeing and fishing. He was much sought after to lead groups on canoe adventures into various wilderness areas, and sometimes took rich fishermen—known in the north woods as "sports"—out to find big trout, bass, and pike. In the fall, they went out for migrating ducks and geese.

The large response to Davis's question arose from the fact that when in town, Paul volunteered at the soup kitchen. He would serve food, but his specialty was mopping, sweeping, and dishwashing. He seemed to enjoy chores like that. Occasionally someone would bring in fresh fish or game. When that happened, he cooked. On those days, more people than usual would show up.

He was both reticent and gregarious. He liked to be with people, but he didn't talk much. He liked to get somebody else talking, telling stories or commenting on politics, and then sit back and listen. As a result, people felt they knew him without knowing much of anything about him.

This part of the story was roughly what Davis was expecting. But it got interesting when he asked, "What did he drive?"

A young man with a lot of dark hair, black jeans, a nose ring, and a chain draped artfully around his waist answered. Though the young man looked fierce, when he spoke, he seemed friendly and open.

"Well, he had a Toyota long bed. A red one. Maybe late eighties, eighty-six or eighty-seven. Pretty rusty, but ran just fine. And he had an old snow machine."

"Can you describe it? It might be important."

"Well, it was a Ski-Doo brand, yellow and black, from around 1970. I was there when he got it, maybe the winter before last. Somebody staying at the boarding house was leaving the area and just gave it to him. It wasn't running. It sat out in back of the boarding house until this past fall. Paul's son was up here one day. He got it going in about an hour. Then a couple of weeks later, he came back with a bunch of tools and a cardboard box full of parts. He spent all day breaking it down. After that, it ran great. Paul used it a lot."

Davis gulped and hesitated for a few moments. He didn't want his excitement to be too obvious. "He had a son?"

Another man spoke up. He was about seventy, way too thin, broken down. Though dressed in old clothes, he was clean and clean-shaven. "JB. His name was JB something. He's been here four or five times, I'd say, over the last year or two. A very nice guy, and a great mechanic from what I could see. He stayed over at the boardinghouse a couple of times—actually he stayed in my room. Paul's room is a little tight for visitors."

"What was he like?"

"Hmm. Nice. Midthirties, I'd say. Basically very friendly, and he liked to do stuff. He always fixed a lot of stuff when he was here, as if it bothered him when something didn't work."

The old man's name was Mason, but people seemed to call him Dixon. He took Davis back to the boarding house to see Paul's room. They found the super, a resident who took minimal care of things in lieu of rent. His name was Arthur, and he looked a lot like Dixon. He had a key to Paul's room. The key fit a regular old Yale door lock, but there was also a padlock hasp, empty.

As was his practice, Davis didn't go in, just stood in the doorway looking. He pulled out his little camera and took a few pictures. The room was small. It might have been a linen closet at one time. It had no real window, just a transom over the door. There was only room for a bed, a rocking chair with a plywood seat, a low bookcase, well-stocked, and a card table folded up against the wall. The bed was neatly made, with worn, green army blankets.

An open closet held some clothes on hangers, including a lot of flannel and woolen shirts. It also held a half dozen fishing rods of various kinds, and some tackle boxes. In the corner were two hunting rifles. On the shelf above were boxes of ammunition and more fishing gear. On the floor were four or five pairs of boots and several pairs of sneakers.

Davis saw Paul as a writer, as someone who habitually wrote down what he was thinking. He was hoping for the tell-all diaries he'd failed to find in Pliny's little office on the lake. He didn't immediately see anything that looked promising.

He turned and shut the door. "Gentlemen, please stand right here. I'm going to get some tape from my car to seal this off. I don't know if this is related to Paul's killing, but we'll have to go over it inch by inch. Just stand here for a minute, then if you're willing, I'd like to ask some more questions."

He was back quickly with crime scene tape with *Police Line, Do Not Cross* printed on it. He taped it in place. Then the three men went downstairs and sat down in a large kitchen in the back that was used by the residents. It had a big table in the middle and some mismatched but comfortable seating around the edges. It was fairly clean.

"I need to know some specific things. When did you last see him?"

The two men looked at each other. Dixon said, "February, maybe late January." Arthur nodded.

"What about rent? Why wasn't his stuff moved out?"

Arthur said, "Well, he's been here for many years. He was paid up til April—we don't charge much for that space; it isn't strictly legal. He had some good stuff in there. Nobody wanted the room. I was hoping he would just show up. I was a little worried, to be frank."

"Who did he spend time with? What did he do when he was here?"

Dixon took the question. "Well, I'd say you've met his closest friends just now. Us. He had a girlfriend for a while, three or four years ago. Then she took off. Let's see, what did he do when he was around . . . ? He spent a lot of time by himself. He read a lot. He'd sit right here, in that chair, and read. He walked a lot. He spent a lot of time at the soup kitchen. He went to the library almost every day."

157

"Did anybody ever go in his room there, to clean up maybe?"

"Are you kidding? Actually, I did open the door once, after he sort of didn't show up, just to make sure he wasn't dead in there or something. But it was just as you see it. I locked it up again."

"Thanks. I don't know if that room is exactly a crime scene, but we need to search every inch of it. I'm going to set that up for tomorrow, if possible. Can I put my own lock on that hasp? I want to be able to say nobody's been in there since right now."

At first Arthur seemed a little huffy, but then he shrugged. "Put any lock you want on there. I really want you to find the guy who did this. We all liked Paul. Without really trying very hard, he did a lot for people around here. He was sort of the unofficial chaplain. At the soup kitchen, too. Though he wouldn't let us say such a thing."

Davis ran to the hardware next door and returned with a stout brass padlock, the kind you can set to any four-digit combination. He quickly punched in the combination he always used: 2-4-3-6, "two feet, three feet."

He went back to the kitchen where Dixon and Arthur were still at the table. "I'll be back in a bit. I've got to go set up this investigation here, but I'd like to come back this evening and talk some more. Maybe somebody else living here knows something. Actually, can I see the snow machine before I go?"

Dixon said, "Oh, it's not here. He took it with him when he left."

* * *

Davis walked around for a half hour looking for a good cellphone signal. A street fell down the hill to the lake past an old synagogue. By the shore, he was able to call Bert.

"Well, it's him, no doubt about it. He's been living here under the name Paul Baer. I've got his room padlocked at a boarding house. He's been wintering here for ten years or so." He went on to review much of what he'd learned, including the soup kitchen scene and the boardinghouse gang. Then he added the big news.

"JB's been up here over the past year at least. I don't remember JB telling us he'd been hanging out with his dad. It was just 'Maybe I saw him on Mt. Marcy.'"

He continued, "He's had the same room for the last few years, and all his stuff is there. I think we should get the crime scene people in here. I don't think we need a warrant, really. I thought I would go talk to the police and see if we can bring our team over here, maybe in the morning. I'm going to stay at Shaheen's Motel—I've stayed there before."

"Call me after it's set up on your end," said Bert. "I'll line people up to come tomorrow. I'll come, too. I want to see this place."

*   *   *

Davis set things up with the police and got his room at Shaheen's. He found a restaurant and had something they called Italian food. He stopped back at the boardinghouse but nobody was there to talk to, and he didn't feel like searching through the town's many bars to find people. He went back to the motel.

The scene in Paul's room the next morning was comical. There was a photographer, a fingerprint technician, and two other specialists, all trying to function in a room big enough for one person at best. A Tupper Lake patrolman was trying to find somewhere to stand. Bert and Davis were downstairs with Janice, drinking coffee in the kitchen. She had insisted on coming. They took turns coming upstairs to check on things.

Five of the residents at the boardinghouse had set aside the morning to watch the proceedings. Three of them were hanging out in the upstairs hall, getting in the way.

Davis didn't think the fishing tackle or guns would tell them much. The fingerprints would be interesting. But his main hope was that the secret journals, the key to the scriptures, which explained everything, would be there somewhere. He was hoping one of the techs would walk up to him, hand him some notebooks, and say, "I thought you might want to look at these." But that didn't happen. The techs left two hours later with a bunch of clothing bagged up, a large envelope of papers that would be interesting to sort through, a lot of fingerprint information, and some odds and ends.

After the techs had left and before they locked up, Davis put on latex gloves and looked through the books. Janice and Bert watched from the hallway. There was some theology, some Niebuhr and Tillich, Dietrich Bonhoeffer, and other writers he'd never heard of. There were copies of two books written by Paul himself. One was a collection of sermons, the other a book called *Jesus in Modern Politics*. But most of the shelf was a motley collection of literature, some serious novels, and a lot of mystery stories. There was not one adventure story and nothing about fishing or hunting. There was a small pile of magazines: a *New Yorker*, an *Adirondack Life* and some others. There was also a shelf of poetry: Donald Hall, T. S. Eliot, Frost, Dick Lourie, Jim Schley. Except for the theology, Paul's tastes in books were like Fred's own.

There was a pile of maps which included the Adirondack canoe wilderness, Algonquin Provincial Park, and other remote canoeing areas. As far as he could tell, there were no matchbooks with coded messages. No envelopes fell out of the pages.

It occurred to him, perhaps for the first time, that there might not be a complex, interesting, intellectual explanation for why Paul had paddled away from his ideal life on the ideal island with the ideal wife. He might have just left. He might have just gone fishin' and neglected to put a note on the door to that effect.

After the technicians drove back to Vermont, Davis, Bert, and Janice repaired to a diner on Main Street. Its sign read "Breakfast All Day." It was a big place, with few customers at 2 P.M. They found a booth that was set apart. They ordered short stacks and coffee and "Pure New York State Maple Syrup $1 extra" and talked it over.

There were two interesting facts. One, the yellow Ski-Doo, which was not in Tupper Lake. Two, JB had been here and had kept it secret. Davis wanted to talk that through with Bert before taking any action. He was also interested in Janice's take on it; she had a quirky way of thinking he liked, different from his and Bert's.

Bert was the moderator, at least at first. "OK, what have we learned about Paul that helps us?"

They all sat there without saying much for a couple of minutes.

Janice listed some of the basic things that were now clear. "Well, of course he'd been here, with a low profile but established identity. We don't know what documentation he had, but he must have had some. We should find out where the Baer persona came from. He'd been doing a lot of guiding and odd jobs. This might be work he could do under the radar, without filing taxes."

Bert cut in, "I'll keep a list." He wrote down "documents, tax records. Is there an original Paul Baer . . . ?"

Janice continued. "He was living on very little. I think it's important that he was part of a community, though. He wasn't wandering around. It may be small, but he had a home. It might have been fairly simple for him to make this switch. The people of Burlington don't overlap with the people here. I could imagine him coming over here with a little cash and just starting up. As long as he'd figured out the ID problem. Actually, though, he'd only been here about ten years. He could have been wandering in the wilderness, literally, for years before that. He knew how to survive anywhere."

Davis interjected, "To me one of the more interesting things is that there's not much drama here that we've found so far. We may yet find something, but so far I'm not seeing, oh, I don't know, a shootout, a pregnant girl, a nervous breakdown, or anything like that. It's all very low-key."

Janice asked, "Do you think he was depressed or had some sort of breakdown? I'd like to comb over that with the people who knew him when he left. People take off as a kind of suicide. Maybe he was going to kill himself and thought better of it."

Bert said, "It's interesting that his life here wasn't that different than his life before. He was outdoors a lot, read and thought a lot, and had a little ministry."

Davis was still thinking about the missing papers he kept hoping to find. "He and Pliny and Paul's dad, John, were all writer types. They had a special building on the island to do their writing in. I think for these men, writing was as basic as eating. I'm having trouble picturing him living twenty years without writing about it. I just can't believe there isn't a laptop somewhere, a bunch of poems under a floorboard, a pile of notebooks." Davis was getting obsessed about a category of evidence that he had absolutely no reason to think existed.

Bert wrote down: "Check in at the library, look everywhere for manuscripts, talk to T.L. Librarians, lockbox? Talk to Pliny about D's writing habits." Then he said, "He's a smart guy. I don't see him as the kind of guy who wouldn't use a computer."

Janice steered the conversation back toward more concrete evidence. "I think the Ski-Doo thing is obvious. The old machine he had here is the same one the professor saw on the lake heading toward Burton with a cargo sled behind it."

The two men nodded. That much seemed clear.

Bert added, "I forgot to tell you, there was a set of planks in the truck when we brought it back, with those iron brackets to make a ramp for a snow machine or a lawn mower. They're working on the truck now."

A waitress cleared away the pancakes and wiped globs of syrup off the table. She topped off their coffees.

Bert always wrote things down the minute they popped into his mind. He scribbled: "find the girlfriend."

Davis was enjoying this conversation. He liked sitting around with them. Dick Fowler wasn't that interesting a guy, though very dogged and productive. But Janice would make a good detective. Maybe she already was. "OK," he said, "what about JB? He's admitted to seeing someone who looked and walked like his father on Mount Marcy on Labor Day 2006. So, he's lying to us. Why would he do that? Is he the killer?"

Bert said, "It's possible to picture JB being out there on the island, kills his father, takes him to Burton on the Ski-Doo. But the part I have trouble with is the mess in the house. I don't think JB as we've seen him would trash his own place. That's totally unlike him. I can more easily picture him as our skier. But why would he lie to us?"

Janice said, "I think that's easy to explain. He'd been seeing his father secretly after running into him on Mount Marcy. I think that part's true. But he wouldn't have been able to tell anybody about it. It would make his life too complicated. It would ruin things for his father, who had created some sort of new life. This way he had his father in . . ." As she spoke, Davis noticed that she could keep track of a lot of facts and intuitively add in the missing pieces in plausible ways. ". . . of course," Janice was saying, "it's possible, if JB was in touch with his father, that other friends or members of his family were, too. Maybe Pliny or Paul's sister also were in communication with him but didn't know JB had been."

Both men gave her a similar skeptical expression. It sounded far-fetched. But Bert wrote down: "Who else knew Paul was alive? Who else is lying to us?" Out loud, he said it again: "Who else is lying to us?"

Davis added, "If I were in his shoes, even if I'd made a life, I'd want to see my son. I'd want to see my best friend. That might gnaw at me after a while." He changed the subject. "How do we approach JB? Are we trying to pin something on him?"

Bert answered, "I think it's simpler than that. You get him up to Burlington. Just mention Tupper Lake. He'll come. Get him in a room, give him a nudge, and see what he says. But let's do another day's work here first."

They decided to stay over that night. Janice would find out about Paul's use of the library and its computers. She would try to learn if Paul had a lockbox in any local bank. She'd also try to identify the woman Paul had been involved with.

Bert would start looking for Paul's legal persona. He'd start at the Tupper Lake Police and work with Ethel on figuring out exactly who Paul Baer

163

was, whether he was an invention of Paul Brearley's or whether Paul had inhabited an available identity of some sort, perhaps someone who had died. He'd be looking at birth certificates, passports, licenses, even fishing licenses. He'd call Ethel and get her working on it, too.

Davis would pump the people at the soup kitchen, at the boardinghouse, and at any other places Paul might have gone to. He'd try to find out where he had worked, and talk to employers and coworkers. He'd ask about Paul's state of mind, how he seemed to people. Maybe somebody at the food shelf or the boarding house would know about Paul's girlfriends. When he was clear about what he wanted to say, he'd call JB. He'd say something like, "JB. It's Sgt. Davis. Guess where I am: Tupper Lake!"

The next day, they met at the diner around two o'clock to compare notes. Bert had determined that Paul Baer was known at the bank and had a small savings account. Almost all of his transactions were in cash. They didn't think he had a credit card, or if he did, they hadn't seen it. There was no lockbox. The police had never taken an interest in Paul. He'd never gotten so much as a parking ticket, never drove over the limit. He was not part of the bar scene there, nor had he been found drunk. He did have a driver's license with his photo on it. He had a Social Security number, and he insured his truck in the usual way. The snow machine was also registered.

Back in Vermont, Ethel was working on finding out where the Baer identity came from, whether there was a passport, where he supposedly was born, and whether he had ever paid any income tax.

The librarians all knew Paul, who had been one of their best patrons. As elsewhere, he had been friendly but reticent. They'd wondered where he was. Janice spent a long time with the head librarian, Mary Bouchard. Usually, in cold weather, Paul spent several hours there three or four times a week. He had a routine. He'd read the papers, then spend an hour or two in the reading room on whatever book he was involved in. He sometimes read history books or current biography, but he also went through a lot of mysteries and novels. After his session of reading, he usually spent at least an hour and sometimes longer on one of the library's computers. They took some satisfaction from the fact that they had no idea what he did on the computer, but that their system blocked a lot of objectionable sites, and anyway he wasn't the type.

Mary Bouchard did not remember the long-term girlfriend that Dixon and Arthur recalled. But she said Paul had gone out with several fortyish local women for short periods and, with some reluctance, gave out the names of three of them.

Janice spent two hours on the library computer looking for Paul Baer. She was good with computers and liked puzzles, but her attempts to guess his email address didn't go anywhere. She thought a pro might be able to get somewhere.

When they had done all this work, they were only slightly ahead of where they had been after Davis's first meeting with the people at the soup kitchen. But when they went back to Vermont, they were way ahead of where they'd been a week earlier. Janice stayed in Tupper Lake, looking for the ex-girlfriends. She found two and arranged to see them the next day.

Davis was tired when he got home to the boat. He put together some leftovers and had a beer. The lake was rough, with winds coming in from the north. He sat down at his little breakfast nook, thought for a minute, and called JB. He left a simple message: "JB, it's Fred Davis. Please call me," and added the number.

Chapter 15

JB'S CONFESSION

JB answered Davis's call later in the evening and left his home in
Poughkeepsie early the next morning to see him. His first impulse had
been to refuse to come up. He couldn't deal with the situation as it had
unfolded. But soon he realized he had no choice.

He was in no hurry to get to his destination. He used every back road
to delay his arrival. He decided to go up Route 22, then cross the lake at
Essex and follow little farm roads the rest of the way. He couldn't bear the
traffic on the interstate or the thought of driving seventy miles an hour. He
might explode.

Since he was about fifteen years old, he had gone out of his way to keep
things simple. His father and Pliny could take care of the deep thinking,
and he'd take care of the power mower, tune up the outboards, repair the
shutters. His life plan was: do your work, be helpful, find a nice wife, have

some kids, help out with the basketball team, and that's about it. Keep it simple.

But since he'd run into his dad on Mount Marcy, this plan had slowly delaminated. At first thought, it seemed OK to spend time with his father and sort of neglect to mention it to anybody else. It would be a separate little department in his life. Two or three times a year, he would go see this new version of his father. They would spend some fairly awkward time together, then he'd go back to regular life. JB couldn't exactly refuse to see his father. And he couldn't exactly deny his father's insistence on keeping it secret.

But before long, this situation led to a growing sadness. He didn't mind keeping a secret from his mother or Pliny or the others at the island. His children didn't care one way or another. But it had been torture to keep it from his wife, Penny. Even before his father had been killed, he was beginning to feel a little desperate.

As he drove north, he had to pull over every few minutes to calm himself. At Whitehall, where Lake Champlain met the Champlain Canal, he took the little road down to the lock and got out. The canal was just waking up. The marinas were open, the lock was in operation, but only one boat was going through, southbound. A few minutes later, a couple of canoeists heading north paddled into the lock. The lockmaster closed the gate behind them and let the water out slowly.

As JB watched, he went over things one more time. Detective Davis knew he had been in touch with his father in Tupper Lake. JB didn't know if the police had figured out that he was going to Osprey Island to meet his father, was out there on skis, went to Burton Island, or moved the truck. There was no crime in having seen his father in Tupper, but it was still a huge problem for him because he would have to deal with his family. In a sense, he'd be a new person, a complicated person he'd never wanted to be. His life wouldn't be as transformed as his father's, but it would be transformed. He'd be the person who kept an important secret from his family. At best, he'd have to own up to this and make peace with everyone.

167

But what if the police figured out somehow that he was at the crime scene and saw the body, and even moved it? That would be much worse. It was a bigger secret. It might be illegal. The police could even imagine he was somehow involved in the killing.

He got back in his truck and drove north on Route 22. His driving was passable, but he was having trouble focusing. He wasn't really seeing the other vehicles. The anxiety was worse than anything he could remember, worse than when his children were born, worse than when his father disappeared. At those times, there wasn't any guilt attached; he just had to survive whatever happened.

Once he crossed the lake on the Essex–Charlotte ferry, he'd be only an hour from Burlington. St. Albans was another half hour north. But the ferry had just left. He wandered around on the dock while he waited for the next one.

It wouldn't be hard for the police to place him in Burlington and St. Albans. He had used his credit card to buy gas in St. Albans and made a cellphone call. Later he'd used his card in several bars in Burlington. They could certainly trace that if it occurred to them to get suspicious of his movements. Should he hold that part back and make them figure it out? Would they have any reason to check?

The ferry arrived. He rolled on, got out of his truck, and climbed the stairs to the upper deck. It was warm, but the lake was choppy. In spite of everything, it was a pleasure to look out over the lake, as always.

The worse thing would be if they figured out he had moved his father's red Toyota. He was pretty sure it was a no-no to not report a crime, but it's a crime in itself to move or destroy evidence. As he thought back over everything he had done, he realized it was possible there was no evidence to show that he moved the truck. His fingerprints on the car wouldn't prove anything since he'd driven the truck in Tupper Lake and was going to own up to that. He probably had his gloves on the whole time he was moving it. He did touch the ignition key, but if he was lucky, so did several other people after him. He definitely had had his gloves

168

on when he handled the bicycle, and there was nothing to tie him to the bike. He hoped.

He rolled off the ferry and drove out toward Route 7, the road up to Burlington. But he turned left before he got there onto a small, quiet, beautiful road that ran through the farms and along the lake. The farms themselves were soothing. He passed a couple of dairy farms, orchards, and fields of feed corn, just planted. Fields of hay, a foot high, waving in the breeze. The occasional view of the lake calmed him down. He decided he would talk about the trips to Tupper and leave the rest out. His own nervousness shouldn't be a big problem—the part he was confessing to should account for that. When he got home, he'd talk to Penny.

Maybe then he could also talk to Pliny, and Pliny could talk to everybody else, including his mother. Maybe things would blow over before he had to see his mother, Abby, Helen, and the rest. Pliny was good at complexity; maybe he'd enjoy being a buffer.

*   *   *

Davis and Bert were in their office waiting for JB. Though they had a lot of new information from the trip to Tupper Lake, they decided to talk to JB before sorting through everything. Also, Janice was still over there; she might learn something important. While they waited, Davis set up to make coffee. They talked about department politics for a few minutes.

By the time JB walked through the door, he had calmed down. Davis introduced Bert. The two detectives didn't do good cop/bad cop; Vermont is a peaceable kingdom. But Bert's presence there, keeping notes, asking occasional questions, had an intimidating effect. Their last meeting was a friendly chat. This was official, with notes being taken.

Davis began, "As I said, we've been to Tupper. Why don't you just tell us the real story now? We can't solve this case if even our friendly witnesses aren't telling the truth."

"Well, you know already. I knew my father was alive and spent a little time with him."

"Why didn't you tell us this before?"

"Basically, my father asked me not to. He made me promise not to talk about it. It would mess up his whole life."

"JB, please. He's dead, you can't hurt him now."

"There's another reason. I kept this from my family at his insistence. When people find out, I'm in a tough situation with all my family and Paul's family. I'm going to be totally in the soup. I could have told them something important and didn't. I was hoping you'd figure it all out without embarrassing me. And I don't know anything about the killing. I'm not sure that anything I know would help you."

Davis decided to back off for the moment. "Tell us a bit about what your father's life was like. You spent a lot of time together. What did you talk about? How did he explain leaving your family? What was he doing with his time? Did he have relationships with women? Did he tell you why he left?"

JB was feeling a bit more comfortable. Maybe he'd get out of this in one piece. "Well, he told me he'd been doing a lot of guiding. He was good at that. He worked through certain resorts and outfitters. He didn't need a lot of money. He did occasional carpentry. I think he'd had girlfriends. Once he mentioned another child, a son who would be about ten years old now, but he hadn't seen him since he was a baby. I can't remember the mother's name."

"Was he happy? Depressed? You must have gotten some sense of what happened when he left," said Davis.

"I don't know if I can explain this to you very well. It's not that easy to ask your father 'Why did you leave us twenty years ago?' or 'Were you depressed?' And how would he answer that question? We danced around the subject a lot, but it's not really my department, questions like that. We communicated by doing things together. Our visits were short. If we'd spent a lot of time together, I might have been forced to ask those questions. I asked him what he was doing, how he lived, where he went. He asked about my family. He has grandchildren he's never met, only seen across a campsite at Mount Marcy."

"Did he take you to the soup kitchen? I should say, *when* he took you there, what did you see? What kind of life did he have? Did he have close friends?"

JB liked this part of the conversation. It didn't threaten his position. "I don't know. He seemed to have a pleasant life, an orderly life, a routine. People really liked him there, appreciated what he did. He liked doing the soup kitchen. He had a bit of a family there, between the soup kitchen and the boardinghouse. A little like life at the island, actually—a small, little, predictable world, seeing the same group of people every day. He seemed fairly calm to me."

"Can you tell me more about the girlfriends?"

"Well, he mentioned the ten-year-old son. That's all that came up. I never met anyone. He didn't give me a blow-by-blow account of his personal life. Tell me, do either of you discuss such things with your dad, or your sons? Well, we didn't, either. We did a little fishing, a little hiking. I'd say we were just getting acquainted. Starting over."

Bert put in, "Could you list the specific times you spent with him? We're trying to get a sense of his movements. We think someone might have seen something the day he was killed, or the next morning."

Davis and Bert had discussed this question before the interview began. They knew JB had been lying, but they didn't know how much. Janice had guessed that maybe JB was the mystery skier. Who else could it be? They were fishing, but particularly hoping to find out if he was the skier without accusing him of it, at least not yet. If he was, he would be a real witness to the crime—the first other than the professor, whose evidence was vague.

JB started listing the times of the visits. But as he did, he saw where they might be heading. He had seen his father seven times after Mount Marcy and before the killing. He ticked them off slowly, as if he were having trouble remembering the dates. But in fact, he was frantically trying to decide what to do when he got to the eighth meeting, on the ice. He was getting red in the face. His lying skills had improved in the last couple of years. He was good at omitting facts and giving out misleading information without it showing. But he hadn't gotten to the point of being able to deliver absolute lies with a straight face. He knew the situation called for a casually tossed-off lie, but he couldn't really bring himself to do it.

"OK," he said. "Give me a cup of coffee and I'll tell you about it." JB stood up and walked about the little office. He wasn't crying, but almost. He banged into a bookcase, the corner of Fred's desk. Then he walked out into the hall. Bert started to get up, but Davis put out his hand. In the hall, JB walked around a bit, getting his breathing under control. After a minute, he came back in and shut the door.

Davis gave him some coffee. He could see that JB, at whatever cost, physically *had* to tell this story. Not telling it had made him almost sick.

"It's really simple. I was going to meet my dad on the first. I stayed over in Burlington the night before and drove out to the lake the next morning, early. From Shantee Point, I could walk right out to Osprey Island. I brought my snowshoes and my skis—one or the other would work. It might be just a mile or so out to Osprey. I put on my skis. It was pretty good skiing; there were some snowmobile tracks for part of it. When I passed the tip of Woods, I heard Dad's Ski-Doo come out from the island. It doesn't sound like the newer ones. I couldn't see who was driving, but there was a cargo trailer on behind. I could see that it wasn't my father driving."

Bert cut in, "Did the driver see you?"

"I don't know, but he'd have to have been looking. I had just cleared Woods Island."

"OK, go on."

"I didn't know whether to follow the cargo sled or go directly to Osprey. I followed it to Burton Island, and by the time I got there, the Ski-Doo was gone, and I found my dad. I stood there a minute, and then I left. What could I do? I skied back to my truck. I wandered around Burlington, drank a little too much. I got a room out by the airport and went home the next morning."

JB was feeling much better. He realized he couldn't have held this back. But in the same moment when he saw how much better he felt, he decided to hang on to the part about moving the truck. The release had recharged his capacity to dissemble.

There was one other thing he didn't mention. He'd moved the body, just a little. That part he would keep to himself. Nobody ever needed to know about it. It was private, just between him and his father.

Bert said, "I'm sure there's a lot more you can tell us. How fast was the machine going? What did the driver look like—what color outfit, for example? Was he big or small? Do you know the exact time? Did the man see you? What did the load on the cargo sled look like?"

JB could answer these questions without getting into trouble. "You know how, when you see a man in a little aluminum boat he looks really big, but you see the same guy in a big speedboat and he seems little? Well, this snow machine was relatively small, and this guy looked huge on it. I think he's a big person. I don't remember what he was wearing. I'm sure he was going flat out, which on that cargo sled with a load might have been thirty or thirty-five at the most. The load was just a lump. I couldn't tell you much about it. It was covered."

Davis asked, "What about at the lean-to? What did you see there?"

"Just a track in, and the body sitting there."

They talked for another half hour, but no new information came up. JB had settled into his plan. He'd told everything he was going to. He would go talk to Pliny then go home to Penny.

When JB left, the two detectives sat there without talking for a while.

Bert spoke first. "He's holding something back, but I don't know what."

Davis agreed. "Hmm. Do we charge him with anything? He's lied to us, but I don't think he's the killer. His story works with what the professor told us. I'd rather not make a criminal of him. At least not yet."

*   *   *

Pliny had the island to himself. Everything was set up for the summer: shutters down, docks in, water heaters turned on. The spark plug on the mower had been cleaned. Champlain was warmer than the mountainous parts of Vermont, and the grass in mid-May was already getting out of hand; he had a lot of mowing to do.

The other islanders had gone back to their regular lives. They'd start drifting back to the island at their usual times later, in June or July. The excitement was over.

Pliny spent a lot of time thinking. Of course, he had always spent a lot of time thinking. Though he had his writing projects to occupy himself, he was unsettled. He was watching a bit too much TV. He fished in a desultory way. He realized that as bad and upsetting as the situation was, he was having fun in a way. It was something important to do. He enjoyed sorting through things with Detective Davis. They should talk some more. Maybe he'd look one more time for Paul's fabled diaries, the ones that would explain everything. He felt more cheerful as he walked down to his office hidden in the trees.

As he reached the building, his cellphone fired. It was JB, and he seemed upset. Pliny arranged to pick him up in St. Albans in an hour and a half. That gave him an hour or so to go through things in the lakeside office one more time.

There was an old oaken file cabinet in one corner. Each of the three men had a drawer, and most of the contents had to do with writing projects. When they weren't writing articles or books, they corresponded with a lot of people and wrote sermons on subjects that were bothering them. Often a late conversation over brandy, as the sun set, would end up the next day in three different sermons, filed away for later use.

Pliny opened Paul's drawer, the middle one. It had been opened only two or three times since Paul disappeared. This was Pliny's second search of the middle drawer. There were several drafts of Paul's two books and numerous articles. Usually there would be rough copies, then a perfectly typed final draft or a carbon copy of it. The sermons were interesting. Where Pliny's own were usually written out word-for-word, double-spaced, with key points capitalized, Paul's consisted of a short list on one side of a three-by-five card. Often there was a scriptural reference, a line of poetry—Paul knew a lot of poems by heart—and a few key words.

Pliny remembered sitting in the audience as Paul delivered sermons from these minimal notes. Paul could deliver the whole talk with no hesitations. He would effortlessly bring in a joke or anecdote at the right time. His delivery had a light, conversational tone, as if he were making it all up on the spot. He was sometimes serious and ardent, but not overbearing or lecturing. He would bring things neatly to a close in exactly fifteen minutes. If Cass was there, she'd give him a little nod at twelve minutes. When she wasn't there—which was often—he'd have somebody else keep time. It was as smooth as his tennis game. But like his tennis game, the effortlessness came from years of practice.

Pliny's own sermons were competent and heartfelt, but he couldn't do what Paul did.

The file drawer also held files full of notes for other writings, including one fifty-page handwritten manuscript, the first three chapters of a book. He looked through every page of every file. Most of the items were vaguely familiar—he'd proofread most of them for Paul long ago.

Whatever he'd expected to find, it wasn't there. The only thing left to search were the books on the shelves, though he didn't really think there would be anything to be found among the leaves.

An hour later, he picked up JB at the public dock in St. Albans. JB looked completely depleted. On the ride back, they said almost nothing. Pliny grilled some steaks and threw together a slightly wilted salad. After supper, JB told the same story to Pliny that he'd told to the detectives. They talked long into the night. Pliny wasn't bothered that JB had kept Paul's life secret. He'd have done the same thing. He felt envious; he wished he'd known about Tupper Lake. He'd have driven there in a minute, shown up at the soup kitchen, and renewed their conversations, picking up right where they had left off.

Chapter 16

THE FIFTH TEAM MEETING

The investigative team met the next morning at eight. They had plenty to talk about. Bert was standing by the charts and maps. Davis had tidied up a bit and made fresh coffee. Janice Pearlstein and Dick Fowler were there with their notebooks at the ready. Ethel Collings and June McDonald were there, as was Peter Dooley from the scene-of-crime team.

Bert outlined the basic facts that by now they all knew, the Paul Baer story. He described the interview with JB and added JB's movements to the map. He had everyone do the same to their copies.

Peter Dooley described the crime scene analysis in Tupper Lake to date. "We found a lot of stuff. Paul lived there for a long time in a very small space. Of course we found his prints. Also JB's prints. We have prints from most of the folks at Osprey Island, for comparison. Arthur, the manager, had pawed through Paul's stuff pretty thoroughly. His prints were all over the place. I think he spent a couple of hours there picking through things. I don't know at this point whether he removed anything." Bert wrote down: "reinterview Arthur" as Dooley continued, "We have an envelope full of miscellaneous papers. You'll have a list of them. Mostly receipts from stores, the grocery, hardware, sports store, things like that. No credit card receipts."

Janice went next. "I went looking for Paul's girlfriends. Nobody really remembered much about the woman he first arrived with, the one with the baby. She took off right away. After that I think there were three others over the ten years. I found two of them. They were sort of similar. He'd had relationships of a few months with them. One ended about a year ago, one a couple of years before that. They were really nice women. Both midforties, pleasant, but not glamorous or anything. One had volunteered at the soup kitchen for a while but had a job in a store in Tupper Lake. The other was a nurse. They were both divorced. And they described their relationships with Paul in similar ways. He was fun to talk to. He liked to do things outside with them. Nice in bed, nothing unusual. But after a few months, the relationships sort of fizzled. They described him as sort of lukewarm, too passive. One of them thought the first one, the one with the baby, might have been Terri, maybe Terri Jones. The son would now be about ten."

Trooper June McDonald, the technician who had worked on the photographs taken from Savage Island, was also a computer whiz, and Janice had brought her over to Tupper Lake to see what she could extract from the computers at the town library.

"The librarian," McDonald began, "Mary Bouchard, thought that Paul spent an hour at a time online, sometimes two or three hours. I was hoping to run down his email account. I spent most of a day on it but I didn't find anything. It would be easy to set up an anonymous, untraceable email account. There are several ways to do it. It's legal. The only way to find it would be to find someone who had received an email from Paul."

Bert added to his list "see JB about email."

McDonald continued, "The librarian's impression was that he was doing more than just emails. Sometimes he would sit there with books around him, as if he was writing something. She had no idea what that might be. It was obvious he was an educated person, but she never had a conversation with him about anything he might be writing. He could have been blogging. He could have been writing something and storing it on the web somewhere. There are several ways to do that. For that matter, he could have been writing books, publishing them on the web, and selling them without there being necessarily any evidence that I could find. He could have had a whole second life on the web."

Ethel, who went next, wanted to make her report and go back to work. "I've been trying to trace the Paul Baer identity. I found a Paul Baer, a onetime resident in Malone, New York. He's about the same age and has a roughly similar description. Brearley was using his identity. Baer was born in Malone, had a Social Security number. He was never married and didn't have much of a job record according to Social Security. No prints on file. He paid taxes in certain years but seems to have been a bit of a drifter."

Bert wrote down "find Baer."

Ethel continued, "I'm guessing Brearley found Baer somewhere, Baer died, Paul grabbed the wallet, and Baer wasn't identified. I have a summary on this I'll give to Bert." She started to leave the room, but Janice spoke up.

"Lieutenant, before you go, let me ask a question," said Bert. "Could the real Paul Baer be alive? Why couldn't two men who were leading marginal, cash-only lives use the same identity? As long as they didn't actually cross paths physically, why couldn't they? Couldn't Brearley have been sort of renting the name as a way to get the documents he needed to function?"

Ethel smiled. It gave her an interesting project to work on, a nice puzzle, just the sort of thing that amused her. "I have no idea. But offhand, I can't think of any reason it wouldn't work. Particularly if our Paul earned a bit more money than he needed and the other one was damned lazy." With that, she walked out of the room.

Dick Fowler gave the next report. "I don't have anything that exciting to tell you. I've stopped at almost every house and business between the boat launch and the ferry dock. I've talked to everybody working at or around the ferry at the right times. On both sides of the lake. There are a few people who live near the New York side of the ferry. So far, I've got one confirming report. A man who lives along West Shore Road remembers seeing a solitary cyclist sort of plowing through the snow, heading north at about the right time. That's confirmation, but no new information. Nobody at the ferry remembers anything. They see a lot of old red Toyotas driven by guys. It's not anything you'd remember ten minutes later."

Dick Fowler sipped his coffee and continued. "I also found the boy whose bike was stolen and returned the same day. His name is Petey Tolland and he lives about a mile from the ferry dock on the New York side. He left the bike there because it wasn't working right and then he walked home. The chain jumped off. The funny part is, when he came back, the chain was unjammed, and the bike was working better than it had in months. The seat had been raised. By the way, we've still got the bike. I gave him an old one of mine that I don't use anymore. Other than this, I'm running out of ideas."

Bert wrote down: "go over the bike again."

Davis, who'd been sitting down through all of this, stood up. "That's great. We've got to have that bike gone over with a microscope. In fact, all of this is good work, good thinking, too. We know so much more about Paul, and what happened out there. It's great to know about the victim. But there is one thing we still don't know at all. Who the hell did this and why? Why were these two men there? We don't know if they were acquainted. We don't know the motive. All we know about the killer is that he can drive a snowmobile, doesn't mind the cold, is big, and maybe can repair a bicycle. He can probably spend the night with a corpse without blanching. From everything, I think he's a bit twisted. Unless something falls in our lap, we don't really have good leads to follow up. It's fun to learn more about Paul, but that isn't getting us a lot closer to closing our case."

Bert summarized things. "June and Janice, I'd like you to keep working

180

on the computer angle, and see if you can find the first girlfriend, the one with the son. Ethel will try to get the real Paul Baer to stand up. Dick, you're doing great, just keep doing it. Talk to the same people again, and all the people who weren't home. I'll get that bike looked over again. Any other ideas?"

Davis said, "Well, I've got my default plan. Go talk to Pliny, and look around at Osprey Island."

Chapter 17

THE FALL OF MAN

Davis had been land bound for several weeks. He wanted to get back on the water.

Any excursion benefitted from a destination or task, however contrived. Visiting family, sketching the wildlife, or researching something were excuses he had used. Though perhaps he could have done the trip a bit faster by car, Davis had two goals to justify this trip. One was to meet again with the border patrol where Lake Champlain crossed into Canada now that he knew the date of the killing. He couldn't cross into Canada armed; he locked his service pistol in his desk.

Second, he wanted to chat further with Pliny. That conversation might bring out useful information or ideas, but his real purpose was social. He liked talking to the old man.

Lake Champlain crosses into Canada in two places. On the New York side, it flows into the Richelieu River at the town of Rouses Point. Boaters going from or to Canada go through here. On the Vermont side, the lake terminates in a large lobe of shallow water known as Missisquoi Bay. The bay begins in Vermont, but most of it is in Quebec. Davis went to the Richelieu crossing first. It was a straight shot north from the dock at the Davis Farm.

Customs on the water worked much as it did on land routes, except the checkpoints were docks instead of kiosks. Davis went first to the US Customs dock, on the west side of the river just past the beautiful, high Richelieu River bridge that loomed above the border. Customs operations here shut down in late fall as recreational boat traffic declined to almost nothing, at which point a marina checked through the few intrepid fishermen and duck hunters still on the water. When the lake iced over, the US Customs office closed for the winter.

A mile or so north was the Canadian customs dock. Signs on the water and at the dock made it clear that all boats had to stop there. The Canadians stayed open all year. But as winter closed in, one man could easily keep an eye on the crossing and read a good book at the same time. At the moment, though, several boats were tied up at the dock, and two officers were busy giving their owners the once-over, asking questions and checking databases. After Davis docked his boat, he sat down with Staff Sergeant Jules Richard of the RCMP, the Mounties. He had a tiny office facing the lake. Nothing showed up on the logs for the time in question. In addition to the logs, cameras mounted below the bridge gave a panoramic look at the crossing. These were monitored here, and also at the US Customs office on the Vermont side that Davis would visit later in the day. The film showed nothing suspicious. There were two ice fishermen who came out for a few hours every day from January 28 through February 1, the day of the killing. One fisherman could be seen walking out from Rouses Point, drilling a hole in the ice and sitting on a big white Sheetrock bucket. Periodically he would pull a small fish out of the lake, lift the lid, and throw the fish into the bucket. Three hours later, he returned the way he came. The other fisherman arrived from the north by pickup truck, set up on the Canadian side of the border, and also left the way he came a few hours later. Davis concluded that whatever had happened on Osprey Island had nothing to do with the Rouses Point crossing.

The crossings at Missisquoi Bay were only about three miles away as the crow flies, but to get there by boat, Davis had to head back south, going all the way around the west side of Isle La Motte and then through the narrow gap at Carry Bay. As always, he remembered the exact spot where, years ago, his and Luke's sailboat had been unceremoniously slit open, like a fish being gutted, by a black-and-red speedboat. He drove slowly through the gap and headed north through a channel, which put North Hero Island on his right, or starboard, side and Alburgh Tongue to port. As he left the channel, the Missisquoi Bay Bridge rose above him not far ahead.

When Davis crossed beneath it and entered the bay, it was eleven o'clock. From this point on, he had to keep an eye on his depth gauge. It was a large bay, miles across, but shallow and weedy. Toward August, when the water level dropped, much of it would be too shallow for his boat. Just past the bridge and to his right—off his starboard bow—was the Missisquoi River delta. It was one of his favorite places. Waterbirds of all kinds hung out here, but the area was famous for the great blue herons who nested there by the hundreds. Birders came from all over to see them. Davis remembered the fishing with special fondness; he had come here dozens of times in his life, by canoe, rowboat, or motorboat, and had rarely been disappointed. If time permitted, he had his fishing gear on board; he'd fish a bit, and anchor overnight on the river.

But now he was headed to the dock at Philipsburg. This was the customs dock for boat traffic in both directions. Philipsburg, in tandem with Highgate Springs on the US side, was also one of the busiest highway border crossings in the region. It joined Interstate 89, headed south to Boston and New York, with Canadian Route 133, headed north to Montreal. A large percentage of the tourist traffic both ways came through here, and a lot of commercial traffic also. It could take an hour or more to get through at busy times.

Davis was met at the dock by Inspector Major Charles Rivas RCMP, a large, rather rumpled man with shaggy hair. He looked about sixty years old. He was in charge of security, which largely meant comparing various databases and watch lists with the identities of people and vehicles crossing the border. His job, and his talent, was to be exceptionally suspicious. When a border guard typed a passport number or name into a computer below, he decided who to wave on with a friendly glance, who to hassle a little bit, and who to hold back for a complete screening while a variety of databases were reviewed.

After the briefest of introductions, they got in Rivas's car. "Chuck Jaimeson is waiting for us up at the office." The office was a second-floor room overlooking the crossing. Outside the window, things were moving well; there were only four or five cars in line. In the office there were six monitors, each showing four views of each kiosk station. A man at a desk watched these monitors continuously. Periodically, he used a little joystick to aim one of the cameras at something that had piqued his curiosity. To his right, another desk held other computers, their screens dark.

Facing the two men as they walked in was Chuck Jaimeson. He was also tall, but younger, slimmer, and athletic looking. Rivas made introductions. "Detective Fred Davis, this is Chuck Jaimeson. He's my opposite number on the US side. This is Corporal Stark." Stark had his eyes glued to the screens; he waved without turning around or saying anything. "Detective Davis," he continued, "is interested in January twenty-eighth through February first, particularly on the lake. Detective, this is the written log." Rivas showed Davis a computer with a split screen, one side marked "USA" and the other "CAN." He quickly scrolled back to January 28. The log showed events of special concern for the highway crossings each way. On the twenty-eighth, northbound, twenty-six cars had been searched and three drivers had been detained, one of them driving a large delivery truck marked "Golden's Produce." Photos of the driver and his truck were

185

inserted into the file. The parallel log for southbound traffic was similar. Events on the lake were shown on the same pages, but in green. These were few. A Canadian snowmobiler who had turned out to be drunk had been detained.

As Davis looked through the entries, nothing jumped out at him. The two men chatted quietly, watching the screens absentmindedly. Officer Stark still had not turned his head. After a few minutes, Rivas interrupted Davis. "Since you're mostly interested in the lake, perhaps I should show you the video. It's over here. The US and Canada use the same cameras."

There were three screens. One, marked "Richelieu," showed the crossing on that river, which he had already reviewed earlier in the day. Next to it were two more, one above the other. Each had a similar split-screen setup, viewing the lake border from four vantage points. There were two cameras mounted on the Missisquoi Bay Bridge, which panned gently back and forth across the bay. Another was mounted on the dock where Davis now had his boat. A fourth seemed to be mounted somewhere on the opposite, western, shore of the bay. Davis could see the dock and the bridge in its wide-angle view. The top screen was live; Davis could see his own boat bobbing in the waves. The lower one stored past videos. Rivas reached over Davis's shoulder and showed him how to search for a given date and time.

Starting with January 26, Davis reviewed the video. In fast-forward, it didn't take long. There was nothing of note at the Richelieu River border. But on the Missisquoi Bay side, on January 30, something caught his attention. It was a big, black snow machine pulling a big, black cargo sled. It appeared at different moments in all four of the videos. Sometimes it passed from one section of the split screen to another, but from a different angle.

It was the cargo sled that caught his attention. Most snow machine people don't tow anything. They are basically joyriding. He saw the driver, who seemed unusually large, unload and set up a portable fishing hut on the US side, but near the border. He disappeared inside the shelter for a couple of hours. He came out with his ice drill, drilled through the ice, and fished for a while. A few minutes later, he disappeared inside his fishing shanty again. A bit later, he folded up his tent, loaded it onto the cargo sled, and covered everything with a little tarp. He appeared to strap a large fish, obviously a pike, on top of that. Then he headed off to the south.

Davis looked at Rivas and Jaimeson. "I think this could be my guy," he said, pointing to the screens.

He spent an hour going over the footage for February first and the previous two weeks. The man was there three times each week. He pulled several fish out of the lake in that time. In one shot, you could see him muscle the pike out through a hole he'd drilled about fifty feet from the hut doorway. Earlier on February 1, Davis noted, a second fisherman had fished the same area, arriving by snowmobile from the direction of Venise-en-Quebec, a tourist town at the northern end of Missisquoi Bay. He was long gone by the time the American fisherman arrived. Scrolling back to the twenty-seventh of January, he found the same pattern. A Canadian arrived by snow machine, fished in the morning, right near the line. The man with the big, black snow machine, with the cargo sled, fished much the same spot later the same day.

Davis thanked the men and left with CD copies of the relevant times. These would go to June McDonald. Maybe June could extract some more information. If he was right, they had a photograph of their killer.

It was four thirty. He called June McDonald. "June, can you meet me at the dock at St. Albans in an hour and a half? I think I have video of our killer from the Missisquoi Bay crossing. I'm hoping you can work on the film tonight, and we'll have a meeting about it in the morning." Then Davis called Bert and set up the meeting.

Plowing through three-foot seas coming out of the south, he set out. He was tempted to stick the CDs into his laptop and look them over as he cruised toward Osprey Island. But the story they told was clear. The most likely explanation of the man's movements around Missisquoi Bay was that he was bringing something illegal into the US, and the probability was that it was drugs of some sort. The morning fisherman was delivering the

187

drugs, and he was picking them up, in plain sight, in the afternoon. Such actions would never be noticed amidst the usual movements of fishing. The repetition of the actions on two different days reinforced his theory. It was only a small leap to presume that the snow machine cargo sled seen at the border in the morning was the same one seen the next morning, by two different people, carrying the body of Paul Brearley to Burton Island.

Davis knew the information on the film proved nothing. But it fit. It enabled him, for the first time, to create a narrative he had some confidence in, though it was full of gaps. Particularly, what happened to the big, black snow machine? Davis was convinced they were close to having a rough outline of what happened. Maybe June McDonald would be able to extract something from the videos that would bring them closer to having actual evidence.

The wind, coming out of the south, was picking up. He turned his attention to piloting his boat through the waves. Under the bridge. Past North Hero, past Butler, around Osprey, through the narrow, treacherous gap north of Burton Island, and over to the town dock. June was there. Davis left the motors running and clambered up on the dock with the discs.

"I think it's the guy with the cargo sled," he told June. "But I'm also interested in the other guy who fishes nearby. Something's fishy about him, too." As June nodded, he jumped back in the boat and set out for Osprey Island.

*   *   *

Davis found Pliny in his little writing cabin nestled in the trees. There were several piles of papers and books stacked on the table and on top of the bookcases.

Davis gave Pliny a "Find anything?" look, and Pliny returned a "Not a damn thing" shake of his head.

Also on the table was a bottle of Glenlivet Scotch, the level about two inches down from high water. Next to it were two shot glasses. Pliny had been expecting him.

Davis filled the unused glass and sat down in one of the old leather chairs. Pliny looked much better than he had before. His eyes were brighter, his movements quicker. Davis was quite content to just sit there without saying anything for a bit. He didn't get quality single-malt whiskey that often. Pliny was pawing through a matched set of Thomas Hardy novels looking for loose scraps of paper. He'd gotten as far as *A Laodicean*.

Davis remembered the title because when his marriage was dissolving, Diane, a big Hardy fan, had accused him of being a Laodicean. He'd had to read the book to find out it meant someone who was lukewarm, uncommitted. But he couldn't remember anything that actually happened in the novel.

He said, "Pliny, nobody can say you aren't making a thorough search. I hear JB came up for a visit."

Pliny put down Thomas Hardy, refilled his glass, and sat down opposite Davis. He also was in no hurry to talk. They had the whole evening. It was clouding over quickly, and the room was dark under the best of circumstances. Pliny had one little light on the table. The two men were mostly in shadow.

Pliny spoke first. "JB was pretty upset. He thought you were going to throw him in the clink. I told him I'd have done exactly what he did. I'd have been thrilled to spend time with Paul, and I'd have kept my mouth shut about it. I think my comments did him some good, but they were totally sincere. In fact," Pliny said, laughing, "I could have run into Paul myself and been seeing him all this time, and I'd be right here deceiving you about it with a completely clear conscience. Though I didn't. Actually," he continued, "I couldn't get much out of JB. He tells you the minimum and just leaves it there. He has no instinct for gossip. All he told me was that Paul had lived in Tupper, had a kid he'd lost track of, lived in a boardinghouse, and did a lot of guiding to get by. And that he went to see him, and at his father's request, kept quiet about it."

Davis knew it wasn't correct procedure to give any information away for free. But he liked talking to Pliny and thought he had a right to the complete story. So far, much of the progress they had made went back to Pliny. So Davis told him all about Paul's life in Tupper Lake, without getting into matters of stolen bicycles or red trucks. He could see, as he talked, that Pliny loved to hear about his friend being alive. Davis described the room, the people, and the atmosphere at the soup kitchen. He showed him a couple of pictures on the little screen on his camera.

Davis could see that Pliny was moved, even teary. Pliny said, "Thanks for telling me this. I'm glad he had some sort of life. I can imagine him enjoying living there, how he might have thought about it. I just wish he'd come back here to tell me about it. That would have been something."

Davis walked over to the French doors overlooking the lake. Pliny's comments made him a little uncomfortable. He took the conversation back to the case. "The funny thing is, we know so much more, but we really know nothing."

Pliny went back for a little more of the Glenlivet. There was now about five inches visible above the golden color of the remaining whiskey. He topped off Davis's glass.

"I know all these facts, I guess. Of course, I have no idea who killed him, though I can admit to a couple of leads I can't talk about. But Pliny, I want you to tell me why he left. What was going on here eighteen years ago? Was this a mental collapse? Some sort of quest, like a yogi holing up in a cave somewhere for a few years, standing on his head? An ordinary moral lapse? Did he get some intern pregnant?"

"Did he eat of the apple?" asked Pliny. "Well, you've phrased the question about right. I doubt it. None of your three scenarios quite ring a bell for me. I wish I knew. At the moment, though, it seems I've become obsessed with this, I'm beginning to lose interest. I owe you dinner, let's go eat something. And bring that bottle along. I'll bring my book. Thomas Hardy sort of fits right into this. Have you read this one? You might like it."

The two men had a huge steak and a passable salad in Pliny's kitchen, and some wine. They talked until about midnight, punishing the bottle of Glenlivet a little more. They talked of their days and years on the lake, but there was no mention of Paul Baer, Paul Brearley, or Tupper Lake, New York.

Later, Davis lay in his bunk on the boat with the intention of reading for about three minutes before falling asleep. His cellphone rang. It was his son, Andy. Andy almost never called him, and never called late, because Andy, as a rule, was asleep by nine, if not earlier. Something had to be wrong.

Hiram had fallen as he was finishing up the milking. He'd been up on a five-foot stepladder, putting something on a shelf in the barn, and fallen hard to the concrete floor, getting tangled up with a grub hoe that was leaning up against the wall. Fred Davis's dad had rarely been injured or sick, but he was over eighty. They didn't know yet how serious it was. He was in the hospital, giving the hospital staff a hard time. The old man was indignant that he could be injured at all.

Andy put it simply. "Can you help with the morning milking?"

Andy could probably get the work done without him but was using the situation to get him involved. If so, he was willing. He asked, "What time?"

"Five."

"OK, see you then. I'll be coming by boat." He hung up and called Bert. "Bert, sorry to call so late. My dad had a fall. We won't know until tomorrow how he is. I think he's just banged up. Anyway, I have to help with the milking. I can probably get in there at a normal time, I'll let you know. June has the film. You'll see two guys on snow machines who just happen to be fishing near each other. I think that's a handoff of some kind." After hanging up, he fell immediately asleep.

He was up and making coffee four hours later, at 4 A.M. At four ten, he was underway, running lights on. As he piloted his boat, he chewed on a few chunks torn off a stale loaf of bread with rough hunks of local cheddar and drank his coffee from a thermos.

*　　*　　*

Vermont was always a latecomer to spring. By mid-June, everything was bursting open, the islands particularly so. At the farm, it was one of the busiest times. Andy was preparing his fields. The store was beginning to get regular business, especially on weekends. Luke was getting equipment ready. The man who owned the Thompson was calling every other day about when his boat would be ready. Hazel was all over the place, doing a million things.

Though Hiram was old, his son would have to put in a lot of hours to cover for him. Hiram took care of the cows but also did a lot of other projects that were important without attracting much notice. Fences had to be built and repaired. The barn needed work. The farm roads were a mess. There was a host of such projects that Hiram took care of in the normal course of events. The old man didn't work as many hours as he once had. No one ever saw him hurry or exert himself. But he was deceptively productive. He was a master at knowing the simplest, best, and least costly way of doing things. He took no needless steps, wasted no motions.

As he worked, Fred decided to live at the farm until the situation with his father was resolved. That meant docking the boat at the Sand Bar. If he left it at the dock at the farm, he'd waste too much time and effort worrying about it, fiddling with the dock, and watching the horizon for stormy conditions. He could move back on board when things had settled down and he didn't need to be at work at five in the morning.

One project he could work on would be particularly helpful: finishing up the restoration of the Thompson. That would free up Luke for other things. There was a lot of work left on the boat's hull and trim that he could do evenings and weekends. Two other old boats sat on trailers, waiting their turn.

Luke had also called Diane. She'd be pitching in, too.

Davis liked working with his son. After a quick review, he remembered how the whole milking process was done. Once he'd gotten a report on

Hiram—basically "It's too early to tell, we'll know more tomorrow"—they didn't talk that much. But he liked being around Andy, and he liked being around the farm while the whole family was worrying about Hiram. He would go see him in the hospital in Burlington later in the day.

He got to the St. Albans barracks around ten. June McDonald had been working on the video since six. It wasn't possible to see what state the machine was registered in. Snowmobiles didn't have plates, like motorcycles, but numbers plus a small decal, like boats. They were not visible in the photos. But the pictures were clear enough to see the shape of the machine from various angles.

There was no guidebook for identifying snow machines by their silhouettes as there were for airplanes. But June had something better. Her boyfriend Herb was a snowmobile nut. To a car nut, a '54 Chevy looks nothing like a '55. To Herb, it was equally obvious that they were looking at a Yamaha Apex Mt 162. A big, four-cylinder machine designed for off-trail use.

At ten thirty, Janice, June, Ethel, and Dick joined Bert and Davis in the larger meeting room. Ethel handed out a list to everyone. There were seventeen Apex Mt's registered in Vermont. Of them, fifteen owners had fishing licenses.

June played a hastily put-together best-of version of the video material. It showed the machine from several angles. The driver was a large man inside a puffy snowmobile outfit with a fur-rimmed hood. That's all that was clear. Several images showed him moving around his portable ice fishing shelter, which was basically a modified tent. The photographer had used a large wide-angle, and most of the views of the man were oblique and out of focus.

"My boyfriend says this is a Yamaha Apex Mt 162. I have no idea what that means, but that's what he says it is, maybe a 2007 model. Ethel's list is of all the Vermont registrations." None of the pictures of the Canadian fisherman were very clear. He came from Venise-en-Quebec and returned there, never going near Philipsburg. June McDonald continued. "We don't

Sam Clark

have as good a read on the Canadian guy. We think the machine is an Arctic Cat."

Bert wanted to be very careful about the fifteen people who owned the Apex Mt. "We actually have no evidence linking this snow machine to any crime. Even if we find the person who owns this particular one, we have no evidence that he had anything to do with our killing. We just *think* he might be the guy. I'd like to just very quietly learn about all these people, where they live, what they do. What they were doing on the last day of January and the first day of February. For now, we don't bother with the two who don't have fishing licenses."

Ethel stood up. "Later today I'll have pictures of those who have photo-ID driver's licenses. We'll know if any of them have a criminal record, particularly anything in the drugs or smuggling or gun violation areas."

Bert was excited but cautious. "We have to go slow here. If we find the right person, he's dangerous. I think he's smart, alert. We don't want him to start shooting, or head to a villa in Barbados where he has a secret identity all set up. Let's just slowly work our way through the list, maybe take a few snapshots. And we don't know if this is a Vermont machine. If we don't get very far with the Vermont list, we'll have to start on New York. Then maybe Quebec. New Hampshire and Massachusetts aren't out of the question, either. That's a lot of snow machines to check out."

They had rarely seen Bert so animated.

"Also," he said, "we have no evidence that the person in these pictures did anything more distressing than catch a bunch of very large northern pike. He could be just fishing. But I want to say, this is a shadowy guy. I'm a little scared of him, of what he might do. If we ever do find him, I want to do it in force. So don't do anything that could reveal that we're interested in him. If you go to the corner store and ask a bunch of questions, he'll hear about it and figure out what we're up to."   This was guesswork, but both Fred and Bert were beginning to have a feeling for the kind of person they were looking for.

194

*　　*　　*

Forty minutes later, Davis walked into his father's room at Fletcher Allen Hospital, on the uphill side of Burlington. Hiram had an IV in one arm and a cast on the other. His head had a big bump on one side and his face was bruised. It looked like he was trying not to move.

Davis was shocked at how bad his father looked. "Good grief, Dad. You look horrible." His father had looked old for a long time, but he had never seemed this vulnerable and shrunken, even when he'd had serious illnesses. He'd had a bout of cancer in his seventies, but even then he'd looked vigorous by comparison.

Hiram didn't seem too concerned. "Well, look on the bright side. My legs are fine, and I broke my off-arm. I should be able to work one-handed pretty soon. Though it really does hurt, to tell you the truth."

"What happened?"

"Well, you know that wooden stepladder I repaired? I was up on the part marked 'this is not a step' when my repair let go."

Luke and Fred had been trying to get Hiram to splurge on a new stepladder for a couple of years. Fred realized he should have taken the old wooden one, sawed it up into kindling, and just bought a nice, stable fiberglass one without further discussion. But he hadn't. "It's the cracked ribs that hurt the most, frankly," his father said. "My big toe hurts quite a bit, too." A nurse came in and checked the dials. Hiram kept talking as she took his blood pressure. "I hear you're milking. Thanks. Hazel and Luke and Andy are going to need all the help they can get. I hear Diane's going to chip in, too. You know me, 'One man doing ten men's work.'"

It was sort of a private joke, but one shared by almost every dairy farmer in the state. There had been an early morning radio show in Vermont for about forty years featuring Bob Bannon. During those decades, the show was heard daily in most of the dairy barns and milk houses in the State of Vermont. Bannon's humor was largely fueled by the fact that he told the same jokes every day in a totally deadpan style and a beautifully deep voice.

At four in the morning, Bannon was his own engineer and announcer, did the ads, read the news, and selected the music, as well as doing the actual show. He had alter egos to read some of the ads, but they all sounded like Bob Bannon. One of them was called Colonel Smedley. Each morning, Bannon introduced himself as "one man doing ten men's work."

Fred asked, "When will they let you out?"

"Well, they think I might have dinged my spleen a bit. I fell on a grub hoe—that's what got the ribs. And maybe the spleen." Davis didn't quite know what a spleen did but knew it wasn't something to be trifled with. "When they're sure I'm not dying from that, I can limp home. But I won't be good for much for a while, except supervision. So Freddy, thanks. I appreciate it. I don't think I've done anything I can't recover from. Can I ask you to do a few things for me?"

Davis thought, *Maybe he's mellowing a bit.* He pulled out his little notebook. On the page opposite "Ask Pliny about Paul's state of mind that summer" and similar reminders, he wrote: "fix fence behind calf barn, pump up wheelbarrow tire, get light bulbs, truck inspection, call farrier." At the top of the list he wrote: "stop at Robinson's, get new ladder."

*   *   *

From the hospital, Davis drove directly to the farm. He worked for a couple of hours on the Thompson, then joined the others for supper. After dinner, he went back to the boat barn. Diane had been out to help with the evening milking but had left before dinner.

His routine for the rest of the week was much the same. Milking, race into work, leave early, see his dad at Fletcher Allen, back to the farm. See Diane in passing, as she drove off to Burlington. Work on the Thompson for an hour or two.

On June 6, Hiram came home, but he was in bed most of the time and made no attempt to do anything. He was still taking a lot of painkillers but was walking around a bit.

Fred found working on the boat soothing. He wasn't a great mechanic; he left that for Luke when he could. But he had always enjoyed the woodworking part. He suspected that he might be better at it than at detecting, or lawyering, which had been the original life plan. He got along well with wood. A straight, rectilinear piece of wood might initially complain when asked to assume the tapered, curved shape required of boat parts, but once it got the idea, it would cooperate. Sometimes, it was a more satisfactory relationship than he had with people, or cows.

Often, after he closed up the shop for the night, he would find his mother alone on the front porch, rocking in her favorite chair before going to bed. Sometimes he'd spend a few minutes beside her. Though she always made a point of seeming peaceful, she was obviously worried about Hiram. She knew Hiram's fall was a turning point, whatever anyone said. In indirect ways, she let her son know she wanted him back home permanently.

Diane started staying over on the weekends, sleeping in one of the guest cabins. Fred left that decision to her. He thought they were getting more comfortable with each other, out of their involvement with the farm and concern for Hiram. They talked a bit about what would happen to the farm when Fred's parents stopped working, became infirm, or died.

Hiram improved slowly. They had a little party, with a beautiful orange fiberglass ladder decorated with ribbons. It was the heavy-duty kind, with steps on both sides, as stable as a stepladder could possibly be.

Over the next eight weeks, Davis worked flat out. While doing all his projects at the farm, he was also working as much as possible on the Osprey Island case and a couple of others.

Soon the Thompson went back to its owner. A 1937 Chris-Craft replaced it in the boat barn. The owners had put a huge hole in the front deck trying out an innovative way of extracting the heavy craft from the water. The finish needed to be redone, also—no small task. The repairs would cost a lot more than the original price of the boat.

By mid-July, Hiram was on the mend. He started coming out to the barn at five as before, itching to get back into his routine. He was almost ready, although the whole experience had in fact taken something away, probably permanently. He was diminished in little ways. The parts would all work, but not quite as well as they had. If he wanted to avoid another catastrophe, he'd have to slow down, but Hiram wasn't ready to admit it.

Though Davis was exhausted, he wasn't as eager as his father to get back to his former routine. It felt like a turning point, but toward what was unclear.

*   *   *

At work, Bert, Fred, and Janice were working their way through the snowmobile lists. There was nobody in Vermont to fit the bill. Two were dead, one was female, two were off at college, and three were about five feet six inches tall, obviously not the person who had been seen by the professor. The rest were out for other reasons.

The New York list was longer, and it was more work to check off each person.

When he wasn't working on other cases, Dick was going door-to-door on South Hero, North Hero, around St. Albans, and over in New York, but had turned up nothing.

June McDonald, who also had plenty of other work to do, occasionally looked through her videos and played with them digitally, hoping to see something new.

At the police lab, the stolen-and-returned bicycle sat in a corner. Larry Bates, who had gone over it several times, would sometimes look at it and think, *This bike must have something more to tell us.*

Chapter 18

NO ROOM AT THE INN

August 3

As the wind quickened, and the boat's engine started to cough and miss, Eddie Zieroff thought, *Getting this boat might be in the category of "seemed like a good idea at the time."* As gas prices breached $3.75 a gallon, motorboats were a good deal all of a sudden. Older ones, particularly older ones that used a lot of gas, were an exceptionally good deal. Boats like this one, which vacuumed up gas faster than you could pour it in, were almost free.

The boat was a twenty-two-foot cruiser—almost the smallest boat you could fairly name a cruiser—with an enormous 200-horsepower Chevy V8, basically a car engine, married to an external drive that looked like the bottom half of an outboard motor. It was what in boat lingo was called an I/O, meaning inboard/outboard. It was an aluminum boat from the early

'80s, and it had an open cabin with two seats and something called a cuddy under the front deck. The cuddy was a bunk with almost no headroom where two people could sleep, at least theoretically, if they weren't too big and were very good friends. A lot of boats like this were sitting in front yards on their trailers with For Sale signs on the windshields. Eddie and his brother Jimmy had bought this one four days ago.

It was legal, legitimately registered in New York State. It had the life jackets, lights, flares, fire extinguisher, anchor, horn, and other safety stuff it was supposed to have. It had none of the electronics modern boats had, but the lights worked if you tapped on the switch just right. It had once been a sharp-looking unit, but now the upholstery was torn, the plastic surface worn in places down to the rough fabric beneath it. The vinyl coatings glued to the gunwales were cracked and curling off.

The brothers had been hired at the International Paper plant together, and they had moved from Albany up to an apartment in Ticonderoga for their new jobs. Ten weeks later, they had been laid off together, with two weeks' notice. A foreman at the plant owned the boat and jokingly suggested that since they'd been laid off, they should buy his boat and have an adventure taking it up to Canada. They'd never been to Canada, so it was obviously a good idea.

They had done some camping in the past and had all the gear. They were good swimmers. Jimmy had even been on the high school swim team for a semester. The big problem was that they had never really done any boating other than the occasional canoe rental with girlfriends on small ponds in city parks. A boat dealer gave them a copy of the boating rules and sold them a book of nautical charts covering the whole lake. He also gave them a trifold brochure that listed places to buy gas, get groceries, and empty out the boat's toilet holding tank, had they had such a thing.

After a practice run in the narrow part of the lake around Ticonderoga, they judged themselves ready.

They were extraordinarily lucky at first. The wind was mild and from the south, pushing them up the lake. When they went full speed, the boat pounded the waves like a clanging cymbal, but at twenty miles an hour, it ran well enough. The motor ran like a top, though the aluminum hull amplified the normal rumble of the Chevy into an earsplitting roar, similar to the thunder made in amateur theatricals by shaking a huge piece of sheet metal.

The trouble began around four o'clock, when they passed what they believed, correctly, was Burlington to their right. The motor started to sputter. By the time the Burlington–Port Kent ferry crossed in front of them, the engine was beginning to slow down; it still ran, but it wouldn't accelerate properly. It had a cough. The waves chasing them now had fifty miles in which to gather, and they were big. The waves were scary at three feet. The boat would climb up the front side of one wave and come crashing down with a huge *bang* into the valley on the far side. The bags of camping gear and food boxes jumped around at each crash, and the fishing rods slid all over the place. They slowed down.

Eddy's natural mode was to hope for the best and plow on. But he was getting a little concerned. He handed the wheel over to Jimmy and found the right pages in the book of charts. It was hard to read it with the bouncing, and the pages blew in the wind.

He said, "Jim, it's dinnertime. Why don't we find a nice place to stay for the night. Maybe we can figure out what's bothering the engine."

As Jimmy drove on, Eddie, who was not a great map reader, looked for a place to spend the night. They had plenty of food and beer; all they needed was a safe place to dock the boat. As they viewed Valcour Island to their left and the Grand Isle ferry crossing ahead, the motor was holding with its new, bronchial voice. Every mile, the wind seemed to strengthen. The map showed a passage that led to a more protected part of the lake, which seemed to have stores, marinas, and a couple of island campgrounds. This was the Gut, which led to the Inland Sea.

Usually boaters had to know where this opening was to find it. Today it was easy to find because five other boats were streaming that way. What the two young men didn't realize, since they didn't have a marine radio, was that the Coast Guard had issued a storm warning, and with it, a small craft advisory. Basically, the message was, get the hell off the lake, and quick. It wasn't a perfect storm, but for Champlain in August, it was way above average. The waves were now four feet, and Jimmy had no idea how to manage a boat in such a sea.

They followed the other boats into what was essentially a shallow, weedy lake, perhaps two miles across, with a well-marked channel to the drawbridge that led out to the Inland Sea. It was a good thing they had boats to follow, as they didn't know how to read the buoys that marked the channel. Jimmy's mind tended to wander, but he was concentrating now.

He said, "Eddie, get on the phone and find us a place to dock overnight." Eddie liked to take charge, but Jimmy was more competent in a tight situation. The sailboats were collecting up near the drawbridge. Their masts were too tall to clear the bridge, and they had to wait for the drawbridge to be raised. The littler boats could slither through the gathering pile of big, expensive boats and slide under the bridge. Slowly, Jimmy, who had no idea of what the protocol, the rules of the road, might be, threaded his way through, following in the wake of a bright blue, modern fishing boat. It was nerve-wracking; he had never done anything like this. Though less rough than out in the Broad Lake, the waves still pushed the little boat this way and that. Jimmy was happy to get under the bridge without crashing into another boat or the rocks onshore.

To escape the din, Eddy crawled down into the cuddy, shut the door, and looked at the folder that had a list of potential local marinas and mooring sites, with phone numbers. He called the marina just beyond the drawbridge, Ladd's Landing, first. It had been full since noon when the warning first went out. The marina at City Bay really didn't rent out dock space overnight. North Hero House had dockage, but it would have cost them their entire supply of cash for one night. At Burton Island every one of the dock spaces was either full or reserved.

That left anchoring for the night or possibly camping without permission on one of the islands that had primitive camping. They had planned to spend their nights safely tucked in at a marina dock, where they could walk to a cheap restaurant or a bar that served sandwiches. But the boat did have an anchor with a very long rope.

After they cleared the bridge, they were in a long, narrow bay. As he drove past the marina, Jimmy was feeling relieved; the waves were less violent. But as soon as he left the protection of Ladd Point, big waves pounded them from the right, though not as huge as those on the Broad Lake.

Burton Island was directly across from the bay, but they couldn't go there. More to the north was a group of several islands that looked promising. As they pulled out of the bay, the wind was pushing them that way anyway. Eddie climbed out of the cabin and pointed northeast. "There's no space anywhere," he said. "There's a storm warning. Go there, that's the best bet."

It was scary crossing toward the islands. The waves pounded them from the south, and they could see black swirling clouds following the waves toward them. Jimmy thought, *That's all we need—lightning in an aluminum boat. If the Lightning gets close, I'm swimming to shore.* Jimmy couldn't find a line of travel that cut down on the pounding. But soon Eddy could see which island was which, and he guided them to the most protected spot, a little harbor created by a bean-shaped island marked Osprey on the chart.

The harbor was almost calm, enveloping, and relatively peaceful. While Jimmy maneuvered the boat, Eddie precariously crawled up onto the front deck, unlashed the anchor, chucked it overboard, and signaled his brother to back up as he paid out the rope, which had been tucked in a locker beneath the deck. The boat drifted seventy or eighty feet north, and Eddie tied off the line. The boat stopped with a little jerk, and then an abrupt *thump*, as if the lake bottom had pulled back. They were about 150 feet out from the dock, the boathouse, and the three cottages that lined the shore. On the island, nobody was braving the weather. If they were there, they had gone inside.

For the next hour, the two men nervously watched the sky. They worried whether the anchor would hold. But gradually the storm passed to their west, there was a bit of clear sky, even a touch of sun, and they turned their thoughts to dinner. They had a twenty-four-pack of Bud, a bottle of Jack Daniels, and a large bucket of chicken from the Colonel, with coleslaw and biscuits. Eddie found his camp stove, and in a few minutes he had managed to impart a little bit of warmth to the food.

Though the wind had abated, it was still blowing, and they had no idea what the night would bring. They decided to take turns standing watch. But they had gone through a lot of the beer and half of the whiskey, and they both slept through the night. When they got up to pee, they could see that nothing terrible was happening.

Eddie awoke the next morning a little groggy, around nine. The other side of the bed was empty. He looked out to see a lovely, calm morning, bathed in sun. Jimmy had lifted up the boxy cover that enclosed the engine and was fussing about. He had made a pot of coffee and was on his third cup. In a few minutes, he found the problem, one of the few problems he was in fact equipped to solve at present: a loose spark plug wire. Pushing it back into place with a grin of satisfaction, he started up the engine, which ran as intended again.

While he was accomplishing this, Eddie was making a half dozen eggs and half a package of bacon and thinking *We're mariners! This might work out after all.*

An hour later, as the sun shone, Jimmy started up the engine and Eddy climbed up on the deck, which this time was not threatening to flip him overboard. He hauled in the seventy-five feet of rope slowly and started to pull up the anchor.

Usually an anchor holds when there's a lot of rope out, the angle of the rope almost parallel to the water. When you're right over the anchor and pull straight up, it's designed to come free. But it didn't. He pulled the rope around to the back deck of the boat, and the two men tugged on it together. Jimmy drove the boat toward the island, to pull from a different direction. It felt like the anchor had been bolted to the floor of the lake. They tied off the rope and had another cup of coffee.

Finally, Jimmy said, "I'm going to swim down there, see what's holding us." He got out his flippers and a diving mask and jumped in. The sun was shining, so visibility underwater was much better than usual. He disappeared for half a minute, then surfaced. He scrambled up into the boat.

"The fucking anchor is caught under a snow machine. Unless we can lift a snow machine, we'll never get it out. Looks like quite a new model."

They could have simply cut the rope and cruised off, though the officials at the border might wonder why they had no anchor, should they inspect their safety gear. But they decided to call it in. After all, they weren't in any hurry, and there might be something in it for them, a reward or something. By then, there were several people at the dock, watching the show. Eddy waved to the kids. Two of them, about ten years old, jumped in a canoe and came out. The boys told the brothers that they were indeed, as they had thought, on the north side of Osprey Island. Eddie told the boys what they had found at the end of their rope, and that they were calling the cops.

Eddy called 911, which directed him to the Vermont State Police. The dispatcher sent them to the Coast Guard, and also alerted the state police scuba dive team. Both groups already knew all about Davis's case, and they knew that whatever they found would probably have something to do with the Brearley killing. The dispatcher also called Detective Sgt. Davis. Then she called Eddy back and told him to stay right where he was. "Don't move," she said. "We'll be there as soon as we can."

Over the next two hours, everyone on Osprey Island gathered on the long porch, opposite the little cruiser. On that day, it was about fifteen people of all ages, including Pliny Winthrop. Coffee, iced tea, brownies, fresh bread, and other goodies appeared. It was a regular party. Every few minutes, someone would row or paddle out to the stranded boat and offer the two young men something to eat, which they accepted in every instance and consumed immediately.

The Coast Guard had a big, rugged, thirty-five-foot boat that had every sort of equipment on it, including a powerful winch set up as a crane.

It looked like an oceangoing commercial fishing vessel. An hour and a half after the call, the boat slowly cruised up to Eddy and Jimmy's boat. On it were Coast Guard Petty Officer Joshua Dale, who was captaining the craft, Seaman David Scott, Fred Davis, and Edward and Peter, state police divers.

Officially, Davis was an observer; it was not his boat. While the captain kept the boat idling in its position, Seaman Scott lashed the boats together and asked the two men to join them on the larger craft. He heard their story, looked at their IDs, and asked them how it had all happened. Somewhat against their instincts, the two young men told the truth.

As they were telling their story, the two divers put on their Aqua-Lungs and went in the water. Less than two minutes later, they were back on deck.

"There's a little ridge down there, about twenty feet down. The anchor is completely buried under the snowmobile, right next to the ridge. I'm thinking the machine was sort of teetering on the ledge. These guys hooked it with the anchor and dislodged it, and then it rolled off the ledge onto the anchor line. Does that make sense, Peter?"

"Yep, that's got to be it."

The men went into the water again. Edward was toting a camera in a waterproof case. Peter had a floodlight with a battery pack strapped around his waist. This time they were down for five minutes.

Seaman Scott, with the assistance of Captain Dale, set up a small crane, basically a tripod bolted to the deck at the stern, with a projecting arm, cables, and an electric winch. The divers came up again and handed the photography equipment to the men on deck. Scott handed them the cable from the crane. They went down for a third time. When they reappeared at the surface of the water, Edward signaled Seaman Scott to reel in the cable until it was taut. Then they climbed back into the boat, keeping their gear on in case the machine got loose and they had to go in again. This was fun for them; they didn't get many opportunities to use their diving skills. Seaman Scott then slowly reeled in the cable, like a fisherman reeling in a fish in slow motion.

The machine came out of the water tail first, dripping water and mud. The Coast Guard boat was pristine white, with a spotless gray deck; Scott let the snow machine drip, then lowered it again into the water a couple of times for a nice rinse. Then he raised it and swung it over the boat. With two men guiding it by hand, he lowered it onto the deck.

It was the largest size machine, a Yamaha, black with red flames painted on the sides. Though still muddy, it looked new. They quickly found the VIN and the model number. Davis called the numbers in to Bert.

Davis went ashore in the kids' canoe and talked to the folks on the porch. None of them knew anything about this, and he didn't expect them to. He knew exactly when the machine had gone in the water, and none of these people were anywhere near Osprey at the time.

A few minutes later, Bert called back. The machine was listed to a Seward Tyler, age fifty-four, residing at 3 Martin Lane, Port Douglas, New York. It was one of the little lakeshore lanes on Brown Point, roughly opposite Burlington. According to the New York registry of motor vehicles, the machine was a Yamaha Apex Mt 162 model.

On the long porch of the cottage where everyone was watching, Fred grabbed Pliny. Pliny had also understood what the snow machine meant. Fred said, "If the papers or any news media hear about this, we'll never see this guy again. Make sure nobody here says a fucking word." He was imagining this guy Seward Tyler reading the headline in his morning *Free Press*: "Snow machine recovered from Lake Champlain." If that happened, he'd be far, far away by lunch.

Two boys paddled Davis back out to the Coast Guard boat, and he immediately gathered the divers, the Coast Guard crew, and Jimmy and Eddie and gave them the same admonition: media silence. Then he called Bert.

"Bert, it's me again. Who knows about this snow machine and Tyler?"

"So far, just me."

"Good. We have to keep it that way, or he'll be gone."

"Got it."

They let the two men go off to continue their adventure, after taking their phone numbers and other information. There was no reason to doubt their story, and in fact, it had been confirmed by the people on Osprey Island, who'd been watching since the young men arrived the evening before.

*   *   *

Later that day, Bert Miller and Fred Davis met for supper at the Vietnamese restaurant in Winooski. It was only four thirty, and the place was not yet crowded. Bert ordered the chicken soup, the house specialty; Davis ordered the #25 again.

They went over what they knew about Seward Tyler. There was surprisingly little information out there. He was fifty-four years old. The snow machine was registered, as were three boats, a thirty-six-foot cruiser, an old Glasspar G3 Ski Boat, and a sixteen-foot Grumman aluminum boat with a ten-horse Evinrude motor. All these boats were 1972 models. Tyler owned a 2003 Subaru Outback and a Ford F-150 pickup with four-wheel drive. He owned the house on Martin Lane. He had no criminal record, not even a speeding ticket, and his fingerprints weren't on file, at least not with his name attached to them. His real estate taxes had always been paid. It wasn't clear how he earned a living, if he needed to earn a living. Google turned up nothing.

He did not appear in the police records of New York or Vermont. He wasn't on the radar of the state police in the Port Douglass–Keeseville area.

Even though they had no proof that Tyler was their killer, the snow machine put him at the scene. They had enough to get a search warrant. It would all have to be done working with the New York State Police.

As he hunched over his huge bowl of soup, Bert said, "You'd think his name would have come up at some time."

The two men ate silently for a while. Neither of them doubted that Tyler was their man. Something was bothering Fred Davis. But he couldn't put his finger on it.

Bert had given up on the chopsticks. The big ceramic spoon was a problem, too. He was trying to gather a bunch of noodles and a chunk of chicken on a fork.

Davis hadn't figured out why he was apprehensive. There was a little itch in the back of his brain, and he couldn't get in position to scratch it. "Tomorrow, I'll take Janice with me and drive by his house. Then maybe we'll cruise past his place by water. I don't want to take a cruiser over there, it'll set him off. I'll go in my truck and just drive by."

Bert said, "Maybe they'll find something on the snow machine when they go through it."

Chapter 19

SKIP AT REST

Around the same time, on Martin Lane, Skip Tyler was sitting in his favorite chair, looking out over the lake, smoking a cigar. He had been less active than usual. He hung around the house a lot, walked around his neighborhood. He did a little aimless fishing in his old aluminum boat, catch and release. Usually in summer he would make one or two drug runs up into Canada in his cabin cruiser. That had been his primary source of income for a long time. This summer, he had been a middleman in a few deals, but his boat remained in storage at a marina in Rouses Point. His most profitable activity since winter had been stock trading, selling short; he had a feel for the collapsing market. But that only took an hour or two of his time each day.

Maybe it was time to plan a trip somewhere. Paris. Greek islands. He could take a cruise. His own cabin cruiser wasn't even in the water yet, and it was already August.

Skip was capable of great effort for a period of time, but these times usually were followed by hibernations. He enjoyed doing nothing. Killing Paul Brearley gave him a feeling of quiet satisfaction. It was a wrong righted. He liked replaying the movie of the killing in his head. The thirty-six-year delay between the final tennis game and the true match point made it all the more delicious. It really was the high point of his year.

Skip was a combination of deliberate and spontaneous. His approach to smuggling meth by snowmobile was methodical, studied. He planned out everything, mapped out his moves, literally plotting them out on nautical charts. But he could instantly alter or ditch a plan when circumstances required. When his plan for bringing in the meth seemed risky, he dropped it without a second thought. Then later, when Paul showed up at the door, his response was immediate.

In everyday matters, he was often relaxed to an extreme. He could spend a whole day just staring out his window at the lake. He could fish for hours without getting impatient. But while in these mental states—as when he sat in his chair smoking his cigar—he was hyperaware, too. It wasn't as if he was nervous or worried. He just took in a lot more sense information than most people. He noticed odd noises most people would screen out. When driving country roads, he'd notice a deer or a bunch of turkeys at the far corner of a field that most people would never see. He never ran over animals in the road, because he saw them before other drivers would.

He thought this quality kept him alive and unknown to the police.

At the same time, he knew something could go wrong, and he had done everything he could think of to plan for the day when some policeman would find him. He had erected alternate identities in two different places, which he could drop or pick up as needed. He spent a little time each year inhabiting these personae to keep them plausible. And he had worked out a variety of ways to make the switch if the time came, with all the links in place should they be needed. The inexpensive motion sensors in the drive and along the road were another line of defense.

He had one other attribute that made him a formidable opponent: He really didn't give a shit. He more or less liked what he was doing, but if it didn't work out, if he was busted, or caught or killed, he could accept that. That was one change since the day thirty-six years earlier when he had played that match with Paul. The fact that he cared that day weakened him. Now his underlying indifference gave him a kind of edge. It enabled him to make quick adjustments, or read situations realistically, and react in surprising ways.

Chapter 20

THE CHASE, DAY ONE

avis and Janice left the next morning in her aging Honda Accord. They crossed to New York on the Grand Isle ferry. There wasn't a direct route along the water's edge; they had to go inland to Keeseville, then back out toward the water. Bay Road paralleled the water. Short roads led down to the shore, with a few cottages on each one. Martin Lane was one of the last of these before Bay Road dead-ended. On their map, there were three houses on Martin Lane and the middle one, number three, was the one which belonged to Seward Tyler.

As they drove down Bay Road, Davis was getting the funny feeling again, as if the hairs on the back of his neck were standing up. His heart rate was going up. Then he remembered: he had been here before.

Janice saw the change and asked, "Are you OK?"

"Let's just do this, and then I'll tell you about it." Davis had the map in his lap as Janice drove. "Take the next left. It's Martin Lane. When you go by the driveways, don't stop and don't look. Just drive by slowly. I'll make notes. I don't want to stop or even significantly slow down."

She turned left onto Martin Lane, driving slowly as if trying to keep the car from getting damaged by the rocks in the road. As they passed number three, Davis looked down the drive. But he remembered more or less what was there. He took a quick photo.

There was a single house at the end of a straight drive about a hundred and fifty feet long. The house was right on the water. The driveway was wooded on both sides. It was an unusual house for the area, a two-story, modernist white stucco block with big plate-glass windows. There were a few panels of diagonal wood siding, like huge postage stamps, pasted on the house. The entry door had once been painted a bright red but was now faded. It looked like an architect must have drawn the house in the '60s to make a statement. But the bright white paint was dirty. The lot was overgrown; the woods on either side came right up to the house, the trees rubbing against the house in places. An old Subaru sat in the drive and next to it, a blue Ford pickup.

At the end of Martin Lane, they turned around, as if they'd been lost, or just aimlessly exploring back roads. As she drove back, he said, "I can't look. It would be too obvious. But you can."

After they had passed Tyler's driveway the second time, Davis started to calm down. Soon they were in Port Douglass and on their way back to the office.

"Well?" she asked.

"I'll tell you about it when we get back." He called Bert and arranged to meet on their return. They drove to Keeseville, then back to Port Kent, stopped for a snack, and crossed again on the ferry. On the boat, they took the metal stairs onto the upper deck. They each had a cranberry cream cheese muffin and a cup of truly undrinkable coffee. Davis said, "You know, you can hardly get a cup of coffee this bad in Vermont anymore."

There were light, one-foot waves. It was sunny and clear. A bunch of gulls were following a school of fish that looked like little wavelets shimmering on the water. A couple of cormorants cut across the bow of the ferry. They seemed much more purposive than the gulls. They were in a big hurry, skimming just above the waves, going somewhere in a straight line.

Davis looked at Janice and said, "How do you like bass fishing?"

She gave him a puzzled look. "Huh?"

*   *   *

The team gathered in the squad room. Davis passed out several copies of his photo, looking down the driveway at 3 Martin Lane. He began, "My closest friend is Luke Walker. He's my brother-in-law now and is part owner of the farm. We've been friends since we were about seven. When we were seventeen, we spent the winter building a plywood sailboat called a Lightning. It was a popular class of racing boats back then. About our third trip out, heading north up near Carry Bay in the Broad Lake, a speedboat came charging through the opening of the bay and smashed into our boat.

"There were cans of beer flying everywhere, including onto my head. The motorboat was a Glasspar G3 Ski Boat, red and black. It was a very modern-looking boat for water-skiing. It had a great big Merc on it, at least big for back then. At the back, the gunwale was low, about eight inches above the water, and sharp as a knife. It sliced a huge hole in the side of our sailboat. I thought he had sunk us. When the dust settled, there was nobody in the ski boat. But a minute later this guy hikes himself over the side. Our boat was sinking, his was unhurt. He was a big, redheaded kid. He looked at us, popped open another beer, smiled, and just took off without so much as a word.

"After we limped in and repaired our boat, we spent several days looking for the guy, trying to locate his boat. We cruised all along the shoreline. We found the boat at a dock next to a cruiser on Brown Point. The house was a big, white modern thing, brand-new."

215

Bert, Janice, and Dick were getting the picture.

"We waited for a dark and rainy night, then drove down there. We snuck through the woods around the house, took the boat out into the lake, pulled out the drain plug, started it up, aimed it east, and set it going. Then we went home, and as far as we were concerned, that was the end of it. We never saw the guy or the boat again.

"I don't think we thought much about it after that. We went back to racing the Lightning. But I'll never forget the look on that boy's face as he sped off. He was having fun. He didn't regret what had happened in the least. It's definitely the same house, and he still owns the boat. I think this just confirms our conjectures that he's a violent, smart, ruthless person. He's dangerous. Let's figure out how to get him.

"Bert," continued Davis, "I'm hoping you can figure out a legal way to arrest this man before he takes off. I want to take a look at that house up close from the water. We need a way to snuggle right up to the shore, study the lay of the land, and get some pictures without attracting his attention."

The answer was obvious to anybody who had spent time on the lake, or any other lake in North America. Bert and Dick spoke at the same time.

"Bass boat."

If they went past the house in an official boat of any kind and Seward Tyler was around to see it, Tyler would be gone in hours, never to be seen again. If they cruised by in Davis's boat or the Lyman Islander, at the very least Tyler would notice. He'd start thinking about it. But the lake was full of bass boats. These were low, flat skiffs with powerful engines, separate electric trolling motors, and fishing seats sticking up out of the decks like mushrooms. They were usually big, fast, and garishly painted. Fishermen in search of bass would come right close to shore, often just twenty or thirty feet out. Then they would work their way along using their silent electric motors as they cast their lures toward the shore where the bass were waiting, hoping for a cheap lunch.

Tyler wouldn't be alarmed by one more, and they might get a few pictures of the house and grounds as they idled by. Janice had done only a little fishing and was happy to play her part.

The legal dimension was more complex. They didn't really have enough to charge Tyler with murder. Their case was circumstantial. If they were lucky, they might find definitive evidence in his house. Once they had his fingerprints, they might be able to match them to prints on Osprey Island that had not yet been identified. But the actual warrants, arrest, searches, and extradition would have to be done by New York State Police, under their laws. If he got out on bail, they would never see him again.

Bert said, "We may not have proof yet that he killed Paul Brearley, but we do have him for some crimes. He dumped a vehicle in the lake—that's illegal—and he polluted the lake on purpose, also illegal. It's not enough to keep him without bail."

Davis stood up. "You work on that. I'll line up a bass boat."

*   *   *

Brian Allen lived on West Shore Road a mile from the Davis Farm. He had a large bass boat, which he treated with great solicitude. It never spent the night in the water. After every use, he gently tugged it back onto its trailer, put on the custom canvas cover, and tucked it away in a small barn built for that very purpose. It was the same black-and-red color scheme as the G3. But where the faded graphics on the G3 were modeled on the pastel two-tone cars of its era, the red flame design on the bass boat was bright and fantastic with lots of sparkle, like the graphics in superhero comics or video games.

Brian and Davis were old friends. Davis stopped by on the way back to the farm. Without getting into details, he explained the basic situation and where he wanted to go and asked for the loan of the boat.

After a minute's hesitation, Brian said, "You know, Freddy, I've never let anybody else even *drive* that boat, even with me in it, sitting in the next seat. Here's what we'll do. I'll take you and your partner fishing. You show me where to go, and we'll fish there. That little section of shoreline and

Willsboro Bay could be worth the trip anyway. For fishing, I mean. It'll be as easy as anything to just put in right here. Say, six o'clock?"

"I have to milk. Can we go later, say, nine?"

"OK, see you then."

Davis was eager to discuss the new developments with Luke in detail. Fred often discussed cases with his friend. Whatever rules of confidentiality might apply, it never occurred to Fred that they applied to Luke. Of course, in a sense, Luke had as much right to the story as Fred did; he'd been there at the beginning. Fred couldn't wait to bring Luke up-to-date, and knew he would get a gratifying response.

It was the last chapter of a very long story. Or he hoped it was the last chapter. But that evening, Luke had to be out at a meeting. Davis gave him the bare outline by phone. Fred had previously arranged to have dinner the following night at Osprey Island with Pliny. He decided to take Luke along and tell the whole story to them both. After all this conjecture, it would be fun to lay things out. It would be like Hercule Poirot or Nero Wolfe gathering all the principals in the case in the drawing room, brilliantly laying out his deductions to everyone's amazement. And Pliny actually had a drawing room.

Davis knew he wasn't really supposed to share inside police information with a civilian like Pliny, but he viewed Pliny as part of the team. The old man had more than once provided important information, particularly identifying the body about a month before the police would have, working on their own. Also, as a minister, Pliny should be able to keep his mouth shut. It would all be in the *Burlington Free Press* in a couple of days.

* * *

Brian, Davis, and Janice met at the boat launch at nine the next morning. They were underway by a quarter after. The boat was fast, and they were near Brown Point in about a half hour.

As he thought about it, Davis realized that it was much better to go with Brian. Experienced bass fishermen have spent thousands of hours combing along dozens of shorelines and flipped their lures toward untold numbers of rocks and weeds. There was a casual purposiveness about their movements that was very distinct. By comparison, Janice and Davis by themselves might have seemed fake. Tyler might have become suspicious.

They started fishing in Willsboro Bay, just south of Brown Point. That way they could get their routines down, talk about how they would snap a few pictures unobtrusively. By the time they got to Tyler's house, they might look like they knew what they were doing. On the inside of Willsboro Point, they hit a hot spot. They were gliding silently between a big sailboat, moored offshore, and a big dock, no doubt belonging to the sailboat's owner. At the same time that Janice and Brian were pulling fifteen-inch bass out from under the dock, Davis got into a handsome pike lurking under the sailboat. After the excitement, the fish went back into the lake.

There was no difficulty identifying Tyler's house. It was probably the only big white stucco house on the lake. A brown but mowed lawn led down to the aluminum dock. The G3 was tied up on the north side of the dock opposite the old aluminum boat. There were tangled woods on both sides of the house, then other, smaller cottages on either side. A family was out on the lawn of the house just to the south. A bunch of eight-year-old boys were running around, while a couple of moms tried to keep them away from the water. The camp to the north seemed unoccupied. The dock sections were still stacked up ashore like pancakes on a plate.

Sound carries over the water, and they didn't say that much as they fished their way very slowly past the stucco house. Brian, silently controlling the boat with the foot-operated electric motor, held a position near the dock, and again where the lawn gave way to woods. There was no sign of anybody watching them, but someone inside could look out without being seen. They slowly glided past, flipping their lures this way and that. Davis had Brian continue to go slowly past this second, unoccupied, house. He took two pictures. He was interested in how their quarry might get away if he thought cops were arriving in his driveway.

It was a different situation than would be found in a town, where roads could be blocked off. Here there were roads to block, but also entangled wooded areas on two sides and the entire lake on another. It wasn't hard to imagine Tyler jumping into the G3 and disappearing quickly. Also, there were miles and miles of wooded land to the west. It gave Davis a lot to think about.

*   *   *

That evening, Luke and Davis went to Osprey Island in the old Lyman Islander they had restored as teenagers. Like them, it was fifty-three years old. For the old boat, it was "use it or lose it." If it didn't get to run through its paces on a regular basis, it might lose interest altogether and head into retirement. It would start to leak more than it already did. It could end up as a planter, filled with flowers, slowly melting into the ground, which was the fate of a lot of old wood boats.

Pliny's place was looking a little better. The little lawn was mowed, and somebody had put fresh stain on some of the trim. There was a rocking chair on the dock attached to the boathouse. They were welcomed on the porch by Pliny and his daughter Abby. Fred wasn't expecting Abby to be there, but after a moment's thought, he decided to go ahead with the plan of telling the story, as much of it as he knew. As it happened, her being there gave him a first glimpse of the part of the story that had been most obscure: a motive for the killing of Paul Brearley.

It was cocktail hour on the porch. The bottle of Glenlivet was there on a round wicker table along with a couple of beers and a bottle of red wine. Some crackers and dip were on an old, chipped willowware plate. The four of them sat in the comfortable wicker chairs for a few minutes, mostly looking out on the lake. All of them had spent countless hours sitting and looking out like this; it was one of the chief pleasures of life for everyone on the lake. They didn't need to say much.

The wind was calming down, as it often did in the evening. A couple dozen Canada geese swirled around noisily a few times, then headed off to the south. It was a good time of year for fishing. One bass boat with two very large men in it cruised silently by right in front of them, twenty feet from shore. The men were flipping their lures toward the shore, over and over. One of the men gave them a perfunctory wave of the hand. Farther out a little family group, a couple and two kids, were worm fishing out of a tiny aluminum boat. The bass fishermen didn't catch anything, but the family was pulling in perch and sunfish every minute or two. The bass fishermen were completely silent, but the family was talking noisily. Their dog had his front paws on the gunwales and barked whenever they pulled in a perch.

It was cloudy; there wouldn't be much of a sunset. They went inside.

Dinner was in the paneled dining room with the rustic, vaulted ceiling. The table was covered with an old-timey red-and-white checked tablecloth and was set with the good dishes. Pliny's cooking was limited to steaks and hamburgers and the occasional limp salad, but Abby cooked real meals. She had made a lasagna and a nice, fresh salad. Luke brought some of his bread, baked that afternoon, and a pie from the farm store.

His audience was ready to hear the story, but Davis wanted to deliver it in the time-honored way—in the drawing room. They had plenty to talk about anyway. They had shared the same lake for a lifetime; there were any number of stories to tell. They had all been there in the good old days.

Pliny had a fire going in the living room and had located a rather antiquated bottle of brandy. The picture of the six men on the front dock was back in its place on the side table with the birch bark top.

Davis told the story of the boat barn. He told the story of building the Lightning. He told the story of the fateful tack past the opening into Carry Bay. He had printed out a picture of the G3 taken that morning at Tyler's dock, and he passed it around. The whole tale hinged on the peculiar shape of the boat, the way its lines resolved into a low, knifelike projection at the back, like a lateral fin, clad in chrome. Most any other boat of the day would have bumped the sailboat, maybe putting a big crack in the hull. But the G3 sliced it open like a can opener.

Davis started to talk about repairing the Lightning, but Luke piped up with a vivid description of how the boat hobbled its way to the marina just inside Carry Bay. "When we let down the sail, most of the gash came back above the water. The boat was about half full by the time we made it to the dock." He described his panic as he tried to get the little outboard started and his despair at the thought of his new boat sinking, the first boat they had built from scratch. Davis had never heard Luke describe his feelings about this part of the story, but he wasn't that surprised; he'd felt much the same.

Davis told about their search along the shorelines for the boat and finding it on Brown Point. The most dramatic part of the story was their midnight trip to seek revenge.

"It helped that the house lot was wooded on both sides. We parked up on the road and could walk all the way down to the dock without anybody seeing us. It's a good thing they didn't have a dog! We paddled it out quite a way."

Luke broke in, "We even brought an extra paddle just for that."

Davis picked up the story. "We paddled it out maybe a hundred yards, then started it up. There was no key, but Luke had it going in two seconds. I don't think they could have heard us. It was a noisy, windy night, blowing north. We pulled out the drain plug, secured the wheel with some fishing line, and let it go headed west. Then we dove in and swam ashore."

Luke added, "Sweet revenge."

Davis smiled. "It was really scary swimming in from the boat. We'd drifted out pretty far. But we're here to tell the story."

Luke said, "And that was the end of it. We didn't really tell anybody about it. Freddy's father would definitely not have approved. He'd have sent us back there to apologize and make amends. We just treasured it in our hearts as a very warm memory. The family thought we'd gone to

Plattsburgh for illegal beers! My wife didn't know about it until I told her about it this morning."

Pliny and Abby had watched the recovery of the snow machine off their main dock. Davis told about tracing the machine back to Seward Tyler and finding his address on Brown Point. He told about realizing where he was as they turned onto the little road.

"When we turned onto that road, I recognized it right away. Then I remembered that Seward Tyler had a G3, and I was totally certain. I was also terrified. I still remembered this guy's look when he took off and left us there sinking. As I said, he was enjoying the situation. I wonder if he sliced up anybody else just for fun with that thing. Maybe he sharpened that trim on the side, like a James Bond boat. I'll have to check that when we see it."

The two men seemed like seventeen-year-olds as they told the story. In their minds, they were right back there.

Then Davis fast-forwarded to the fishing trip. He passed around another picture, showing the house and its setting. "It was a little strange going by there in the bass boat."

"I wish I'd been there," Luke said. "I want to be there when you nail this Seward Tyler."

Pliny was suitably impressed with the drama of the story. He was enjoying a series of events that made his year much more exciting than was usual for a man in his eighties.

Abby, though, was fidgeting in her seat. Finally, she got up, poured herself about a tablespoonful of the brandy, and sat down again. "Good story. Actually, I think he's known as Skip."

She was enjoying incredulous looks from all three men. They were being upstaged. In the spirit of the evening, she started her story at the beginning. As she talked, Davis could see the gears turning in Pliny's brain, trying to remember back.

"Paul found the G3 after you sent it across the lake," she continued. "He was fishing out by the Fill and found it in the weeds, half sunk. He

Sam Clark

stoppered it up and towed it all the way back to the Sandbar. The ranger there found out who owned the boat. This wasn't that noteworthy an event. But Skip's dad made him come out here to thank Paul for rescuing the boat. Helen was right there when they walked up. She told me all about it. Later, there was a cookout, and we all skied behind that boat."

Pliny walked over and picked up the picture of the boat. "Actually, I skied behind that boat. Pulled me up like nothing. I think that was about the last time anybody got me on water skis."

Abby continued her story. The surprise factor was big, but the story was short. "We had a couple of picnics with Skip's family. I've been to that white house. We skied down there, too, but it was way too rough. I think Paul played tennis a couple of times with Skip. After a brief period, we never saw any of them again.

"Actually, Skip came on to me—I don't know what we called it then—but there was something a little creepy there, and physically he was so big. I ran the other way."

Later, as they cruised back to the farm, Davis had Luke take the helm. He was busy thinking. Did this change anything? They already knew Tyler—now Skip—was a little strange. The new information was that Paul and Skip knew each other, or had for a few weeks one summer, almost forty years ago. And that the friendship, as far as anyone knew, had been short.

*   *   *

Milking was getting easier. Hiram was feeling better and picking up more and more of the work. Fred and Luke were planning to spend the rest of the morning working on the old Chris-Craft. It was a rich person's boat. It was when new in 1938, and it was now that it was being restored.

The boat was off its trailer, on a temporary yoke they had built to hold it low to the floor where they could work on it. Luke, as usual, was working on the engine. The top half of the engine had been winched off and was sitting on a workbench. Another bench had various parts spread out. The cushions were stacked in a corner. All the cleats, lights, chocks, and other brass parts were arrayed on a piece of plywood on a pair of sawhorses.

Fred had a selection of power sanders hooked up to a vacuum system. He was carefully sanding the boat down to the wood, but all he could think about was Skip and the big white house. He was picturing two or three New York State Police cars pulling into the drive and imagining what Skip would do. He had the photos of the site spread out on the plywood next to the brass hardware and also a gazetteer open to Brown Point. Every few minutes, he'd put down the sander and walk over to look at these exhibits.

The Chris-Craft was a shared project, but so, in a way, was Skip. Luke was thinking along the same lines as his friend. When the vacuum went silent every few minutes, he walked over to the photos, and the two men looked them over together.

Luke said, "I can picture a clever escape in almost any direction except right out the driveway."

Davis added, "Those woods are really dense. They'd be hard for the cops to climb through, but he could have paths that went through there on either the north or south side. With just a little warning, he could walk right out. And then just hike out along the railroad tracks, or through the woods to this other road, here." Route 28 was parallel to Bay Road, and less than a half mile inland.

Luke said, "For that matter, it wouldn't be hard to just swim along the shore then dodge back up on land. He might not even be noticed."

"How would we counter that? You'd have to have a boat just offshore, with a big light, if we went in there at night."

They worked for another few minutes. Fred stopped sanding and walked back over to his map. "To cover all these routes would take dozens of police. I'm not sure the New York authorities will be able to do that."

Luke asked, "Do you think he'd try to split by boat? He'd be pretty vulnerable if he went out into the Broad Lake. But maybe he'd make some sort of short hop, and then escape by car somehow."

"I think he's a man of style. He'll want not only to get away but to make us look bad. He'll take the G3."

They started to go back to work. But Davis asked the obvious question: "How would we prevent that?"

"Easy," Luke said. "Just take the propeller nut off. He'll start to back up, the propeller will go flying off, and he'll be stranded."

This defense had the advantage of style, too. It had a *Spy vs. Spy* quality. A very large threaded nut kept the prop secured on its shaft. The idea was that in a forward direction, the natural spin of the propeller pushed it against the motor. But in reverse, the propeller would tend to spin off its shaft, immobilizing the boat.

Fred got the idea immediately. "We could do that from underwater, or a diver could. I have a little trouble believing the New York people will want to go that far."

"Do they have to know?"

They went back to work for a few minutes, then the big vacuum stopped again. Fred said, "There's only one problem here. This guy is much bigger than us, and he's not afraid of a little gunplay." After a moment, he said, "And I am."

As the morning wore on, they looked at hiking scenarios, flight by boat, and the idea that Skip would have a plan to swim his way out of there. That wasn't as unlikely as it might seem. With scuba gear, or even just a snorkel, he could get away without having to swim that far. He could work his way along the shore, or cross a short gap to Willsboro Point, and then escape by car somehow.

Or, maybe the unoccupied house next door was part of an escape plan. He could have rented it. But they often came back to the idea that he'd use the G3 for the first leg of an escape, on aesthetic grounds. They viewed him as a stylist who wanted to do things with flair.

*   *   *

The team met yet again that afternoon: Bert, Davis, Janice, Ethel, Larry Bates from the lab, and Dick Fowler. They all seemed excited. It was surprising to see Dick there. He had almost disappeared. He was knocking on doors early, late, and on weekends and was rarely seen by the others. He had stopped at every house or farm with any kind of view of the lake near Burton Island or Osprey. For example, even though almost no one was on Butler Island in winter, he had talked to many of the landowners in case they had made a midwinter trip out there. He had visited every dwelling near St. Albans that had a water view or was near a boat launch. But today he had emerged, and he looked like a kid with a show-and-tell.

Davis started off. The story of his childhood encounters with Skip, and the fact that Skip and Paul Brearley had once known each other, was interesting. But for the moment, it didn't change much from a policing point of view. It was mainly of interest to those who had become obsessed with the victim, and his killer.

Larry Bates went next. "We've been through the Yamaha. I got a mechanic from the Yamaha dealership to come look at it with me. I don't know that much about these things. He found two housings that weren't supposed to be there. To me they looked like part of the machine. The finish matched, same kind of bolts. But they were compartments. So far, we've found some fragments of plastic from there, maybe from plastic bags. The compartments were waterproof, and we have some good prints from inside them. We're working on them now." He passed around photos of the fake housings.

Dick couldn't hold back. He had made a half dozen copies of two photographs. One was a summer shot of the boat launch at Hathaway Point. Someone was launching a boat at the ramp, and there were several trucks with boat trailers parked in a row along one side. Dick had taken it that morning.

The other picture was a winter scene, after a new snow. It showed a black Ford F-150, with a little ramp on the back. A large man was loading a smallish, yellow snow machine, which had a distinctly retro look. On the snow beside the truck was a black cargo sled. The photo was a bit foggy, but the license plate on the truck was readable. Dick's presentation had exactly the effect he was looking for. Dead silence, bated breath. In a few seconds, Bert said, "Bingo."

Dick was smiling. "I've knocked on about a thousand doors. There are a bunch of camps down there on Hathaway Point, of course. On about my seventh pass through I found a guy who owned one of these camps. He was out there on February first to shovel off the roof of his camp. He's got an old trailer with a little porch. He thought the roof was going to cave in from the weight of the snow. He saw a guy go by with the F-150 with a big Yamaha in the back and didn't think anything of it. Then he went back the next day because he couldn't remember if he'd locked up his camp. He lives right in St. Albans. He walked down the road and saw the same guy—well, you see it there. My witness is retired, and a bit of a snow machine buff. He's been riding since the first ones came out almost, or so he said. Anyway, he recognized the yellow Ski-Doo for what it was. It seemed interesting to him, but also not quite right. Why would a guy leave on one great snow machine and return on an antique piece of shit? He took a picture with his cell phone. That's the picture." Dick had missed a lot of the clever banter around the case and a lot of the detective deduction sessions. But he knew this was the goods. He'd pulled a nice three-foot pike through the ice.

There was a brief round of applause, initiated by Janice. But Bert wasn't really surprised. He'd been in contact daily with Dick and knew what he was up to. He also believed that criminals leave evidence, and if enough people look long enough, they will find it. There were some truly unsolvable cases, but usually cases were set aside because interest waned or other, more important ones pushed them aside.

"Nice work," he said. "Actually, very nice work. I think this gives us all the evidence we need. I'll go talk to the state's attorney and get formal charges set up."

Then Davis said, "OK, now let's figure out how to catch this guy."

*   *   *

Later that day, as Davis was sitting in his office thinking about their improbable and slightly illegal plan, his phone rang. It was Larry Bates from the police lab.

"Fred, I forgot one thing in all the excitement. I found some prints on the bicycle. I've got it leaning up in the corner of the lab here, and I've been thinking it might have a bit more to say. I went over it again and found a nice set on the bottom of the rear fork. They belong to JB. No question. I think he had a bit of oil on his fingers and was tuning the thing up a bit. They are very pretty prints. Just thought you'd like to know. Goodbye."

Davis sipped his coffee for a few minutes. Then he called JB's cell phone.

"JB. It's Sgt. Davis, up in St. Albans. I want to tell you a couple of things. We know who killed your father. And we're going to pick him up. Probably tomorrow or the day after. Another thing. We found your fingerprints, clear as day, on a certain mountain bicycle."

JB didn't say anything.

"I want you to come up here and tell me why I shouldn't charge you with tampering. At the least. Not tomorrow, I'm busy. The day after."

*   *   *

At seven that evening, Detective Sergeants Fred Davis and Bert Miller sat down with Lt. Ethel Collings. She was in charge of working things out with the New York State Police.

Ethel said, "I just got off the phone with Major Harold Ryan. He's head of New York State Police Troop B out of Plattsburgh. I knew him at Plattsburgh State, and we've worked well together over the years. He thinks we have more than enough for a search warrant, and almost enough on the murder charge. He and I are suggesting we send two detectives to interview Tyler, one from his office, Detective Trooper Jim Harris, and Bert. He says Harris is smart, but also tough if there's any rough stuff.

You'd drive up in an unmarked car, in plain clothes, start by saying we've found the snow machine by chance, and what does he have to say about it. Then sort of slide into the killing. See how far you get. There'd be two more troopers in another car just outside the drive. In addition, surveillance would be set up all around, on land. He's already got someone watching Tyler's movements.

"Bert, you and Harris would bring the warrant with you to search the house, outbuildings, and all vehicles including boats. You'd have an arrest warrant on dumping the snow machine and drug possession, suspicion of trafficking in narcotics. That's because of the added compartment on the machine and some meth residue we've found in there. We can hold him for a while on that.

"They'll have one police boat just around the corner, but beyond that, we'd be responsible for surveillance on the water. They don't want to know too much about what we're doing."

Fred asked, "When does this happen?"

"Noon tomorrow."

Chapter 21

THE CHASE, DAY TWO

New York authorities had agreed to send three cars. One, unmarked, would gently cruise past Skip's driveway and set up farther down Martin Lane in hopes of blocking that line of escape. The two detectives would be approaching the house in an unmarked car. A third cruiser with two troopers would pull into the drive of the house just to the north, number one Martin Lane. The New York State Police boat would be around the corner, ready if needed, with four troopers.

The border between New York and Vermont wiggles its way down the middle of the lake. At Brown Point, it's about four miles from the New York side. Three high-speed Vermont police boats were ready to get involved if Skip crossed this line. The line wasn't visible on the lake itself, of course, but it appeared clearly on GPS receivers. Davis hoped the Vermont boat captains would be willing to forget to check if the occasion called for it. Trooper Jones was on one of these boats, with a powerful scope mounted on a tripod.

Officially, this was a New York operation. But, by chance, a number of Vermont officers had decided to take the day off. Janice was fishing Willsboro Bay with her new friend and fishing mentor, Brian Allen, arriving at ten thirty. The bay was just south of Brown Point, enclosed by a long arm of land called Willsboro Point. The point was covered with little roads with summer houses on them, but all of them funneled to a single road leading out toward Willsboro. Janice and Brian were going back to the same spot where they had caught a bunch of fifteen-inch bass and incidentally had an excellent view of all water routes headed south away from Skip's.

Davis had also taken up fishing again, and at eleven thirty, he'd set up on the outside of Willsboro Point. At first he had wanted to take the Lyman Islander. But once burned, twice shy. He realized that if Skip did get away in the G3, he could slice open the Islander even more effectively than he had the old Lightning sailboat, many years ago. Instead, he brought the old Boston Whaler twenty-one-foot utility that the Davis Farm had had for many years. It had a white Evinrude fifty-horse engine, only about twenty years old. Practically new. The Whaler was an incredibly rugged boat, literally unsinkable, and much heavier than the G3.

With his boat anchored, Davis sat almost motionless, his fishing pole resting in his hands. The others might use the latest lures; he had a couple of night crawlers on a hook, with a nice, red-and-white plastic bobber. It matched his red-and-white-checked shirt.

Dick was in another borrowed bass boat, which was tied up at the boat launch in Port Douglass. He had been there since before dawn and had been out fishing several times already. This was a particularly fast boat, twenty feet with a 200-horsepower engine.

They saw themselves not as active participants in the arrest, but as observers. If by chance they saw something interesting, it would only be neighborly to let the New York police know. If Skip entered Vermont waters, he was theirs.

Luke was also taking the day off. The farm had a huge stake-bed truck used for transporting tractors, hay bales, or crops headed to market. Exactly at noon, he positioned himself at the neck of Willsboro Point. If he got a call from Janice or Davis, he could block the only road out in a couple of seconds, and then find a safe place to watch what happened.

All of this was marginally legal. The New York cops wouldn't be pleased. Bert and Davis suspected they wouldn't be surprised. But there was one little action that was not legal. Edward and Peter, the divers who had pulled the Yamaha snow machine out of the lake, had arrived with Dick. Just after dawn, the three men went out. As they neared the house next to Skip's, the two divers put on their scuba gear and slipped into the water. Peter was carrying a long socket wrench with a 1-1/8-inch socket and Edward a two-foot piece of two-by-four and a large flat-head screwdriver.

They positioned themselves under the aluminum dock. From there, they could watch the house without being seen. They watched for five or ten minutes. Edward was the lookout. No one seemed to be about. While Edward watched the house, Peter took the screwdriver and flattened two little metal tabs that locked the propeller nut in place. He jammed the two-by-four between the prop and the housing. Then he used the long wrench to remove the nut. This operation took three minutes.

They dropped below the surface and swam away.

*   *   *

Skip woke up at a comfortable hour of eight and made himself a cup of coffee. Then he went into town for breakfast, picking up a *Times* and a *Wall Street Journal* on the way. He sat at his favorite booth. The waitress knew what to bring him, and when. He was partial to the blueberry waffle, with maple syrup and just a little sour cream. He had to watch his cholesterol.

Gas prices were down just a bit, he read. Obama looked like he had figured it out. Merrill Lynch was selling off huge quantities of toxic mortgage securities at penny stock prices. The pundits in the Journal were of mixed opinion. Some were looking ahead to a strong '09. Others were looking for a downturn that could last a year. Skip thought, *Time to sell.* When he got home, he'd make some online trades.   Back home, he made a second pot of coffee and then sat in his favorite chair to read the rest of the paper. The most fun story concerned a soulmate of Skip's, a man named Samuel Downing III. Downing had been a hedge fund manager with a weakness the law uncharitably characterized as fraud. On the day in June when he was supposed to report for his prison sentence, Downing faked his suicide—his car had been found on the Bear Mountain Bridge in Upstate New York as if he'd jumped to his death. But nobody saw him jump, and no body was found. A few days later, he was sighted lining up to get on a plane a Logan Airport in Boston. At his second arraignment, he claimed he was too mentally distraught to enter a plea because of his drug therapy. Skip thought, *A man after my own heart. He really knows how to hedge.*

He started to doze around eleven thirty. He pulled his baseball hat down over his eyes.

Skip had set up four motion sensors and two cameras. Any significant movement on Martin Lane or on his own driveway or in his side yards set off a beep. A light on a control box showed which location had fired. One camera showed his parking area, the other the entrance to his driveway, along with a short section of Martin Lane. Above the control box, a small TV with a split screen monitored the cameras.

The beeping didn't usually mean much. It went off whenever a car went by. Sometimes animals in the woods set it off. The driveway sensor almost never fired because few people came to the house. He picked up the brim of the hat to look at the monitor, then let it fall back over his face.

At five minutes past noon, the control box lit up. First the sensor for the road itself fired twice. Then the driveway sensor fired. He looked at the little TV screen that showed the driveway, and his position was clear. There was a car there with two men getting out, and a state police cruiser was pulling in next door. In a moment, the doorbell rang.

After a moment's thought, he went with plan A. He was already packed. He was always packed. A backpack with everything he needed was on a table by his back door. All he had to do was get to somewhere where he could steal a car—one of his few mechanical abilities—and he was gone. He put his laptop in the backpack. This bag held everything he needed to renew his life elsewhere: some clothes, two passports, credit cards, cash. A side pocket held his revolver. Without exactly rushing, he went downstairs and out the basement door onto the back lawn.

If he was challenged from the water, he was not afraid to play rough. The G3 itself was much faster than it looked. All he needed was a couple of minutes in any parking lot or driveway, and he was thoroughly familiar with the most convenient possibilities. Willsboro Point was right there, and he knew where the unattended cars would be. He had keys for two of these cars in a pocket of his bag.

Fred and Luke's plan called for Skip, in a panic, to back quickly away from his dock. As he reversed, the propeller would spin itself off its shaft, leaving Skip stranded, a ripe fruit nicely presented for the New York State Police to pluck. But Skip was not at all in a panic. While the police were knocking on his door, he calmly untied the boat, started it up, and backed it out slowly and quietly, slowly enough that the propeller stayed in place. Then he pushed the throttle lever forward in one quick motion.

He loved the way the boat leaped forward. The bow rose up at a sharp angle, like a whale breaching. As it gained speed, it leveled off. The New York police in their boat a hundred yards offshore were taken by surprise. Their boat was faster than Skip's, but his was quicker off the blocks. Skip had the additional advantage of knowing exactly what he wanted to do. By the time they decided to give chase, Skip had shot across the bay and beached his boat next to a dock at the tip of Willsboro Point.

Detective Sgt. Fred Davis saw this from his boat not a hundred yards away, just off the point. Janice saw it from her similar position inside the bay.

At first Skip thought, *I'll never see this boat again.* But then he stuffed the keys in his pocket. *You never know. I might be back here in a few minutes.* He jogged up the lawn with his green bag. Skip had walked here many times and was on chatting terms with many of the residents. He knew of eight possible cars he could commandeer with little trouble. One family kept their car keys on a little board on the kitchen wall, neatly labeled. He had once borrowed a Camry from another man and made himself a copy of the key at the same time. The camp where he beached the boat was owned by an old man named George Smith and his wife Arlene, who had lots of grandchildren visiting each summer. Smith kept an old, battered, black Honda Civic for their use, and the key lived on a little nail inside the garage door. Skip had spent quite a few evenings chatting with the Smiths.

He grabbed the key, threw his bag onto the passenger seat, set his handgun on top of the bag, and drove off. Mr. Smith was tending his garden plot, his back to Skip. He was a bit deaf and didn't hear the engine at all. If he turned around, he might just think that one of his dozen grandchildren had taken his Honda to the store. It was true in a way; he was almost one of the family.

Skip had imagined situations like this many times. Over the past years, he had successfully eluded the police, but he'd been lucky. This was the first time he was in their sights, his first chase scene. But he felt he was in a reasonably safe position. The cops from the police boat would be close behind him, but they'd be on foot. A single road exited the point, and he would be there in about four minutes. It would take the cops at his house at least twenty minutes to drive there, racing along with their sirens screaming. If he made it off the point, he had many routes he could take to get away, and he wouldn't have to stop and consult his map: he knew them all. In a pinch, he had his gun. In a funny way, he thought, this was the most fun he'd had in a long time. He was driving fast, but not breakneck. No need to panic. In a few hours he could be picking up his new life. A few hours after that, a lot of money would disappear from Seward Tyler's accounts and reappear in other accounts that would never be traced.

For Fred, the idea that Luke would block the road leaving the point with the farm truck was the backup plan. Really, it was the backup to the backup of the backup plan. He wouldn't have agreed to it otherwise. Though he had anticipated the possibility, he was surprised to see it really happening. He had thought the trick with the propeller would work perfectly.

The backup plan was simple. Luke was sitting in a driveway where the road led off the point, just past a sharp turn. If needed, Fred would call Luke. Luke would simply pull the truck forward and block the road, and then retire to safety behind a nearby rock. Very possibly Skip would turn around and try to escape by boat.

As Fred saw Skip beach the G3, he immediately cut his anchor line with his knife, turned his boat south, and headed toward the narrow neck of the point. He had long since picked out a place to dock. But as he sped toward the neck, he got very anxious. His planning had already come unglued. What if Skip saw Luke? What if he shot Luke and drove off in the truck, for God's sake? That would be just the sort of thing Skip might do. All sorts of dangerous things could happen, and if they did, Luke would probably be the loser. As he remembered his and Luke's last encounter with Skip forty years ago, and how Skip had reacted then, he started to shake.

He decided not to call Luke. Better to let Skip go. Maybe the New York police would catch him. Too much risk. He started to calm down.

But Janice did call Luke. "He's headed to you by car, I think."

Luke shut his cell phone and almost immediately heard the car coming. He started the big truck and pulled into the road according to plan. The roadway was wooded, and Skip wouldn't see the obstruction until he made the turn. Luke didn't have time for the part of the plan where he would jump out of the truck and retire behind a rock to await developments.

Skip, getting a little more nervous as he approached his point of escape, made the turn too fast. As Luke watched, Skip veered right to avoid the truck. He was a good driver, but the car glanced against the stiff steel edge of the flatbed, right at his eye level. If he'd hit the truck much harder, Skip could have been beheaded. But he made the turn, just smashing out the window and putting a crease in the side of the Civic.

Luke couldn't help noticing that the basic shape of the gash was not that different than the one the G3 had sliced in the side of their sailboat years ago. But this time the outcome was a little different. Skip wasn't able to calmly regroup and drive off as if it never happened, casually popping open another beer. Instead, the car came to an abrupt stop against a two-foot pine tree at the side of the road just a few feet from the cab of Luke's truck.

The front corner of the old Civic was crushed. The steering wheel was pressing against Skip's chest. It might take the jaws of life to get him out. His left leg was torn up. Though Skip couldn't see exactly what had happened, he knew it hurt, and he could see a lot of blood.

His travel bag was sitting on the seat beside him with the gun on top. He was looking up at Luke. It didn't look like he was going to get back to the G3 for another breathtaking chase across the waves. He needed the police to come and get him out before he bled to death. But there was one thing he could do. It was agonizing to move, but he slowly reached over to grab the gun. Luke could see this happening, but he was scared, frozen. He tried to start the truck, but in his haste, he flooded the engine.

But as Skip reached for the weapon, another man walked up to the blown-out window. He was dressed in jeans and a red-checked flannel shirt. It was Davis. He reached in and snatched the gun by the barrel. He walked around to the driver's side and dropped the weapon on the ground.

"Not this time, Skip."

For a moment, the two men just looked at each other. There was no suggestion that Skip knew who he was looking at. He didn't say anything and neither did Davis. They must have looked at each other for ten seconds, but it seemed like a minute. Davis leaned down, wiped off the gun barrel, and stood up.

Luke, recovering his equanimity at the sight of his friend, calmly restarted the truck, clunked it into reverse, and backed up. Like any rural Vermonter, he gave his friend an understated wave as he forced the shifter into first and headed home. Davis answered with a smile and headed calmly back toward his boat.

Their earlier attempt to serve Skip up on a platter to the New York officers had failed, but Skip was definitely not going anywhere soon.

A few minutes later, as Luke drove home at thirty miles per hour, he had to pull onto the verge twice to let the racing police cars stream by.

Skip sat pinned to his seat, bleeding. It wasn't the fact that he would soon be caught that bothered him, or the fact that his chase had ended against a tree. That was a risk. He'd taken that risk.

More, it was the return of a feeling he'd had when the red Toyota pickup disappeared, and years ago when the G3 disappeared one night. It was the feeling that there was someone watching him all the time, someone who knew more about the situation than he did.

When three cruisers skidded to a halt next to the Honda, they found the wrecked car with a big, red-haired man behind the wheel, just passing out from loss of blood. A .32 caliber revolver lay on the ground. Nobody else was there.

Luke was heading home by land and Davis by water. Janice and Brian were calmly fishing in the bay, and getting some hits. "No point in wasting a good fishing opportunity," Brian said.

"OK with me," Janice answered. "I'm off today." She liked Brian, and he was cuter than her boyfriend.

Chapter 22

EVIDENCE

By two o'clock on August 8, Skip had been extracted from the stolen car with the jaws of life and rushed to the Champlain Valley Physicians Hospital in Plattsburgh. He was only half conscious. He'd lost a lot of blood. Surgeons were putting his leg back together and finding out he had three broken ribs but no serious internal damage. By 5 P.M., he was in a recovery room with a New York State Trooper on the door, though Skip wouldn't be going anywhere soon. He had not yet been charged.

The stolen Honda Civic was a treasure trove of evidence. Skip had been unable to part with Paul's wallet. It was a keepsake, a trophy, and it was in his pocket when he was extracted from the car. They had the revolver, which had been sitting on the ground outside the Honda Civic, though there was nothing positive tying that gun to the killing except that it was the right type of weapon. In Skip's garage, they found Paul's old snow machine and the cargo sled, outfitted with additional clever compartments.

They had enough DNA to build an entirely new Paul Brearley from scratch if they only knew how. There was some on the cargo sled, some on the wallet, and some from a blood smear on a pair of Skip's gloves they found in his garage. Now that they had Skip's fingerprints, they were able to find matches from the house on Osprey Island, in spite of Skip's efforts to wipe the place down. The best prints were from the underside of the toilet seat.

As soon as Skip was fully conscious, they had all they needed for a very solid arrest and arraignment in New York, followed by extradition to Vermont.

The search of the stucco house didn't yield much new information. Narcotics dogs had gone wild in the house, but the samples they found were minute and still being analyzed. Skip didn't himself use drugs. He was a beer guy. Skip's computer was mostly used to manage his investments. They were looking into the financial evidence, trying to locate bank accounts.

*   *   *

Two days later, on August 10, Skip was healing rapidly, but not quite ready to be charged. Trooper Jim Harris was on guard most of the time; he'd lost Skip once and didn't plan to lose him again.

Detective Sgt. Fred Davis was in his office looking through the evidence one more time. They had more than enough for an arrest. All they lacked was a bullet from Paul's body to match the .32 Skip was carrying. They would keep looking for that at Osprey Island. Yet some of the basics were still unknown. What was Skip doing there in the first place? They knew from their examination of the Yamaha that the machine had broken down there; the shift cable had come free right at the transmission. But they didn't know exactly what Skip was doing on the lake, except that it probably involved drugs. They didn't really know what had led to the shooting. They didn't know if either man remembered their meeting decades earlier, or recognized each other at the island, or expected the other to be there.

They didn't need to interview Skip. They had enough to convict him. The only better evidence would have been eyewitnesses armed with cameras at the moment the trigger was pulled. They didn't need to cleverly trick Skip into revealing information in order to make the case.

Davis frowned as he looked over the list. He wanted everything tied up. Even more, he wanted a better understanding of the underlying story: why Paul left, why he returned, why he went to Osprey Island that day, and why these things had led to his death. He knew he would probably never know. He'd have to settle for giving Skip a nice, long jail term.

Davis couldn't participate in Skip's interviews because of their history. It would ruin the legal case, poison the evidence. He would be accused of bias, and fairly so.

He joined Bert, Janice, and Ethel in the squad room.

Ethel said, "They're planning to charge Skip with the murder tomorrow afternoon and read him his rights. The doctors say he'll be mentally recovered by then and not on anything stronger than Tylenol. In a few days he'll be able to walk, he'll be arraigned, and we can extradite him back here. Tomorrow morning might be our last chance to talk to him before he has a lawyer and goes silent on us. Bert, take Janice over in the morning and get him talking if you can. I'd say, Bert, you go in there for a bit. Then have Janice go in a little later. Maybe a woman will get something from him a man couldn't."

Davis wanted to do these interviews himself. He wanted to see if Skip recognized him from the crash scene, if he remembered the man in the flannel shirt who disarmed him. He wanted to find out what Skip knew or thought or remembered about Paul. He wanted to find out if Skip even remembered destroying a small sailboat with two boys in it years and years ago. At the same time, he thought Janice might be able to get him talking where he or Bert might not. It would be an opportunity for her, questioning her first murderer. At the beginning of the case, only a few months ago, Janice had been the neophyte, coming along for the ride, the apprentice. But they had learned that in addition to ordinary competence and reliability, she was smart and good at puzzles, at filling in the blanks. A police investigation mostly consisted of filling in the blanks. When these conversations took place, he'd be in the hospital waiting room downstairs, waiting.

*   *   *

At ten the next morning, Bert, Janice, and Fred arrived at the hospital. Fred waited downstairs. Skip had been moved to a regular hospital room at the end of the hall. Trooper Jim Harris was seated at the door. Skip was sitting up in bed reading the *New York Times* as if it were an ordinary day. He had a cup of coffee on the rolling hospital table in his lap. His movements were a little awkward; he had a sling on his left arm. He could use the fingers but couldn't move the arm very far. His left leg was in a full cast. There was still a bandage on his forehead.

Bert walked in by himself. He said, "I'm Detective Sgt. Bert Miller of the Vermont State Police. We've really got about all the evidence we could want. Some guys found your Yamaha with their anchor, waiting out a storm. They holed up in that cove overnight. We have a photo of you loading Paul's snow machine on your truck. For example. There's a lot more. Photos from the border. DNA. It's great having Paul's wallet. Why did you hang on to that? There are a few things you could clear up for us."

"Really."

"For example, what were you doing out there in the first place? We know you shot Paul Brearley, but we don't know why. What happened?" He waited a long minute. Then, "Why did you sink your snow machine? Why were you out there that day?" He moved a chair closer to the bed and sat quietly. Maybe Skip would try to develop a story line that left him largely innocent.

Bert sat there for another forty minutes, asking questions, mentioning little pieces of evidence, but the last word he heard from Skip was "really." Skip seemed calm, unruffled, not that interested in what Bert was doing. He continued reading his paper, sipping his coffee.

Though Skip was in a hospital bed under guard with two casts and a head injury, he seemed utterly composed, as if he'd just gotten back from walking his dog and was enjoying his morning paper.

In fact, Skip's outward calm wasn't a pose. He really was comfortable there. At the same time, he was thinking about ways to improve his position. It was like when he was driving, just rolling along, but also scanning the fields for deer, watching the road far ahead for fox, turkeys, or potholes that might require a response. So far, though, scanning the road ahead hadn't led to much.

He was bothered by the unexplained things that had undone him. The Yamaha snow machine was practically new, top-of-the-line Japanese technology. It should never have broken down near Osprey Island. The disappearance and reappearance of the red Toyota. It wasn't just that these things caused his capture. It was that they slightly altered his sense of himself. He always saw himself as the person driving events. Usually that was true, but not now. It was like the time when his boat vanished in the night. Skip was an empiricist. These things bothered him.

Bert thought Skip might be tiring a little; he'd slipped down an inch or two in the bed.

After another ten minutes, Bert walked out, without a parting word. Ten minutes after that, Janice went in alone. She was in uniform and didn't introduce herself. She sat down in the chair and pulled it closer to the bed. Looking at a piece of paper, she asked, "Skip, what about work? It says here you did a little real estate work, and worked as a stockbroker for a bit. Why did you stop?"

Skip smiled. "If you didn't have to work, would you?" Skip seemed to have a knack for comments that shut down a topic.

"Tell us about the day of the killing. What happened? Why kill Paul

Brearley?" Silence. She continued, "Was Paul meeting you there?"

"Paul who?"

Janice said, "We know you knew Paul as a young man. We know you spent a lot of time together, water-skiing, visiting back and forth. You tried to date a girl from Osprey Island. A girl named Abby. She says you were a little creepy. She says she ran away."

Skip wasn't quite ready for this. He thought that part of his life was far enough in the past to escape notice. He wanted to get his answer right. He was silent for a minute, as he decided on an approach to this line of questions. He was tiring a little. His arm hurt. He needed more Tylenol.

"Really?" he said.

"Tell us about your relationships? Ever been married?"

"No."

"Girlfriends?"

"Not at the moment." He wasn't giving out names. But Janice thought the energy level in the room spiked.

Janice said, "I really don't get it. What do you do with yourself?"

Skip picked up his paper and awkwardly flipped to the financial page. Except for discussion with the orthopedist and requests to the nurses, it was the last time he spoke that day. Janice sat there another five minutes, then left.

As she walked out, Detective Trooper Jim Harris walked in. He formally arrested Seward Tyler on charges of murder, breaking and entering, drug trafficking, and the sinking of the snow machine and read him his rights. Skip maintained his silence. There was nothing to gain by speaking.

*   *   *

On August 13, two days later, on their morning rounds, Skip's internist and orthopedist determined that his arm had fully recovered, though his ribs still hurt. The leg cast would stay on for several weeks, but he could walk on crutches. That afternoon, Skip was indicted in a Plattsburgh courtroom, where he continued his policy of silence, except to say "not guilty." He was immediately extradited and transported to Vermont, where he was placed in the St. Albans Police jail.

Janice and Bert interviewed Skip, with his lawyer Farrell Dodd present, four more times over the next two weeks with no results.

Chapter 23

MORE EVIDENCE

The search for new evidence continued, though everyone had other cases to work on, too. Bert, Janice, and Davis continued to meet about the case, though less often.

Ethel had found out that Skip had inherited enough money to live on, mostly the proceeds from his parents' other homes, and some investments. He wasn't a big spender and had no family other than a sister who lived in California. By phone, she claimed not to have seen or spoken to Skip in fifteen years. He had attempted to make an honest living at one point, working as a real estate agent for one period and as a stockbroker a few years later. During the periods when he held an actual job, he seemed to be honest in his dealings.

*   *   *

Bert, Davis, and Janice met at the Vietnamese restaurant in Winooski one week after Skip's return to Vermont. As usual, Davis ordered the #25, Janice and Bert the chicken soup, and as usual Bert was having trouble with the big pottery spoon. Janice was doing it all with the chopsticks, no problem.

Bert said, "We need more on the drug angle. We don't have strong evidence there. We know he was dealing and transporting, but we can't prove it." He turned to his partner. "Freddy, talk to them at Rouses Point again. Find out if he took that cruiser into Canada. Talk to them at the marina. Let's find out what he does with himself. Find out if he travels, and how he pays for tickets. He's got to do something! See who he travels with. Janice, I like the relationships angle, there has to be something there. It's odd that there's no relationship history."

Janice said, "Well, we don't know that he's been single. But he can't have been just sitting in that white house all this time, watching his monitors."

Bert said, "Well, maybe he has been mostly sitting there. He didn't go to the gym, wasn't in the tennis club. He was recognized in local stores, like the hardware and grocery, but made very little impression on people. A few of the summer people on Willsboro Point remembered him but had no new information about him; he was just a neighbor to chat with in passing. In the diner, he was friendly but not chatty. He had a credit card, but it was only used for mundane purchases like gas or food. There were no airline tickets on it, for example." After a moment, he said, "From what we've seen so far, he doesn't seem to need much human companionship."

*   *   *

The next morning, Detective Sgt. Davis drove back to the marina at Rouses Point, the New York town that sat where the lake narrowed to become the Richelieu River. It had once been an important port; mansions lined its main drag. The mansions, and the town, were now a bit down-at-heel, but the place was still important to boaters, and there were several big marinas along the water. A beautiful arched bridge looped over to Vermont. The pilings for the old railroad bridge still stuck up out of the water, like dead trees in a swamp. Two stone breakwaters reached far into the bay, protecting the marinas. Davis could picture a time when trains lined up at the station and freighters were three deep on the docks.

Between the marina docks and the road was a scrubby field. In winter, it would be covered in boats shrouded in white plastic, propped up by groups of rugged tripods made of pipe or heavy timbers. Most of the boats were still in the water, but a few were sitting there unused on their stilts, some with For Sale signs.

The most interesting was a shabby, forlorn, forty-foot houseboat sitting right on the gravel. The long and narrow steel hull might have once been a canalboat, but the cabin on top looked as if it had been framed up over a long weekend by amateur carpenters who were a little under the weather. The boat was decorated like a hunting camp, with dark paneling inside and a lot of male clutter. Firewood and some old furniture were lashed to the roof. Through the window, Davis could see deer antlers on a wall plaque next to a calendar for 1976 with a picture of Farrah Fawcett in her red bathing suit. On the outside there was a hand-lettered sign: "No girls allowed." Davis thought, *If you see the boat, you can pretty much tell what the owners are like.*

Next to it sat Skip's cabin cruiser. Davis walked around it twice, slowly. The last time he had seen the boat, it had been brand-new, a shining fiberglass trophy. The fiberglass had lost its sheen, but otherwise the boat looked well cared for. They already had a warrant to search it.

Propped up on stilts like this, it was hard to inspect the inside of the boat without a ladder. But the hull, propellers, and keel were at eye level. A really good boat, like his Lyman Islander, looked elegant in or out of the water. Most of these more modern plastic boats looked ungainly ashore, like a too-tall teenager.

Davis would leave the inside search to the crime scene team. But as he made a final circuit, he noticed there were two holes in the boat's keel, about an inch in diameter and perhaps four feet apart. He had never seen holes like that in a boat's keel. They had no nautical purpose. But he knew exactly what they were for. He snapped a picture with his little camera. He took a tape measure out of his bag and measured the location of the holes and the distance between them.

He wondered if the crime scene people would figure out the holes, or even notice them. While they searched the boat, he would search the route the boat would have taken north when in use. Before leaving, he talked to the marina owner, a sunbaked man in his fifties named Harris McNeill. Davis found him on the gas dock, where a large cruiser was having trouble docking in the stiff wind. It was like parallel parking where the road was moving up and down and side to side at the same time. The big boat was threatening to bang into the other boats at the long dock. Davis helped bring the boat in safely. The two men talked on the shore while a teenage boy filled the boat's tank.

McNeill had just the remnants of a Maine or old-time Vermont accent. "Of course I know Mr. Tyler. He's come here longer than I've had this place, and that's been fifteen years. This is the first year he hasn't launched the boat. Usually he puts in June first. We pull it out again on October first. We don't see him in between, except maybe once or twice for diesel. But I see him go by headed north maybe three or four times a year, and he comes back several days later."

Davis asked, "Who's with him?"

McNeill said, "Nobody. Maybe once he had a woman with him, I'm not sure. That's unusual. Most people have a girlfriend, kids, or a buddy. I've never seen anybody with him, though they would never let him go through the canal solo; I've tried. They are very strict about having two people on board at the locks."

The big boat had been gassed up and was ready to set out. McNeill said, "Listen, I've got to get this guy out of here before he destroys one of these million-dollar sailboats. He doesn't have a lot of control over his boat." He tipped his hat and moved toward the dock, where the dock boy and the boat's owner were untying the vessel. Then he turned halfway back. "I'll tell you one thing, though. Tyler didn't say much, and he wasn't that friendly a guy. But he could really drive a boat. Even in a wind like that, he'd bring in that big boat of his sweet as could be."

Davis said, "Mr. McNeill, we're going to have to search his cruiser. There will be a crew up here in an hour or two with a warrant, and they'll be here several hours. It shouldn't disrupt what you're doing."

McNeill nodded and turned back to the dock.

Davis called Ethel to set up the search. "Ethel, could you have them go through Skip's cruiser? It's up on a cradle at Rouses Point. They're going to have to spend all day at it. There are about a thousand compartments that could be important."

Davis got back into his car to work his way north along the Richelieu River. At both customs docks, he confirmed McNeill's description of Skip. On average, Skip had made trips three times a summer, almost always by himself. He was polite, well-dressed, and completely cooperative. The Canadian customs people had never had occasion to search the boat or have more than a casual interview with him. The Americans at the US Customs dock, always more suspicious, had searched the boat once, three years ago. The agent who had made the search was still working on the dock, and he remembered making the search. Two men and a dog had spent an hour at it and found nothing.

Davis's next stop was Saint-Jean-sur-Richelieu thirty miles downriver. This was a little city at the southern end of the narrow Chambly Canal that bypassed the white water sections of the river. It wasn't a big canal, like the Erie, but an intimate little thing with a towpath and small, narrow locks. As the canal had been restored, the town had become a tourist destination for boaters, walkers, and cyclists. When Davis stopped in at lock 9, there were a dozen cyclists using the old towpath and several determined runners. Three families with small children were watching the boats go through the lock from behind a railing.

Nobody at the lock remembered Skip or his boat. Once they collected their fees, the lockkeepers didn't think about individual boats. But they assured Davis that if Skip Tyler had gone through the lock, there would have been two people on board to handle the ropes that positioned the boat in the lock. That meant Skip must have had someone to help him, or recruited someone on the spot.

At lock 8, the story was the same, but Davis thought the fortyish woman he talked to might be holding something back. She seemed to recognize the snapshot of Skip that Davis showed her. He wondered if she had let him go through solo, perhaps accepting a small gratuity in return. Or maybe she knew him better than that; he took her name in case he wanted to pursue this later. He stopped at two more locks and heard basically the same story, or lack of story.

He had better luck at his last stop, a marina near Sorel where the Richelieu joined the Saint Lawrence River. According to the dock boy, Skip was a regular customer there over several years and a big tipper. Skip would often tie up there for two or three days at a time. A variety of people, male and female, would be seen in and around his boat, coming and going through the day. It was a big marina; they didn't pay a lot of attention. It was generally a party scene, with quite a bit of drinking. Skip always paid cash.

Davis headed home. But what he learned at the marina opened up a tangible new area of investigation. He would be back, or perhaps Dick Fowler or another member of their team. They'd have to work with the Canadian authorities.

*   *   *

The scene-of-crime team spent two days going over the thirty-five-foot cruiser. A boat is not easy to search. It has dozens of odd-shaped compartments with odd-shaped voids between them, some of them almost invisible. It would be easy to contrive ways to hide things. A cruiser has a galley with even more little compartments and a head that does not invite careful search. You'd have to be completely knowledgeable about a particular model of boat to be able to tell the difference between a compartment that held a large chunk of foam flotation, or maybe some cleaning supplies, from one that was transporting drugs. At the border, it would take many hours to search a boat of this size, and a complete search was impossible.

After two days, the searchers had found sixty-four compartments, cubbies, voids, and access panels. Some they had inspected with a tiny camera on a flexible stalk, which could look in places beyond the eye's reach. They had drilled a few holes to insert this device into cavities that seemed suspicious. Dogs had sniffed their way through the boat. They found nothing. Not being boaters, the searchers never noticed the two one-inch holes in the keel.

Davis, however, was already looking for something that went with the pair of holes, and as a boatbuilder he had a pretty good idea what it would be. He called the New York State Police and arranged to go to Skip's house again with a New York officer for another look around. They spent two hours at it, but nothing suggestive came to light.

But on his way home, Davis passed one of those self-storage rental places with row upon row of garagelike compartments and pulled in. The owner was there and looked at a photograph Davis showed him.

"Skip? Yeah, I know Mr. Tyler."

By five that afternoon, they had a warrant. Davis and the New York State Police officer were standing at the door to Skip's storage compartment. It was one of the half-sized units, with a four-foot-wide door. The owner opened the door.

They saw some old furniture, fishing gear, a couple of boxes of books, some tools, and a fiberglass construction. It was about six feet long and two feet wide, a slender and aerodynamically shaped box, something like the ski carriers people put on their car roofs. It had a slot down the middle about two inches wide. At each end were flat flanges with holes in them. Davis took a tape measure out of his bag and determined that they were one-inch holes and that they were four feet apart, center to center. Around the perimeter of the box was a row of bolts about six inches apart. Obviously the unit separated into halves, like a clam. Neither of the detectives touched it, but Davis took a few photos. Then they sealed the little rental unit. The gadget would fit perfectly on the keel of Skip's cruiser and never be noticed.

Davis called in. They decided to meet later that evening. The technical search would be the next day.

*   *   *

At the next interview with Skip, Bert slid three photos across the table. One showed the storage room with the door open. One showed the fiberglass container opened up like a suitcase lying on the paved driveway in front of the container. Next to the fiberglass unit was a large German shepherd looking at the box and straining at his leash. The dog handler's hand was just in the frame.

"Skip, it's interesting. By coincidence, that slot there is about the same width as the keel on your nice, old cruiser."

Farrell Dodd cut in. "I think we're done for today."

*   *   *

Bert, Janice, and Davis met again that afternoon and were joined by Ethel Collings and Dick Fowler. It was time to regroup.

Dick had been looking for any records of Skip's travels. He had begun his search in Plattsburgh. "I've been stopping by travel agents. I got as far as the E's. But after talking to them, I realized I was probably wasting my time. If I were Skip and I wanted to skip town without being noticed, I'd get my tickets online, pay by credit card, and then board at some very busy airport, or a remote one. Albany or Manchester maybe. The last thing I would do would be to show my face to a travel agent. Though I'll keep looking if you want me to."

Neither Davis nor Bert answered quite yet. They wanted to hear everything. Davis was thinking Dick should go back up to the marina where Skip had docked his boat in Canada, near Sorel.

Ethel, who was usually matter-of-fact about everything, was excited. "We've broadcast our information about Skip—the prints, the ballistics information, the photos, and so on. There's a very determined investigator down in Panama. One of these guys who checks everything three times. First he looked through his collection of crimes involving thirty-two caliber revolvers like Skip's. He found print matches on two of those cases. Both drug killings. He had a slug from one of the cases and it matched our ballistics information. He's taking our photographs around right now. It could be a while before he knows any more. He's sending reports on the crimes that go with the gun."

Her next announcement was more important. It would give them real information. "And we've found the real Paul Baer. He's a homeless guy. He's in a hospital in New York City right now; they just took out part of a lung. Apparently he's been living there recently but had been in Albany for years. He looks sort of like our Paul." She smiled. It was one of the more demonstrative gestures they could remember her making.

Davis spoke next. "That's brilliant. OK, let's finish this." The case was dragging on, and he had other things to think about. "Bert and Janice, I think you just keep doing what you're doing and sort things out with the state's attorney. Dick, unless somebody has a better idea, I'd like you to go to that marina in Sorel. Maybe also dig into the marina in Rouses Point. Just do what you do. I'm going to the big city."

As they stood up, he added another thought. "No deals. We don't need to make a deal. I'd say hold back with all this new Panama stuff, see if you can string him along a little and get him to tell us what really happened on Osprey Island."

*   *   *

Davis made three calls. The first was to Bellevue Hospital to make sure Baer would stay put. They told him the old man wasn't going anywhere soon, maybe never.

Then he called Cassandra Brearley, Paul's former wife. He had her on his speed dial. He'd called her every two weeks all summer, but she was screening her calls and never picked up his. This time, she did.

"Detective Davis. I wondered if you'd given up on me."

"Ms. Brearley, I'm going to be in New York tomorrow. Will you talk to me?"

"Yes. My stupid son would be in jail, or heading there, without you. You could have busted him over his father's truck. So I owe you for that. Call me when you get here, we'll set something up."

The third call was to Pliny. By now, he had Pliny on speed dial, too.

"Pliny, it's Fred Davis."

"Hi. How's the case going?"

"Except for the fact that we don't know the most important things, fine. We have plenty of evidence. But that's not why I'm calling. We've found Paul Baer. The real one. He's in Bellevue Hospital, in rough shape. I'm heading down there in the morning. Do you want to come along?"

It was hard to keep the two Pauls straight. But the real Paul Baer had known their Paul for a long time. He might be too sick to talk or know nothing new. But they might get lucky.

"When do we leave? I have to go to New York anyway."

*　　*　　*

They left early the next morning. Davis's route followed the water: along the lake, along the canal, then along the Hudson, parallel to the route he would have taken by boat had the summer gone as planned. It was sunny, warm, a good day for a drive in the country.

The two men had spent a lot of time together, always talking about the case. But they had all day, and their conversations expanded.

Pliny told Paul about the churches where he had worked and some funny stories about pastoral life. He told him about two years spent in Africa, in a mission school. He told him about his wife. She had been the minister's wife for twenty years, then gone back to school to be a teacher. She'd been dead for fifteen years, from cancer. He'd never wanted to remarry.

Davis asked him, "Why did you become a minister?"

"Well, all the Plinys are ministers. I didn't figure out until I was standing in a pulpit for the first time that I didn't have to do it. But it suits me. I like to be busy, but I don't like to work too much. It's one of the few jobs where you can draw a salary for sitting in your study half the time.

"In college, I felt called to it, and I'm glad I've done it. It's an odd thing to do, though—I know that."

Davis told Pliny the history of the farm and about his decision to leave. He told him about his abbreviated legal career, how he drifted into police work and found ways to spend time in or around the water.

He told him about the boat barn and his love of fixing up old wooden boats. Pliny's openness about his own story made Fred a little less guarded than he usually was. "Sometimes I wish I had just stuck with boats," he said. "I'm OK with people, but I really know how to relate to a piece of wood."

Then he talked about his marriage. How he met Diane, their life together, coming up to Vermont, her success as a lawyer. "I think our separation started when I figured out I didn't like being a lawyer. When I got up in front of a judge, I didn't feel, *Oh, this is where I was meant to be,* but *Oh no, get me out of here.* I didn't like being indoors all the time. I didn't like the trickiness of the law, its relativity—my client, right or wrong. I'm moralistic. When I defended a crook, sometimes I wanted to lose the case. I thought police work might be closer to my way of thinking, and it has been. And I get to be outside most of the time.

"But Diane's family," he continued, "were immigrants. They were all about moving up, being professionals, becoming prosperous. To her, being a cop was going backward. Her uncle and two of her brothers were cops. Of course, that was just one issue. I think my work got in the way. She could work all day on some horror of a case, then come home and be normal. I'd get all wrapped up in things. I wasn't always there for her. I wasn't always there for my son, either. I missed a few soccer games and school concerts. I forgot a couple of birthdays and anniversaries."

They were driving along Route 4, just crossing the canal. "You know, I'd like a redo on those years. I could do it better now. To tell you the truth, I want her back. And my son, too."

Davis had never exactly said these things out loud to anyone before, though Luke understood them without discussion. They had passed across the screen of his mind a few times, sort of blinking behind his other thoughts, enough to upset him, but never in big letters, nice and clear, in simple, declarative sentences across the middle of the screen.

"You know, Pliny, you are good at this. You just sit there, and I start confessing."

A moment later, Pliny asked, "Does she know that?"

Fred's mind had drifted. "Know what?"

"That you want her back."

"Well, she's probably figured it out by now."

With a little smile, Pliny looked at Fred. But Fred was looking at the road ahead. "You might try telling her. 'Diane, I want you back more than anything'—something along those lines. You know, a stronger hint might do the trick."

Fred was eyeballing a nice-looking wooden rowboat on a trailer behind the car in front. Pliny said, "Of course, that's one of the great things about being a minister—you're supposed to dole out a little advice, even if people ignore it."

They were in New York by noon. Baer was hooked up to various tubes and monitors, barely able to move. The doctors didn't know if he'd recover, but the old man seemed to have surprising powers of recuperation for an alcoholic with lung cancer. He was a tall, scrawny man of the same general type as Paul Brearley—sort of rangy—and he had a distinctive round white beard, which looked weirdly familiar to Davis.

Fred told him about Paul Brearley's death. The old man—he wasn't that old, really, but he looked it—was obviously shaken by the news. His face dropped. "I'm so sorry to hear that. I liked Paul a lot."

He was happy to tell the story.

"I ran into Paul in Malone, maybe fifteen or sixteen years ago. I used to like to spend the summer up there. I'm from there." Malone, New York, up near Canada, was a good place to disappear into. "I had a bit of a life then. I would work sometimes. I had a room there every summer. I like to fish. I'd get odd jobs to keep alive, but I was barely making my rent and having trouble covering my bar tabs. I like to do my drinking in bars. I don't go for the lonely-guy-with-a-paper-bag thing. I like people!

"Anyway, one summer—I'm not sure exactly which one—I met Paul. He was on the next stool, spending more time than necessary on a pint of beer. He was never a very accomplished drinker, strictly amateur. Well, we both noticed that we looked alike. He said, 'If I had a beard like that, nobody would be able to tell us apart.' I was a lot bigger then, a big, strapping man.

"It turned out he needed an identity—and I didn't. Basically I sold him mine. Or maybe it would be better to say I sold him a fifty percent stake in it. You could say he invested in me!" He started laughing and coughing and didn't stop for a minute. He was enjoying telling his story.

"I leased him myself for two hundred and fifty dollars a month. You could say I agreed to do his drinking for him so he wouldn't have to bother. Sort of a drinking subcontractor. Every month, I'd get an envelope with some cash. I'd email him where to send it, usually general delivery somewhere. It's hard to build a new identity from scratch but surprisingly easy to share one. He got duplicates of my license, Social Security card, etcetera. I think he may have paid taxes, I'm not sure. I think he might have had a credit card, too."

Davis realized he was getting a bunch of new leads to follow up, things

259

Ethel and Janice could run down quickly. He liked the real Paul Baer. "You emailed him?"

"Well, wherever there's a public library, I have an office. People like me spend a lot of time in libraries. That's why we are so wise." More laughing and coughing. "The two of us usually got together once or twice a year, somewhere in the North Country. He was fun to talk to. My brother. My twin, I guess."

"I don't suppose you remember his email?"

"Of course I do," replied Baer. "We used the same one—debaer@NCmail.com. He used it a lot more than I did—he did some business with it. Guiding customers would contact him that way. I could track his movement through these guiding deals. A customer would email him, or a guide service. He had some camping buddies he liked to go on more serious trips with up to Canada, way the fuck up there. They'd go out in the wilderness in a canoe for weeks every fall. I never could really understand that part of his life. Why put yourself through that kind of effort? But it was fun for him. You know, the challenge."

"What did you talk about?"

"Nothing fancy. With the right guy, I like to talk a little philosophy. Nothing wakes me up like a good debate about religion. He'd do that a little; he was smart and educated. But really he just wanted to talk about ordinary stuff, politics, the weather. He took me fishing a few times. That guy knew how to fish, I'll tell you. If I live, I'll miss him."

Davis thought, *Will the real Paul Baer please stand up? This one might not be doing that anytime soon, if ever.* He said, "Here's my email and phone. Stay in touch when you get out of here, will you?"

"Thanks."

Davis started to get up to leave, but Pliny reached out his hand. Pliny wasn't really supposed to be there—this was police business, and Fred was supposed to ask the questions. But Pliny wasn't leaving yet.

"What did our Paul say about his life? Did he talk about it? Why did he leave? Did he give you any explanation? Actually, do you have any papers of his that might tell us something?" Davis had never seen Pliny so agitated.

Baer didn't answer at first. He looked like he might be nodding off. "Give me a minute, I'm thinking back." After a minute, he continued. "I don't know of any papers offhand. Though you could look in our room in Malone. Sometimes he used my little room in Malone. There might be something there."

Baer closed his eyes for another minute. Davis could see Pliny was about to press him and signaled with his hand to wait.

Finally the old man started talking again. His voice seemed a little stronger. "In a way, Paul was one of my closest friends. When I first met him and we started talking about sharing my identity, so to speak, he had to tell me something. Basically he said he had walked away from his life, that he had a wife and son. He wasn't some sort of crook on the lam. That's all he was willing to say.

"I love to talk. I'm happy at any point to tell you about my extensive love life or any other intimate stuff I can get you to listen to. And I love gossip. It's fun to hear about personal stuff, the juicier the better. I tried every way I could think of to gently pry out Paul's story. He was very good at not answering in a polite way or changing the subject. I think I was the only person who knew that he used to be somebody else.

"But clues leak out," continued Baer. "Over the years I picked up a few things. He'd been a minister, written books. He was from New England—I could tell that from his voice, from the places he talked about. He was a big reader. I could see what he was reading. He made some comment that let me know what year he walked away from his life. He mentioned Lake Champlain quite a bit. He'd go back there in the winter, which was pretty strange until I thought about it. I could see he'd been an athlete just from the way he moved. Once I saw him hitting tennis balls with some high school kids. It was obvious he'd played a lot of tennis. Well, that tells me his family had some money. You don't row or swim or play tennis if your family doesn't have money. After a few years,

261

I had a rough idea about his life. He was an elite kind of guy, to put it all together. And of course, he was very well-spoken.

"Sometimes I'd just say, 'Tell me about your life.' I think he enjoyed being a little cryptic with me. Occasionally he'd be more forthcoming—usually out on the water someplace. Once I asked him straight out, 'Why did you leave? Why did you walk away?' And he sort of answered me. He said, 'Well, if I knew then what I know now, I'd never have left.' I asked him, 'Well, what have you learned?' And he said, 'I learned that in the end, it's easier to solve problems than run away from them. And I learned that you can ruin your life, throw it away, in one day.' That's a word-for-word quote. He said it exactly like that.

"About three years ago, I figured out who he was," finished Baer. "It's amazing what you can figure out with Google if you have time on your hands, and I do. I found out the whole story, Osprey Island and so on. I've actually read his books. In fact, I have a signed copy, which I bought used over the web. It's inscribed, 'Frida, thanks for coming to my talk. You contributed a lot to the discussion.' I wonder who Frida was. I didn't tell him I'd found him out. But I did needle him a little, drop a few hints. If you go to that room in Malone, you'll see that book."

Pliny said, "Paul, I hope you get better soon." He was writing down his email on a scrap of paper, along with his phone numbers. "I want to stay in touch with you. Before he left, Paul was a very important person to me. I care how he died, why he left. For twenty years, I talked to him a lot and knew what he was thinking. I'd like to find out what he was thinking about for the next eighteen years. I'll come visit you anytime you want, and if you want to visit me, just call me anytime. And if you know of anything he might have written, I'd really like you to tell me."

The two men walked out into the midday sun. Pliny took a subway downtown to Wall Street to see his broker. For Davis, it was a half-hour walk to Cass's apartment in Union Square.

*   *   *

Cass was a striking woman. She was fairly tall, dark-haired, buxom but trim. She looked like she spent a lot of time at dance classes of some sort; her feet pointed out a little, like a dancer's. She radiated a lot of energy. She must have been extremely distracting in her twenties and thirties. Her hair was still long and straight but there was a lot of gray in it. She might have had the same hairdo back then. But her outfit was up-to-date, fashionable in a New York way. They walked to a coffee shop near her apartment.

"Just call me Cass, please. Where's Pliny?"

"He went to see his broker."

"He knows you'll get more out of me if he isn't here. I'm sure he has a lot to talk over with his broker. I think he's even older than Pliny."

"Thanks for seeing me. I know none of this is easy. Obviously you know things about Paul in 1990. I've been trying to understand him, why he might have taken off that way, and I really don't understand much."

"Well, it's not that complicated. About two weeks before he left, I told him I was divorcing him. I have to say, I've never really talked about this. Only a couple of my girlfriends know anything about it, and they get a very edited version. I don't like to be known as the woman whose husband disappeared then came back and all that. It's too disruptive to my life. This is just between us. I don't think anybody at the island really knows this stuff."

Davis decided not to interject too many questions. She knew what he needed to know, and he didn't.

"Paul was a very beautiful boy, unusually beautiful. For quite a few years I thought we were doing pretty good. He was so *successful* at everything. Everybody loved him. He was no nice, so balanced. He was so nice to me. He did the dishes, stuff like that. We were a great team—we got a lot done as a couple. You know, a minister isn't just a minister. He's a small organization, and the wife is the VP, or maybe the CEO.

"But I was on edge sometimes," continued Cass, fidgeting with her cup. "I didn't know why, exactly. Our personal life seemed good. There

263

was sex there, but there just wasn't *Paul* there. That's what I figured out later. He was playing a role.

"People used to think, Oh, Paul ran off with another woman. But actually, I met someone. I went to a retreat that winter, a meditation thing. There was a guy there. He wasn't particularly a hunk or a jock the way Paul was. He didn't write books. He wasn't eloquent. But he was *there*. He was totally present. That was a whole new thing for me. A whole new idea about sex, and about talking to someone.

"Anyway, after agonizing about things for a few months, I told Paul I was leaving him. I think he couldn't imagine that anyone would possibly want to leave him. He was really vain, actually. He was vain about his modesty! But he asked me to explain why I was leaving him, and I did. I told him what happened at the meditation retreat. And you know, I think he understood what I was saying. In his own way, he was honest. He knew how to listen.

"I don't know exactly what happened between that conversation and him vanishing. I've often thought, why not just have a divorce, like anybody else, with a year or two of suffering, some trouble for JB, and then everybody moves on? Was that too much to ask? But no. He has to make a big deal of it, wrestling with an angel, identity crisis, confrontation with self or something. What's wrong with just an ordinary divorce and some tears? Here we are, twenty years later, living through it all over again.

"And the funny thing is, I don't really know why he left. Why didn't he try to sort things out with me? Fight for me? That hurt. He didn't want to put up a fight. If I had to fill out a form on this, 'why my husband left me just because I was leaving him,' I wouldn't know what to write down. Somewhere in his head were a bunch of thoughts I never got a hint of.

"It's a shame, really. Such a beautiful boy. I'm pretty happy now. I have a nice, ordinary life. But sometimes I think, Paul and I came so close. To getting it right. I wish one of us could have fixed things. That would have been something. Maybe now we'd know enough to talk it through."

She stood up. "Thanks for keeping JB out of trouble. He wouldn't do that well in jail, and he couldn't afford a fine, for that matter."

*   *   *

As they fought the traffic out of New York the next morning, Davis told Pliny about his conversation with Cass. The manic driving perfectly matched Pliny's inner state. He didn't disbelieve it, exactly, but he couldn't imagine a situation where Cass would rather be with somebody other than Paul. He was sure that Paul would have been just as incredulous. It didn't fit the family myth.

Cass's story didn't establish what was going through Paul's mind, but it opened up several plausible explanations.   Before talking to Paul Baer, it seemed improbable that Paul Brearley could go eighteen years without discovery or catastrophe. But Baer's explanation made it simple. Baer's comments were also the best window they had into Paul's thinking during his exile.

Davis drove on the New York side of Lake Champlain all the way to Plattsburgh, where they could take the ferry back to South Hero Island. Later, he remembered the journey as one of the oddest experiences of his life.

The two men talked very little. It wasn't exactly a conversation. One of them would say something. Then there would be a few minutes of silence, and then the other person would respond. They were giving their minds a chance to react to all the information they had. Maybe an actual discussion could come later. The conversation said more about them, Davis thought later, than it did about Paul Brearley.

"I don't think we should assume," Pliny began, "that Paul, during the whole remainder of his life, had as bleak a view as he expressed to Baer. He didn't describe Paul as acting depressed all the time or anything like that."

Davis disagreed. "How could he *not* be in misery after what happened? I can't imagine that." Davis had thought a lot about Paul's actions, ideas, and motives, but less about his mental state from one day to the next. He thought Pliny didn't want Paul to have suffered too much anguish. "Given what we know about him, I can picture him seeming normal or

265

even content to other people. But when he's by himself, which we know was most of the time . . . I don't know." As he was saying this, he didn't realize he was also talking about himself. But later, he could see it.

Ten minutes later, Pliny said, "Well, he was schooled in suffering, he'd studied it. I think to us, he and I and his dad, we had contrary ideas about mental anguish. On the one hand, it was part of one's spiritual work—it meant you were seriously engaged. On the other, we are admonished to enjoy life, to praise God."

Another ten minutes passed.

Davis was remembering Cass's comments. "Cass describes him as out of touch inside. Maybe being out of touch was unbearable to him."

This was an hour's conversation, completely unsatisfying. They didn't have the answers, and they never would. Davis's last comment might be as close as they ever got to understanding Paul.

The last part of the ride was like a guided tour of the case. They drove near Skip's house on the lake, through Plattsburgh, down the long road to the ferry, past the park and ride. They got their ticket and waited with a half dozen other cars for the ferry to load. From the dock, they could just make out the blue silos of the Davis Farm.

Davis asked, "Pliny, are you going to Malone to look at Paul's—and Paul's—room?"

"There's nothing there." The ferry was just pulling in. Pliny continued, "Maybe he tried to write about it but couldn't really figure it out. I can imagine him getting out a notebook or opening a file on his computer, if he had one, and then just sitting there."

*　　*　　*

Pliny did not go to Malone. Davis spent some time in Tupper Lake, but he didn't learn anything new. Dick stopped in at some more travel agents, but his trips to Sorel were more productive. A young man named Giles, who pumped gas at the marina, remembered Skip and his boat. There was sometimes a bit of a party scene on the cruiser. He remembered a couple of French guys, Quebecois, who were there a lot with their wives or girlfriends. He remembered the women—not young or skinny, but comfortable in their bikinis. There was a lot of drinking. Giles was invited on board once and got stoned in a big way. Nothing that outrageous happened. The owner— he didn't remember his name but recognized the picture—kept to himself.

It was a link, but not really proof of anything, except that Skip knew some other people and spent time with them. All the information went to the Canadian authorities.

From a policing point of view, the team had all they needed. Case closed. The state's attorney had plenty of information to convict. At the same time, they had leads on other, related crimes, and followed them up when they had time.

But with all that, there were still questions that bothered Fred Davis. What happened on the island? What was Skip doing there? What had been going on in Paul's mind all that time? They weren't much farther ahead now than they had been in June.

Chapter 24

DOWN ON THE FARM

Davis was sitting at the Champ Diner near the Grand Isle ferry dock at his favorite table looking out over the lake. The milking was done, and he didn't have to go to St. Albans. For October 1, the weather was surprisingly benign, calm, sunny, and warm. Tourists were converging on Vermont from all directions to see peak foliage, but they weren't coming here. The lake was shutting down. People were trailering their boats and having them shrink-wrapped in huge sheets of white plastic. They were shuttering their cottages, draining down the plumbing, mowing the lawn for the last time, and dismantling their docks.

He had his *New York Times* and two eggs over easy with bacon, the thick Canadian bacon that had helped the police team figure out where the breakfast sandwiches had been made.

According to the *Times*, gas was a bargain at $3.11. Obama was up by six points. Economists and commentators were combing through Geitner's plan for the economy. Palin's team was lowering expectations for the vice presidential debate.

When he'd bought the boat on April Fool's Day, he'd pictured himself this past summer out on a long, long tour, like the ones he'd taken with Luke in their salvaged cruiser when he was in college.

But between the Osprey Island case and his father's accident, the boat had spent the summer at the dock at Apple Island Marina, getting grungy. He'd had one three-day trip. Soon he'd pull it out of the water, clean it up, and tuck it away in the barn. Since his father's fall, his life had been refocused on four things: the Brearley case, life on the farm, the boat barn, and Diane.

Though Skip's case would drag on in the courts, Davis's involvement was now minimal. The state's attorney had not been that interested in Skip's offer for reduced charges in exchange for information on the drug trade. Dick, knocking door-to-door and dock to dock at the marina in Sorel, Quebec, and working his way back to Montreal, had found a thread of information and was slowly, gently tugging on it. Ethel, in her determined way, was unraveling Skip's life in Panama. If he ever got out of prison in Vermont, Skip would be welcomed into prisons in New York, Canada, Panama, and probably a few other places.

Davis had frequently fantasized about having a little chat with Skip along the lines of, "You should have driven a little slower when you destroyed my sailboat forty years ago. Ha ha! He who laughs last . . ." or words to that effect.

Their little team had done a good job reeling in Paul Brearley/Paul Baer, and later Seward Tyler. Back in April, Fred had been feeling dissatisfied with his life as a detective. He had been thinking of going back into the law or trying to make a real business out of restoring boats.

But the Paul Brearley case had revived him. The victim was interesting, the perpetrator was interesting, and their relationship was interesting. There had been a nice crop of witnesses, too, people worth talking to.

He liked working with Bert, Janice, Dick, and the others. They complemented each other. Bert was organized, Janice was smart, competent and intuitive, Dick was dogged, and he himself was a bit of all these things. In Davis's experience, there were no brilliant Sherlock Holmeses or Nero Wolfes, armchair geniuses who deduced things. But a smart, slightly obsessed crew of people who worked hard and talked to each other could be very effective.

He had worked on crimes before that were difficult to solve, but usually there was nothing particularly interesting about the victims and the people who victimized them, who were often their relatives or acquaintances. It might be satisfying to right a wrong or jail someone who deserved it. But often he would just as soon not have met any of them. He needed a nice, hot shower to wash them away.

In the two years he had left before retirement, he hoped to keep his little team together and have some appealing victims to avenge and worthy crooks to do battle with. But that might not happen.

His father had recovered and was back at work. But he would never get back the strength he'd had at that moment when he was perched at the top of the old ladder, reaching for something on a high shelf, and the patched leg of the ladder had given way. When he tumbled down, he was beginning his slow tumble off the edge of the world.

Since he was about twelve, one of Davis's core principles was that he had to get away from the farm, that he wasn't cut out for farm work. That he couldn't stand working with his father. But here he was, thinking about, anticipating, his projects back on the farm. And not really being angry with his father. One of the two of them must have mellowed. It would have been fun to make that cruise through the Erie Canal, but he liked being almost indispensable at milking time. He wasn't sure he trusted the others to get things just right. He didn't want to come back and find his tools misplaced. It was still awkward working with his son, Andy, but a little less so. He thought if he didn't watch out, he might, in a moment's inattention, come to like farming.

The boat repair work seemed to take care of itself. Right now, they had an old Penn Yan Swift in the boat barn that needed to be totally rebuilt. It was one of Fred's favorite boats; he'd been wanting to work on one for about thirty years. Behind that was a sailboat so old that nobody knew who had built it. That would take all winter to fix up. Davis wasn't sure he'd enjoy that work if he had to do it full-time. In two years, maybe he'd find out.

None of the thoughts about work and the farm were surprises to him. But now he was uttering them to himself in ways that could lead to action rather than the inadvertent drift that was his usual method of making his way through life.

But then there was the fourth topic—Diane.

They'd spent quite a bit of time together that summer. They'd helped each other with chores a few times. There had been a few walks along West Shore Road. They'd taken their grandchildren out on the lake in canoes, in the Islander. They had washed up the dishes together.

Though they'd come close a couple of times, they hadn't spent the night together since Hiram's accident, and Fred hadn't tried to push it. In the past, it was usually her decision, and he was always happy to comply. There had been no serious discussions about their relationship. A couple of times he had started to talk about it, but the conversation had petered out.

His ruminations about Diane often got somehow conflated with the boat. Early in the summer, when he was docked at the Sand Bar, he sometimes lay in his bunk and imagined that she might show up. He'd feel the boat rock a bit as she stepped over the side. There she would be.

He imagined the trip south through the Champlain Canal. When he was first planning the trip, Luke was to join him for that part of it. But he imagined arriving at lock 12, the northernmost lock, and Luke wouldn't be there. Instead, Diane would be on the walkway above the lock, waving. Luke was usually trying to engineer their reunion; he would have set this up. It could happen that way.

Then he and Diane would cruise through the locks together, negotiating

271

their issues as they negotiated their way through the locks, catching the slimy mooring lines with the boat hooks. When they got to lock 1, they'd be together. It wasn't so preposterous in a way. A canal was slow and peaceful, a good place for a reunion.

He kicked himself. If he wanted things to change with her, he would have to say it out loud to himself and to her. This was territory he had avoided for many years. It was simple. He would be happy with her, and unhappy without. He didn't want to end up like Paul Baer, either one of them, lost when he didn't have to be.

He paid his bill and walked out to the shore by the old breakwater and thought about what he would say to her. A half hour later, he called her.

"Diane, it's me."

*   *   *

When he got back to the farm, he decided to clean up the boat in preparation for putting it up for the winter. Also, to make it tidy for Diane. They were having dinner on the water.

Just sitting quietly and unused on the lake, a boat is slimed from below by the weeds, encrusted by the zebra mussels, and the decks above get begrimed by the birds, bugs, and overhanging trees. He had a lot of scrubbing to do.

But as he was setting up, an ancient, pristine black Volvo pulled up by the road, and Pliny walked down to the dock. He was wearing jeans, a wool shirt, and a sweater that looked as old as the Volvo. On him, this outfit looked dapper.

Pliny clambered right into the cabin and sat down at the little booth. "I brought you something." He pulled a book out of a bag. It was the signed copy of one of Paul's books, the collection of essays, that the real Paul Baer had kept on a shelf in Malone. "I took Paul Baer up to Malone to get his stuff. We both thought you should have this. In honor of our adventure. Do you have any coffee here?"

Davis had been wanting to go over things with Pliny, who had been a partner of sorts in the whole project. In a couple of minutes, he produced two cups of coffee and sat down with his friend.

"Well, Pliny, how are you? I thought you were leaving next week."

"I was. But being alone on the island in my house started to get to me. I kept looking at that photo, the one of the six of us after repairing the dock. It seemed so magical and beautiful, as if these families would go on generation after generation, doing good things, having fun, working together. But not long after the photo was taken, Paul was gone and John was beginning to fail. I don't really get along that well with my own son. It's really just me and JB now from that group. I realized that moment on the dock was the high point. It's over now. We have a new group photo with different people. Move on."

Davis asked, "How are you feeling about the whole thing? How's JB doing?"

"Well, let's see. JB is struggling. I think it will take him a bit to get back to being the person he's best at being. But he's getting there. We've spent the last few days closing up the island and working on my dock. But I think he's eager to get back to his business and away from all of this.

"By the way," he continued, "you probably know this, but Cass is your biggest fan. She knows you could have made big trouble for JB. We all appreciate it. We have enough problems without JB in jail, or whatever they do to people who mess up the evidence."

Davis asked, "Does she know I told you what she told me?"

"That she was going to leave Paul back then, and told him about it just before he vanished? Yes, she assumed you told me about it. But she asked me to keep it to myself if I could. I don't think she wants the whole family talking about her. I don't know if I can really keep secrets from my own children. We'll see. She talked to JB about it."

"Was that why Paul left, do you think? Because of what Cass was doing?"

"We'll never know, will we? But here's what I think. I think he must have been a little shaky already. Since he was often questioning everything, it's

273

not hard to imagine. Then, if she said, 'I'd rather be with somebody else, some ordinary guy,' that could have thrown him. Why would she leave her family and this handsome, smart, loving, successful guy? Maybe he thought there must be something basically wrong with him, something he didn't understand. And were that true, it's not hard to figure that he'd feel he had to search for whatever it was. Or maybe he was an ordinary guy, really—jealous and vain—and just acted like an idiot.

"But I'm tired of thinking about it," Pliny continued. "You and I should just let him go, and worry about ourselves. That's what I really think. Have you learned anything new about the case?"

"No. We never got very far trying to trace Paul on the Web. I think Janice is still working on it when she has nothing better to do."

Pliny looked out over the lake for a minute and sipped his coffee. "Here's my question to you. Why did Skip kill Paul?"

"Well, the obvious answer would be Paul could identify him and he needed Paul's snow machine. He had never been identified for any of his criminal activities. But I think Skip liked a dramatic gesture. I think it was fun for him. Bert and Janice interviewed him over and over, and he wouldn't say a word about it."

Pliny asked, "And how are you doing? You seemed pretty involved in this. It wasn't just another case to you. How did it affect you?"

"It made me think a bit. I got very involved with Paul. Or the idea of Paul. I thought there was some secret there I needed to know, apart from the criminal case. But the more I learned, the more I came to see him the way Helen did, as a very well-presented, talented, articulate, in-shape, lost soul. There was more to learn from JB than from him. In a funny way, it helped me figure out a couple of things."

"Hmm?"

"For one, I'm moving back here. I'm going to spend time with my dad while he lives, which could be a long time, come to think of it, and with my son, who I've been estranged from, or maybe semi-estranged. I have to retire in two years. Probably I'll fix rich people's boats, unless rich people can't afford to get their boats fixed. And I'm going to see if I can get my wife to move back here with me. Simple, isn't it?"

As Pliny was putting on his jacket, he said, "I'm actually on my way to see Paul Baer in New York. I like him."

"How is he?"

"Well, he's recovered surprisingly well. He's in remission, at least for now. He's not that old, really; he's got some strength left. But if he drinks, he'll die. That's what the doctors told me. I'm going to try to get him someplace to live, if I can, and try to keep him out of trouble. He's my link to Paul. I like to talk to him. We're becoming friends. He told us he likes to talk philosophy. Maybe I'll try to find out what he means by that. My kind of guy."

Davis couldn't quite figure out whether Pliny was trying to save Paul Baer or wanted something from him. Maybe it was a simple friendship. "Well," he said. "Good luck. He could use a friend. I'm sure you'll be a good one."

After Pliny left, Davis stopped by the farm store. The place was full of what Vermonters uncharitably referred to as leaf peepers. His mother was at the register explaining the different kinds of apples and jams they were selling. She could make a pretty good story out of a bottle of raspberry jam.

Diane was scooping ice cream and helping customers carry bushels of apples to their cars. Davis fixed himself a dish of maple ice cream, watched Diane for a minute, then walked back down to the dock.

*   *   *

Supper on the newly cleaned boat was basic. A little soup from the kitchen to heat up, some wine, half a loaf of bread, and a couple of slices of Siberian peach pie. The lake often quiets down in the evening, and it did on this one. They sat outside on the little back deck, but it was cooling down.

In part of Davis's mind, he wanted to take the reunion he had imagined spread all along the length of the canal and condense into one quick and efficient talk. But he knew better.

He said, "I like being here on the farm. I'm getting to know Andy again. It's nice being with the kids every day. My dad needs help now; I'm actually needed. To tell you the truth, he's a little easier to deal with than he once was. I think he wants my help. I'm moving back to the farm, at least while Hiram is alive."

She didn't respond right away. She sensed he wasn't done. She wasn't going to let him off the hook.

Finally he said it. "Diane, I want us to get back together. I don't know what decisions I'm going to make about work a year or two from now, but I want to live here with you. Permanently. Being with you has always been the most important thing, I just didn't always know it. Now I know it." There was really nothing to add to this.

For a few minutes, they sat there watching the sun set over the Adirondacks. It was getting colder.

They were almost close enough to touch. Now Diane was avoiding the issue. Studying the sunset, she said, "I give it a nine point four, maybe nine point five." She said, "Let's go inside, it's a little cold."

Fred grabbed one of the old family quilts and pulled it across them. A lot of the most important decisions in their lives had taken place beneath old quilts that his mom had discarded as unfit for respectable use.

"Freddy, it's been obvious to me for a couple of months that you were getting a lot out of being on the farm, and if you hadn't told me you were going back, I'd have brought it up myself. Your father loves having you there. He told me that more than once. I think you are really his favorite. He just never could see beyond the farm, that's all. I'm sure he's overjoyed to have you home.

"I know where you'd like this conversation to go. I don't know what I want to do. I'll tell you this: I'm thinking about it. But I've been seeing someone else. I've waited a long time for you, Freddy."

They sat for a long time without saying anything. It was dark. Davis said, "You're right, it is cold. Let's go inside."

ABOUT THE AUTHOR

Sam Clark grew up in Poughkeepsie in the Quaker Community there. As a child, his family had a place on an island in Upper Saranac Lake, in the Adirondacks. They lost the place later, but The Island still lives in much of what Sam builds, and certainly in The Inland Sea.

Sam came to Vermont in 1960 to attend the late lamented Woodstock Country School. After College at Amherst, he moved to Plainfield, Vermont. He has been a designer, builder, and cabinetmaker since 1970, working in Central Vermont and Cambridge, Massachusetts.

Sam has been involved in a series of worker-owned woodworking businesses (co-ops) in both locations. His partners and he were part of a sea-change in building, the rise of owner-builders and of "design-build". The idea that the person who builds or remodels a house could be the designer, in collaboration with the homeowner, is common now, but back in the 60s and 70s, it was a radical idea.

He has written several books on design and building, including The

Motion-minded Kitchen, and The Independent Builder, which are still found on the shelves of older builders, and some younger ones.

Sam has always been interested in the history and people of New England, and the ideas that took root here. He had often attempted to write about this subject with little success. But on November 4, 2008, the day Barack Obama was elected, he was hit by a car while biking, not far from his home in Plainfield. He couldn't work for a few months, but he could still type. He decided to approach this subject again in the form of a mystery novel.

During this period, he had gotten back into boating, and his family had a spot, with a dock, in a trailer park called Montani's, in Keeler Bay, on the eastern side of South Hero Island, in Lake Champlain. This sequestered part of the lake is known as the Inland Sea. It seemed natural to locate his story there.

Sam says, "it might seem absurd to jump from writing building books to writing a novel, but to me principles to live by, and principles to build by, aren't that different. You could argue that constructing a detective story isn't entirely different from constructing a building book, or a house."

Also Available from Rootstock Publishing: